A DESERT OF BLEEDING SAND

A DESERT OF BLEEDING SAND

A DESERT OF BLEEDING SAND
BOOK ONE

LUCIA DAMISA

A Desert of Bleeding Sand is a work of fiction. While reference might be made to actual historical events or existing locations, the names, characters, places, and incidents are either the product of the author's imagination or are used fictitiously, and any resemblance to actual persons, living or dead, business establishments, events, or locales are entirely coincidental.

All rights reserved. No part of this book may be reproduced in any form by any electronic or mechanical means—except in the case of brief quotations embodied in critical articles or reviews—without written permission.

For information regarding subsidiary rights, please contact the Publisher:
Darkan Press Inc. LLC
Alberta, Canada
www.darkanpress.com
Darkanpress@gmail.com

First Edition March 2025

Edited by AuthorsDesigns
Proofread by Jeanne Olynick
Cover Designed by Olha Volkova
Artwork and Illustrations by Olamide Feranmi Elizabeth
Map designed by AuthorsDesigns
Formatted by AuthorsDesigns

eBook ISBN 978-1-0694190-2-6
Paperback ISBN 978-1-0694190-1-9
Hardcover ISBN 978-1-997731-42-9

Copyright © 2025 Lucia Damisa

*To my parents—for your patience throughout the long journey here.
To Isabella, Peter, Naomi, Benjamin—for always believing my miracle
would happen.*

ABOUT THE WESTERN CONTINENT

The Major Kingdoms of the Western Continent:

- **Thalesai:** the kingdom of humans
- **Dahomey:** the kingdom of azizas (African faeries) and air magic
- **Albion:** the kingdom of wraiths and shadow magic
- **Sarqi:** the kingdom of shapeshifters and earthen magic

The Smaller Kingdoms of the Western Continent:

- Basutoland
- Togoland
- Ciskei
- Lake Chad

The Five Tribes of Thalesai:

- Ussi
- Baihan
- Mizsab
- Kwali
- Esan

ABOUT THE WESTERN CONTINENT

The Three Chambers of Thalesai:

- **The Chamber of Wings:** the king's closest chambermen often made up of advisors, an emissary, and the admiral.
- **The Chamber of Fangs:** the highest-ranking military officers.
- **The Chamber of Claws:** the rulers of Thalesai including chiefs (rulers of villages), dynasts (rulers of towns and cities), and chancellors (rulers of settlements)

The Five Elite Academy Divisions:

Ahimoth Insignia

Ahimoth: Military (the head branch), Engineering, General Studies

Gergesenes Insignia

Gergesenes: Military (the head branch), Healing, Engineering, Philosophy, General Studies

Nergal Insignia

Nergal: Military (the head branch), Healing, Engineering, Philosophy, General Studies

Felax Insignia

Felax: Engineering (the head branch), Philosophy, General Studies

Quartus Insignia

Quartus: Five Healing Academies

The Elite Academy Student Representatives:

ABOUT THE WESTERN CONTINENT

- **Dathan Issachar** (Gergesenes Military Academy)
- **Ibhar Ghed** (Ahimoth Military Academy)
- **Lysias Ohel** (Quartus Healing Academy)
- **Mishan F'larin** (Felax Engineering Academy)
- **Zair Nebah** (Nergal Military Academy)

GLOSSARY OF TERMS

- **Al'Qtraz**: which translates to the *Sand Palace:* Thalesai's royal palace is located in Ari'el.

- **Airran**: a betrothed man.

- **Aiyena**: a betrothed woman.

- **Ari'el**: the capital city of Thalesai.

- **Barghests**: tigerlike beasts with red fur that feed on guilty people.

- **Ironteenth Fighters:** the Majesties' elite guards. They are made up of twelve swordsmen, twelve archers, and twelve spearmen.

- **Khosa/Khosana:** a title for the male and female nobility in Thalesai.

- **Kiniuns**: great lions with white fur and blue incisions on their faces. They stand taller than horses.

- **Siyvas**: Thalesai's currency.

- **Spaeman**: a divine seer and advisor for the king.

- **Zenana**: the queen's special and closest group of female courtiers from the four tribes.

Zair Nebah
Baihan/Esan · 18yo · 5'7"

Negral Academy (Military)
↦ Skilled in hand-to-hand combat and uses cursed magic
↦ Favored Weapon: Bow and Arrow ⌅

1

ZAIR

Danger.

Its sulfuric smell traveled in the hot desert winds, down the tall dunes circling the academy to taunt my senses. I almost called out a warning, but no one would believe the girl with the evil eyes.

"Utterly profane," a Mizsab tutor spat. Her nose ring glinted as she glared down at us from a classroom's balcony. "This tribe of humans with aziza blood tainting their veins. That it's Visiting Day doesn't mean *they* can come and smear this academy!"

Her vicious stare scraped over my face like talons.

I silently listed the positives as my sandals tapped on the winding footpath.

At least the balcony's shade is a good reprieve from the Sahara Desert's heat.

She isn't throwing things at us.

My sister didn't seem to hear the woman's words of rejection.

At eighteen years old, I'd learned that however small, focusing on the good always made the spite easier to swallow. But even those couldn't silence the warning chimes in my ears. Trouble traveled on the wind to the Nergal Healing Academy.

The academy remained oblivious, its majestic buildings rising around us in a network of halls and stairs that emanated steam in the heat. White marble tiles adorned the soaring walls and sable banners fluttered from the mahogany posts that lined the footpaths. A guard wearing a headscarf against the sun led a wild dog—a hulking canine with long fangs and piercing eyes—into our aisle.

I squeezed the callused oak of my longbow as the canine's black and flaxen fur brushed my skirts. It sniffed and snarled at us. The guard watched, anticipating a howl of warning. But the beast didn't smell any trouble.

Jaw clenched, the guard finally led the wild dog away without apologizing.

"If only I had an elite soldier's rank," I whispered to my father, who towered like a great rock beside me, "then they would respect us."

"You are worthy of respect even without a rank, Zair," he said, his gray-streaked brown hair framing his passionate expression. "Never doubt that."

Perhaps in theory but not in reality, papa.

My mother's copper bangles jingled as she waved me closer to her. Although she stood a few inches shorter than me and wore flat old sandals, they weren't the reasons she appeared timid here in the academy. The balcony above cast shadows over her downturned rosy lips. "Zair, do you feel it too? The chimes of trouble in the air?"

A chill rippled under my skin.

"I do, mama." I glanced toward the sand dunes, understanding her need for my confirmation. The threats our family faced out of people's hatred for her tribe forced us to constantly look over our shoulders for enemies. But this aura of danger... it prickled my skin like tines.

She touched my father's arm, her head barely reaching his chest, and leaned close to keep my sister from overhearing her. Sarai's keen senses were yet to mature fully, and mama would not want to frighten her needlessly.

"We should tour quickly and leave, husband," my mother murmured.

His thick brows fused. "Leave? We've just arrived and traveled a long way to visit the academy. We need to take our time. Make sure it's a suitable academy for Sarai."

She shook her head, her veil rippling over her maroon cotton blouse. "The atmosphere is unsettled. The air wails like a grieving mother."

My father glanced at me, taking in my tight grip on my longbow. If my older sister, Niah, had been here, she would have affirmed the hum of danger too, but she had volunteered to stay home to attend to my mother's customers. My father knew the instincts we had inherited from my mother's tribespeople did not give false warnings. If we were troubled despite the heavy security in the academy—the stoic swordsmen patrolling every corridor and archers watching from the balustrades—it was safer to leave soon.

"Should we warn everyone?" he asked.

My mother glanced at the library's colonnade where two librarians frowned at us. "Our abilities warn against different kinds of threats. It could be that someone is watching and waiting to harm our family alone. Even if the danger is to the academy or someone here, they'll scorn our instincts rather than listen to them because..."

Because we are so despised. Her unsaid words pierced my stomach like needles, and I glanced at the granite floor to hide my wince.

"Alright," he said grimly, his light-brown eyes darkening both with apprehension and resolve. "We will leave soon. Let Sarai have a quick visit first."

A few feet ahead, my little sister fluttered on like a butterfly, anxious as my family toured the domed academy that ran along the eastern borders of Thalesai.

The teachers will love you, I wanted to reassure her, but I couldn't promise her that.

"Nergal's healing academy is very different from its military academy, Zair," Sarai exclaimed, waiting until I joined her on the open bridge of the second level. Her footwear clapped eagerly on its mosaic tiles. "Even the healing students' uniform is less severe than the military's. I like it very much."

My mother had styled Sarai's hair into a neat bun, very different from my sleek zigzag weaves that rippled down to my waist. Sarai had also insisted on wearing a black caftan with silver trimmings to imitate the Nergal uniform colors that its students proudly displayed. Whether it was the Nergal's Military Academy, Healing Academy, Philosophy Academy, or the Engineering branch, our colors were the same. Just like our insignia: a fox's head with its mouth wide and its fangs ferocious.

"You will look wonderful in their uniform," I said.

Her golden eyes brightened with pleasure. "I'll score the highest in the exams and make you very proud!"

A lump formed in my throat, and I nodded. Thalesai's elite academies were built solely to train the future rulers of the kingdom. The smartest, strongest, quickest, and most innovative youths to inherit the leadership mantles someday. As our rivers coursed to kingdoms with magical people who were more powerful than us humans, Thalesai needed intelligent rulers to thrive.

Sarai looked precious, like a cub, and I grew antsier over the wind's whispers of dawning trouble.

"There are so many classrooms in the healing academy too," she observed.

"Indeed, our classrooms *are* fewer," I agreed, seeking a distraction from the bell-like ringing in my head. In a few moments, we would be gone. "We military students enjoy our training pits far more than we enjoy books and classrooms."

The Thalesain soldiers who overthrew our oppressors in the War of Beasts hadn't battled with quills and paper.

"But reading is your favorite pastime," Sarai chimed with a conspiratorial grin.

I lightly flicked her nose. "Hush or you'll ruin my fierce reputation."

She giggled.

"And, thankfully, only the guards here carry weapons, rather than students and teachers clanking like gongs with every step they take," my mother teased.

Still, she couldn't hide the worry edging her lips. The same full lips my sisters and I had. Just as we had inherited her midnight hair, brown-gold eyes, and beautiful oval face that lit up with rare smiles. She had pulled her maroon veil low over her face to conceal her eyes, but Sarai and I went without veils. Not even against the blistering sun. While he left my mother to make her choice, my father would not hear of it that his daughters hid in shame while he was present. The double, golden rings in our eyes proclaimed our mother's Esan tribe to any who looked.

And look they did, bristling like sidewinders. The teachers in silver robes and black turbans striding briskly by us; the students ambling in and out of classrooms, balancing tomes and jars of experimental medicine; the guards with sheathed adaswords before every entryway.

As our sandals thudded past their stations, the guards gripped their hilts as if the steel could incinerate us with a mere touch. *We are more human than aziza. And steel doesn't even burn aziza, only pure iron, you fools.*

"Oh, this place is big!" Sarai remarked as she tipped her head back and surveyed the structures marching for the sky amid the yellow sand dunes. "I have to train here."

My father patted my shoulder with his huge, brown paw of a hand. "Keep studying and working hard like your sister did. And after you turn eleven next year, you just might."

I smiled at his praise and took Sarai's hand.

"Did you know that the study of herbs dates back centuries before even Thalesai was formed?" Sarai asked. "To ancient civilizations like Mesopotamia and Sumeria?"

Resisting the urge to squint suspiciously at the gangly boys jogging toward us, see if they were the reason for the warning, I tilted my head. "I didn't, but I know these teachers would be eager to have a student who does."

Sarai's face lit up like a bowlful of stars. The boys jogged by to greet their parents at the other end of the bridge. The source of danger was still out there.

We climbed down the stairs, dipping into the academy's bustling main complex. An archway leading to the herbal garden loomed ahead of us. *Onward Always*, Nergal's slogan, was carved into it. Sarai squealed, startling some teachers who were conversing in the grand peristyle.

"Can we walk faster?" Sarai whispered.

We chuckled at her enthusiasm. The Academy's herbal garden seemed to whisper an invitation as its green and yellow blooms peeked and bobbed through the entryway. It scented the air with jasmine and moist earth. Cultivated with decades of research and passion by intelligent healers, it was a paradise for any who loved the healing arts. My passion was soldiering; my father dealt in fabrics, and my mother and older sister were teamakers. We weren't quite as excited at the prospect of staring at grasses.

"We won't stay long, *ami*," my father warned.

"Yes, papa! Did you know that if I'm admitted to study here, I'll be the first ever Esan student in an elite healing academy? Just as Zair is the first Esan military student." Sarai was fairly skipping now.

"Now, Sarai, you and your sister are *Baihan*. Your father's tribe. And you deserve every privilege of the Baihan tribe," my mother corrected firmly, even though my father didn't mind Sarai's words. He had never equated being Esans with treachery like everyone else did.

"But people don't care which tribe we truly are from, only which we look like," Sarai countered innocently, but my mother flinched.

I opened my mouth to hush Sarai. To tell her never to imply that our mother was the cause of other people's cruelty toward us. A horrible noise split the air like a roar of thunder, stunning the school into stillness.

"What was that?" I clung to the bow strapped across my chest, spinning toward the sound. My heart slammed as my senses screeched a tune of peril.

"Saints preserve us. The sky!" a man cried from two stories above.

My eyes darted upward and my stomach twisted. The sky, a clear blue arc moments ago, was now swirling and darkening like a cauldron of murk.

"Trouble has come," my mother whispered, her face stricken.

The sound slashed again, so loudly it stabbed my ears like a blunt blade. I grabbed Sarai's shoulder and set her behind me.

"Zair?" she called shakily. "I'm scared."

Heart racing, I turned and gave her the determined smile I did when people spat at us on the street or our food ran out. My 'we will be alright' smile. "Courage, *ami*. We'll be home in no time."

"Courage," she echoed.

My father clutched the hilt of his adasword, his large body moving to shield us as more students rushed out of the classrooms.

I nocked an arrow and was moving to stand beside him when

crooked light ripped from the sky, blackening my vision for a heartbeat. It landed in the complex and erupted. Shock jarred through me as flames ate across the complex like an angry serpent. The group of teachers conversing in the peristyle moments ago vanished into its smoky mouth.

Oh saints.

Screams rent the air, one of them Sarai's. My protective instinct soared over my horror as my father turned to us with wild eyes.

"Hide!" he shouted.

"It's the mercenaries," I said, my heart lurching. I trained my arrow in the direction of the flames. "Isn't it?"

My father didn't get a chance to answer. Light sparked and fire exploded between us. I cried out as the force slammed me against a pillar. Pain gnawed up my back. Heat singed the hair on my skin.

Ears ringing, I pushed to my feet. Where were they? Where was my family?

"Papa! Zair!"

The panic in my sister's scream dropped my heart to my feet.

"Sarai?" I ran, stumbling blindly through the smoke toward her voice.

"Zair! Help me!"

I ran faster, calling for her. Another bolt of lightning split from the riotous sky to smash the building ahead. Walls crumbled and I flung myself beneath a stairwell. Many students, teachers, and visitors scrambled into any cranny they could find. Others ran from the enemies we couldn't see.

Guards shoved through the chaos for the flames. Their faces held no fear or confusion. Only determination masked their brisk movements as they yelled for people to take cover.

These attackers making lightning fall from the sky to smite harmless healers *were* the dreaded mercenary groups. They'd been ravaging Nergal's academies to abduct students for months and had made academies intensify their security like forts. No one knew *what* they did with the missing students. Now they had come for Nergal's Healing Academy.

"Sarai!"

My father's desperate voice reached me in the chaos, and I

scrambled out from beneath the stairwell. No answer came from Sarai.

I watched the next lightning streak dive like a bone trident, jagged like the worn threads on lines of yarn. An ancient instinct within, a trickle of aziza heritage, sensed the corporeality of the lightning.

It wasn't evanescent. It was *solid* light. Crafted.

Without hesitation, I harnessed my innate speed, moving so fast it was like time slowed.

Yarn.

Guided by that roaring ancient sense, I aimed my weapon at the three-pronged light tearing through the sky. My hands shimmered softly. The soft white glow of magic rushed over my bow and arrow. My arrow released with a snap and twirled in a swift, straight line like a proud hawk.

My arrowhead struck the sinuous light. It pushed into the light like a blunt knife pushing at skin.

My joints faltered as the first lightning streak collided into the second, and the third until they were stumbling midair like a three-legged drunk. My arrow ripped through all three and fire layered the sky with the monstrous explosion that ensued.

People screamed even louder. I staggered as my bones buckled from the use of my magic. Hot ash poured from the sky, and I threw my arms over my head.

By Osime, how had that worked?

My shock faded to dismay as I sighted my sister. Two figures with cloaked faces hurried through the fumes, dragging Sarai along. She fought them like a mad cat, tears pouring down her cheeks.

Swiftly, I nocked another arrow and shot. At the last second, my target swerved aside, his eyes wide as they zapped to me.

"Get away from her!"

The other man threw Sarai over his shoulder. I fired at him, but the first raised his sword and intercepted the shot. My arrow clanged against the blade and bounced away. After using magic to destroy the lightning, I was too weak to pursue them with my enhanced speed. I loosed another arrow, then another, moving forward. The first retained his position as the guard, his sword moving with shocking skill, blocking as quickly as my arrows fired.

A cry of trepidation left me. "Let her go!"

"Zair!" Sarai pleaded.

Steel surged in my spine. I aimed two of my last four arrows and sent them flying. The mercenary's eyes widened. He slashed his sword downward to deflect the first shot. He couldn't keep my second arrow from slamming into his shoulder. Blood spurted as he stumbled backward with a cry.

With a burst of hope, I nocked my last two arrows.

The two men exchanged a glance, quick communication passing between them.

The second mercenary hugged Sarai to his chest as a shield, and the first stumbled to stand behind them. *No.* Ignoring her wail, he grabbed her hair to expose her neck and brandished his scythe.

It happened so fast.

Sarai's face shone with terror and plea as she saw me. "*Zair.*"

"Stop!" I screamed.

In a blink, he slashed his blade from her shoulder to her chin. Blood spurted and Sarai's body slumped on the ground.

The world stopped.

The mercenary glared at me, smoke churning around him.

Attack! Kill them both! the soldier in me shouted, but shock held me frozen as I stared at Sarai's body. My lungs closed.

"You've thwarted our mission," the mercenary snarled as his partner tried to drag him away. "But she possesses magic that will serve us, and we've marked her. She's ours now. We *will* come back and take what is ours, I vow it!"

My joints unlocked. With a screech, I began to release another arrow. But they threw themselves behind the black walls of smoke, disappearing from my view.

Dazed, I jogged for Sarai. My mother screamed, my father shouting as they reached her first.

"Mama! Is she...?" I couldn't say it as I reached them. I *couldn't* breathe.

"She's alive," my mother said quickly as she cradled her youngest to her chest, her face agonized. "But the bleeding will kill her. She needs a healer."

Quiet suddenly rolled over the academy. No more cries. No explosions. Just the mercenaries' vow to come back for Sarai ringing in my ears. When minutes passed without flashes or fire, the survivors crawled out of hiding. Wailing filled the air between destroyed buildings.

My father raised his tear-streaked face from Sarai, my rage and sorrow reflecting in his eyes. "Guard your mother and sister. I need to find a healer."

He disappeared into the curtain of smoke, and with trembling knees, I took a defensive position in front of my mother.

Papa will come back. We will find Sarai a healer.

And then I'll hunt down those bleeding mercenaries. I would destroy them before I let them take my sister from me.

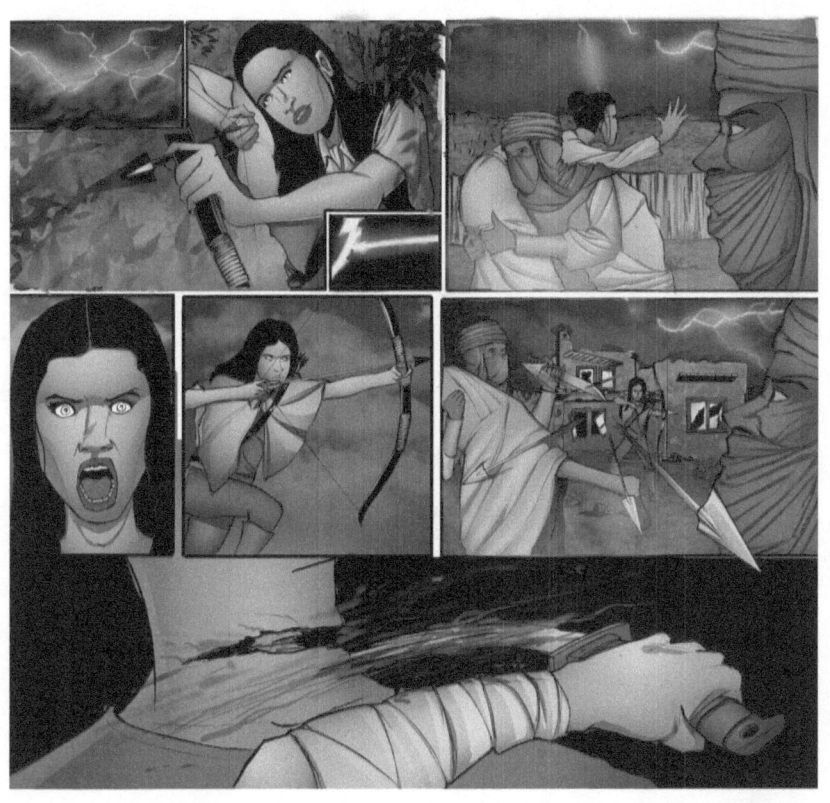

2

DATHAN

Five Hours Earlier

If I effectively crawled through my dorm room's window and climbed down this end of the academy's fence, my escape would be complete.

Yes, and if you were a groundhog, you could use your claws to burrow underground.

I scowled at the mocking thought and turned to the settlement nestled between my school, the Gergesenes Military Academy, and the reddish rock walls of the valley. Canopies fluttered in the Sahara Desert's baking winds. Flat-roofed houses glowed in the sunrise.

I leaned against the fence. Scaling the academy's hefty walls would be downright lethal. Yet it was my only chance of escaping the school before the Commandant chose Gergesenes' representative for the king's coronation in a few days.

"You could snap your neck, you know."

I jerked like a thief caught stealing, but it was only Jaziah. His broad form strode toward me in his dusk-blue leather uniform, a bandolier of knives gleaming across his chest. Beneath his unruly dark hair, a frown masked his face.

Releasing a long breath, I moved away from our academy's

fence, and plastered on a careless smirk. "Shouldn't you be patrolling the next street, Scholar?"

Go back, Jaziah. I need to plan.

"Why aren't *you* patrolling your assigned street?" he queried. "The supervisor just asked me where you are. He's annoyed you left your post. He could fail you on the *Guarding and Patrol* course."

My shoulders twitched and I instantly whirled toward my assigned street, my adasword's hilt warm as it brushed my wrist. Blast it, I hadn't expected the supervisor to start his survey this soon. Final exams were fast approaching for year-five students. Our exams *and* test scores would determine if we would graduate from the academy in five months. I couldn't score anything less than a distinction if I wanted a chance to join the kingdom's elite military unit.

The kingdom's elite military unit.

Conflicting desires clashed within me like a sandstorm. The need to hide myself against the yearning to thrive. Self-recrimination stabbed through my chest like a frigid knife.

My best friend fell into step beside me, still awaiting an answer, so I said, "I was merely taking a walk down Thalesai's memory lane."

It was the best excuse I could give him and our supervisor. Gergesenes Military Academy *was* built on a battlefield. The site of the first battle in the War of Beasts—when four of the five human tribes united and battled out the magical races that had invaded and ruled our lands for centuries.

"My friend," Jaziah said, clasping my shoulder, "we have lived on this 'memory lane' for five years. Try again, this time with more passion."

"It's about perspective," I returned, shrugging his hand off.

We entered my assigned street. It cut through the market which the modest settlement was built around. Baihan folks wearing scarves against the sun haggled loudly in the stalls. Large jars of colorful spices lined shelves, their scents mixing with the smell of poultry and dust.

"Perspective? Hmm. Don't tell me." Jaziah looked over his shoulder at the academy's fence. "The king's official coronation begins in a week. And since the Commandant of Gergesenes'

Academies might choose you to represent us at the palace, you now see the fence as an escape ladder since it's the only way you can evade the Commandant's order. You know, instead of grabbing the honor as *hundreds* of other elite students would."

Sometimes, I felt lucky to have someone who knew me almost as well as I knew myself. My family had settled into the mansion opposite his family's ten years ago. Unlike the other neighbors' children who had been wary of my reticence, Jaziah had pushed and prodded for a friendship until I had yielded. Since then, we'd been brothers in heart. At times like these, however, his perceptiveness made my heart stumble.

"Wrong." I avoided his peering grey eyes, scanning a display of ornate Baihan mirrors with the brass finish my mother favored at bazaars. I ensured my face and eyes gave nothing of my turmoil away, a skill learned the hard way at school. But every muscle behind my leather uniform was as taut as my blades.

"The penalty for leaving without permission while school is in session is twenty lashes and a suspension," Jaziah warned. "Yes, we weren't suspended that time we snuck out like scallywags to attend a revel. But remember how our backs bled from the whipping? How being locked in the school's dungeon for three days felt like *dying*?"

I squeezed my blade's hilt against the memory. I'd only survived down there for that long because Jaziah had kept me from drowning in my thoughts with his whining. Since then, there was nothing we dreaded more than facing the Gergesenes Academy's student board. Yet if I stayed and was sent to the coronation, my greatest fear could manifest.

My bones chilled and I shook my head firmly. "What about the penalty for wrong accusations? I wasn't planning on scaling fences, you mother hen."

He huffed. "You can lie to your ladyloves but not to me, Dathan Issachar." He moved so that he was walking backward and facing me, his jawline set. "Each of the five elite academies is sending one student from its prime branch to the coronation. To showcase Thalesai's bright future to our people and the foreigners alike. Would I *kill* to represent the whole of Gergesenes Academies and our Baihan tribe at the coronation? To mingle with the nobles?

The Majesties, the generals, dynasts, and even the foreigners from other kingdoms? *Absolutely.*"

My chest prickled with longing and I fisted my hands. The side of me that craved the honor didn't matter. I couldn't risk my family's freedom by drawing the wrong type of attention.

"But if *you're* chosen," Jaziah continued quietly, stopping in front of me, "I'd know it's because you deserve it. Why are you so averse to receiving accolades when you work harder than many students I know?"

The question hovered heavily between us, one he'd been asking me for the past ten years. Why did you decline being part of the tour to visit the kingdom's prime garrisons when it was for the top ten students in our class? Why do you only fail the tests where the rewards are trips to the engineering bases in the north to see our greatest weaponry? Why do you turn down all of my father's invitations to the palace when I know how much the palace intrigues you?

But I never shared the answer with anyone, not even him. I didn't study or work hard for the accolades. I only wanted to make it into our kingdom's elite military unit and become so strong that no one could oppress my family ever again. The accolades were a great honor but would shine a light on me that I couldn't risk. If I'd known that striving for an elite soldier rank would lead to me being Gergesenes' representative at the coronation—because the illustrious event just had to coincide with my last year as a student—I would have dulled down my performance even if the mere thought of it hardened my gut.

"You know I avoid attention like the plague," I reminded him and nodded to our supervisor, who had returned to scan my street.

The brawny man's annoyance eased when he found me in position this time. I needed to return to the school's fence and make my escape plan. But since Jaziah was determined to play guardian, I supposed I was stuck being a good student.

Jaziah snorted as we resumed patrolling.

"Everyone who works hard enough to gain admission into the kingdom's elite academies wants attention. We *are* trying to occupy leadership positions, aren't we?"

"The elite soldiers aren't those kinds of leaders," I protested.

"They are the leading military unit." His face grew grave. "I mean, look at the Nergal Academies. Those bleeding mercenaries have been attacking their academy's branches along with farming villages. Yet, there are still younglings lined up all over the kingdom to take Nergal's admission exams next year."

Mentions of the Nergal attacks always ignited a flame of anger in my stomach. The elite academies admitted the best students from every Thalesain tribe, but each academy still had a tribe that it was mostly populated by. The Gergesenes and Nergal Academies were Baihan-populated. So news of Nergal's attacks hit us deeply because these were fellow Baihan youths being ravaged.

"*You're* a prime student too." I brushed aside his defiant hair from his eyes, a habit since he never let me trim his hair as low as it should be. "The Commandant might choose you to represent Gergesenes."

His eyes lit up at the prospect and I suddenly wanted him to receive the honor more than anything. But then he sighed dramatically. "I'm traveling to the Nergal Healing Academy in an hour to see my cousin for their Visiting Day."

I frowned at him. *Skies, he really is leaving me as the Commandant's choice!*

"I might be back before the Commandant chooses in four days. If I'm not and he chooses you, however—"

"*Please!*" a young male voice cried. "*Stop!*"

Jaziah and I halted and scanned the market, listening closely.

"*I'm sorry!*"

"It's coming from the spring!" I shouted, bolting for the sounds of splashing water and struggle.

Memories flashed through my mind of a younger me pleading with those exact words. Helpless with no one to save me. I ran faster, bursting into the settlement's spring. Baihan women had abandoned their buckets and chores, gathering at the center. The smell of soap and mud filled my lungs as I pushed through the crowd to the cobalt spring.

An angry merchant gripped a small boy by his collar, burying his head beneath the water. I ignored the boy's rags, the worn bag of potatoes tossed on the rocks, as I shoved myself between the merchant and the boy.

"Get away from him," I ordered.

The merchant didn't expect the intrusion. In one moment, I was pulling the boy's head out of the water. In the next, hands shoved my back and my world turned wet. I plunged out of the shallow spring and stood, dripping from head to toe.

Jaziah restrained the struggling merchant. "Stay still, *osao!*"

"That beggar stole my potatoes. The punishment for thievery in this settlement is *death*," the merchant fumed.

The women argued amongst themselves, divided on who to support. The boy panted as he crawled away from the water.

"He's just a boy," I said. "I'll pay for any losses, but by Osime, do not take his *life*. Are we this callous and indifferent to his suffering?"

My words rang through the spring. The women fell silent. The merchant's eyes flickered. No longer did he glare at the boy like a little demon, but he seemed to see the neglected child he was.

He sighed. "Those potatoes were not cheap. I lost my temper."

Moments later, the man affirmed that he was calmer and Jaziah released him. I gave him all the *siyvas* I had with me and made him vow not to harass the boy again. The boy stayed hidden until the merchant disappeared, then he crept out from behind the rock and ran to meet us.

"I didn't mean to steal, Scholar," he mumbled, still panting. "I don't like stealing, but I was hungry."

I looked at Jaziah. We'd never needed many words to read each other. Jaziah nodded and handed me two copper *siyvas*.

I gave them to the boy. "I suspected you were a smart boy. Next time you're hungry, join the people the academy feeds, alright? Asking for help is better than stealing—and it will keep you alive much longer."

The boy's lips wobbled as he gazed at the coins. He bowed so low that his little nose almost touched the ground. "Prosperity upon you for helping me, Scholars."

Ten years ago, I'd been as scared as you, pleading for help, but none came. Swallowing a rush of emotions, I nodded and he raced toward the hawkers selling boiled corn.

The market women praised us as they returned to their chores. Jaziah turned to survey my drenched uniform, then held my gaze.

"Another soldier might have agreed that the boy should be killed for theft."

I sighed, suddenly very weary. "He'd be a monster."

He nodded slowly. "You deserve the honor of representing Gergesenes in the palace, Nath. Accept it, and remember that whatever happens? *S'neh gi dhala*. You and I will overcome."

I made myself repeat our mantra, one we'd made during a particularly hard drill at the academy, that had carried us as a team through many challenges. But after he squeezed my shoulder and left to his post, guilt pressed down upon my chest.

I'd just lied to my friend. I would do whatever it took to avoid the king's coronation. Otherwise, if those who'd hunted my family into hiding found out we were still alive, we wouldn't survive their vengeance a second time. I was not powerful enough to protect them yet.

But I wouldn't stop until I was.

3

ZAIR

Pain and guilt constricted my chest until breathing hurt. I'd failed Sarai terribly. I should've held on to her when the attack started. I should've wielded my arrows quicker and impaled those mercenaries. But I'd failed.

I needed to fix it.

Parents of students poured into the wrecked academy, splitting to join one of three groups. Those in the makeshift infirmary that was busy with healers who had barely survived the attack themselves. Those on the heels of the soldiers here to investigate, demanding answers about their children's whereabouts. And those on the smoldering quadrangle, weeping as they searched under the broken pillars and stairs because they didn't want to believe that their children were part of those taken.

It was a world of pain, and as the day darkened into evening, I drowned in it.

My parents repeatedly called me over to the infirmary, but I moved with the group, dogging the soldiers' footsteps.

"I'm a military student," I said to the junior soldier jogging down the steps to deliver information to his superiors. "Please, let me join your team to pursue the mercenaries."

"Esans don't help anyone. They abandon the people who depend on them," he snapped, his uniform shining like a clamshell amidst the smoke and blood.

My chest twisted. "This has *nothing* to do with tribes!"

He whipped around to face me, his body radiating such hostility that I almost stepped back.

"Indeed? This academy took every measure to strengthen its security against mercenary attacks. Yet I'm to believe it's a coincidence that on the day you Esans visit, the mercenaries just managed to find a way around those defenses?"

I shouldn't be so shocked, yet the words lashed at me like a slap.

"You... you think my family had something to do with the attack?"

He studied my expression as if scouring for an affirmation of his suspicions.

"Those mercenaries attacked with fire from the *sky*," I said, trembling. "If my 'Esan blood' gave me even a quarter of that ability, my sister wouldn't be fighting for her life right now."

Guilt filled his eyes. Still, rather than apologize, he cleared his throat and turned around.

"We'll find the bandits. Stay out of our way while we work, for your own sake."

I watched speechlessly as he marched on. Of all the insults my family had received for my mother's tribe, this accusation of attacking children had to be the worst.

"Zair."

Drawing a steadying breath, I turned toward my father's voice with a brittle smile. "Yes, papa?"

Wariness pinched his tired face as he stared at the retreating soldier. "Sarai is finally conscious. She's asking for you."

I'm the soldier in this family, yet my sister was marked right under my nose.

The anguished thoughts twirled in my mind as I caressed Sarai's hair in our tiny lamp-lit bedroom. Our older sister was in the small tea garden outside, trying to calm her own disquiet by weeding. Beyond our walls, the southern quarters of Ari'el buzzed with activity as the night markets opened. Had it been a normal school break, I would be sitting on our flat rooftop with my sisters, talking about the day's events. Or reading a book while also keeping an eye on our crime-riddled quarters.

Tonight, I just wanted to hold Sarai.

She slept so peacefully only because my arms were around her on our shared bed. Even after I failed her, my little sister still felt safe with me. The ache inside my chest expanded until it felt like my entire body hurt.

Since we returned from the academy two nights ago, she'd become a shadow of herself. Too quiet. Jumpy, even when the healer had covered her wound. Staring with horrified eyes each time a door opened.

My throat lumped. "I'm so sorry, *ami*."

The door swung open and I stiffened, relaxing only when our parents entered. They sat on my older sister's bed with red-rimmed eyes. My mother had been sobbing in the washroom, where she thought we couldn't hear her. My father hadn't slept since our return. He was afraid those brutes would come and steal his youngest daughter if he shut his eyes for a moment.

We watched her, hearts in our mouths.

"Zair," my mother began gently. "It's time you returned to the academy."

My hand faltered. I drew a breath. "I know I have to, but Sarai..."

"No *buts*, Zair."

"One more day, mama..."

"You requested a three-day break to travel to the Healing Academy with us," she said. "It's been four days. The Nergal Military Academy is strict, and we can't let you lose your admission when you're only months from graduating."

I swallowed thickly. How could I concentrate at school when Sarai wasn't safe? Shadows danced over the bandages on her neck and chin. The wound would scar, and she'd never forget for even a moment that the mercenaries were coming back for her.

Saints, just like that they had stolen my sister's security.

Anger flushed through me and I fisted my hands. "You're right. I should return to the academy where I can find answers, glean what the Nergal Academies know about the mercenaries, and go after them."

"Don't do anything that will cost us you too," my father snapped. "Don't you think I want to chase after the mercenaries myself? But if Thalesai's soldiers are yet to find them, what chance do we have?"

I bit back a frustrated scream. Nothing killed me like this gnawing helplessness. The world was a hostile place for my family. I'd entered the Nergal Military Academy against all odds so that I could train to defend them. Now, at the first collision with real danger, I'd failed.

Reading my expression, my father rubbed a hand over his weary face. "Zair."

"I'm sorry." I couldn't stop saying those words.

He stood and squeezed my shoulder. "We cannot let those bastards ruin our entire lives. We'll do everything in our power to keep Sarai safe and trust that our soldiers will destroy the mercenaries soon. But you must return to school and keep fighting for the future you want."

My future would never be the same without Sarai in it. I couldn't just sit still and hope. I had to fight to save her.

"I'll leave for school tomorrow," I whispered and continued caressing her soft hair.

Saints, please let this not be the last time I hold my little sister.

"To *study*, not to infiltrate your Commandant's office, yes?" my father asked worriedly.

I reached forward and squeezed his hand, but I couldn't promise him that.

THE EVENING BREEZE rippled through my plain skirt and blouse as I stepped out of the kitchen door into the little tea garden surrounded by a wooden wall. My mother had woken Sarai to change her bandage. My father stayed close, telling Sarai a story to create an illusion of normalcy. Since it was decided that I would be returning to the academy tomorrow, I had a request to make of my older sister.

Niah knelt between beds of healthy plants, their rich scents blurring the odors of refuse that piled up along our street. She looked up at the soft squeak of the door, her face drawn with sadness, her callused hands covered in dirt. My heart squeezed.

"You've done enough work tonight, Niah. It's time to rest," I urged, glancing around the garden that she and my mother lovingly maintained.

Most areas in the southern quarters of the capital, including ours, were made up of filthy streets and crooked houses. And while I longed for the day that I could earn a good rank and move us to the better areas of Ari'el, my parents had striven to build us a home in the southern quarters that was warm and cared for. The walls and doors of our four-roomed house were small, yes, but they were sturdy, protecting us from the elements as well as invaders. Our rugs were old but kept clean with my sisters and I going to the nearby well every fortnight to wash them. My father, a cloth merchant, made sure to provide lovely fabrics yearly for my mother to sew into new drapes and beddings that beautified our house.

That same conscious care—in spite of our situation—was shown to the tea garden.

"*Rest* is going to be a strange word for a while," Niah said with a sigh, rubbing her hands together to rid them of dirt. "But you're right. Tiring myself out in the garden won't solve anything. I should tire myself out in the kitchen instead."

Amusement whispered through me as she held out her hand to me. I went to help her rise and we stood at the same height.

"I'm returning to the academy tomorrow," I told her.

Conflicting emotions zipped across her expressive face as we walked back to the kitchen. I was the military student but my older sister was also very protective of our family. Whether it was affront or anger she felt against bullies, it all showed on her face. Right now dread and understanding warred there, and my stomach flipped.

"What are you thinking?" I asked as we entered the lamp-lit kitchen, shutting the door and cold air behind us.

Two cabinets rested against the walls, filled with old utensils for cooking and tea-making. The single window opened above the stove, layered with wooden bars to keep thieves out. Through the light curtain, I scanned the dim street outside. Only a few Baihans rode by on treasured horses. The others walked quickly or in pairs, avoiding the darker alleys so the pickpockets and robbers couldn't attack them.

"I understand that you must return to the academy and complete your fifth year. You've worked hard for years to not. But with Sarai in danger, I worry about you leaving my sight. It's laughable since I'm no fighter." She gave a sad laugh, then swallowed. "But... I want our family to stay together where I can watch over everyone."

"It's not laughable. If it were possible, I would bring you all to the academy with me so we can stay together." I glanced briefly at her. "I have a request, Niah."

I opened the warm pot of vegetable rice. Its mild aroma tinted the kitchen, spiced simply with salt and ground crayfish. I ladled modest portions into the clay bowls with chipped paint that Niah set on the cabinet beside me.

Niah halved three boiled eggs on a plate and shared the cuts into the bowls since we couldn't afford to all eat full eggs. "You want me to write to you if the danger heightens around Sarai, even if papa and mama decide it's not serious enough to summon you."

Her guess was accurate.

"Will you?" I turned to face her, my tone pleading since Niah tended to agree with my mother on most things. "I can't leave if I'm not certain I can return in time to defend Sarai if our fears come to pass."

She swallowed thickly, arranging the bowls on the trays as she considered my request. Finally, she rubbed my shoulder in a reassuring gesture. "I'll write to you if things change for the worst. I promise."

I placed my hand on hers. "Thank you, *jidi*."

She lifted a tray of food. "Will you promise to stay safe when you leave?"

"You know I've been sleeping with my bow by my bed since year-one."

"That isn't a promise to stay safe," she countered.

I looked at my feet. She would smell it if I lied to her.

Hesitation radiated from her, but then she sighed and headed for the parlor door, worry weighing down her shoulders. "I'll pray for you every night."

"I'll appreciate it," I said softly. I carried the second tray and followed her out of the kitchen, a bit relieved. Now that I knew Niah would keep me informed, I could focus on keeping an ear down at Nergal. Listening for any information that could help me free Sarai from the mercenaries.

4

DATHAN

I must be long gone before dawn.

News had spread. The Commandant would choose Gergesenes' representative for the king's coronation ceremony tomorrow. Jaziah had not yet returned from the Nergal Healing Academy. I had hours to get out of school.

I shoved open the arched windows of my dorm room and bats squawked as they scattered into the cold night. Climbing down four floors of the smoothly-marbled, Agra-inspired wall in the dark would be punishing, but I wasn't exactly swimming in choices.

Bracing a leg outside the window ledge, I made to swing the other over the pane. Fingers grabbed my arm and yanked me back into my dorm room.

No. No. No!

I stumbled when my boots met the granite and my soldier's instincts surged. I shoved off the viselike grip, spun to face my restrainer, and gulped hard at the sight of the Commandant of Gergesenes Academies.

A Baihan tribesman in his forties, he was a mountain of a man with intelligent eyes that inspired instant respect. Or fear. Depending on what side of his goodwill you were on.

"Sir!" I stood at perfect attention, blood pounding in my ears.

"What in the sheols do you think you're doing, Issachar?" the Commandant roared.

"Training, sir!" I lied without pause.

His warm-mud eyes narrowed. For a dreadful second, I was certain he'd grill me for answers. He took a deep breath as if seeking calm. A gesture he made quite often with all the rascals under his wings.

When he spoke again, he looked less likely to devour my head.

"Follow me to my office."

"Yes, sir."

Blast it.

Broadly-built boys in nothing but shorts or bare backsides jumped aside in the dorm's passageway as we tore through it.

"Looks like Issachar's in trouble," someone announced.

I rolled my eyes as more heads popped out of doors.

"What did you do to get the Commandant so incensed, Issachar? Teach us your wise ways!"

"Close your wide mouths, you vagabonds," the Commandant barked over their snickers.

Their lips pressed together, holding back foolish grins.

We jogged down four flights of stairs and burst into a tame night with fewer staff striding past and crickets chirping. The dunes were silvery pyramids calling me to their obscurity. A dusty breeze teased the sweat beading on my temples.

If only Jaziah had returned from his visit to the Nergal Healing Academy, he would've known how to silence the voices of alarm with his insistent encouragement. That did it. If Jaziah didn't return by tomorrow I was riding out to find him, or else this dread flooding my chest would drown me.

For tonight, I tried a diversion technique on the man whose school taught it to me. "Sir, Scholar Jaziah would make a great Gergesenes representative at the king's coronation. Don't you think?"

Sheols, even my voice sounds desperate.

The Commandant opened his mouth to speak but then looked away. I frowned, noticing how the tension in his shoulders rivaled even mine. Grimness tightened his face, his eyes hard as we crossed the warren of dorms coated in Gergesenes' dusk-blue and black colors.

I was smart enough to fall quiet and observe.

Students boomeranged in and out of the lamplit buildings. The studious ones read in the classrooms, and the overeager year-one pupils clanged training swords on quadrangles. Oval doorways gleamed with the Gergesenes insignia: a great hawk with its wings splayed proudly, our slogan *For Honor* engraved underneath.

The night seemed normal, save that the watchtowers rising from the academy's four ends were manned by twelve archers each with nocked arrows. That was far more than the usual four archers: two guards and two students-in-training keeping easy watch.

In my five years at Gergesenes, I'd never seen the watchtower guards poised for attack. My stomach hardened for a different reason. *Trouble.*

We arrived at the administration block with its gleaming marble walls and flat roofs, and strode briskly for the Commandant's office. It was oddly dim and quiet. Before I could ask the Commandant the reason why, we reached his office.

Armors clinked as soldiers lingered in the hallway, but these weren't Gergesenes Academy's guards.

"Open the door," the Commandant said.

I did as ordered and waited for him to precede me. His usually-bright office was warm and dimly lit, like there was a presence here that no one could know about.

Exquisite plasterwork of hawks ornamented the ceiling, reflecting on the spit-shine glass tiles. An armchair shrieked against the tiles, and the Admiral of Thalesai rose from it.

Ten sheols.

My soul almost leaped out of my body. I gawked at the man who commanded the kingdom's forces. He'd saved the late king from an assassination, dug out every rogue group that started tribal attacks across the land, and kept our borders impenetrable. Lithe and a bit weathered, his exploits were sung about during our grueling drills. The soldier every aspiring and existing soldier strove to imitate.

"You better not drool on my tiles, Issachar," the Commandant said dryly.

I came to attention and gave my best salute. "Sir."

The Admiral looked me over, from the black scarf keeping my hair from my face to the muscles stretching my sleeves, down to the dagger in my boot. His expression betrayed no thought. My skin stretched taut as I wondered what verdict he would come to.

Unimpressive for a soldier? Passable?

My lifelong aspiration to join the Majesties' elite soldiers would be lost if he dismissed me as unimpressive. A familiar hollowness spread in my chest. Guilt, for this incessant desire to join the kingdom's elite soldiers when I should be content with a regular military rank that would surely keep me out of the public eye. Yet the Ironteenth Fighters received advanced combat training that would hone me into an indomitable soldier. A man who could defend my family from everything.

Finally, the Admiral turned to the door where the Commandant stood. He gave the Commandant a nod.

"At ease, Issachar," the Commandant said before sitting behind his hand-carved desk.

The Admiral resettled in his seat, his brocade tunic and bronze Baihan armbands gleaming in the dimness.

How was he familiar with the Commandant? *Wake up, you awestruck slug. Of course, they know each other.* There were times I forgot the Commandant was a retired general of Thalesai.

"I'm sure you're wondering why I've summoned you," the Commandant said, his mien still tense and somewhat... mournful.

Clasping my hands behind my back, I said, "For the king's coronation."

"It begins in two days."

Saints no. "Yes, sir."

"You are one of the best student's this academy has seen. Therefore, I've chosen you to attend as Gergesenes' representing student."

My chest caved in but I kept my face composed. The Commandant didn't pause to wonder why I wasn't dancing around his office, or at the very least, thanking him profusely. Anyone else in my place would've been.

"But I'm not sending you to the Al'Qtraz only to honor the king." A pause. "I also want you to root out a snake."

My mind cinched on that. I frowned. "I don't understand, sir."

The Admiral answered, "I'm certain, Scholar, that you know of the mercenaries infiltrating Thalesai's borders, attacking small villages, and abducting students from academies."

I swallowed. "Yes, sir."

Neither man spoke for a while, the Admiral *tap-tap-tapping* his fingers against the table.

He finally said, "Facts prove that the mercenary unit is aided by someone in the leadership circles. The information that helps them plan flawless attacks against our well-guarded institutions isn't one peddled on the streets or shared as far as our border areas where they target. That is information shared behind the palace's closed doors."

He let the words sink in.

"The mercenary unit is also known to use advanced weaponry that common bandits cannot afford. Based on these, and other classified evidence, we've come to the conclusion that a Thalesain leader is funding the mercs."

The revelation hit like a blow. The depth of treachery.

"If the neighboring kingdoms—our former oppressors—sniff these weaknesses in Thalesai," he said weightily, "they could scheme to infiltrate us again."

And we could fall back to the days of bondage.

My shoulders stiffened against the fate. Yet what did this have to do with me?

"The king's first decree as ruler was a ban on handlers in the palace," the Admiral continued.

"By handlers, you mean spies, sir?" I asked carefully, a ticking starting in my head.

A brief nod. "His Majesty knows that the palace is one of the tensest places in the kingdom, especially due to the conflicts between the Ussi and Baihan chambermen. He believes that if the chambermen retain their spies, prying into each other's affairs and plotting sabotage, the tensions will continue to worsen. And if the rulers of the tribes are in dissent, the rifts in the kingdom would never be bridged. So he has decided that during his rule, the Al'Q-traz will be a neutral ground. No spies or covert activity.

"While this decree is commendable, it has put me in a tight spot where I have to choose the least suspicious person possible to infiltrate the palace and gather information."

Skies above, he could not mean me.

"As a student invited to the king's coronation," the Admiral said, "no one would expect you to be a spy. And if indeed you are one of Gergesenes' prime students, then you can help me find what I need."

I kept my face composed but my mind swirled. Attending the coronation would not only set me up to be found by the man hunting my family, becoming a *spy* as well would cost me a position in the Ironteenth Fighters if I was caught. He wanted me to break the king's rules.

It went against everything Gergesenes taught me.

Your fealty is to the King of Thalesai. Protect the king at all cost.

Besides, I was no 'handler' but a warrior in training. We took practical courses on the *Art of Espionage* in year-four, yes, but that hardly made me a spy.

Yet superiors did not ask in the military. This was an order.

"Issachar has excelled above his peers in combat, weapons, disguise, and intelligence training," the Commandant affirmed to the Admiral. "If any student can maneuver the tight security in the palace, it is him."

"I sense doubt from you, Scholar Issachar," the Admiral noted.

"Allow me to settle it." The Commandant regarded me with something akin to grief. "There's also the issue of the abducted students."

Not fair. He was playing a card I could never ignore. I knew torment too well, was *sickened* by the mere thought of it, to not rise up to help Nergal's missing students if I had the chance.

"Our military is scouring the kingdom to rescue them, and the king is sparing no expense for this search," the Admiral continued, placing a fist on the table. "However, my soldiers are constantly five steps behind the mercenaries. They seem to know our every move before they are even finalized. Only someone in the close circles of the Al'Qtraz can know of the military's rescue plans, alerting the mercenaries before their camps are found."

A chill swept through me.

The Commandant said with a grave expression, "We need you to uncover who in the palace is aiding the mercenaries *and* what they want with the students they take. Before the Gergesenes Academies fall victim to their next string of attacks."

I swallowed, but otherwise kept my face expressionless. "Yes, sir."

"And Issachar." Sadness dimmed his eyes. "I know you have doubts. And there's no easy way to share this report, but if you need further motivation—" he hesitated, "—then do it for Jaziah."

The ticking grew louder in my head. "I don't understand, sir."

That was a lie. Jaziah hadn't returned since he left for the Healing Academy, but he was a soldier. I'd refused to even assume that he'd been caught up in the raid.

"Jaziah was at the Nergal Healing Academy during its attack. He was among the youths captured."

The confirmation shattered the glass walls I'd built around myself, knocking the air from my lungs. *No.*

"It can't be." Horrific images of my friend in chains clogged my throat with bile.

The Commandant's eyes were bloodshot now. "It is. Find the traitor, and perhaps we can rescue Jaziah before it's too late."

5

ZAIR

The desert dawn was a roll of coral and azure, the surrounding sand dunes rising and falling tan clouds. The crisp air bit my face. Usually, dawn brought me peace; the gentle hours to soak in the new day before I had to face my peers' scowls and titters in the classroom. But now that the mercenaries had marked my sister, I would only find the dawn peaceful again when they were destroyed.

It didn't help that the Commandant of Nergal's Academies tense presence beside me made my stomach cramp. Our boots thumped silently against gravel as the academy's mudbrick stables grew closer. Two hundred and fifty voices reciting the Nergal Academy's pledge resounded across the landscape. My mates continued the morning assembly on the main quadrangle where she had summoned me from. Something told me I wouldn't be joining them in our *History of Thalesai* class either this morning, or in the dining hall for morning tea.

A petite woman with a big presence, the Commandant was grimmer than usual. Her pristine jacket and trousers highlighted her toned physique. Little scars from her days in battle splattered over her cocoa-toned face and hands, her dark hair in a single braid.

Four sergeants halted their patrol to salute her, then frowned at me as she gave them permission to carry on. I didn't recognize them. They had to be from the new squad sent to increase the academy's security. Even the academy's civilian workers—cleaners and cooks—had now been ordered to carry weapons everywhere.

Ma'am, do you know of any child that was marked *by the mercenaries? What became of them?*

It was too tempting to ask her directly. Throughout my five years in this stone labyrinth, she'd never paid attention to me, not even with how high I kept my scores to earn her approval. Now that she'd summoned me, I itched to ask to be recruited in the efforts to find the mercenaries.

She led me through the stable doors into the familiar smell of sawdust and straw. We passed Lantern's stall, the first horse I had been trained to ride in year-one.

I started, "Ma'am—"

"You were at the Nergal Healing Academy during the attack a week ago," she interrupted me, her voice composed.

The invasion of her third school in only four months had to be eating at her. But she'd worn a controlled air when she'd promised us at yesterday's assembly that our schools would be made safe again.

I swallowed hard from the raw memories of the attack. "Yes, ma'am."

The Commandant halted before a stall with a saddled gelding, but still, she didn't look at me.

"Do you know what will be done to the kidnapped students?" she asked. "How the abductors keep their captives subdued, even when their captives outnumber them?"

My throat thickened. The answer was explained in gruesome details in our history tome, *The Red History*.

Bleakness entered her eyes. "The abductors break their spirits. They starve and beat their captives until they lose both strength and will to escape. During our searches, we've encountered signs that this is what is being done to my children."

My stomach wobbled. If we couldn't protect Sarai, she would soon be one of those children.

The Commandant's face became drawn, accentuating a scar along her brow. "This is the third attack on a branch of our academy in four months. The reason they keep taking more students and as many as fifty at a time—is because the ones in captivity are dying. We've found bodies. If the rest are not recovered soon, the torments will kill more of them in a few weeks too. And then another academy will be attacked to gather more students. An academy that could be our very own—until the mercenaries meet whatever goal they have."

Horror stabbed at my lungs. My lips parted but I didn't know what to say.

I'd destroyed their lightning with my arrow, I almost blurted. But I couldn't mention practicing anything that sounded like magic. It made people treat me like I was a freak. Especially my classmates.

"I'm sending you on a mission, Scholar Nebah. This school has equipped you with every key skill a warrior needs. Hand-to-hand combat, weapons training, espionage, gesture-reading, and endurance. Are you willing to serve your school and kingdom?"

I didn't hesitate. My boots snapped as I stood at attention. "Yes, ma'am."

"Good." Fire burned in her eyes. "You'll attend the king's coronation as an invited guest. And there, you will land a blow that will cripple these mercenaries who dare harm my children."

My chest leaped. *An opportunity. An opportunity to help Sarai.*

Hay crunched as she preceded me into the stall and there, the Commandant of Nergal spoke in a lethal voice.

"Intel came from above. There's a traitor in the Al'Qtraz funneling information and resources to the mercenaries. It's the reason they have diligently countered all of Nergal and the military's efforts to rescue the students."

My spine tautened. Someone in the palace was sponsoring the mercenaries?

"You'll attend the coronation as our representative. Once you're in the palace, you must sieve out the poison in the water."

Staggering understanding came of the statement used as a code in Nergal. "Espionage is forbidden in the Al'Qtraz," I blurted. "Apprehended spies are executed in the city's square."

I'd seen two dead bodies with slit throats in the city square, displayed on poles for days after in warning. Was that the reason she chose *me*? I had Esan blood, therefore I was expendable if caught. And if I ever exposed her as my sender... she could deny me.

"I know it is forbidden." The Commandant's eyes flickered but her tone remained unwavering. "But it is a risk that must be taken. Or else Thalesai's younger generation might never be safe again."

My mind spun. I was being sent to spy because the other students of this school's lives were treasured above mine. That had to be the reason. It burned in my ribs. Yet this could be it. My one chance to protect Sarai. "What would I do with the traitor?"

"When you find the betrayer amongst Thalesai's rulers, you will assassinate him."

My head fell silent. "Assassinate."

"Cut off the serpent's head and leave no trail behind. Once the traitor is gone, the mercenaries will lose their intel and provision. They'll be weakened and our soldiers will find them."

Assassinate.

She angled her head toward a small bag on a horse, packed with tools to aid my mission as a spy. But she wasn't sending me only to find the traitor working against her academy, but to end the traitor's life.

"You'll have only twelve days, marked by the seven ceremonies of the coronation: the Receptions, the Tour, the Blessing of the King, the Best of Ten, the Queen's *Vyji*, the Crowning, and the Gifting. Twelve days, Scholar. Can I trust you with this assignment?" she asked, leading the horse outside by the reins. "Can I trust you to let no one and nothing stop you?"

I wanted to balk. The weight of it was too great.

I fisted my hands against the fear. I couldn't let the enemy take my sister.

Footsteps shuffled by a canopied bench a few feet away. Someone stalked off, as if they'd been close by, watching us. The figure was feminine, but a viridescent veil concealed her face. Even hurrying off, she possessed the regal bearing of someone who knew her worth.

Was it she—whoever she was—who ultimately wanted a student spy from Nergal? Who gave my Commandant permission to go against the king's order and infiltrate the Al'Qtraz? I glanced at my Commandant who didn't look twice at the intruder.

They're definitely acquainted.

I had to be sure of her reasoning first before I threw my neck under the blade. "Why me, Commandant?"

She couldn't know what had happened to my sister, and she had never before acknowledged me.

"You're a student of the Nergal Academies and a citizen of Thalesai, are you not?" she replied vaguely.

She did not want to admit that I was expendable. I ran my fingers through the horse's mane. Perhaps I could save Sarai while also proving myself to the Commandant. If I stopped the traitor singlehandedly, the Commandant might finally *see* me. There was also the Best of Ten contest that was held during every coronation. If I triumphed at this Best of Ten for the Nergal Military Academy, it would be impossible for her to dismiss me. And then she might recommend me for an Ironteenth Archer's rank when I graduated in five months.

If I came out of this alive.

The Commandant halted. "If you doubt you can succeed at this mission…"

"I don't. I will do it," I said and prayed to the great Osime that I indeed could.

"Good."

You must sieve out the poison in the water.

Can I trust you to let no one and nothing stop you?

My mission sang a daunting song in my head as I rode through the gates of the military academy built into the southwest of the Geidam Dunes. In the early afternoon, the flat sand-and-rock landscape dotted with cacti spread out to kiss the wide open sky. Hot breeze whistled over my skin and dust grazed my throat. I was a lone figure on the sweltering terrain with the dunes rising behind. My only companions were the occasional rattlesnakes slithering from under rocks to check if I was a giant rat by chance.

As the hour passed, the wide Tiz valley soon colored the desert with the emerald of palm trees and the cerulean of the Niger River, welcoming me to Ari'el's gates. The smell of spices and dry air submerged me in the city's bustle. Ari'el was a city of hope, a symbol of human perseverance. Thousands of domes steamed under the orange sunlight, streets slashing through with horses and people in breezy attire.

I halted under an arched, windy bridge where six beggars always gathered. Lowering my eyes, I placed a copper *siyva* in each of their leaky alm-bowls.

"Oh, thank you!"

"Saints bless you!"

It was almost all I had, and maybe it was from understanding dejection, but I couldn't pass beggars by without helping in some way.

Oh, Osime, I prayed silently, *help us all find peace in our lives someday.*

I flicked my horse's reins, battling with the desire to stop by my home. It wasn't far from the gates, but if anything had happened to Sarai, my older sister would've sent me a message.

Focus.

Anxiety and hope twirled in my belly with each clop closer to the Al'Qtraz. It gleamed in the distance like a giant mother-of-pearl. Behind it, red-gray mountains curved like tongues licking the sky. It was the greatest honor to be present at the coronation, but I had not been sent there to be honored.

My arms throbbed dully as I pulled the reins, halting at the base of the thronging hill. Lords and ladies rode vibrant carriages and decorated camels up the cobblestone street built into the hill. Servants followed behind them in wagons that groaned under the weight of chests and bags. Painted glass and terracotta statues of the past Kings and Queens of Thalesai in their tribal ensembles held lamps as they lined up the hill at twenty-feet, drawing reverential stares.

At the hill's top, the beautiful palace of pale sandstone and marble soared for the heavens. Golden domes and white pillars shone under the late afternoon sunlight.

"The palace was built over a century ago," a passing Kwali merchant with his tribal ear-piercings told his young daughters animatedly. The two girls sat on his camel's back, along with bundled items, while he trekked and led the animal by its reins. "Expert artisans across the kingdom were summoned and tasked to craft a magnificent wonder for the first human king."

I surveyed the small, exquisitely garbed family. A chameleon's strongest defense was blending in. If I could merge with the palace's crowd, a harmless friend, I and my mission would be less conspicuous.

I added tentatively, "Our tutors swear that no effort was spared in the quest to build a palace that rivaled the other kingdoms'. Even though our tutors were not alive then."

The children giggled at my wry tone, encouraging me.

"You see, little ones, the Al'Qtraz, *the Sand Palace*, was built after the five human tribes merged into one kingdom. Then the Aziza King doused it and this entire hill with a night enchantment to fight off magical attacks."

The girls gasped in awe. So I didn't add, *"His peace offering for tyrannizing us."*

I smiled, knowing it was also more than that. The azizas couldn't afford to lose human resources entirely. After the war, their leaders sought to give us a great gift, seeking acceptance as Thalesai's trade partners despite their past as our slavers. Thalesai's king accepted the palace magic only after his seer confirmed its purity.

The Kwali merchant nodded, but then he looked up and saw my Esan eyes. His jaw clenched and he led his camel away. "You're a long way from Dahomey, creature."

Just like that, my trepidation worsened over this stay in the palace. Alright. If I couldn't blend in by making them accept me, I'd make them avoid me instead. Drawing in a breath, I flicked my horse's reins and rejoined the dozens streaking toward the arched entrance.

Clad in my school uniform of midnight leather, a starlight-silver cape, and a silver brooch of Nergal's insignia, the guards only needed to see my Commandant's letter and seal to allow me to pass. Still, they shot me warning looks before they moved aside for my horse. Could they know? That despite being a military student, my purpose here was to eliminate a leader they guarded?

Don't be paranoid. How could they possibly know?

They had more advanced training to analyze people than I did, but I had also learned how to avoid being read.

I swung off my horse and a stable boy seemed to materialize, taking the animal away. Another guard at the inner gate led me through an ornamental yard with starflowers lining the paths and alabaster fountains spraying lavender-scented water. As my boots thudded on the cobbled paths, I quietly recited my plan of attack.

Study the gatherings, seek suspects, investigate them, find concrete evidence... and eliminate the culprit.

Beside a tiered fountain, I recognized a uniform. One of the elite academies' representatives was early.

The broad boy wore the Ahimoth Military Academy's uniform —red leather and a black cape cinched with a silver brooch of a bear. Ahimoth ranked number one amongst Thalesai's five elite academies. Yet everyone knew it was because the academy's owners were Ussi tribesmen. With a majority of the Chamber seats occupied by the Ussis, Ahimoth had numerous sponsors and the most advanced teachers, grooming more Ussis to hoard more leadership seats someday.

"Once another representative arrives, the three of you will be led into a parlor to wait for the others," the guard said brusquely when we reached the student, then left.

The student surveyed the yard, his bearing prouder than the nobles strolling toward the palace's grand entrance. His fierce scowl and reddish hair might as well have been warning signs blaring, '*Avoid this boy if you don't want to complicate your mission.*'

I bit my lip, impatient as I scanned past the perennials and climbing flowers to the tall, golden domes of the palace. Where were the other students?

"Oh saints, *yes*."

"Hush!"

Two young women giggled as the embroidered hems of their amethyst skirts slid past my feet, their glances fluttering toward something behind me. I turned around.

A young man in dusk-blue leather displaying the hawk insignia of Gergesenes strode my way. For a brief moment, his stunning eyes and sculpted features stole my breath. What did the saints do?

Spend decades carving his sharp jawline, those high cheekbones, and slightly uptilted eyes?

A thin bronze band glittered around his curly umber hair, signifying his Baihan roots. He had to be around my age, maybe a year older. Nineteen. That striking face was stonier than the Plateaus of Rahbat spreading under the eastern sky as he surveyed the yard, standing taller than almost everyone here. From the innate confidence in his every step, I couldn't tell who would be the most arrogant. Him or the Ahimoth student.

I suddenly felt small, out of my depth, and I hated the feeling. I lifted my chin. Unexpectedly, our gazes collided, and my chest gave an odd flutter. He peered into my eyes, brows lowering as he took in the unusual rings in them. His were hazel... beautiful and piercing.

"Bleeding sheols!" the Ahimoth boy exclaimed.

I broke Gergesenes' gaze and turned. Ahimoth pinned me with his focus like a scythe. I realized too late what he was contemplating.

"The Nergal Academy sent Esan scum to contaminate the palace with aziza blood?"

I wasn't braced for the derisive words uttered so loudly that across the yard, heads snapped over to me. My stomach hardened. He'd just howled to the pack and pointed me out as the prey.

6

DATHAN

I pinched my nose in irritation as the Ahimoth student opened his oversized mouth. Today marked Jaziah's fifth day in captivity. I'd left Gergesenes this morning with an ache in my chest because he hadn't been there to readjust my collar as always since the academy's twilight waking hour made dressing up tricky. Jaziah was in danger. And yet this mission to save him—my presence in the palace—could damn my family.

After the Admiral had left Gergesenes, I had weighed the risks and asked the Commandant to send another student to the palace. When I couldn't tell him what I avoided here, he'd sternly held my gaze and asked if I would leave my friend to die when I could save him.

It was hardly a question. Yet the answer could cost me everything.

And as if that wasn't bad enough, Ibhar Ghed had been sent as Ahimoth's palace representative.

"You dare to look up at the palace with those snaky holes in your head, Esan girl?" he spat.

"My name is Zair. And you're one to talk, Ussi boy," the Nergal girl retorted in soft tones.

Zair. A rare name. Her sable hair had been styled in neat zigzag weaves that then flowed down to her waist, enhancing her fierce expression. Despite her severe stare though, her face shone with more beauty than most women in the yard. Her almost ethereal features harkened to her aziza heritage, I quickly realized.

"What is that supposed to mean?" Ibhar demanded.

"Ibhar," I warned.

"This isn't your field, Dathan!" he snapped.

"Indeed?" Our academies competed at the winter butteball tournaments. He played dirty and didn't care who he crushed to win. Not when his father, a chamberman, was there to bribe and threaten board members to save Ibhar from punishment. After he'd crippled my teammate two years ago, along with his dreams of being a soldier, I made Ibhar my mark to beat on the field. We rarely ended matches without exchanging blows.

Here he was again, in the Sand Palace, revealing his inner worm.

Zair had flinched from his insult as if slapped, yet didn't attempt to shield the vivid feature of her hated tribe by bowing her head. Guilt stung my chest because, like others in the yard, I stared at her eyes too—those double golden rings around their dark depths.

But while I had no love for the Esans, I loathed bullying more.

"You would act dumb—like you don't know why your type isn't welcome here?" Ibhar let his voice resound, deliberately drawing attention. "Your presence threatens everything the coronation stands for. What did the Esan Empire do during the Invasions when humans had been battling enemies on all fronts?"

"Scuttle over to merge with the azizas for protection, abandoning fellow humans to suffer the oppression and indignities!" a regal Baihan noble sneered, fueling Ibhar's mood. "Only to be reduced into aziza slaves in the same year they signed over ownership of the Esan Empire."

Ibhar nodded.

"Stop this," I hissed as shame and anger stained Zair's face.

More people buzzed toward our gathering like calves to milk. They would happily take their resentment for the azizas out on this girl.

Ibhar barked on. "And then *after* humans had spilled their blood in the War, you Esans thought you could escape aziza territories and trickle back into the unified human lands like you have a right, pregnant with spawns tainted with aziza blood."

They'd birthed a new generation of children with the strange gold-ringed aziza eyes that now characterized the Esan tribe.

"How could I forget?" she returned tightly. "Till this day, the other tribes still punish the Esans for their ancestors' misdeeds."

"Misdeeds?" Ibhar laughed bitterly. "You call abandoning your kind 'misdeeds'. Your eyes are enough to prove that word puny."

"And the freakish abilities too," a Mizsab nobleman added, gesturing his gold-patterned hands. "How they can *smell* lies like..."

"Like dogs." Ibhar smirked as Zair recoiled.

"You want to pick on someone, Ibhar?" I challenged softly. "I'm here."

My dislike for the Esan tribe wasn't shaped by the past but the present. A majority of the Esan tribespeople were dishonest rats. Using their abilities to become smugglers of contrabands and thieves. Greedy with a hunger for *siyva* that overrode honor. Yet if the girl was here representing Nergal, it had to mean she was one of the decent Esans. Nergal's Commandant would never send her here otherwise. Ibhar was smart enough to know this. He chose to ignore it.

"Leave this place now, azishit," Ibhar spat the slur.

Onlookers echoed the insult.

Embarrassment dimmed her eyes, only partly hidden by her resolve.

"I was invited here by the king. You have no authority to tell me what to do."

A growl escaped Ibhar. He didn't like being put down by anyone, least of all an Esan girl, in public. He crowded her and rammed a fist to her cheek.

People gasped. I saw scarlet. The girl's cheek reddened but she didn't cower, as if being hit by strangers was her reality. Instead, with focused agility, she whipped around for momentum and slammed her boot against his right knee. Ibhar stumbled from the force, his honed balance the only reason he didn't fall into the fountain.

Scholar Zair had more in store for him.

Her hand shot to her portable club, her focus cinched on Ibhar's head. *Blast it*.

Before she could do something she'd regret, I dived between them and nudged her arm downward. Wrong choice.

The weighty club slammed into my shoulder, might've broken my shoulder blade if the steel plates in my uniform didn't absorb the impact.

Clenching my teeth against the throb, I gripped her wrist. Her gaze remained on Ibhar, chin hardened with disappointment that she hadn't put a dent in her target's skull. My anger flared and I shoved her hand down before the soldiers saw her weapon. The wooden clubs were designed to wound assaulters but when wielded against vulnerable body parts, like the head, they could do much worse than wound.

"He struck you and you struck him back. That's enough. *Walk away*."

Her gaze finally tore from Ibhar to me, wavering between remorse and defense. The gold rings there sparkled with eerie beauty.

"Sorry. But don't think you can tell me what to do either, Gergesenes," she hissed, then stepped around me and strode for the entrance. The guard must've announced that it was time for us to go in.

Frowning at her, I touched my throbbing shoulder and shot Ibhar a warning glare as he fumed. "Behave yourself, Ahimoth, or deal with me here too."

He growled, righting his brooch and cape.

The palace guard halted at the magnificently carved entrance and waved a hand. "Come along, Scholars."

Taking sharp strides, I caught up with the guard and Zair. Ibhar bounded close. The three of us fell into step behind him, entering a vast foyer and then taking a turn into an airy passage that buzzed with courtiers. I couldn't resist the urge to study Zair. Head tilted, she soaked in the gilded columns that framed the rococo ground floor passage and its floor-to-ceiling windows that overlooked the dipping sun. Ibhar almost towered over her, yet if I hadn't stepped in to apparently offer myself as his shield, she might've beaten him to the ground with her aimed hits.

"Your skills out there were lethal," I said to her.

She blinked at me in surprise, but then her lips pressed together. She turned and stared straight ahead.

My breath stalled, but I gave a disbelieving laugh. "You intend to ignore me."

"I'm not here to form friendships with rival academies, Gergesenes," she replied, the light from the chandeliers glowing on her smooth skin.

I squashed the observation and stared ahead too, annoyance rippling through me. Point taken.

I took in the feast unfolding as we climbed down terracotta steps into a glowing courtyard garden. Like treasured trinkets dangling on a woman's ear, hundreds of quartz lanterns glittered on hydrangeas wrapped around pillars and the lower branches of redbud trees.

"It's stunning," Zair breathed.

Tension made me see the garden as little more than a field of sparks waiting to incinerate my life.

Jaziah is out there in this cold night, likely starved and freezing.

An ache squeezed my throat.

Dozens celebrated the welcome of the king's guests in flowing richly-dyed gowns and embroidered robes with beaded caps. Long sapphire pools snaked between broad-leaved plants. The lanterns gilded the furniture set on the white granite floor between tall figurines of dahlias and lavenders.

Members of the king's three Chambers mingled. Dread and anticipation whipped in my chest at the prospect of meeting with them. Dread because there remained a chance I would run into those that hunted my family like dogs years ago. Who still haunted my dreams. Anticipation because I could launch straight into seeking out the traitor.

One lesson we'd been taught in the *Art of Espionage* was that there was always something that gave a rotten egg away. A smell, a taint, you just had to pay attention.

"Now, *this* is a party." Ibhar adjusted his chunky gold rings and veered toward a gaggle of girls in vibrant lace gowns.

"Not so fast." Our guard clasped his shoulder.

A maid hurried over as our guard said seriously, "There are

foreigners present, so our elite students must look their best. You're covered in dust and sweat from your long journeys. Follow the maid to the courtyard's washrooms to clean up and wait for the remaining students. Greet the Majesties *together*, then you can mingle."

With that instruction, he left the courtyard. Only the Ironteenth were allowed near the royals. Half of the brutal swordsmen, spearmen, and archery teams manned the balconies and entries in their coal-black armor. Keen eyes trailed the foreigners in our midst. As a sign of good faith, the king had ordered no one to carry pure iron, mirrored shields, or fabric coated in the *napellus* herb—the magical beings' weaknesses that had helped humans defeat their forces during the War. The Ironteenth Fighters were the exception. Pure iron blades sat strapped to their honed bodies, the mirror end of their double-sided shields faced inward, only as long as the wraiths behaved, and the arrowheads were coated in *napellus* in case the shapeshifters misbehaved. If any of the mystical beings sneezed suspiciously in the direction of our king and queen, not even their magic would save them from the Ironteenth's barrage.

That would be me and Jaziah amongst the Ironteenth Swordsmen someday—if I get Jaz out of captivity before the worst happens. I would have the arms and skills to protect the Majesties, along with everyone I loved. Maybe then my father would finally understand my path.

"Isn't this enthralling, Scholars?" the Kwali maid asked us, sweeping an appreciative glance over me as she wove through the ostentatious celebration.

Yes, the same way fire was enthralling until it incinerated you.

Zair likely shared my thoughts; the violent girl moved purposefully but quietly. *She'd apologized.* If you could call it that. While my Baihan tribesmen smiled proudly at me and Ibhar's Ussi tribesmen patted his shoulder, guests spat at Zair's feet and turned their noses up at her. Another person in my place might relish it as vengeance for her assault. But our leaders' hostilities toward a young student bothered me.

She kept her rosy lips and slanted eyes expressionless in a guarded front. Was she as aware that there was no other Esan person in this gathering of leaders?

"I didn't think Khosa Tewasere would make it to the coronation. The man is as old as the generational tree at my villa's backyard. He can barely stand, let alone rule!"

The Baihan chiefs lounging in cushions frowned over the rims of their goblets at a wrinkled Mizsab man who sat two tables ahead, enjoying the dance performance.

"Indeed. His Majesty is young yet he keeps a court filled with ancient men and women. Many of these Ussi and Mizsab nobles are old enough to hand over the reins of power."

Ibhar's jaw tensed at the chief's Binhese remark, but he had the sense to keep his face neutral as we bowed and passed the men. The ceremony appeared harmonious, but a trained eye could see the tension rising between the tribes. The kind that also sparked between us all and the foreigners in our midst.

"I still can't understand why our kingdom waits an entire year after the saints have ordained a king to coronate him." I frowned as a snake-charmer thrust his serpent near my face. "Too much ceremony for a land that should be focused on rebuilding."

"I believe it's sensible," Zair argued in that low voice, as if she was careful never to draw attention her way. "He's to be the ruler of five very... distinct tribes."

Ibhar snorted. "*Distinct?*"

He flung sneers from Zair to me, rival military students he was sure he was better than.

Zair lifted her chin, her head barely reaching my shoulders. "Either way, the king needs to observe. He needs to allow the chambermen to handle the brunt of rulership during his first year. Then he can learn the ropes and decide what kind of leader he wants to be."

"Who would've thought that the girl who tried to kill me with a club would be an idealist?" I asked drily over the nearby thumping of djembe drums.

Her lips parted. "I did not try to *kill* you."

"No, you tried to maim *me*." Ibhar gave her a dark smirk. "You've just made yourself an enemy, Esan girl."

Zair's jaw clenched yet she didn't flinch from his words like she had in front of the crowd. It made me wonder how that mind behind the beautiful mask worked.

"You sound as if we've not had bad rulers since the human lands amalgamated," I said, probing.

"It might not be foolproof, but it has its benefits, Gergesenes," she shot back, quick to grow defensive like all Esan tribespeople.

The thought silenced my debating mood. Wouldn't it be precious to unabashedly be who you claimed you were? Rather than feel with every breath like you were being pulled in two directions. I scanned the festivities more urgently now. I needed to break away from this group and the unwanted feelings Zair and Ibhar stirred within me. Where were those washrooms?

Nobles from the king's three Chambers laughed on their cushions, drinking from silver goblets and eating grilled *suya* as the Ussi costumed dancers entertained.

Which one of you has Thalesai's youths in shackles?

I angled my head to study the dignitaries admiring the peacocks around a garden pond. And jerked to a stop like a boulder had been slammed against me.

Bald head, black skin, with gold studs in his earlobes. Orcus Sarhedrin. The Dynast of Bornoir. He ambled past the pond, hands clasped behind him.

Memories gushed through my mind like a dark river. Ten-year-old me running through a red night, heart racing as I glanced over my shoulder at soaring flames. My mother clutching her side, her face glazed with agony as blood dampened her hands.

Emotions rushed through me as I stared at the man striding arrogantly across the courtyard. Shock, hatred, sorrow, grief, and anger. Anger that had been suppressed for over nine years simmered up my throat. My fingers itched to unsheathe my blade. To walk up to him and run him through. To stare into that hard face with all the hatred in my heart as he gagged on his own blood.

As if he could feel the intensity of my scrutiny, he looked straight at me.

Blast it! I forced my feet forward. His gaze drilled into me like nails.

Flee, before you make your family victim to his vengeance again.

Training kicked in. I drew in a breath to rein back the raging emotions like a corral around wild horses. I relaxed my pace, as if I wasn't steps away from my family's tormentor, and strutted along.

From my corner vision, he shook his head at himself as if quelling a thought, and moved along.

I couldn't help it. The moment I felt his focus shift, mine trained back to him.

He made for one of the archways that led into the palace proper, glancing once over his shoulder. His gaze swept almost calculatingly over the guests as if assessing whether anyone watched him. The subtle furtiveness of his movements ignited my suspicion like a hum under my skin.

"The washrooms are over there." The maid pointed and smiled at us. "Please clean yourselves up and wait for your peers in the courtyard's parlor. I will summon you when the Majesties are ready for you."

"Thank you," Zair answered two steps to my right, and then frowned at my form moving after Sarhedrin.

Ibhar grabbed my shoulder and snarled, "You heard the instructions, slug. We clean up and greet the Majesties *before* gamboling."

"Get off me." I shoved his hand off. Wanted to ignore the instructions and go after Sarhedrin. That *old* flame borne out of a young boy's pain crackled, to rid the world of the man who wanted my family destroyed.

Stop it, I ordered myself, sucking in quiet breaths. *Think*.

Although I now knew he was here, Orcus Sarhedrin could never know *I* was here. I couldn't draw unusual attention to myself. And what better way was there to make myself conspicuous than to disobey orders and go after him?

Protect your family.

Ibhar and Zair went ahead of me to the flat-roofed structure partly hidden by hedges. I followed behind them and tried to pull Jaziah to the forefront of my thoughts. Wherever Orcus Sarhedrin was, I had to stay a hundred feet away from it.

7

DATHAN

Ibhar and I were shown to the men's washroom while Zair was shown to another. We cleaned up in tense silence and as I adjusted my collar, Jaziah's absence nearly knocked the air from my chest. How did a person live with this ache, wondering what their loved ones suffered? With the paralyzing question of whether you'd see them again?

And asps like Orcus Sarhedrin moved freely in the palace.

Ibhar's ring slipped. His hands shook as he picked it up. Ibhar Ghed was nervous. But he also frowned as he noticed my clenched fists and quick breaths. Defensive, we both stiffened and left the washroom. The two other elite students finally joined us on the settees. The young man wore eyeglasses and the dark tattoos of the Mizsab tribe on his hands, while the young woman's earlobes displayed the multiple piercings of the Kwalis. The parlor's clock ticked six o'clock but the maid still didn't call on us.

My feet tapped restlessly, to the others' annoyance, but Sarhedrin was here. He was here.

A shudder worked through me.

Where had he been stalking off to?

"Do you know what we represent here?"

Ibhar's words broke into my thoughts as he walked toward the wall paintings of Thalesai.

"No, we merely tossed on our uniforms and came to gallivant in the palace," I deadpanned.

"Then listen closely, you dullards."

The sarcasm went over his thick skull.

The others bristled but I gave him a tight smile, reclining in my seat.

"The invasions from the aziza, shifter, and wraith kingdoms of the Western Continent crushed the human lands." He stabbed a finger at an oil painting filled with fire and blood. "Demolished us to almost nothing as they waged wars from all sides during the Invasions. They claimed our resources, killed and captured our people for slaves, and advanced in eminence with our backs as ladders." He pointed at another painting of shackles and whips. "Now, they surpass us in might and wealth, while centuries later, we still struggle to recover."

The parlor was silent now, save for the sounds of revelry outside.

"At least they gave us mystical beasts to make up for centuries of oppression," I said wryly, rubbing my eyes.

The humans won the War of Beasts with a secret resistance that spent years smuggling weapons made with objects that weakened the other races' magic, and a wealth of explosives. If our predecessors hadn't been brilliant enough to create dynamites with pitch powder and other weapons before their fight back, we wouldn't be free people today. We all acted like the Treaty of Realms alone kept the other kingdoms in line. But the knowledge that humans had countless stores of this powder—while our engineers built deadlier weapons to counter their magic—also forced the other kingdoms to maintain the Treaty.

"The wraith kingdom was even generous enough to toss their coveted dragon egg into the mix to mollify us," I continued. "If only someone knew where the first King of Thalesai hid the egg."

"The first king didn't hatch the dragon egg because he didn't trust that the wraiths would give humans something that deadly in good form," Zair said, studying my tapping feet. "He didn't want his successors making the grave mistake of unleashing it on the human lands."

"Dragons," Ibhar snapped, "aren't the subject. *Listen* to me.

Despite the peace Treaty that the foreign kingdoms signed, Thalesai is still trying to reach a height so great that our neighbors can never bring us to our knees again. One where we would match them wit for wit, strength for strength..."

"This might be baffling to hear, but we know our own history, Ibhar," I said slowly and the engineering student chuckled beside me. "It's the entire reason behind Thalesai's Amalgamation."

Ibhar glared at me and slashed his hand through the air. "We are the new generation, here to represent the hope of Thalesai's future. You slugs better not embarrass us before the foreigners by acting inferior."

"Scholars, the Majesties will see you now."

We jumped to our feet at the maid's summons, and I drew in a deep breath as we strode after her. *Pull yourself together*. I couldn't let Sarhedrin destabilize me and ruin this mission to help Jaziah.

The maid didn't lead us to the courtyard, but to a larger amaranth parlor with velveteen chairs and furniture edged in glimmering gold. No mirrors or iron. Under the intricate lanterns, the new rulers of Thalesai and their closest councilmen held court with the foreign ambassadors. I struggled to settle my mind as we lowered to our knees on the periwinkle carpet and bowed our heads in homage. This moment, meeting the Majesties, was too important for distractions.

"Your Majesties," we greeted in unison.

"You are here." Queen Yval's pleased and almost ethereal voice filled the parlor. "Look up, Scholars, let me see your faces."

We obeyed. The queen's beauty was envied across the kingdoms. Her flawless skin glowed brighter than the purest honey. Her eyes were clear emeralds glittering in a pool of white, and poets sang that Osime had woven her long, red-gold hair from the dawn itself. Yet even her beauty could not clear the memories of Sarhedrin's men whipping my father until he was drenched with his blood. I wrestled back those images.

Lingering behind her, the queen's zenana—a dainty merge of her closest courtiers from the four tribes—chuckled over Ibhar and the other boy's moony gazes.

"The students are here, Your Majesty," an Ironteenth Swordsman alerted the king.

King Khasar Nogbaisi of Thalesai swiveled from the foreign ambassadors to us. His was a striking presence, a handsome narrow face with sharp eyes and a tall figure bedecked in splendid gold robes and bronze adornments. The king was young, had been ordained by the high priest at age twenty-one so that he would rule long like his predecessors. But that youthfulness radiated as virility. A golden coronet sparkled against his brown skin and raven-wing hair.

A pleased smile curved the edge of his mouth. "Our Burning Hearts," the king introduced proudly to the ambassadors. "These five students are the elite amongst their peers. The future of Thalesai. I'm rather eager to showcase their skills over the course of the coronation."

The atmosphere thrummed like a power clash of light and dark and earth under the combined presence of the azizas, wraiths, and shapeshifter ambassadors. The foreign dignitaries stood, dominant and distinct, as they studied us.

"Ahimoth and Gergesenes are elite military academies," Queen Yval explained, gesturing to Ibhar and me.

Despite her youthfulness, she possessed a sting about her that seemed fit for this pit of vipers called the Sand Palace.

She looked at the other two students. "Quartus Academy trains the best of young healers and Felax trains our innovative engineers."

My brows fused slightly. Zair's throat bobbed. Why did the queen not mention Zair's academy? Because of her tribe?

Perhaps it was from my experience of alienation or the Ussi's unrepentant superiority that made them see anyone else as unworthy, but the queen's slight to Zair tasted sour in my throat. How would Her Majesty react if she knew *my* background then? Raise the first torch to persecute me?

An Ironteenth Fighter's focus fell to my fists—which I hadn't realized I had clenched—and his face hardened.

You're making yourself conspicuous.

I subtly allowed my hands to fall open as the introductions proceeded, and kept my muscles loose.

The queen drifted past Ibhar, her tribesman, and stopped in front of me. My chest contracted. Had she noticed my angry stare?

She peered at me for a moment and said for my ears alone, "There is so much anger and pain in your eyes, Scholar."

My arms shuddered. She might as well have stripped my skin off.

"Do well to tame it," she advised. "There's more at stake in this gathering than you can understand."

I understood only too well what was at stake. "My apologies, Your Majesty."

The king finally made a hand gesture. "Leave us, Scholars. Retire to your suites and join us for tomorrow's feast."

Relieved to survive the first royal meeting without blunders, the five of us released collective breaths the moment we left the eminent circle.

And then the king's instruction sank like a rock in my stomach. We'd been dismissed from his gatherings for tonight. I had to wait until tomorrow to make headway in my mission to bring Jaziah back.

Curse it.

Maids and guards escorted us to temporary bedrooms; something about our lodges not yet being ready. The maids apologized profusely, but I didn't mind. No way I would shut my eyes after encountering Sarhedrin here. The night grew windy and black, and I either paced or stopped to stare at the stars glinting over the distant sand dunes. Wondering in what part of the kingdom Jaziah was and trying not to revisit the memory of Sarhedrin's furtive movement. By the time dawn broke, my hands shook with energy. I wore charm, my weapon of choice today, like a robe and joined the other half of the Reception with one purpose in mind. To make my list of suspects.

8

ZAIR

A day after the queen's public slight, my skin still burned from the humiliation. The Reception ceremonies spanned the two days it would take the guests to arrive. As today's festivities progressed, I overheard a few people talk with vindication about how Her Majesty had 'snubbed the Esan student yesterday'. She had made it clear that I didn't have her favor.

Would the queen have introduced me among the dignitaries if she knew I was here for my sister? My peers?

I swallowed down the sinking emotions and watched the chattering nobles.

With acute focus, I searched for shifty glances, odd body movements, or overly demure behavior—a deflective act often hinting at more beneath the facade. The guests so far were wary, but they also moved with easy confidence.

Saints, with each passing hour that I detected nothing suspicious, I couldn't help but feel like I was losing good time.

The queen's Ironteenth Archers manned balconies, their alertness poignant even down here in the courtyard of flowers and fountains. The twelve best archers across the kingdom, replaced the moment they slacked even the slightest bit in their duties.

"What is it that makes them so revered?"

The accented Turanci—the common tongue—spun me toward

the towering foreigner who joined me among the glittering fountains.

Aziza.

My chest leaped. Why had he broken away from his envoy to come here?

The soft white light of aziza magic rolled over his golden skin, making him shimmer in the sunlight. Black sheer wings with the beautiful, overlapping scales of a butterfly's protruded from his back, the tip of his forewings reaching above his head. His pointed ears and inherent elegance, the faint smell of soil and sugar, set me on guard as he stepped closer. Though young, his gleaming uniform had been designed to intimidate with its silver plates and turquoise weapon sheaths. Yet, beside a being whose blood was mixed in my own, a sense of familiarity lingered and I felt no fear.

"What?" he taunted, his silver hair teasing a perfectly sculpted face. "Would you hoard your histories rather than boast about it to a visitor? You humans often love to brag."

"Ironic coming from folk that constantly flutter their wings, not deigning to let their feet touch the earth," I said, but I'd never been one to turn away from a challenge. I explained with my chin up, "They're our Ironteenth Fighters. A position I aspire to earn someday."

He tilted his head with false confusion. "You humans think *iron* is a number?"

"The Ironteenth unit was formed during the War of Beasts," I returned, warming up to this word battle. "The first human commander of the resistance group had just fallen in a hard battle. His successor took up the mantle in the direst moment of the War, overwhelming enemies with his daring strategies. Even civilians from all tribes began to rally behind him, forming a larger force. Worried about this intelligent and bold human leader—"

He snorted and I wanted to shove him into the fountain.

"The shapeshifters launched attacks to kill him. They killed off his first, second, and third group of guards."

He smirked. "Of course."

"So thirty-six fighters came together and formed the Ironteenth. The protectors that would not be overcome," I said a bit hoarsely. "They were fierce, loyal, and wild. They forcefully took the *kiniuns*—the white lions—from the shapeshifters and tamed them to become Ironteenth riding beasts. The beasts sensed their wild courage and submitted to them. They kept the commander safe as he led humans to more victories and began the wave of battles that drove you, invaders, out of our lands."

Ever since then, the Ironteenth had been a cutthroat rank that left zero room for error. Their trainings turned every part of them into weapons. Take away an Ironteenth's blades and he would tear your throat open with his teeth. Cut off his right hand and he would split you in two with his left. Challenge him with any weapon of your choice and he would best you with it. They moved with calm command, but beneath that sable armor were protectors with the skill of ten soldiers.

Indeed, the *kiniuns* only bonded with and obeyed the powerful.

Before this mission, I'd dreamed of being admitted into their drill camp after graduating from Nergal. Even though the practical side of me had known the chances of that happening were... well none.

There were hundreds of archers with more experience and from more acceptable tribes, awaiting the same opportunity. But now... now, an additional advantage to this mission was that if I proved myself capable of eliminating Thalesai's traitor on my own, the Commandant might give me a recommendation for the Elite Drill Camp.

"Good story," he conceded, adding musingly, "If only your humans were as passionate about you."

The words speared through my chest. Drawing in a breath, I said, "Next time, ask Thalesai's ambassadors your questions." I made to walk away.

"Wait." He held my arm.

I shook off his warm, glowing hand. "What?"

"You are part aziza," he said calmly, yet an edge crept into his voice. "We do not have to be on opposite sides."

Suspicion curled through my throat.

"Speak plainly," I said sternly.

His mouth twitched, his smile devastating. "I had no intention of lying."

Azizas couldn't lie unless they wanted to lose bits of their precious wings in penance. I didn't laugh at his humor. No doubt, a ploy to lower my guard.

He nodded, searching my face as he said lowly, "I know the little flow of aziza blood in your veins means you can smell bold lies like garlic, hear danger coming like bells ringing in your head, and harness our weightlessness to move faster than pureblood humans. What *else* does it mean for you?"

A defensive wall surged in my chest. It meant I could camouflage into my surroundings—a strenuous ability not even my mother or sisters had. Battle lightning too, apparently, but I snipped, "I'm *human*, barely aziza at all. That means *I* can lie and won't perish from pure iron like your people. Why are you naming the cursed abilities your people forced on us?"

Affront flashed in his eyes. They were two shades of gold; dark-gold ringed with gold so light it was almost white.

He said, "Our magic is bound by the king's seer within these borders, willingly given in exchange for the promised safety of all parties. Yet, as a royal guard, I want to ensure my ambassador and the aziza retinue are as safe here as your rulers claim."

Realization dawned and I stiffened. "So you want me to be your eyes and ears, to spy on my own people for you."

"They do not treat you like you are theirs," he repeated, a gleam entering his gaze. "I can help with your aspirations. Have my ambassador praise you to your king so that he would consider you for this Ironteenth position you yearn for. In return, you will give me frequent... assurances that no unexpected plan is being made for us while we're here."

"How dare you?" I hissed.

His eyes turned to granite. "You know, you've been speaking with me for a while. Refuse my proposition, and I could tell them it is you who has propositioned me."

My stomach clenched. "You can't lie against me."

"There are ways to dance around the truth when necessary—and trust me, it is necessary. You humans are antsy, and the pure iron your soldiers used to weaken azizas during the war is used liberally here. Keep me informed on any unexpected plans for us foreigners, and I will help you in return. Otherwise, they will never believe your word against mine."

My throat tightened. Yet he was right. I made the mistake of entertaining him, where too many eyes watched. If he claimed I initiated this discussion, he would be believed in a heartbeat. I'd lose my chance to save Sarai on day two.

A foolish mistake I'd made, lowering my guard. Never again.

"Fine," I hissed. "I will inform you one time."

"Three times before we leave," he insisted.

"*Twice.*"

His shoulders eased. "Alright. We have a bargain."

"Keep your *good word* to yourself. This isn't a *bargain*, only blackmail, and know this." Blood roaring in my ears, I held his golden gaze. "I do not like being manipulated."

He had the grace to blush—a faint sweep of red above his collar. "Take what I'm offering in return."

Repulsed by him and angry at myself, I walked away.

"I am Arno Irmah by the way," he called after me.

Well, go to the sheols, tyrant spawn.

"What is your name?"

I didn't bother to answer him. Instead, my stomach hardened over what I'd just agreed to.

9

DATHAN

The palace's night magic hummed awake as evening fell, and the sentient structure beamed at the peak of the city like Ari'el's own star. As children, Jaziah and I would sit on my parents' rooftop in the icy evenings and gaze at the distant glow until my mother yelled at us to leave the cold before we fell sick.

I resisted the urge to run my fingers through my hair as I excused myself from yet another group of wealthy Baihan youths who eagerly answered my questions about their parents' achievements, but had no information that gave me a lead.

Skies, any of these faces in the crowd could be the traitor, yet none acted inconsistently or suspiciously. I strolled along the pink-leafed trees and kept my expression neutral as I silently ran through each scene since I arrived at the palace.

My thoughts soon returned to Sarhedrin, despite my decision to stay far away from the dynast. His furtive glances last night, the cold calculation in his eyes...

My instincts nudged me to find out why. Only right now, those instincts felt influenced by the past.

You have better instincts than most, Issachar. Trust them.

The Commandant's words echoed in my mind. I completed my circle around the trees, back to the main gathering, and a slight body bumped into me.

Considering I was built like a boulder, the female bounced to the ground and spilled her tray of water over my boots.

"I'm sorry. I'm so sorry!" She knelt at my feet, trembling with her head bowed.

My gut twisted and I crouched, trying not to wince at the clingy feel of soggy shoes. "They *are* gorgeous, but they're still just shoes. I'll survive."

Her head rose and my breath caught. Gold encircled her mocha eyes. Wrapped in sackcloth, she was thinner than a colt. Red welts banded her wrists, and the wraith kingdom's insignia dug into her chin. An Esan slave.

"T-thank you for your kindness, sir," she whispered.

Sorrow poured through me. Even after the Treaty, was this how the wraiths treated the offspring of the slaves they didn't set free after the War?

She fidgeted under my stare, and I cleared my throat. "Let me help you..."

A sharp crack resounded and the girl's head jerked to the side. Gasps filled the air but outrage waned once her Esan eyes were glimpsed.

An obsidian headpiece flashed as a wraith lord, sublime in his dark gossamer coat, yanked at her hair. With milk-pale skin, shadows writhing around their bodies, and the power to walk through solid walls, the wraiths were like powerful spirits. Yet, they bled red like we did. They had no reason to treat us like animals.

"Stand up, wretch!" he hissed at her.

"Release her."

The king's adamantine voice resounded. Disapproval tautened his body, and the merriment lowered to near silence.

"Your Majesty," the wraith lord said with cloying politeness, tightening his grip on the girl. "This slave is our property, bought and brought from wraithlands."

"No human will be mistreated in Thalesai, slave or not. Release her."

Hearing the king's unshaking command, I disagreed with my father and Commandant's beliefs that the king's determination to please every tribe was setting him up to fail.

Forgetting the dozens of watching eyes, I brushed the wraith lord's hands off the girl and helped her rise. Shadows roared like a vicious mouth from thin air and barreled me into a wall. Pain sparked up my bones, my skin icing like death. Screams filled the courtyard.

"Never lay your unworthy hands on me again!" the wraith lord snarled.

Shadows gloved his fists until he embodied the monsters that haunted our history.

I saw one thing: an outlet to unleash all my rage at Sarhedrin and Jaziah's capture. I launched myself at him like a rock. My fists flew into his gut, my iron-hard punches unbalancing him. He vanished into shadows before my fifth blow made contact.

He reappeared on my left, unbalancing me. His hand gripped my throat, cutting off my airflow. "I'll kill you."

I pulled at his wrist with one hand and landed a harder blow to his face. He growled as blood slipped from his nose and mouth. My heart clashed against my ribcage in need of air.

Hands ripped us off each other. He shoved his restrainers away and held out his palm.

"That will be enough!" King Khasar thundered.

The musicians fell silent. The entire garden seemed to hold its breath. My haze of anger faded. *Everyone* stared at me. I swiped my hair over my eyes, lowering my head before unwanted eyes noticed me. Curse it. My heart pounded. I would be dismissed from the palace and lose this fragile chance to save Jaziah.

"He should pay for this!" my opponent demanded, his skin almost completely shadowed. A raging storm cloud.

The Ironteenth shifted like mountain cats about to pounce.

King Khasar's face was steely. "Your magic was to be yielded to my seer before crossing my borders. You heard my terms that there would be no magic in this gathering."

Other kings might have forced the foreigners to shed their magic rather than take them at their word. But I'd heard that King Khasar gave people the chance to act honorably first before he resorted to force.

The wraithland's ambassador quickly stepped toward the royal tent, his shadowed palms open in entreaty. An Ironteenth Fighter blocked him.

"I didn't know that my courtier here neglected that agreement, Your Majesty," the ambassador said. "Accept my sincerest apology. He will be punished as is due."

Bleeding liar. The shock on my opponent's face said so.

"See that you do. I want him out of my lands right now," King Khasar ordered, then spoke in low tones to his Ironteenth Captain. Likely an order to summon his seer.

The wraiths seethed in their dark splendor, but their ambassador gave a bow and hissed words to his guard. "Lieutenant Kerr, lead him away."

Wraith guards led my opponent away, flanked by three Ironteenth Fighters.

The slave girl trembled like a leaf under the attention, but she mouthed 'thank you, sir' to me and hurried off. I lifted my head—and the king stared right at me. His expression was unreadable, and I braced my shoulders as my heart raced faster.

The king ordered, "Music."

He'd pardoned me.

As if desperate to erase the tension, the festivities resumed with gusto. I released a long breath, my heart kicking against my chest. I'd lost the reins of my control enough times. My head would stay down henceforth with my focus on the goal. Not the fire in my chest.

My tribespeople gathered around me to empathize. I snagged the chance to study them closely as they patted my arms, proud that I still stood after a clash with a wraith. Even though we had exploited the wraiths' aversion to mirrors during the war, no one knew the full extent of the wraiths' strengths.

"I suspect that despite the Treaty," the Baihan wife of a chancellor whispered to me, "the wraiths still keep their magical capabilities mysterious to have an advantage when they strike us again."

"His magic looked terrifying, mama!" Her daughter shuddered. "I'd forgotten the wraiths are our deadliest neighbors. Praise Osime, you're fine, Scholar Dathan."

"I'm sure he's thanking his own gods that he is fine too." I shrugged, the inner soldier refusing to accept inferiority to a foreigner.

The women grinned and the mother asked to officially introduce me to her daughter when a bald head gleamed. Sarhedrin stalked past.

Always stalking. *What are you up to, Sarhedrin?* It was time to follow my instinct.

"...and Anesua is an accomplished weaver," the Baihan mother was saying. "The tapestries she weaves for her lounge never cease to delight me."

Keeping Sarhedrin in my corner vision, I smiled at Anesua and said softly, "It would be an honor to see your craft someday, Khosana. I'm certain I'll be delighted by it as I am by your company."

The two women beamed.

"I'm loath to excuse myself, but I can see my uncle calling for me. I'll find you again soon."

"I look forward to seeing you again, Scholar," Anesua said shyly.

I gave a bow and left. Once I sensed the warmth of their gazes shift from me, I drifted behind a tangle of glowing fig trees and leaned into their shadows. Khosana Anesua radiated with beauty and kindness, but it was a set of fierce, golden eyes that stirred my curiosity.

A clear view of Sarhedrin quickly wiped every other thought from my mind. He reached the vacant marble archway. Silvery fountains and plants obscured it from the celebration, beyond the Ironteenth Fighters' view. A person came out from behind it and my nape prickled.

The king's older brother. Caiphas Nogbaisi.

Sarhedrin, the Dynast of Bornoir—one of the wealthiest towns in Thalesai—was an Ussi tribe fanatic. The king's brother, on the other hand, was Baihan. And although King Khasar was known to rule like the lines between the tribes weren't deeper than the Gorges of Sela, it was not *normal* for both men to converge.

My nape tingled: they obviously did not want witnesses from the ceremony.

What could they possibly be meeting about?

I mentally drew an image of the kingdom's map. The king's brother was the human ambassador to the wraith kingdom. His office sprawled on the borders of the wraith kingdom, a direct opposite to Bornoir. Land affairs hadn't brought them together. It surely was not national bonding, either.

What did then? *The mercenaries?*

Yes, there were little threads to grab. And maybe I was latching on to this because I wanted nothing more than to strike Sarhedrin.

But I silenced the doubts.

You have better instincts than most, Issachar. Trust them.

There was a traitor here betraying the people, weakening our already vulnerable lands. One whose mercenaries had snatched Jaziah out of the life he'd worked hard for. This was the first lead I had. I would follow and investigate it unless it led nowhere.

For now, knowing when to withdraw was as vital as knowing when to charge. I'd drawn enough attention this evening after brawling with a wraith. And Sarhedrin could not catch even a whiff of my presence, or interest in him. Tailing these men would have to wait until midnight.

10

ZAIR

I had become an informant to Thalesai's enemy.

No, not the enemy *since the Treaty of Realms...*

Oh, who was I deceiving? Treaty or not, the other kingdoms wanted us to fall. Arno Irmah's blackmail could ruin my mission. My throat ached, but there was no time for weakness. The bark of a redbud tree dug into my back as I tried to focus on the feast instead.

Find the positives. I was in the best place to save Sarai. My cover as nothing but a representing student still stood. Long before Arno Irmah's blackmail could ruin my mission, I would take the traitor down. Calm returned to my mind.

The palace's humming magic filled the evening with a warm aura. After a long day of feasting, the dignitaries' guards would soon start to lower. My senses were ready. I would miss nothing.

A memory zipped in.

They would rather ignore your skills over their fear of the azizas than use them and be stronger, my father had said to me.

I'd asked him why none of my teachers wanted me to use my heightened perception. Skills my mother had taught my sister and I to use to protect ourselves. Our lessons together had been full of delight and awe, and made me believe the abilities were good. Until I arrived at the academy and told my teachers about it.

I'm on our side, papa, I'd said. *I'm training to fight for the human kingdom.*

I know, he had said sadly. *It's the shortsightedness of man.*

But those abilities my teachers condemned... perhaps they could help me save their students now. Didn't this mean the abilities could be something to be proud of? *No*, I chided myself. Magical abilities made me freakish. I had to use the abilities now, for Sarai. I'd do anything for Sarai. But after this, I would continue to ignore them.

The Kwali music swept over the night like a stream, and a wistful light rippled over my chest as young couples—betrothed and married—paired and swayed to the tunes.

Deep male chuckles drew my attention to the Admiral and the First Colonel strolling along the pools. These high-ranking officers chose the archers, swordsmen, and spearmen that formed the Ironteenth Fighters. I could drift over to familiarize like I'd seen Ibhar do, try to gain their favor, especially the Admiral's since even the First Colonel answered to him. It might impress them to know that the only reason Ibhar could hit me earlier was because I'd restrained my enhanced perception. But I couldn't delude myself over the reception I—or that information—would receive.

The Admiral's eyes closed with another deep chuckle that rumbled through the evening. The First Colonel laughed too, or at least his mouth made the sound. His eyes grew flintier than honed knives as he glared at the Admiral. I straightened. The moment the Admiral looked at him again, speaking amusedly, the First Colonel's eyes were bright with gaiety, his red-tattooed fingers patting the Admiral's arm.

It had happened quickly and would easily be missed by many guests. My instincts chimed cautions in my chest. Both were esteemed military men under the king's third Chamber: the Chamber of Fangs. Their interests ought to be aligned. *To protect the kingdom at all costs and keep its torch ever burning.*

The Admiral was a tenacious man who had served the last king and protected the human borders from infiltrators for that long. What reason would First Colonel Remmon have to look at him with such... *hate?*

Could the Admiral be standing in the First Colonel's way somehow? Holding him back from achieving some goal of his due to the Admiral's diligence? And on a grander scale, could this have something to do with aiding the mercenaries? Perhaps the Admiral's duty to find the mercenaries made it difficult for the First Colonel to succeed as their palace plant.

It could be an exaggeration, but it wasn't *nothing*. For my head to ring as painfully as it just had... trouble brewed there.

Hope spiked, but I couldn't invest all my attention on this. It might not be the right trail. For now, I'd first investigate Colonel Remmon, slink into his offices and rooms. Make sure his hatred for the Admiral had not manifested as feeding the worms that ate through our kingdom.

IT WASN'T long after that three royal maids summoned the students to show us to our official lodgings in the palace. Nobles strutted and maids streaked past us in the agave-scented passages. Bright tilework in versailles and pinwheels designs shimmered underfoot and at my sides. Tall gilt frames with oil paintings told of Thalesai's victories and brass ornaments displayed our Burning Heart emblem. Small fountains sparkled under huge chandeliers, and the arches sweeping above me were of embossed pink granite.

While the Al'Qtraz's opulence *was* staggering, I concentrated on its layout and the guards' placing. We had just ascended into the palace's first level, and the frescoed balconies above hinted at five more massive levels.

Skies, but there were armored guards at every twelve feet. *Barghests* snarled at their sides, massive beasts that resembled tigers but were far more menacing. Powerful bodies rippled beneath scarlet fur, their ferocious eyes hungry and sharp. The wraith kingdom had gifted the beasts to the Majesties, and word was that the predators' abilities transcended their physical might.

As if my mission wasn't daunting enough.

"Is Nergal's architecture so inferior?" the other elite female student asked, drawing my attention.

I scrunched my brows. "I don't understand."

Suspicion filled her blue eyes. "You're staring at the palace's build very keenly."

I blanked my face. "It's my first time in the palace, that's all."

Would she report this? Her ears had the multiple piercings of the Kwali tribe and the Kwalis *were* supposed to be neighborly.

Ibhar must've heard her queries, seeing an opening for his. He rammed his shoulder into my arm, almost knocking me into a painted ceramics display. My pale cape swiveled as I quickly found my balance and glowered coldly at him.

"The best students from Nergal must've been picked off by the mercenaries if the Commandant would stoop to sending Esan scum."

"That is not something to joke about, Scholar," the buff guard rebuked Ibhar in a low but unyielding tone. "And you're not allowed to speak of that here. All of you."

For a second, I thought Ibhar would snap at the guard. He was simply a palace guard, after all, not an Ironteenth Fighter as Ibhar might be one day. But Ibhar knew that right *now*, the huge man would likely flatten him in a few moves. He turned a glare on me before staring ahead in silence.

I tried to push his words away, but they struck a sore spot. The Commandant hadn't chosen me because she respected me, or even because she had no other option. She chose me because I was disposable if this plan fell apart.

Swallowing, I let my strides lag until I walked behind the tense group, even though I kept my chin high.

Bow to none but those you decide are worthy, my father had taught his daughters. *Hide not your eyes, my treasures, for they are beautiful.*

Besides, it didn't matter why I was chosen, only that I was in the right place to protect my family. Rather than keep replaying Ibhar's words, I replayed the guard's warning.

You're not allowed to speak of that here.

Only the king could make such a ban in the Al'Qtraz. But *why*? Shouldn't this be where the mercenary problem was most addressed? Why would he bury the issue? It had to be for the foreigners' benefit. To appear like he had his kingdom under complete control. My blood boiled. He hadn't even made a public address over the students' abduction. Parents knew little of the king's efforts to recover their children—or if he even cared. And yet, the foreigners were his priority.

We passed under another arch into an ivory-and-teal bedecked lounge with long windows overlooking the glittering city.

"These are your bedchambers," a maid said brightly, gesturing to the five ornately inlaid doors. "Your bags have been delivered. Let us know if you need anything."

Bickering with that rivalry that simmered during our inter-school competitions, the other students opened doors and wove in and out until they found their delegated rooms. I stayed out of their way. Once they were settled in, I stepped into the last chamber. The bruised part of me expected to find a dirty hovel waiting, but it seemed someone in this palace wasn't made of vinegar.

The walls were coated in gentle and deep peach. Quartz lanterns dazzled over me, filling the room with the welcoming smell of olive oil. The cream ceiling was embossed in the same soft green as the broad velvet cushions shimmering by the open balcony doors. I brushed my fingers over the quilts and gasped at the lush texture. They were rich yellow like the carpet, but bore various designs of desert lilies and jojobas. An indulgence indeed, yet it felt wrong to sleep here when my peers slept in chains and Sarai could hardly sleep at all.

I sighed. "If only my sisters could be here with me. Sarai would be safer."

Moving to the low table closest to the canopied bed, I dropped my daggers and club. From a compartment sewn into my uniform's elbow, I drew out the tiny phial that had felt like an anvil on my conscience all day.

Poison wasn't a soldier's weapon. It was exactly what people would expect from Esans. But I understood why the Commandant chose it. Swift and clean.

Rolling the phial between my fingers, I moved to open the balcony's glass-and-metal doors. Beyond, Ari'el was a bustling field of domes and beaming lights against a backdrop of stars and dunes.

Cut off the serpent's head and leave no trail behind.

Drawing a final breath of crisp air, I closed the doors.

I would launch my careful investigations of First Colonel

Remmon's office when the night was tamer. For now, I pulled out my heavy tomes from my satchel. I couldn't sleep with worries of Sarai and my mission, so I'd study for the final exams coming after the coronation. I opened *The Red History* tome. The most grueling history course where our ugly past was taught to remind us of what had happened, and would recur if we ever let Thalesai fall to the tyrants again.

11

DATHAN

Cloaked in a garment the color of night, I slid out of my rooms and into corners of the slumbering palace that lanterns didn't illuminate. Tonight was for making a suspect list as I mastered the palace's labyrinthine layout. Once I had those pinned, I'd investigate my suspects for even the thinnest threads of treachery. One of those threads would surely grow into a path, leading me straight to the traitor.

A grand rosewood clock that was built for the west wing of the third level ticked. Firm and daunting with every few steps, like a countdown on Jaziah's life. *Don't think like that. Jaziah survived five years of brutal training at Gergesenes. He survived his family's separation and could still make you smile. This won't break him.*

I just had to haul him out of captivity fast. Light footsteps approached. Moving stealthily, I pulled myself into the shadowed crevice of the torch sculpture I'd marked earlier. If silence wasn't vital, I would laugh that my hands still carried a faint scent of the cinnamon cakes my older sister sent to Gergesenes just before I left.

Unwilling to go to that dark place where I couldn't tell reality from nightmare—or sleep, as most people called it—I'd unwrapped her parcel tonight. Her progress as a baker always warmed my heart to see, yet tonight I couldn't eat her gifts. Baking had helped Asahel gain a sense of control over her life after our pursuers' assault left her feeling powerless for years. And while I knew it was now her solace, sometimes her creations reminded me of what had been done to us.

Now, the main orchestrator, the brute who gave the orders, slept under the same roof tonight. Restlessness gnawed at me. I needed to glean something tangible, fast. To be certain Sarhedrin and Ambassador Caiphas were my target.

If there wasn't implicating information...

Go after him anyway and have your revenge.

I battled against the pull of that inner rage. My loyalty to Jaziah and my family's safety came first. If there wasn't proof that Sarhedrin was the culprit, I had to give that lead lesser priority and seek out my true target.

Certain the passersby were gone, I lowered myself from the sculpture without a sound. Murals of the ten saints watched me from the ceilings. Magenta doors and cyan-checkered walls clicked into a neat design. With each pad of my feet, the silence grew eerily absolute and my nape prickled.

You're imagining it. Sometimes silence is just silence.

I pivoted into a hallway. Red elliptical eyes flared in rage. Barghests. Not one but four, five, six of them. In the darkness, they looked like snarling demons.

Bleeding sheols.

The first prowled closer. The others followed, shadows dancing over their goblin faces.

Stay calm. Retreat fast. Holding up a hand, I took steady steps backward.

They followed.

I mouthed, "Good doggies..."

In a blink, the creature leaped to full size. I swung around to bolt. Fangs sank into my neck. Claws bit into my skin as I crashed face-first under its rough weight. I spun to my side and aimed my punches at its head and eyes—its only vulnerable points—as I made to break free. The others crowded me like fresh meat.

"*Argh.*"

My eyes rolled back as the pain began to suck the air from my lungs. I grabbed its thick neck and shoved at it as we locked gazes. Man to beast.

In the next blink, the pain dissipated. The beast fell off me like a scale, watching me warily as it took backward steps. I pawed at my neck, but there was no blood. No wound. Because... barghests were beasts that fed on evil. It had bitten me, *tasted* that my intentions were fair, and now had nothing to hold me ransom.

The creatures growled a warning and as they charged off, they became a muted blur. My feet stumbled, an ache sparked in my back, and the ceiling filled my vision.

What the...?

Disoriented, it took a precious moment to realize I was on the floor.

I rubbed my eyes, but my vision didn't clear. It hit me like frozen water. The beast's bite was *poisonous*. I staggered to my feet and righted myself. My hazy vision spiked up my heartbeat.

Blast it, losing my sight meant losing my speed and a higher chance of getting caught.

Executed.

No, I didn't dare abandon tonight's goal without making progress. My vision had lost its sharpness, but Gergesenes' training had equipped us to navigate terrains with little to no vision. Many sabotage missions were implemented in the cloak of night, forcing us to rely on other honed senses.

Lead with your hands. I became one with the shadows, feeling the walls for support, maintaining my balance up stairs. *Listen.* I changed routes at the slightest sounds of boots, armor, or voices. *Read telling smells in the air.* The strong scents of leather from guards' uniforms indicated the areas they lingered around; I dodged those. With each step, I attuned myself to the changes in the atmosphere's rhythm, optimizing what visuals I had.

The palace watched me; I felt its magic trail my movements like a breath on my skin, waiting for any misstep.

As the hours passed, I managed to sort the vast palace into six definite floors and three wings. I slowly and steadily made my way to the chambermen's offices. The painstaking pace had dampened my collar with sweat when I finally found an office with Sarhedrin's rank on the plaque. *There you are.*

I imprinted big and small details of the area in my mind, the exits and interconnecting passages, the grade of lock on the door and its thickness, while also using the seconds to catch my breath.

Alright. Time to get out of here. Taking further action in this state would be too risky, and the longer my vision remained blurry, the more exposed I felt.

I silently felt my way down the dark corridor for the level's exit, marking quick hiding areas. From the connecting passage, voices echoed. I stopped, moved into the shadowed alcove, and peered over the edge.

Six guards—no three, *three* guards—patrolled the exit and conversed lightly. I stepped back. I couldn't get past them. Curse it, I had to wait them out and the grand clock for this level ticked down the minutes to daylight.

"Prosperity upon you, Khosa," a deep voice echoed, raising the hair on my neck.

The atmosphere shifted slightly, thicker with new tension.

I peered again over the edge of my shadowed alcove. The king's Second Advisor stood in the hallway, arms crossed over his protruding stomach as he stared up at the tall guard.

"Prosperity to you too," the Second Advisor answered. "Have your guards noticed anything suspicious tonight?"

My heartbeat quickened.

"No, sir," the guard said confidently.

"Be sure. The Al'Qtraz isn't what it was weeks ago," the Second Advisor warned. "It is now a garden brimming with thorns, some poisonous."

So the Second Advisor didn't trust the foreign guests either. Good. Now if I could just vacate this place before he learned that even the local guests were not completely trustworthy.

I shifted into the shadows but the sudden movement worsened my vision. My head spun, ruining my balance, and my elbow knocked against a vase. The glass vase slipped and my heart stopped as it crashed loudly enough to wake the dead.

12

ZAIR

The mercenaries whipped the stolen students like they were animals, ignoring their pleas and tears. Sarai was among them, weeping with her clothes askew, her lips caked with blood.

The students' heads turned to look at me, begging me to save them, but I couldn't move.

I jerked awake with a gasp, a clock ticking on the wall opposite my bed. I'd barely been asleep for an hour but it was time. I'd chosen the early morning to creep across the Al'Qtraz because it was when most people slept the deepest.

As I slid on the silent slippers the Commandant gave me, I loathed drawing out the aziza speed deep in my veins like one wrung out water from wet fabric. My bones hummed as the magic blew like warm air through my body, making me light enough to travel with the night wind. The speed was an ability I rarely used. Speed, and camouflaging, left me weaker unlike my other abilities. I would prefer not to use magic at all, but I wouldn't risk creeping around the palace at human pace on my first night. I needed to gauge what I was up against first.

Shadows swaddled me with each stair I ran down and each door I opened. Patrolling guards couldn't see me before I swished past. By a certain window, sounds of boots and a scuffle reverberated from the fragrance garden below. My energy already waned but I halted to peek, and my veins iced over.

Two guards dragged a lithe figure with shackled hands. Black garments swaddled the person. Dressed just like *me*. A spy. They'd caught a spy!

I should run, but my feet wouldn't move as I strained to hear the heated exchange.

A guard yanked the spy's mask and an irrational fear hit: what if I knew the person? The female face wasn't discernible, but I could smell her fear even from up here.

Swifter than a hawk, a guard drew out his adasword and slashed her neck. My gut churned. The executed body had barely fallen before barghests pounced on it. Blood sprayed. I twisted and retched into a nearby vase.

Go back. Go back before they catch you too! my nerves screamed.

I couldn't. I swiped my arm over my mouth.

Taking a steady breath, I hardened my determination against the horror. I kept to the shadows and stealthily moved on at a human pace, staying alert to signs of danger. Finally, my destination spread out before me. Dark frescoed walls. Baroque paintings. Checkered ceramic tiles. If I'd had any doubts that I was in the right place, the maid giggling with the large guard confirmed it.

"*Hiyba*," she chided playfully in the echoing hallway. *Husband*. "Focus on guarding Colonel Remmon's office!"

There was no getting around them as they leaned right against the door. Skies, it was pertinent that I searched the Colonel's office *tonight*. Seek out clues that proved he was a man I needed to follow or not.

But the maid was one of those who'd led us to our rooms. She would recognize my eyes at a glimpse.

A great soldier doesn't wait for opportunity; she makes it.

I needed to distract them. The guard pressed a kiss to the woman's neck and murmured, "How could I possibly focus when my lovely wife brings me my favorite food?"

And then he whisked her away, his adasword flashing as they disappeared behind the balcony's doors. Ha. It seemed the saints' favor shone on me tonight! With long, soundless steps, I moved before the towering door of First Colonel Remmon's office and drew out my lockpick.

"Who are you?"

My heart flew to my throat, my ears prickling. The passage was empty, but I had not imagined that loud voice.

"Answer me!"

It was the painting. The bleeding painting of an armed warrior of old *talked*. No time to freeze. The night magic was performing its duty and trying to protect the palace. The painting opened its mouth wider as if to shout.

"I am not your enemy," I whispered.

Its face darkened and desperation snapped an instinct awake in me. *You can silence him*. The instinct guided me to harness the flow of magic in my veins, dewy vines climbing to the surface. I grabbed the painting's frame. My sparse magic streamed forth in a white flow to the painting. The magic that the Aziza King had placed in the walls as a gift recognized its own. The agitated warrior went to rest.

Relief weakened my muscles, but I shut down the side of me that almost rejoiced to possess magic. Picking the eight types of locks was in year-five's coursework on infiltration and investigation. My stomach sank with recognition of Colonel Remmon's lock. Grade six.

Cracking it would take too long. I quickly analyzed the situation. My senses didn't chime against imminent danger, and I had enough energy for a speedy escape if needed. I blew out a soft breath with a decision made. *I couldn't leave empty-handed.*

Praying the newlyweds took their time outside, I inserted my lock pick and wrench into the lock, and envisioned the internal design of a grade six lock. Applying the right pressures and carefully lifting pins, I manipulated the lock. Finally, the door popped open.

I slid through the crack and shut the door behind me, panting like I'd run miles. Drawing on my training, I calmed my racing heart and allowed the room's silence to wash over me for a moment. Then I drew the candle box hanging on my neck—one with a deep history—and struck the flint once with practiced precision. I lit only one of the three wicks, just enough to illuminate the immediate area.

In the dimness, I marked the faintly outlined window; another way out if I could no longer use the door. I mapped the distance—five strides from the desk, then a climb down the sills to the shadowed courtyard below.

Sliding to the nearest wall, I held my candle up and scanned the contents of the shelf. My ears strained for any sound beyond my own breathing as I silently searched the shelf's tiers. Only medals and portraits lined the upper rows. I flipped through the tomes on warfare on the last row; nothing unusual fell from the pages.

I turned to the hangings along the walls, lifting paintings and tapestries to peer behind them. The walls were bare, devoid of safes and secret messages.

I made for the teakwood desk next, careful of triggers that might set off alarms. By process of elimination, if there was anything suspicious to be found here, it would be in this desk.

Even if you found incriminating evidence, do you think you are strong enough to take on the First Colonel?

I shoved the intimidating thought away. I would do anything for Sarai. I worked my way from the bottom drawers up, picking locks and shutting them when they revealed nothing untoward.

On the desk's top were just more tomes and reports. Disappointment tore at my chest.

Wait...

Pin-thin lines stretched down the table. So thin that they could easily be dismissed as paper imprints, if noticed at all. But while my human instincts might have missed them, my Esan perception honed in like an arrowhead. The lines went in a perfect square about a foot wide. Sliding my fingers down to the edge of the desk, just within the outlined square, I gently pushed the edge upward.

It clicked open. A lid. To a secret compartment in the table.

That wasn't suspicious in itself. Everyone had secrets they kept close, especially in a place like the Al'Qtraz.

But why would Colonel Remmon's secret involve the Admiral's schedule? The document stared up at me as I recalled the hateful look the Colonel gave the Admiral in the garden.

My mind whirled.

Did he possess the schedules of *all* his superiors? So he could coordinate his plans with theirs?

Even as I scrambled for possible explanations and excuses, nothing stuck. I lifted the paper, seeking more schedules arranged underneath it. There weren't any. Just the Admiral's schedule, hidden here as if no one could know he had it. I didn't know what this meant, but I couldn't ignore it either. As the head of the military, the Admiral was the highest authority with the wherewithal to end this mercenary reign of terror. I had to know if *that* was the reason the First Colonel was watching him.

No time to figure it out now, though. The guard could be returning from romancing his wife, and they were feeding spies to barghests.

Grabbing fresh paper from a stack and a quill, I steadied my shaky fingers and copied the Admiral's schedule while disturbing nothing on the desk.

I added: *The First Colonel is monitoring the Admiral. Find out why.*

My candle box and the duplicate schedule disappeared into my clothes. Drawing out one of my tools, a damp piece of cloth from my pocket, I pulled open the door, watching the hallway through the crack. No movements outside.

I slipped out and clicked the lock in place. Drapes surrounded me like a pliant shield as I ran behind them. I made to wheel into the next passage when a familiar voice resounded.

"Carry out a search on this wing!"

The king's Second Advisor. My heart jumped to my throat.

I ran for the door directly opposite the drapes and shoved my lock pick into the keyhole. It was a much simpler lock. Grade two. In the next moment, the door opened, and I slithered into the space.

Thumping boots grew louder against the tiles.

I made to shut the door when a hand grabbed the edge.

The Second Advisor!

13

DATHAN

I grabbed the door before it shut. My heart rattled as I shoved my face between the door's crack, but the figure on the other side pulled the knob, determined to shut me outside.

The guards know I am here.

Those words thundered through me even as I fought the lingering effects of the barghest's poison. The guards would rip the place apart to find me. I knew the drill. I tugged harder at the door, inching it open.

Shock jarred through me as Zair's alarmed face tilted up to mine from the other end of the door. Her eyes widened, my astonishment reflected in their brown and gold pools.

Was my vision deceiving me? After the vase broke, a figure had streaked past the corner of my vision to this door. It had moved so fast that had it not paused by the door to manipulate the lock, I would have almost dismissed it as a trick of poor sight. But the dark clothes selected to blend into the darkness, the urgency, and precision in lock picking told me otherwise. It was another spy. And all I'd needed to race to the only room in the vestibule and share the shelter.

Now Nergal's student gaped at me from the other end. I resisted the urge to rub my eyes, in case the barghest's poison was still distorting my vision. The poison was finally wearing off and it *was* Zair.

"Summon the other squad," the Second Advisor ordered grimly. "Carry out a search on this entire wing!"

Her shock quickly gave way to resolve. She made to pull the door shut in my face. I gripped it tighter and pulled it wider. She wasn't getting rid of me that easily. It seemed like forever until she glowered and shoved the door open. Just enough for me to dive into the musty space without knocking her over. We shut the door a second after an unsheathed adasword glistened into view.

Stars from an open window cast dim light in the carpet closet. Outside, adaswords *zinged* out of their scabbards. Drapes swished. Vases screeched against tiles. Orders were hissed. I held the hilts of my knives. Zair gripped a piece of cloth in her hand.

"Spread out!" the sub-head guard said in Mhese.

If the spy was indeed from another kingdom, they wouldn't have him understanding their intentions. Thalesai's guards, though, regardless of tribe, were fluent in the four tribal languages and taught to speak them at the military academies.

My heart pounded in my ears as footsteps reached our door. Barghests snarled, claws scraping hungrily at the door.

"Pick the lock," a guard ordered.

Blast it! Zair took slow steps backward. I kept my attention on the chaos outside the door, clutching my blade tighter. The beasts would sniff her out in half a second hiding in those carpets. She hissed out panicked words I couldn't make out amid the barghests' snarls. The lock clanked under the guard's expert hands.

Zair gasped. I glanced at her and... she was kneeling on a musty, handmade carpet. An emerald-green tapestry that *floated*. Her fingers glowed white as she gripped its fringes, like she was just as startled.

The carpet moved.

An escape.

I swerved and dived atop it without pause. The taut fabric dipped like a mattress under my knees. And like a gliding bird, it carried us out the window, speeding for the sky as the door slammed open. Winds ripped at us, howling like a thousand wolves. The stars grew closer while the palace shrunk smaller than my fist. The soulmate stars of King Abeel and Queen Sepner, Thalesai's first rulers, dazzled close enough to touch.

How in sheols was this happening?

Braced on her knees beside me, Zair angled a vicious expression at me. "Stop following me!"

"Haven't you heard of student solidarity?" I retorted over the winds.

She pulled her dagger and launched at me. Her blade glowed like a deadly piece of the constellations as it neared my throat. In a swift move, I caught her wrists before she could have me where she wanted, at her mercy, and pressed them to the carpet. One with a blade, the other with a cloth. She tried to slam her forehead into my jaw. I swung my head to the side and yanked on her elbows, throwing off her balance.

She fell forward against me, her soft curves pressing against my body, her silky hair brushing my neck. Awareness jolted through me.

Jerking, like she felt the jolt too, she lurched as far back as I let her.

I pulled a lid over the feverish sensation in my skin and focused on her astounded face. "I'll have to break your wrist if you keep trying to kill me."

"I'll push you off this carpet!"

"Dare it," I warned, "and I'll take you down with me, you bloodthirsty thing."

Hair whipping around her, she made to retort. The carpet swerved as if jerked back by some unseen string, unable to travel too far from the palace. We plunged back for the Al'Qtraz at the speed of light. Zair yelped. My stomach knotted.

Going back. If the guards still searched the closet, we were finished.

"*How* are you doing this?" I queried.

"I don't know." She shook off my hold to clutch the carpet. "I asked the palace for help, and it... fused its magic with mine and guided me to lift the carpet."

I blinked in disbelief, and she squinted as if saying, *Don't you dare insult my tribe*. I glowered at her presumption that I would.

We dipped back through the closet's window into an empty room. Her hands stopped glowing, like a lantern snuffed out. The carpet deflated unceremoniously, but she landed as solidly on her feet as I did. A heavy breath rattled through my ribs. We didn't get caught. Yet.

Relief softened Zair's features, and she retrieved her weapons from the carpet. Certain the external threat was gone, we turned to face the threat within, hands on our hilts.

"What are you doing here?" we hissed in unison.

I scanned her clandestine ensemble, refusing to dwell on the outline of those slender curves that had molded against me. My neck heated. Her full, rosy lips pursed, and I ignored the skip of my heartbeat.

Pay attention, soldier. No, not *to her face.*

She didn't fall when the carpet abruptly deflated despite the unbalancing flight. She had run to the room with unnatural speed and tackled the lock with military precision. She was trouble. But she was not the traitor mobilizing mercenaries.

"Are you a spy in the palace?" Another simultaneous question that dripped with accusation, as if both of us hadn't just evaded our kingdom's guards.

"What in the sheols were you going to do to the guard with a piece of cloth?" I whispered, crossing my arms. "Swath him over the head?"

Sensing I wouldn't attack her if she didn't attack first, she folded the cloth and dipped it in her pocket. Judging from the faint sickly sweet scent, it was seeped in *kaiga*. A scarce anesthetic that could knock even the burliest man out with one deep whiff. How had she gotten that?

"What were *you* going to do?" she threw my question back at me, crossing her own arms. "Stab the king's Second Advisor and alert His Majesty, and everyone else, to the fact that there are more spies in the palace?"

I tore my gaze from that slender nose and smooth skin, ignored the slight quickening of my heartbeat, and glanced at the closet's window—Jaziah would never let me hear the end of it if he knew a beautiful face almost distracted me on a mission. *Almost.* Dawn's pink tendrils coursed through the dark sky. Soon, the entire palace would wake.

"The guards won't stop tearing through this level until they find a snoop, or a reason to explain away their suspicions," I said, growing grim. "We can't get past their search, and yet we need to get out of here."

If we didn't soon, they would surely return to this area and find us.

"There is no *we*, Gergesenes," she bit out, but I could see her mind evaluating the grave circumstance.

The hint of worry in her eyes softened my response. "It's beyond our control, but right now—" I gestured to the closet. "—we *are* stuck in this together."

I didn't add that two snoops running in different directions meant that one could direct the guards' attention to the other to escape. It was the kind of sly choice many Esans would make to save their neck. I wasn't letting her out of my sight just yet.

Zair gave me a distrustful look. "I'll decide what I…"

"Wait. Listen to that," I said as boots *thunked* and a trembling voice rang out.

"Someone is… pleading," she whispered, the pulse thrumming faster in her neck.

My chest clenched tightly. The noise of struggle was close enough to hear, yet too distant to be in this passage.

"What are you doing?" she demanded as I placed my hand on the doorknob.

I ignored her and placed my ear against the door, listening over the pounding in my chest. No footsteps padded directly outside the closet. The atmosphere was still. Empty for now.

She marched over and placed her hand over mine to block the knob. "*What* are you thinking?"

Her touch branded my skin, but I held her agitated gaze to make her understand.

"Whatever is causing that struggle might draw the guards' attention long enough to make our way out of here," I said. "We can stay hiding and miss this chance to escape—to *survive* tonight. Or find out if it's a situation we can exploit."

Taking a breath, I pushed open the door, giving her time to decide. No guard stood in this hallway, but the pleas and clipped demands rang from two hallways down. Hardly far from us at all.

A perilous beat pounded in my ears as I glanced questioningly at Zair. *Decided?*

Her jaw was clenched, but the weight of danger intensified with each scream of pain and she gave a nod.

I didn't miss her deliberately soundless steps as we hugged the shadows, the way her gaze also marked the windows and corners for quick escapes. A blaze glimmered somewhere deep in my chest. We stopped at the archway of the noisy hallway and pressed our backs to the wall.

She placed a finger to her lips, and I would've laughed that she thought I was naïve enough to make a sound if the man's pitiful cries didn't tighten my stomach.

"...and if you don't tell us who sent you right now, steward, I'll rip out your eyes too."

My stomach hardened at the ruthless voice of the sub-head soldier from earlier. And this spy... he was a palace steward.

"Alright!" the trembling male voice shouted. "The Chief of Warro is who paid me to spy on Chancellor Keide. It's the chief! Now, kill me, *please*, and make it swift."

My hands trembled and I fisted them. Zair's fingers curled into her trousers. Moments later, a body thudded on the tiles and bile burned in my throat.

"Take the body away, sergeants. Sub-heads, find the Chief of Warro. Throw him in the dungeons," the Second Advisor ordered coldly.

Blood roared in my ears, but I nudged Zair forward. Already sharing my thoughts, she turned and raced into the next corridor ahead of me. My heart raced. While the carpet had carried Zair and I out of range, the spying steward must've been caught in the guards' search of the wing. The guards must believe *he* was the snoop they had heard when I'd pushed the vase.

I would consider it all later, but right now the search had paused with the belief that the culprit had been caught. This was our one chance out of here.

Zair threw a troubled look over her shoulder, clearly thinking of the dead spy. I clutched her elbow and pointed a firm hand ahead. *Not now.* We slowed at the filigreed archway that led to the main entry, but two guards were jogging up the shadowy stairs. Right to where we stood.

We began to move back, scanning the area.

I jabbed my thumb at the dark glass window beside the archway. Zair paused, certain I'd want to use my escape route first. I nudged her back and surprise flickered on her face before she dived forward, pushing the window open. I scaled into the cold darkness behind her, the ledge so thin that only our heels rested on it. Balancing my weight, I closed the window, just as footsteps bounded closer.

Barghests growled somewhere distant, but the corridor quickly fell silent again.

We slipped back inside and dipped into a tiny alcove above the stairs, to survey the open foyer on the lower level and the voices echoing beyond it.

The snarls from animals grew louder.

I couldn't risk any more beasts catching my scent. I slipped out the *biksod* I'd tucked into my boot—a technique I'd easily devised with a sister who liked to bake with the leavening powder. Zair watched with raised eyebrows as I dusted myself down in the pale substance. Not enough to leave a dust trail; just enough to bury my scent for a bit. I turned to her. She wasn't going anywhere until I found out just *who* she was. I put more *biksod* between my hands and brushed my hands down her arms. Awareness zapped in the tiny space between us.

She almost jumped out of her skin.

She hissed, "What are you doing?"

I held my hands up in a harmless gesture and lifted a challenging brow. "What do you think?"

She tried and failed to hide her impressed look as she realized my reasoning. "You're covering our scents from the barghests."

"Shall I proceed, Nergal?"

She tautened defensively at my honeyed tone. "Give it to me and I'll do it myself."

I could, but... "And lose the chance to brag that my ingenuity helped you? Never." I placed a hand on the wall beside her head. "We are losing time, Nergal."

Her long lashes fluttered, and I knew she'd felt those sparks too when I touched her. "If your hands stray, even a bit, I'll cut you."

Her fire and independence brightened that flicker of light in my chest.

"I don't doubt that for a moment." I dabbed more *biksod* in my hands and swore lightning fizzled in the alcove as I ran them down her arms. Swallowing, I crouched and brushed my hands down her long, shapely legs. *She is beautiful.*

Her breath caught audibly as I straightened in front of her, a current crackling in the air as our gazes locked.

What was happening here?

"Time..." She swallowed. "It's time to go."

She all but fled the small space between me and the wall. Sense returned to my mind. *Stop whatever this is.*

Pulse thrumming, I followed after her and jogged down the carpeted stairs. To evade the patrols, I led us through a longer, dimmer route.

We dipped into a fragrance garden but the smell of death filled my nose. My thoughts zipped to Jaziah and cold curled under my skin as I made out body parts scattered in smears of blood.

"The guards caught another snoop tonight," Zair murmured as we picked our steps through flesh and bone.

My eyes flared. "Someone other than the Chief of Warro's steward spy?"

"Yes. The palace guards are never to be underestimated." She let out a breath. "She didn't scream like the Chief of Warro's spy did. Barghests ripped her apart."

Sheols. The reality that this could've been us, if not for the carpet... and because the other spy had been caught in our place, chilled my blood. I didn't know if the Chief of Warro's spy had good or bad motives, yet a weight pressed on my chest over his execution.

"Thank you," I said.

She blinked in surprise. "For what?"

"For letting me share your... unusual carpet," I said with a small smile.

"I barely had a choice in the matter," she said firmly.

I held back the response that flew to my lips. Made myself accept the comment for what it was. A barricade to end any further affiliation, despite the ripple of awareness that moved between us since that moment in the alcove.

Fine. We were almost fully out of danger. It was time to place my goal at the center of my mind.

We spilled into our vacant lounge as it picked up the colors of the dawn. Without a word, she turned straight to her chamber.

Ah no, she was not getting away that easily. I had questions for her. I followed, pushing the door open before she could shut it, and then locked it behind me.

"What do you think you're doing?" she asked. "We shouldn't be alone together in my bedroom!"

I turned to her. She'd placed pillows underneath a blanket like she was innocently asleep there.

"Are you a spy?" I repeated, taking a step closer to her. She looked almost as wrung out as I felt, yet it didn't dull her ethereality or lessen the tug from somewhere deep in my chest.

No. Whatever this feeling was, it had to stop now. The last thing I needed in the palace was a distraction, no matter how intriguingly parceled it was. Especially if she posed a threat to my mission.

The gold in her eyes flashed in her room's dim light. "Are *you* a spy? I didn't know sneaking about the palace was part of the Gergesenes' syllabus."

I started to retort that *she* had also been sneaking, but I quickly caught on to her. I lifted an amused brow. "You're attempting to deflect. Smart, but Gergesenes is the second-best military academy in the kingdom. Whatever skills you've been taught at Nergal, we've been trained better at them."

She glowered up at me. "What is your purpose here?"

"What is yours?"

We deliberated each other, minds working to figure out what neither would confess.

Nergal had suffered the academy attacks. She could also have been sent here covertly to uncover the traitor sponsoring the mercenaries from the palace. Still, that we could be walking in the same direction didn't make us allies.

When the Commandant and Admiral gave me my mission, they specified one thing: I had to bring the traitor to *them*. The Admiral planned to interrogate the traitor, figure out who else he was in league with, the mercenaries' aim, and where to find the students.

To ensure that when the Admiral grinded the culprits, he would grind them and their operations to ash.

And Jaziah would be free.

I didn't know what her end goal was, *if* we had the same mission. Or who she would take the traitor back to. Nergal's Commandant could've assigned her to spy here, but there had to be someone powerful backing the Commandant for her to dare send a spy into the Al'Qtraz.

Whoever their backer was, they weren't the Admiral. The most equipped soldier to handle the mercenaries.

From the curved windows lining Zair's walls, soft light illuminated the pocket she'd returned that piece of cloth to. What else was hidden in her pockets? Had she found useful details that pointed to the traitor?

No, I was getting ahead of myself. She could be after something else entirely.

Choosing to back away for now, I muttered, "Just don't get caught."

Her cheeks puffed out with her scoff. "So that I don't ruin things for you?"

I shrugged. "If one fox is caught by the shepherd, it becomes harder for the other to succeed in its hunt."

She considered this, then went to open her door. "Thank you for the concern, Gergesenes, but I don't intend to get caught—or executed."

14

ZAIR

I paced my room, wondering what Dathan Issachar's scheme was as the palace's temple echoed with priests and nobles singing early psalms. The ornate clock tolled seven o'clock. The river condensed the hot desert air, sending fog curling through the city's buildings and arches like a milky breath.

Today was the King's Tour; the second occasion of the coronation. I had only ten days left until I ran out of time to save Sarai. My head ached from all the magic use last night and my body felt sapped. Yet it wasn't my biggest concern. I'd never wanted to be the strange magical girl.

What was Dathan Issachar's mission? Was it the same as mine?

Every part of me protested the possibility. He was strong and smart. Clever too. Who would have thought to utilize *biksod*—a *baking* ingredient—as a tool to camouflage scents? A vision rolled in of that intense moment in the alcove. My skin warmed from the vivid memory of his strong hands running down my arms, his fingers encircling my calves, the power in his honed body mere inches from mine...

Realizing what I was thinking, I exclaimed, "Stop it, Zair."

He had only been focused on his survival and hadn't wanted me to compromise it. No man could have real interest in me.

It had been clear to me for years... Young men my age would always be repelled by my roots. None of them would ever see past my eyes and accept me. I swallowed. After hearing people curse my mother for ruining my father's life by 'using her Esan wiles' to trap him, and making him and their children pariahs, I knew that love and marriage were not in my future. My chest squeezed, but I pushed the old ache away.

Scholar Dathan was nothing to me but another student with interesting skills and hidden motives. If we had the same target and he caught the traitor for whoever sent him before I did, I couldn't ensure that Sarai was freed from the mercenaries' clutches.

Hurrying through an engraved doorway, I padded into a rose-and-brown bath chamber reflected in embellished mirrors. At the center was a wide pool with fuchsia vases overflowing with lilies and lavenders around it. I undid my hair plaits and brushed my fingers through the silky tendrils. I dipped into its fragrant water and hurriedly washed. Wrapped in a towel, I rushed back to the room and pulled the Admiral's schedule from my pocket.

What part of the Admiral's agenda was important to Colonel Remmon? Every meeting listed here seemed, well, important. Fine. I'd keep an eye on Colonel Remmon during each event until more clues slipped. They always did.

I swiveled and spotted a new attire laid out on my bed. Good thing I'd thought to pull out my pillows beforehand. With foreigners in the palace, even the maids would be attentive and wary, reporting odd sightings back to the Ironteenth.

"With guests like that blackmailer Arno," I murmured bitterly, "they'll be justified."

I slipped on the gauzy azure skirts. The dewdrop embellishments on the hem brushed the carpet, hiding my ragged slippers. I glanced at the wardrobe where the oversized slippers the academy had provided me with sat. It made me wonder if they had intended to send another student to the palace before the attacks. Perhaps afterward, the Commandant chose me since I was dispensable and sent me off with the student's items. I pushed the stinging thought away.

My blouse hugged my skin in goldenrod and a silver-embellished collar swirled up my neck. Even before Nergal drilled into us to *dress for respect*, my father was a cloth merchant—I'd been born with a passion for fine clothes. These were especially lovely.

My old bronze bracelets jingled as I made a single zigzag plait by my left ear, another by my right ear, and brushed the rest to flow down my back. I lined my eyes with cheap kajal and applied perfume oil before heading out of the chamber, scenting of spiced honey.

Presents filled the lounge's center table. *Gifts from courtiers for the students!* Red silks, perfumes, books of folklore. Each had names attached. Briefly setting my worries aside, excitement flickered in me as I checked them.

I loved storybooks. Amid their pages I was never an outcast.

But there was no gift for me. I should've expected it. Still, my chest dipped.

The other students' doors were shut, but delicious aromas tugged my empty stomach to the balcony. I hadn't been able to eat at the feast yesterday with countless eyes on me.

"Where are the other sluggards?" Ibhar's voice came from the balcony.

The sun warmed my cheeks as I entered the carved balcony with a gold-and-blue view of the capital. A long, low table was heaped with platters of crispy akara, fresh bread, sauced eggs, the creamiest yoghurt, diced sugarcanes, and pots of spearmint leaves. The curved marquetry chairs around it had been spaced so far apart that one would think the maids knew of our interschool rivalry for the highest positions in the kingdom. Perhaps they were afraid we'd claw each other's eyes out if we sat too close.

Only two of those chairs were occupied though, and for a weak moment, I considered forfeiting breakfast if I had to eat with just *them* for company.

Dathan's head perked up, his bronze circlet glinting as he pinned me with salient eyes of green and gold and brown. His painfully handsome face was fresh in the morning light, as if he had just washed too. His curly hair fell to his broad shoulders, brushing his sapphire tunic and neck scarf.

In just one night, we had brawled on a soaring carpet, worked together to escape guards, and shared a tiny alcove with... unsettling sensations. My verdict was that he seemed to threaten some old, firm wall inside me and I needed to stay away from him.

"Here's one, but *she* sure isn't a sluggard," he answered Ibhar.

He rose and prowled toward me like a lion.

Set him on defense before he takes the offense.

"Doesn't look like you slept well," he said, his scent dark and zesty as it swirled around me. "Thinking about me?"

"Yes," I said simply. "Of all the ways I'll beat you at the Best of Ten."

Ibhar frowned, his attention bouncing between us.

Dathan's mouth quirked. "Cocky. What a match we'd make if I didn't suspect we are colliding stars."

Before he could say whatever made him rise, I added, "A rule we're taught at the Nergal Military Academy is to learn our surroundings. The palace is full of people who once had us in chains—some who still have Esans as slaves in their kingdoms. Last night I was surveying to make sure I'll be safe here. Was that also your reason for wandering at midnight?"

His eyes narrowed. "I was sleepwalking and happened to alert guards and beasts in the process. How is that for excuses?"

By Osime, he was intimidating. As keen as a hawk.

I swallowed. "I don't know, but now that we've confirmed the palace is well-guarded at night, we have no reason to continue... roaming. Which means if I find you creeping about again, I'll have to report you."

Good. Scare him into giving up on whatever mission he has.

For a moment, I was sure I'd succeeded as his head jerked back. Then his eyes flashed like green flames, his mouth curving in a humorless smirk. "Alright, Nergal. Two can play this game of sabotage. I best not find you 'surveying' either."

With that, he headed back to his chair. My heart still raced, but I released a long breath. So what if my plan backfired a little? At least he didn't know he intimidated me.

Dark circles tinted Ibhar's eyes like he'd had a rough night. He grumpily buttered thick slices of loaf.

Could he have been out spying? *No, please. Not him too.*

A look flickered over Dathan's face that said he'd read my thoughts. Was he wondering the same about Ibhar. But what reason would Ibhar have to seek out the traitor? The Ahimoth Academy was owned by Ussis, who cared little about the other academies or their missing students. Relying on assumptions was risky, but I doubted Ahimoth would risk their star pupil's neck by sending him to spy in the palace over attacks on Nergal academies.

Hunger pinched at my stomach, reminding me of the meal waiting. I made my way to a chair farthest from the young men. Coming from the southern quarter's slums and an academy that followed a strict diet, this meal was a feast.

I'd just settled into the chair when Lysias and Mishan—the healing and engineering students—burst through the doors with excited energies. Mishan, the Felax Engineering Academy representative, adjusted his glasses by his blonde temple, his hands adorned with the black geometric tattoos of the Mizsab tribe.

Both chattered as if between yesterday and this morning, they'd somehow become friends. Considering their academies weren't competing for limited positions in the same fields, it wasn't that odd.

Lysias's honey-hued hair rippled in the warming breeze, her four earrings of golden moons twinkling. Her fuchsia-and-gold skirts glistened as she chippered, "Prosperity upon your day, Scholars."

She moved around the table, keeping a distance from me and then Ibhar, like he scared her too.

Without awaiting a response, she continued cheerily as she sat, "The Al'Qtraz truly is as exquisite as they say. My bath chamber has more mirrors than my entire dormitory at Quartus!"

I wanted to agree, but although the Kwalis were a neighborly people, I couldn't assume she'd want to talk to me. Her eyes held wariness, being amongst other tribes and rival students, but she also seemed... open. Determined to extend a hand of acquaintanceship.

"In all my years of studying components, I've never understood women's obsession with their reflections," Mishan said wryly. "And I live with *three* Mizsab women so I'd know."

Indeed, the Mizsabs were very passionate people—*or* impatient, depending on whom you asked. It had made their soldiers a pain in the backside during the War of Beasts.

Lysias waved him off. "Have you all seen the itinerary for the coronation? It's packed. Everyone was talking about it after the morning's psalms in the palace's temple—"

"Will you shut up?" Ibhar snapped, startling everyone. "You're giving me a headache with your stupid twittering."

Lysias shrunk, plucking at the tablecloth as her cheeks reddened. I seethed, but tried to focus on adding sugar to my tumbler of spearmint leaves. Speaking out would only worsen the situation.

Dathan looked at Ibhar as if only slightly curious. "Why so grumpy, Ahimoth? Didn't sleep long last night?"

Ibhar froze, and as I sipped my minty tea, I realized Dathan was fishing for confirmation. Any sign that Ibhar could indeed be a spy too. Why would the question disgruntle Ibhar if he had nothing to hide?

Ibhar surged to his feet like an erupting volcano and flung his glass, drenching Dathan in yoghurt. Lysias and I gasped. Mishan exclaimed.

"Stay in your lane, ricemaggot," Ibhar snarled.

Ricemaggot. It was a Baihan slur as we were large producers of rice. Angry words filled my throat, but I felt especially *wary* of Ibhar.

Dathan glared at Ibhar's retreating form, his jaw clenched tight enough to crack. He was restraining himself from reacting, I realized, because he had his answer. Ibhar's intense defensiveness meant he hid something.

The moment Ibhar left the balcony, the air became less choking.

Mishan hesitated, then offered an embroidered napkin to Dathan. "*Kele.*" *Sorry*.

"*Ishe,*" Dathan thanked him in fluent Mhese and took the napkin, but rose and left the balcony.

I might have no fondness for Dathan Issachar, but Ibhar was such a menace!

Lysias and Mishan served their breakfast and talked quietly as they ate. With the distance between our chairs and the clatter from the vast yard below, I couldn't hear much with my human senses, but their attention frequently flicked toward me. They had to be talking about my Esan roots; everyone did when they looked at me that way. I could only imagine how surprised they'd be to learn that while my mother was Esan, I was Baihan—a tribe with more prominence than both of theirs.

But attempting to correct people's assumptions made me feel like I was ashamed of my mother. She faced enough discrimination. The last thing she needed was to receive it from her children, whom she loved with everything.

I was forcing down the last of my buttered loaf when a guard blocked the doorway in his glinting armor. We greeted him and he responded courteously.

"The tour of Ari'el will commence soon," he said. "You students are expected in the outer courtyard in fifteen minutes. Nergal, the Royal Advisors insist you make yourself unseen today."

Lysias gasped softly. Avoiding their eyes and hiding my chagrin, I nodded firmly and searched for the good in the situation. We were riding around the city today. I would see my family. The sting eased and a small glow filled my chest.

The guard left and we stood up. Mishan went to knock on Dathan and Ibhar's bedroom doors. "We leave in fifteen, slugs!"

Lysias and I grabbed veils from our chambers, protection from the sun. By the time I reemerged, my dagger tucked into my waistband, the others also approached the doorway.

"Seems we best friends are heading to the outer courtyard together," Dathan said with sardonic cheer. He now wore a pristine white tunic with a black silk neck scarf and trousers.

"You're more delusional than our Baihan king if you think your lowly tribes are worthy of Ussi friendship," Ibhar spat.

"Ah, typical Ussi. Zero understanding of the word *humility*."

"Saints above!" Mishan threw up his hands, striding ahead. "This is why we minorities avoid gatherings of the major tribes."

Dathan and Ibhar scowled at him and although he was skinnier than them, he was almost as tall and scowled back. The air strained between us, and it didn't help that I quickly attracted glares and snide comments from courtiers. But Lysias looked at me differently now. No longer as if I had claws and fangs, but like the guard's harsh order was... shifting a thought she had.

Then again, I could be imagining what I hoped to see.

We descended the sweeping velvet stairs to the ground floor, ambling past some Kwali chiefs. Mishan's gaze lingered over his shoulder at them for a moment.

"I also heard something interesting after the temple's psalms," he said. "The king stripped the Chief of Warro of his title and imprisoned him. The chief had been spying about the palace to find reasons for Chancellor Keide's new wife to annul their marriage. So that the chief could proposition her."

Lysias gasped and Ibhar's head jerked backward. I couldn't help but slide Dathan a secret look, and an understanding zapped between us. The second spy last night had nefarious motives. I could've sworn Dathan's lips parted in a relieved breath.

"Well... the Kwali Chancellor's wife *is* very beautiful," was all Lysias could think to say about the interesting situation.

Amusement whispered on my tongue. Dathan and Mishan chuckled. Even Ibhar snorted, easing the strain.

Lysias's eyes sparkled with delight when we reached a ground floor passage of blue-washed walls with red flowerpots arranged along the walls. Open arches revealed bejeweled ensembles as the nobles sauntered into a long stone yard embellished with dewy hawthorn hedges and fountains. Horses huffed as dozens of stable boys prepared them for mounting. Thalesai's guards shone in their ceremonial wear—ivory armor and black capes—bearing adaswords and longbows.

"I have to applaud the wraiths." Lysias considered their shimmering gathering. "Those flowing dark gossamer and obsidian headpieces? Sublime. Although I could do without the shadows."

"You mean the very element that holds wraith magic?" Mishan smirked. "I prefer the shapeshifters' attire."

He gestured to the hefty beings glowering at their horses. "The topaz-studded shemaghs and damask robes make the feral beings seem almost humane. If only their hair wasn't tastelessly long."

Dathan snorted amusedly. "*You* mean the very element that holds shifter magic?"

"Our dignitaries look wonderful," Lysias said with gentle pride. "No flaws whatsoever."

My nape tingled against a presence closing in on me before I saw the shoes striding beside mine. Peeking sidelong, my heart stumbled. The king's Spaeman.

Saints above. Why was he here?

I'd only ever seen the Spaeman from a distance during royal addresses. And even that far, the king's seer's presence made one feel exposed. He was the king's divine guide. While many disputed that he possessed mystical powers, asking why Spaemen hadn't predicted the Invasions if they were so powerful, much about them —from their longer limbs to their frosty eyes—was beyond our normal. The Spaemen's tribe, age, and everything that made us comfortably human, were unknown.

My chest squeezed until breathing became difficult. What if he *was* a seer? Was that why he sought me, a mere student nowhere worthy of his attention, out? He would expose me as a spy to the king. What would happen to my family?

"I would tell you to beware."

His smooth voice cut through my thoughts, his focus ahead as mine was.

"Yet before we are forged into our true selves, before we find our true purpose in this world, we must first walk through fire."

"I don't understand, Khosa Spaeman," I said with false calm. Inside, my belly clenched in knots.

"You will," he said with something akin to regret.

With those daunting words, he walked off in a flash of white. Lysias took tentative steps closer to me as we emerged in the moist, clear morning.

"His presence is nerve-wracking, isn't it? What did he want?" she asked.

"I don't know. He spoke in parables." My voice shook slightly.

Ibhar sneered. "He must want to cleanse the palace's atmosphere of her half-blood taint."

I folded my fingers against the stab of the insult.

Lysias's mouth pinched, but she continued speaking to me in a lower tone that sounded oddly... kind?

"Do you think he can really read minds and tell the future?"

The question only heightened my panic. "I don't know," I murmured and moved faster for my horse, certain the look on her face wasn't disappointment.

"You believe the foolish rumors, Quartus?" Ibhar mocked.

"My name is Lysias," she said stiffly.

"There has never been proof that the king's Spaeman has the ability to do more than fling his freakishly long limbs about and stare all mysteriously, *Quartus*."

Lysias just shook her head.

Dathan muttered, "If the Spaeman was a seer, he would've nipped the mercenary issue in the bud before it escalated to this point."

Was that why Dathan was here then? To indeed find the traitor and nip the mercenary issue before it escalated further?

I might've believed the Spaeman was ordinary too. But my mother often told us tales of Spaemen averting people's futures.

THE KING and queen settled in a regal, oval carriage of white and gold crafted for the occasion. The Ironteenth rode beside and in front of them on the *kiniuns*. Great lions with snow-white fur that stood taller than the horses, their menacing faces incised with glowing blue symbols. I had always wondered what the symbols meant, and if I made it into the Ironteenth I could finally find out. Their broad bodies contracted as their maned heads scanned the procession, their eyes full of intelligence.

The rest of us lined up in rows behind the royal carriage, from the most important dignitaries to the least at the rear. Each row had seven to ten dignitaries either riding astride, sidesaddle, or in a caleche. We, the students, rode seven rows from the Majesties, close enough that the king turned in his seat and sighted us easily. He nodded in approval.

Royal guards took flexible positions at the edge of the rows, to ride back and forth as needed to guard the parade.

With the Majesties' orders, our royal party rode down the hill and into Ari'el proper.

Colonel Remmon rode with other high-ranked soldiers two rows behind the Majesties. While my heart still skipped after encountering the Spaeman, Sarai's marking and the ticking clock on the missing students' lives fueled my persistence to tail him.

Sunlight gilded the capital nestled between the cerulean Niger River and the golden sand dunes. Houses in shades of blue with metalwork doors and decorative stucco surged in rows that framed our procession. The residents—wealthy merchants and landowners in tasseled silks—cheered for their new king and queen.

"Long live King Khasar!" men declared, blowing handfuls of salt over our procession. A show of adoration.

"A union that will lead the kingdom to greater glory!" women sang about the union of tribes with the royal couple, waving cymbals and dancing.

I couldn't tell if the foreign ambassadors—riding in the second row behind the Majesties—felt the marvel Ari'el always awoke in me as we proceeded into the northern Baihan quarters. As the colors morphed, revealing queues of green walls, red-tiled roofs and oval-shaped doorways.

"Prosperity, Scholar Dathan!"

"Marry me, Scholar Dathan!" wealthy Baihan girls crowed.

Dathan's mouth quirked as they blew him kisses. Mishan caught one of the 'kisses' and pressed it to his heart, making the girls giggle. Lysias rolled her eyes at him, her veil fluttering around her shoulders. The sun was still too mild for us to wear our veils.

My mouth quivered over their playfulness, but I didn't dare let the smile out. Not when disgusted looks were thrown my way. Rather, I focused on the city spread out wide around me, a potent feeling buoying in my chest.

Pride in Thalesai, in my city.

Humans might not be able to morph into feral beasts like the shapeshifters or fly like the azizas, but our land had progressed immensely since the War. It was beautiful again, unlike the paintings I had seen of our ravaged lands and the broken human slaves. Our people were stronger, smarter, and bolder.

I glanced toward my home in the southern Baihan quarters near the rear gates. Eagerness buzzed in me to see my family and make sure Sarai was well. For them to watch me ride with the royals, an honored guest of the king. They would be so proud.

Our horses trooped into the Halim Market, where hundreds of storied shops with colorful verandahs were built in a vast circle. A city within a city. Red awnings fluttered from sand-colored buildings, protecting basins of onions, dried peppers, cherries, colorful purses, and hand-painted pottery from the sun. Some ladies in the procession admired the attractive displays while the lords conversed easily. I kept assessing each of them for suspicious behaviors, but we were outdoors.

It seemed everyone was on their best behavior, including First Colonel Remmon.

"We were told that this coronation tradition symbolizes the king and queen acquainting themselves with the people they are to rule. It is a noble tradition."

I stiffened at the voice sent into my ears with aziza magic and whipped my head to glare at Arno Irmah. He had moved from his position in the fourth row and now rode with graceful ease beside me. If I was suspected to be consorting with foreigners, I could be thrown in a dungeon.

"You said you yielded your magic to the Spaeman."

"There is innate magic we cannot shed. This small trick is one of those."

"Shouldn't you be guarding your ambassador?" I rebuked quietly.

"That is what I am doing here beside you." His silver hair shone sharply like his uniform, his wings folded tightly away from the crowd.

He ignored my glower and instead stared, appalled, at a showglass filled with delicate combs in pearlescent cream. "By the god Ix. Are those combs crafted from *bones*?"

"I'm an odd choice for a tour companion, don't you think?"

"Why?" he asked. "Because you stand apart for being part aziza?"

I held still for the coming insults about being an outcast that didn't fit anywhere.

"When people can't understand a unique thing, they treat it as an oddity. I believe things that stand apart are special," he said.

I frowned at him, but his ethereal face was calm and earnest. It made me answer him.

"They are combs made from bones. *Aziza* bones, to be precise." I arched a smug brow, but quickly froze.

From beside the Majesties' carriage, the Second Advisor watched me as I spoke with an aziza soldier.

Arno snorted amusedly. "You are a fascinating little liar."

I bit out, "I've heard nothing that might threaten your party and have no reason to believe that'll change."

He studied me for lies. But if I was lying again, he would smell it in a heartbeat. I rode to the other end of the students' row, and the Second Advisor unpinned me from his scowl. I glanced at Dathan to see if he'd picked up on my affiliation with an aziza guard. He wasn't watching me, thank skies, but alertness tightened his jaw. He was watching *someone*. Yet he'd draped his black scarf over his head—concealing his focus. Clever hawk.

Buyers and sellers stopped their haggling over goods to cheer for the cavalcade. Storytellers jumped from mats to gather around us. Children around Sarai's age stopped pestering sugarcane hawkers to jump and wave. In front of the throng, an emaciated beggar girl stood with slumped shoulders in her rags. The neglect written all over her hit me in my chest, and I quickly held out my last copper *siyva*. "Here."

Her dirt-streaked face brightened, then she looked up at my eyes. She glowered, about to slap away my hand, but then she halted. She swiped the coin, turned, and disappeared into the crowd without a word of thanks.

At least my show of concern would mean something, ease her neglect... wouldn't it?

The noise became overwhelming. The royal guards went on keener alert. There were still those from other tribes who chafed at being ruled by a Baihan king and that his title would be sealed in only ten days. *Ten days.*

The streets leading out of the market grew narrower. The Iron-teenth ordered the procession to split into the four streets as planned, and then converge on the main boulevard ahead.

"Scholars, you take the Saii Street since the Aniel Street is farther. Meet us up front!" a guard called over the noise, waving us vigorously down an alley. "Don't make us wait long for you."

Mishan nodded and led the way down the alley.

Why was the guard's ceremonial cape wrinkled, as if he'd shoved it on hurriedly? Ceremonial wear was *always* to be neat.

That rule had been beaten into us in year-one when many of my classmates had still been scruffy rascals. And *why* was he bearing a scythe rather than an adasword? But bodies moved like a gushing river around me. My horse was carried along, down the alley before I could pay attention to the noise in my head. Two lower-ranked soldiers rode behind us.

We cantered down the empty alley with the intention of reaching the boulevard before the rest of the party. We were too disciplined to make the Majesties wait.

My skin prickled as we rode farther, hooves echoing like we were in a forgotten tunnel, no end to the alley in sight.

"Wait!" Dathan called. "Halt. Something isn't right."

The others must've felt the same. They pulled on their reins as quickly as I did.

"It's too quiet here," I said, scanning the vacant roofs. "Too empty."

If we were following a route around the market as planned, excited children would cram the roofs, eager for a glimpse of the Majesties.

"The exit shouldn't be this far," one of the soldiers agreed as they unsheathed their adaswords. They wouldn't take their task to defend us lightly.

Dathan glanced over his shoulder, his brows knitted as that sharp mind worked. "We should leave the way we came, sirs. It's the—"

A knife lodged in the first soldier's throat and sprayed blood on his horse. Shock blasted through me even I unsheathed my dagger, looking around. But the attacker was hidden. Two knives ripped into the second soldier's eyes with sickening precision. Lysias and Mishan shouted as he slumped to the ground.

"Turn around!" I screamed, but it was too late.

Figures cloaked in black fell from the roofs—roofs that were vacant seconds ago—like ghosts with masked faces and surrounded us.

Dathan's first dagger pierced a bandit's shoulder and the bandit shouted as he dodged the second dagger. Dathan already moved, swinging off his horse and sprinting for a fallen guard's adasword.

I kicked my horse into a gallop to cover Dathan's back as sharp objects flew in the air. Pain flashed in my thigh and two darts protruded from my skin.

Keep riding! my brain ordered. *Get out of here.*

But my limbs had become watery, my eyelids sinking anvils. My horse dropped like a boulder, also hit by whatever poison coated the darts. Pain seared my left side as I slammed into the dirt beside one of the impaled soldiers.

My heart dashed with the need to fight, with helplessness.

Arms came around me, ripping off my weapons. They dragged the four of us into a wagon and threw bolts of coarse fabrics over us. The last thing I saw between gaps in the cloths were the dead soldiers being hauled away.

15

DATHAN

A fetid odor crept into my lungs, drawing me to consciousness. Pain jarred through my head as I forced my eyes open.

What was happening?

The soldier in me began to catalog my surroundings even before my mind fully woke. A dark room reeking of blood and filled with cobwebs. No windows. Only the slight cracks between the ceiling and wall allowed air and bits of light in.

Nothing looked familiar. Because...

Captured. The word clanged in my head. The memory of our ambush and the dead soldiers in the alley filled my sluggish mind, jolting me. *Escape.*

I made to lunge to my feet. Jangling metal yanked me down, flinging my back against the wall. A groan escaped me but the pain quickly became the least of my concerns. My eyes flared on the shackles binding my hands and feet to the wall.

Trapped.

My throat tightened with dread. More unwanted memories flooded my mind. I fought them. I needed to focus on getting out of here, returning to my mission. But the tide dragged me under.

The tiny, dark cellar that had felt like a coffin. My family hiding there for five days and in utter silence for fear of our hunters overhearing us. Fear that they would hurt Asahel worse. Asahel's silent tears clawing at me until I could hardly breathe from her pain.

Separate the past from the present, the Commandant's steady voice drifted through my wild mind. *Else they will merge and cost you the future.*

Sweat dripped down my temples. My wrists trembled in my shackles. I struggled to get my shaking under control as bodies rose like the awakening dead from the floor.

Lysias and Mishan.

Terror glazed their eyes, but there was also control. Military student, engineering student, or healer, one did not aspire to join Thalesai's Chambers without learning to master fear. Danger would always lurk when the tribes converged.

Metal clanged to my left. I whipped my head, only to find Zair. Anger and panic masked her face as she studied her shackles.

The shackles had little allowance. Our ambushers knew they had elite military students in their cells and weren't taking any chances.

"Just what the kingdom needs with foreigners present and sniffing around for weaknesses. Another group of abducted students to reveal that there are enemy groups afflicting Thalesai," Mishan said roughly.

"D-do you think our captors could be organ-harvesters?" Lysias whispered with wide eyes, half her face darkened with dirt.

"I thought so at first." Zair's forehead fused in thought. "But from the recounts of people that escaped them, organ-harvesters kill their captives immediately."

Flames of anger crackled in my ears. Organ-harvesters were another group of bandits with motives no one understood. Why were they greedy for their fellow humans' organs? What were they doing with hearts and lungs and eyeballs?

I could never place myself in their shoes enough to glean the motive. Each time organ-harvesters were caught, they killed themselves by poison consumption before interrogation.

"They're also always on the move," Zair continued as she studied the cell, "rather than maintaining bases like this one."

"And since we are not random victims taken for our organs,

we're more likely their specific targets. Brought here *because* we're academy representatives in the royal procession," I said.

She gave a nod. The bandits had to know that taking the king's guest students from the procession would launch a host of soldiers after them. It couldn't be a careless move. It had to be a part of their plan.

I struggled to keep my thoughts in the present. What if the king's procession *was* the main target, then? We'd been lured down that alley by that bastard in a scruffy guard uniform. Their attack was carefully executed. Pulled during a crucial moment of the Majesties' coronation: the first public event.

An agonized scream rent the atmosphere, followed by shouts of plea. A sickening slurp of blood and the hacking of flesh silenced the scream. The shouts became muffled sounds of horror, the smell of blood stronger.

Lysias scrambled back against the wall, small noises leaving her throat. Mishan began to tremble without control.

"They butcher people down here," Zair breathed.

A butcher's block.

"Ey!" I called firmly and three pairs of scared eyes cinched on me. "Do not fade on me. I need those sharp minds working at full capacity if we don't want to be down here when the butchers reach our cell. Alright?"

Bits of courage returned to the cell even as another string of terrified screaming started. More memories assaulted me.

"We students are a prominent part of the King's Tour," I said. "Our absence wouldn't be overlooked by the people. Their cheers would quickly transform into confusion when they look for the representatives of Thalesai's future and don't see us."

"Ibhar should be there since he didn't ride down the alley with us," Lysias said bitterly, scrambling away from a scorpion.

"An Ussi student present while the others aren't won't reassure the other tribespeople that their own student reps are fine," Zair whispered.

"If anything, it'll wake their outrage," I agreed. "And if it's suspected that we'd gone missing during the procession, it would kill the enthusiasm King Khasar has received. Make him appear incompetent."

"The crowds would discard praise and demand our presence," Zair said. "Showing the foreign ambassadors that Thalesai isn't half as unified as we claim. That we're as big a threat to ourselves as they are to us. It'll completely discredit the king to the people of Thalesai. And... this might ultimately be what our abductors want."

"King Khasar is Baihan," I muttered thoughtfully. "The Chamber of Wings, the king's first councilmen, consist mostly of Baihans and Ussis. This abduction could've easily been plotted by Ussis, who don't want to bow to a Baihan king. Or Mizsabs, Kwalis, or even Esan folks, to discredit him."

My head pounded with a new urgency. I'd made a vow. To protect the king at all costs. I couldn't allow this to be done to him.

Within, my spirit roared against powerlessness.

Green eyes worried behind his dusty glasses, Mishan whispered, "Judging from the light between the cracks, it's noon. We were taken in the morning. It won't be long before our absence becomes a major concern and raises panic. If it hasn't already."

A cell door slammed and our shoulders jerked.

"We need to get out of here and salvage that procession," I said, hoping the shudders working through me weren't evident in my voice. "It's our duty to the king."

"I don't w-wish to be the raincloud on a sunny idea." Lysias tugged on her wrists; her shackles jangled. "But we're sort of in a bind."

Indeed the situation appeared hopeless. The shackles were of enforced metal. We were placed far enough apart that we couldn't manipulate each other's chains. If only I could settle down, I could think of something. But dark spots danced in my vision as my father's cries filled my head.

A *slam* drew my attention to Zair. She kicked against the rusted door again.

"Guard!" she called in a whiny tone that was so unlike her, it startled me.

"What are you doing summoning them?" Mishan demanded.

"Guard!"

She kicked and called out until the sounds grated on even my nerves. But I read the firm set of her lips. Zair had a goal.

"If you keep up with that, they *will* kill us and sell our organs," Mishan snapped.

The door banged open. A man barged in swiftly and his whip cracked around the cell like vicious tentacles. Zair cried out. Mishan groaned. Lysias screamed. The strap lashed against my chest, across my back, and fire ate my skin. The flogging continued until bile pressed up my throat.

Was this what Jaziah was *enduring*? The male halted his whip midair. Behind his face covering, he took in the fire burning in my eyes while my peers writhed on the floor. The deep rage there stopped him short.

His hand lowered. "Those changing eyes... They look like old Sosthene's eyes."

The breath knocked from my lungs, and my boulder of rage shattered into pebbles. I threw my gaze to the ground and scrambled backward.

The guard stepped closer.

"I need to relieve myself," Zair gasped.

The male paused, a new knowing to him as he studied me, then he looked at Zair. "*What?*"

She clenched her teeth. "*Privy.*"

He rammed his boot into her thigh, and his callous treatment gutted something inside me.

"You get no privy break, Esan scum!"

Zair's eyes shuttered at the insult. "Why are we here?"

"Shut up!"

As he barked, I scanned his body. No key dangled off him, which had to be Zair's reason for luring him here. If we couldn't see the keys, we couldn't swipe them.

And we needed them because this man knew who I was.

"If you are going to kill us, you might as well tell us why," Zair said.

Lysias's attention darted from Zair to the guard as he growled, "Forthrightness does not always win respect, girl."

The guard's hand brushed over his crotch.

It was a quick gesture, one performed absently. Very easy to miss. But the contact of his hand near his crotch produced the lightest *tang*.

It could be a very long dagger nestled there. It could also be just what we needed.

"Now be as silent as a carcass, or lose your tongue." The male smirked at me and stormed out, slamming the door so hard that cobwebs poured from the ceiling.

Lysias gave a half-sob in disgust.

Zair and I spoke simultaneously: "The keys are inside his trousers."

We turned startled looks on each other. Mishan and Lysias gaped at us, wondering how we'd managed to notice that through the whipping.

"We need to get him back in here and retrieve that key," I finally said.

"He'll whip us to death," Lysias countered.

"That's his goal," Zair cautioned. "To scare and demoralize us into submission. If we don't escape now, his whipping will worsen until we can barely *think* about fleeing."

"What if we don't succeed and retrieve the key?" Lysias's mouth trembled. "They'll kill us like those people screaming."

"What if we do succeed? We'll be safely out of here," Zair said with a gentleness I hadn't seen from her before, and yet it flowed so naturally. "Let's focus on that. Elite military students have training on how to escape captivity. And also... miracles can happen."

Mishan swallowed, his eyes bloodshot, but he nodded. Lysias nodded too.

I tipped my chin at Zair, my breathing growing shakier with every moment trapped in here while that man who'd gleaned my identity was out there. *I have to silence him.*

"Do you want to lead this one, or should I?" I asked Zair.

"I'll follow," she answered.

Anyone else would presume she was demurring to the soldier she considered better skilled. But while she kept to herself, nothing about Zair since I'd met her was demure. She went toe-to-toe and fought to prove herself. We were potential rivals, likely after the same target, and she wanted to feel me out. To see what she could be up against.

Right now, my sole goal was getting us all out of here. I was more than willing to take the lead. In the most controlled voice I could manage, I leaned in and told them my plan.

"You see these shackles? They are restraints, but we are going to turn them into weapons."

A few minutes later, the walls vibrated with our yells for the guard. "Privy!"

Zair kicked against the door. The rest of us rattled our shackles in a riot that would shatter even a High Priest's patience. At least, the sounds distracted me from my mind's torment.

The door banged open. We instantly quieted as the male barged in like a bear primed to rip us apart. He raised a scythe this time.

Zair lunged up as far as her chains allowed and shoved him forward with all her might. He was far bigger but taken by surprise, he fell right in our middle—where our chains gave us enough allowance to strike.

He opened his mouth to shout, but the air had been knocked out of him.

Mishan and I struck both his temples with the shackles before he could scramble up. He slumped back down, my hard stare the last thing he would ever see.

Mishan's face paled as blood seeped from the man's skull. "Is he... is he *dead*?"

I didn't answer. I might've neglected to explain what happened when you rammed metal into a man's temple with the force we used. But the bandit was a traitor to the realm, he'd tormented us, and would've gone after my family.

He'd begged for this fate. I'd only answered him.

Lysias avoided the blood as she frantically searched beneath the guard's waistband for the keys. I'd calculated they would be closer to her end. But her hands now trembled so badly, she could barely search his lower body.

"More will come looking for him soon," Zair whispered urgently from her position watching the door. "We won't get another chance."

Lysias swallowed and nodded.

"Try to calm down," I said. "We have some time."

A costly lie, but while Quartus might be the best teachers of the healing science, they clearly hadn't taught their students about scouring the dead. She needed gentle encouragement.

Our breaths rattled in the silence like some distorted clock counting down to our deaths. After terror-filled moments where I became certain we'd be caught and butchered, Lysias raised a key triumphantly. "I have it!"

"Less celebrating, more unshackling!" Mishan whispered.

"Sorry." Lysias quavered as she began unshackling herself. "I've just n-never been captured before."

How lucky. Her movements became steadier. She broke free, relief filling her eyes with tears.

"Zair next," I urged.

Although Mishan shifted impatiently, he didn't contest it. Admiration filled me. There wasn't time to explain that Zair was a keen-minded soldier. If the situation worsened, she could buy Lysias time to unshackle Mishan and I with fighting skills that Mishan didn't have.

Thud. Thud. Thud.

The four of us jerked still at the echoes of heavy footsteps.

"Someone is coming," Zair said with alarm.

"Hurry, Lysias," I hissed.

She rushed to unshackle Zair's ankles.

"Mishan next," I said, even as the horror deep in my veins woke.

Lysias made quick work of Mishan's chains and scurried over to me. Zair ran in front of the door, grabbing two shackles from the ground.

Lysias had unlocked my hands and one of my ankles when a masked male filled the doorway. His focus landed first on his fallen accomplice, and his eyes rounded.

He opened his mouth to yell for reinforcement. Zair's shackle slammed into his stomach. He tipped backward. Zair dropped her weapons and grabbed his tunic, dragging him forward to stumble inside the cell instead. With a fluid jump and kick, her boot slammed his head with a ruthlessness that banged him face-first to the ground. He didn't twitch.

"Skies. You are lethal," Mishan breathed.

Panting, she eyed Mishan with distrust, as if expecting him to attack her for defending herself.

Mishan shook his head fervently. "No, Zair."

No time for small talk. With my manacles opened, I shot up to my feet. "Let's go!"

We ran down a tunnel-like passage. Sharp arguments and the snarling of dogs reverberated from behind doors. We made little sound, barely breathed. Shackles could only do so much damage against scythes. Worse, they could use their poisoned darts against us again.

An open cell exposed corpses, dozens of them, butchered and piled to the ceiling. *Skies*. On instinct, I halted and blocked the doorway with my back. Lysias was sobbing quietly, already passing the threshold of her endurance.

"Don't look in," I whispered as the three of them ran past me, each surmising what the overpowering odor meant.

At the passage's end, a narrow stairwell spiraled upward. Zair led in a jog and I flanked the group.

"I need... I need help," she said hesitantly at the top, her hands pushing against a metal lid that sealed the cellar.

Mishan hurried past Lysias and together, they shoved the lid open with a loud screech of metal. Light poured into the stairwell like rain. Anticipation and panic heightened over the noise we'd made. So close.

A door burst open and someone boomed, "The prisoners are escaping!"

"Quick!" I ordered from the step's bottom.

The man barreled for me. I swung my shackle for momentum, a makeshift morning star as I gauged him. He reached the proximity I wanted. I released the manacle. It splattered blood from his head as he crashed. I threw myself up the stairs into a buzzing afternoon.

Yells erupted from below. Knives flew out, barely missing my chest.

"Shut the door!" I shouted.

Zair and Lysias shoved down the lid just as veiled faces crowded the stairs, and held it down. I charged for a water-filled tank.

Blast, it was too heavy.

Mishan appeared beside me. He grabbed one end with all his might and we pulled the tank. The young engineer might be lanky, but he was strong.

"Move!" we shouted.

Zair and Lysias jumped aside. The lid jerked upward. Mishan and I pushed the tank over it.

"It won't hold them down long," Zair said, panting.

"Well, until we figure out our next course of action, we're at its mercy," I said, running my fingers through my hair.

Grey stone walls rose around us in a wide, broken arc. Shops, with colorful roofs made of painted, downturned canoes. Sounds of the bustling harbor echoed around us. We were in the Secruvi Market.

We'd been shackled in one of the storages built underground for the merchants' goods.

The pounding against the lid continued, yet for the first time in hours, air made its way easily into my lungs. I sucked in a large amount and let it out with the horrors. The hair on my nape twitched. I whirled. Zair was studying me.

I squared my shoulders. "If we needed further proof that they're not novice bandits, the fact that they can afford cells in Secruvi is it."

Zair allowed the topic change and glanced at the sky, her face streaked with dirt. "It's late afternoon. We've been absent for too long."

16

ZAIR

My nerves strung tightly, the restlessness to escape this marketplace overwhelming.

"Now what?" Lysias asked.

"We rejoin the procession as quickly as we can," I answered.

An urge I'd learned, that had become part of me like a cloak sewn onto my skin since entering Nergal, arose. The constant need to prove myself worthy.

If the four of us rejoined the king's procession at once, I would fade into the background yet again while the other students would be praised as the heroes. But if I was to reach there first, to be the student who saved the procession from falling apart, I might stand out. It wouldn't do much to erase the disdain, but at least I would be on people's minds for something good.

Besides, something else had been eating at me since I awoke shackled in a cell. My parents would be waiting on our street to see me. If I wasn't there when the procession passed... My stomach cramped to imagine their panic. Worse, they knew that if we encountered trouble, my rescue wouldn't be a priority like the other students. The worry would eat them up.

My slippers *thwacked* as I broke from our haggard group and ran for the far edge of a building where a horse's tail swished. The time for teamwork was past.

A dozen horses lazed in a corral. The stable boy's eyes bulged when I burst through the wooden gate in all my filthy glory. His brown skin paled. "A-aziza!"

"I'm part of the king's retinue. If you lend me a horse to rejoin the procession, I can assure you that your master will be paid handsomely for his service to the throne." Even as I spoke, I had already mounted the horse.

The poor boy was too terrified to stop me. I urged the horse on with my knees, galloping past the other students as they ran for the corral.

As the horse's clops echoed through the vacant alleyways, I couldn't help but think about Dathan Issachar. He'd looked out for everyone in the cell despite appearing tenser in captivity than I'd expect from Gergesenes' best pupil. He could've had Lysias unshackle him first and left us behind. He could've run past the cell that smelled like a hundred corpses and let us see whatever was in there. He had put everyone before himself, even me. He'd done the same last night, letting me climb through the window he spotted first before he did.

I didn't know what to make of him.

I knew the route the procession would take to ensure it touched the key areas in Ari'el; traveling every street and quarter of the city in a day was impossible. So I galloped the horse along quieter alleys of the route, halting to ask for directions. Finally, the sounds of the royal cavalcade buzzed.

In between the buildings, I caught glimpses of the Majesties' carriage flanked by the Ironteenth Fighters. As I arranged my hair, dusted the dirt from my face, and draped my veil to conceal blood spills, I wondered if the fiend who'd planned our ambush, who was working to discredit the king, lurked amongst the nobles.

If only I could see the disappointment on their snaky face the moment I rode in.

Taking a deep breath, I guided my horse between the storied coral-and-brown stenciled houses of the western Mizsab quarters. Dozens of hooves crunched on gravel, fabrics rubbed on saddles, carriage wheels whirred. My heart lurched as I sidled into the activity. The three guards who now manned my end of the procession looked stunned by my appearance, but parted for me to rejoin the procession.

The overall number of palace guards had reduced by half.

They went searching for us.

The three guards scanned behind me for the others as I settled my horse behind Ibhar's. The redhead took no notice of me. Good. I was glad to bypass his welcome.

Why didn't he ride down that alley with us?

The other nobles around noticed my presence and sucked in breaths. Stern whispers rushed amid the human dignitaries. More tense guards turned and saw me.

One of the guards on my end rode closer and snarled, "Where are the others?"

"They are on their way, sir."

Confusion slashed his face. "On their way from *where*?"

"It's a long story, sir." And I didn't have the energy just then to relive it. "But they are coming back. I promise."

Distrust etched into his sun-tanned face. His mouth twitched to blame and barrage me with demands. But he was smart enough to realize I knew the risks of returning to the procession if I had harmed them. So he ignored the eyes prompting him for answers and took his place beside me, waiting to see if my word was true.

His presence unnerved me further, but a thicker tension prickled at my senses. It shivered through the royal party, steamed within the crowds lining the wide street.

Hands were lifted in respect and a few people called out words of praise. Yet the jubilating from earlier was absent, faded like color from a once-vibrant fabric.

One could say it was because the king was Baihan and the queen was Ussi, and these were the Mizsab quarters. But it wasn't that sort of tension.

It was worry. Concern that their student, Mishan, as well as the others, were nowhere in sight and yet the cavalcade was proceeding like it was whole. There was growing distrust in their rulers.

"Where are our children?" someone suddenly cried.

Agreeing noises followed. The foreigners were already exchanging looks, joining heads to mutter. Their thoughts were clear: *The citizens look mutinous? Is Thalesai not as unified as is portrayed?*

Because a kingdom that was divided against itself would fall easily. A kingdom that was united, however, stood firm.

"Your people no longer look happy, Your Majesty," the shifter ambassador called from his horse behind the royal carriage. "Is there... aught we can do to help?"

Like take your kingdom from your hands?

The guard beside me stiffened. Skies. Was I too late?

I couldn't be.

"Ride ahead," the guard ordered, but I was already ahead of him.

I shifted from where I'd shrunk like a chameleon between Ibhar and the guard, and moved forward. Stood out.

Queen Yval was the first to spot me as my horse cantered near her archers. Her beautiful face seemed like it had aged ten years in mere hours. But through the fake smile she wore, relief eased her meadow eyes.

I mouthed, "We're alright, Your Majesty."

In the crowd, attention followed the queen's. And although I might just be the loathed Esan, my reappearance proved that matters weren't quite as out of hand as they feared. Ibhar noticed me then. He frowned, obviously chafing that I might just have saved the day.

Well, he could choke on it. He hadn't spent hours chained underground, fearing for his life. He had no right to have an opinion about me today.

One by one, Lysias, Mishan, and finally, Dathan rode into the procession beside me. They'd also scrambled to conceal signs of our attack so that to others, they merely looked ruffled riding against the desert wind.

Rumblings began amid the human nobles, small exclamations of relief.

I glanced at First Colonel Remmon—was he angry that we had returned? Nose twitching, he spoke with his comrades and kept glancing at Lysias. He neither looked happy nor sad.

Queen Yval leaned closer to the king and spoke. He didn't quite turn to look at us, but the tightness in his shoulders visibly eased.

The further we rode into main roads sloping downward to the

gates, the livelier the streets became. Until the cheering and blowing of salt resumed, wiping away previous tensions and distrusts like snake prints blown off sand. Real smiles filled the faces of the nobles again while the shapeshifters silently sulked.

"Long reign the King and Queen of Thalesai!"

"May Osime bless the Majesties of Thalesai!"

We'd succeeded. We *had* saved the procession!

Within the jubilations, my gaze clashed with a whitish-blue one. The Spaeman.

My heart skipped. Riding beside the royal carriage, his ancient stare was keen, as if prompting me to *realize* something...

His parable. *I would tell you to beware...*

Our capture was what he'd meant about fire and warnings. As realization dawned on my features, he gave a small nod and returned his focus ahead. My frozen lungs resumed function.

But why not warn us *explicitly*? I clenched my teeth. Why let us endure the torture? Risk the king's reputation? Had he 'seen' who our captors were?

Or could *he* have orchestrated the ambush? And then spoken ominously beforehand just so if we managed to escape, suspicion wouldn't be cast on him because I could say he'd warned me? No one knew his tribe. He could be just as against a Baihan king as others were, and knew exactly where to strike to discredit him.

It was a possibility. Yet nothing about him made my senses tingle.

He terrified me to my bones, yes, but not because I thought he was a devious snake who would try to ruin the king.

"What is your business with the Spaeman, Nergal?" Dathan asked lowly amid the noise, his eyes penetrating despite carrying traces of anxiety. "This is the second time you've both exchanged quiet communication."

The girls whose calls he ignored to speak with me were not pleased. Their glowers burned my skin like acid.

I answered his unbalancing question with one of my own. "What had *you* so shaken in chains? You must've been trained for hostage situations."

His eyes widened. I'd hit a sore spot. Whatever it was, it

allowed me to ride ahead and escape his implication that I was stalking the Spaeman. If anyone heard him imply such a thing, more trouble than I could handle would come after me.

The procession made a turn at the roundabout of the Burning Heart emblem, its five streets stretched out to the central districts. We galloped to the palace, passing the mammoth Epistle Library that my sisters and I loved to visit.

My sisters! I'd missed the procession past my home. My parents would be beside themselves with worry.

News about the Majesties blew faster than sandstorms through the kingdom, I reassured myself. Our return would surely carry to my family and soothe them.

We'd been lucky. There were hundreds of students still in captivity without hope of freedom. Parents who wouldn't be reassured of their safety. And if I didn't work fast and find clues, those students might never see home again.

THE SUN WAS NO LONGER brash but wan as it lingered above the rolling dunes. Its muted gold glazed the Al'Qtraz, birthing a breathtaking sight that soothed me after a desperately ugly day.

The aziza lords were now circling in the sky, sunning their magnificent wings before the desert night breathed its harsh cold.

"Ari'el's cold nights are unfavorable to our wings," the ambassador had huffed to the Royal Advisors before the retinue took flight like golden birds.

The five of us students barely hopped off our horses before a palace guard bounded over.

"The Majesties have summoned you."

From the yard, we were marched straight to a lounge on the eastern wing of the ground floor. Scarlet drapes fluttered over the warm metal accents of tea trays and lamps. Woven rugs depicting flames muffled our footsteps. Metal-carved lattice windows revealed the darkening sky and the early stars winking across it.

Their ceremonial regalia of ornamented blue satins splayed grandly around them, yet as King Khasar and Queen Yval sat on a banquette, I was reminded of how young they were. The two royal advisors making up the Chamber of Wings and the Admiral were also present, flanking the Majesties.

The Royal Advisors often made me think of a candle and clock. The Baihan First Advisor was the candle, with his trim and tall physique, and white beard. The Ussi Second Advisor was the clock, with his short and rotund form.

"Scholar Ibhar, you were at the procession throughout the day," King Khasar stated.

"Yes, Your Majesty," Ibhar answered more reverently than I'd thought possible.

"Then leave us."

With a deep bow, Ibhar strode out.

"Have a seat, Scholars," Queen Yval said softly, sweeping her bejeweled fingers toward the banquette opposite them.

We obeyed. A low table with brass candlesticks stretched between us.

"Tell me what happened today, where you went, and leave nothing out. I want to believe you four are not irresponsible enough to leave the procession for half of the ceremony to gallivant," King Khasar demanded quietly, his expression a merge of anger and disbelief.

His assumption shocked me. We would never sabotage our king like that. I shifted forward on my seat to answer. To also tell him to ask the Spaeman about our attack.

The candle—the First Advisor—raised his hand to quiet me.

"Not you." And with his other hand, he prompted Dathan to do the explaining. "Scholar?"

My cheeks burned with humiliation. Of course, no one would want me to speak to the Majesties.

Queen Yval's regard fell on me. I was too ashamed to peer directly at the disgusted expression she surely wore, so I kept my focus ahead and willed the tears not to fall.

Dathan swept his palms over his thighs, his forehead fused as if deciding how best to phrase our encounter. He settled for, "We were attacked and abducted shortly after leaving the Halim Market, Your Majesty."

Shock slashed across the nobles' faces like a claw. Queen Yval gasped. The Admiral straightened, his shock slowly burning into fury as he noticed the rumpled attires and bruises we had tried to cover with veils—telltale signs of our maltreatment.

"Explain," the king finally said.

Dathan gave the gritty summary of our trickery into the bandits' trap, being shackled in filth and whipped, the killing and corpses, and our hairsbreadth escape. Before the clock could speak, Dathan went on to describe precisely where the cell was.

While he remained respectful, Dathan was furious over our assault and was telling the king in hardly subtle terms that he wanted the culprits found.

The king's eyes glinted as he regarded Dathan. Glinted with something very much like admiration. Though the exchange lasted a millisecond, my stomach clenched.

The atmosphere dampened as the royals and chambermen's faces shuttered like gates. They already had a theory over why we were attacked, I realized. They would keep it within their close circle.

"I applaud you, Scholars. For not only breaking free from captivity, but also your diligence in returning to the procession after such torment," King Khasar said. "There could be no greater show of your loyalty to Thalesai, of your worthiness to be here. You saved today's procession. May the torches in your hearts never burn out."

He hadn't spoken to me directly, but I *was* part of the four. His accolade warmed my chest.

"The Admiral will investigate your capture and bring the bandits to justice." His face hardened. "What was done to you will not go unpunished."

Dathan gave a small nod.

"You should retire to your chambers to rest. Whatever you want to help you recover from today's ordeal, you need only ask," Queen Yval said, her voice filled with gratitude.

Something Second Advisor Drake clearly did not approve of.

The short man seethed indeed like a vibrating clock to see the Majesties praise mere students profusely.

The First Advisor stepped forward to lead us out of the lounge. "I know what it is to be captured and tortured. How it scars and changes a person. Come along, young heroes. You deserve a good night's rest."

17

ZAIR

With each click of my heels up the broad steps, the First Advisor's dismissal replayed in my mind. Being silenced before the Majesties throbbed like a sore in my chest. Was I really so worthless?

It was during moments like these... that I couldn't help but wish I didn't have Esan eyes. The secret thought choked me with guilt. It felt like I blamed my mother for my hard reality. I didn't.

My mother was my pillar. I wouldn't trade her even for the loftiest Ussi woman. It wasn't her fault that her ancestors had abandoned their kind during the War or later abandoned their new land for their forsaken one when that turned out to be a worse fate.

I just wished, in moments of weakness, that I'd inherited my father's eyes.

Self-recrimination suffused me, and my head ached with too many dispiriting thoughts. In the quiet stairwell, I nodded to the few guards standing by the hand-painted vases and paintings depicting Thalesai's history.

I'd chosen to take this route rather than the general one with the others when Dathan had strode up to me, all ruggedly handsome even after capture, and said, "You're an impressive fighter, Nergal. Good job."

There was a light in his hazel eyes that he hadn't regarded me with before. It was an earnest, poignant light a girl could grow to crave.

But I'd given a nod of acknowledgment and steered away in search of a different route up.

I didn't want his praises, or to speak with him at all. Yes, the rational side of me knew it wasn't he who had shut me up. But it *was* Dathan who was deemed worthy while I wasn't. Who was deemed better.

Besides, I preferred he didn't know when, or if, I went to my rooms, so he couldn't watch to see if I snuck out again.

Breeze suddenly ruffled my clothes. The flapping of wings heralded Arno before his tall form entered my line of vision. I glanced around the stairwell, barely relaxing even when I confirmed no one could see us consorting. Was today not trying enough?

"Very stealthy for a royal guard," I said stiffly.

"You are stealthy. Now, multiply that by three and that is my stealth level." He touched his silver brow in aziza greeting, falling into step beside me.

"I have no information for you. Not unless you want me to lie." My slippers clapped against the marble with my faster march.

His butterfly wings fluttered and he kept pace, gliding above the ground as smoothly as oil rolling over glass. "You were gone from the procession for a long time."

I eyed him sidelong. "You're monitoring me too?"

"We are all monitors at this perilous gathering of kingdoms." When I volunteered nothing, he said, "I suppose you won't tell me where you went, or why you now have a large bruise on your neck."

"Why are you here?"

He sent his voice directly into my ears, and I yelped from the warm, vibrating sensation.

"I overheard some *dephaseui* talking during you students' absence."

My head snapped to him. *Dephaseui* translated to 'shapeshifters' in Gallic, the aziza's official language after the magical Franks had colonized them centuries back.

His mouth quirked over my wide-eyed interest.

"They said you humans are better on your knees, flogged and

ordered about. They believe you are savages playing dress-up in satins and gold. They are giving Thalesai a few decades at most until humans destroy it and are 'ripe for plucking.'"

Heat blazed through my ribs at the unrepentant predators. The Majesties should toss them out of our land and warn them never to return!

And yet. If only Arno knew how close to the truth that final statement could be. If the mercenaries continued to destroy institutions, if the king continued to handle the matter so narrow-mindedly, Thalesai would crumble on itself.

A realization dawned. "You're spying on the shifters' party too. And the wraiths."

That conversation wasn't one the shifters would utter carelessly, not with their magic bound here.

Arno shrugged, which looked comical with his wings still waving.

"A wise guard does not watch the doors and windows for enemies alone, but the chimneys as well."

"How inspiring," I said. "Why are you telling me this?"

"You refused my offer to put in a good word on your behalf for your Ironteenth aspirations. And I can't teach you magical tricks since my magic is bound here—"

"I want *nothing* to do with your magic."

"This way, our bargain stays two-sided. Why are you ashamed of having magic?"

"I'm not *ashamed*—"

"Lie."

I scoffed. "I just don't want to be any more abnormal than the eyes already make me."

He frowned darkly. "I see my speech during the procession had no effect."

Huffing, I glanced away to focus on what was important. We couldn't allow these vultures to see the opening right there, waiting to be used.

Arno gazed through the passing windows where stars abounded over the sand dunes. "Ari'el."

"*Where the stars touch the dunes*," I mumbled its meaning.

"I hear those constellations," he said, pointing to the ten stars arranged into *A.S* in the sky, "are the heaven's ode to the last human soulmates."

"King Abeel and Queen Sepner."

Soulmates were so special, that even the sky immortalized their union.

"Ari'el is beautiful," Arno confessed, and then his mouth twitched. "But not as much as my city in Dahomey. It floats on the sea with islands that sit in the sky, built with the wondrous magical abilities you're so ashamed of."

I sighed wearily, slowing down as we neared the students' lounge. My body throbbed after today's attack and my head ached down to my eyes. Worse, I hadn't slept a wink last night or eaten since breakfast. Unfortunately, there was no time to rest. Today had been chaotic. I hadn't paid proper attention to my prime suspect, First Colonel Remmon. I needed to amend that. See if he'd done anything else that pointed to him being the traitor.

Swallowing, I turned to get rid of Arno first.

"You can't come into the students..." My sentence died off. He was no longer beside me. Or in the stairwell. I hated to admit it, but that was indeed stealthy.

Could the traitor, whoever they were, have been the orchestrator of our abduction? It was possible since they already aided the assault of other students.

As I passed the third level's atrium and strode quickly through the lounge, my stomach tightened with unease. Too many scattered pieces rose every moment. Were they even connected? Which should I pay the most attention to?

My breaths came out fast and choppy as I closed my bedroom door behind me. What if I was chasing the wrong scent, and because of it, the traitor's deeds worsened right beneath my nose? What if I was too slow to protect Sarai?

When a mind tries to absorb too many things at once, it will absorb nothing. Take it one sentence, one page, and one book at a time.

It was my father's advice years ago when I had started studying for the Nergal admission exams. There had been arithmetic tomes, grammar tomes, basic science tomes, and philosophy tomes I'd had to memorize. In the first week, when I'd been overcome by a fear of disappointing him after the sacrifices he'd made to help me succeed, I'd tried to cram it all at once. I had only succeeded in making myself ill.

Since then his advice helped me whenever I grew overwhelmed. One clue at a time.

Skies, I missed my family.

Jogging over to my wardrobes, I pulled out my black garments, gloves, and soundless slippers. I expertly painted the fast-drying clay two shades darker than my skin tone over my face. I sketched careful lines as we'd been taught, adding twenty years to my face before the clay dried. The palace was rowdy. If I was sleek, I could slither about the gatherings and overhear something that pointed to the traitor. I would begin with Colonel Remmon, the Admiral's stalker.

Dathan was right. Today's bandits had a wealthy sponsor. Business boomed in the Secruvi Market due to its closeness to the seaport, so the rents cost enough to buy an entire house in middle-class areas. Colonel Remmon could afford to pay for a storage cell there.

DRESSED TO SLINK, I held my breath as I waited for the patrolling guards to pass. Then, I snuck into the servants' route on the adjacent passage. I had discovered the separate route this morning when the liveried servants had emerged from the curtains to clear our breakfast. A route to prevent them from running into nobles with mops and food trays. I had many plans for it.

The dim passage wound like a serpent within the palace's walls. A slashing black-and-white checkered tunnel with many mouths that I swore was alive. I listened to servants' conversations and brief exchanges over whom they were headed to serve.

"I'm going to serve the First Colonel."

I followed those servants rolling their food trolleys down the slopes toward one of many doorways. This doorway opened to a softly-lit lounge on the ground floor. Too tired to risk using aziza speed, I dropped on hands and knees and crawled behind the drapes as the servants piled in with food.

They served the food and hurried off, revealing Lysias's presence. She was a dainty beauty sitting next to the burly Colonel, and while a smile tilted her lips, it seemed forced.

"Eat with me," Colonel Remmon offered with a flirtatious smile, gesturing his red-tattooed fingers to a bowl of grapes.

Skies, he was at least twenty years older than her!

Lysias shifted uncomfortably in her seat. "I'm not hungry, sir."

"There's no need to call me *sir*. You know my first name, sweet Lysias."

She turned up that forced smile, standing up. "Well, thank you for taking the time to listen to my project pitch, s-. I'd like to go rest now."

"Of course. You've had a terrible day."

He stood and yanked her into a hug, ignoring her squirming as he ran his hands intimately down her body.

She pushed out of his arms. "*Sir!*"

He leered. "Concerning your project, come find me in my room soon, and we'll discuss the funding. May the torch in your heart never burn out."

Lysias bristled, but she strained to keep her smile and stalked out.

Disgusting man!

I barely breathed, didn't dare move, as he ate quickly—as if he had somewhere to be this late at night. He stood and left the lounge.

Rather than attempt to trail him out, I climbed out a long window behind me into the night. The shadowed walls were my shield as I followed him from outside. I drew out my camouflage magic, just for a moment, as the gate loomed in front. A hum vibrated deeply in my chest, and magic swept over me like a warm tide. Exhilarating yet draining bursts of light rushed under my skin. Magic, like a cloak, painted me in the immaculate hues of the gate's arches, shielded me into nothingness as I slipped past the keen guards saluting the First Colonel.

Remmon and I exited the gates, and began down the cobbled hill road.

Walking.

I quickly stemmed my magic before it drained me even more; still, my arms shook with fatigue from using the ability. Why was the colonel not riding? Why were his assigned guards not accompanying him?

Maybe he merely sought an evening stroll. Maybe this meant nothing. Still, I followed, heart pounding in my throat as I crept behind the line of glass and terracotta statues that gleamed in the moonlight.

He is a thousand times your superior, a voice warned. *He will crush you if he catches you spying.*

I wasn't an ant to be crushed. I was a scorpion that wanted to sting those who threatened my little sister.

As if the night winds carried my thoughts to him, his head whipped in my direction.

I flung myself behind the painted statue of a queen and drew a breath for calm over the blood roaring in my ears. Moments later, clothes fluttered in my corner vision. He was moving again.

Off the hill, the Ciasille Square consumed us in its riot of sensation. Roasted meat sizzled on grills beside elaborate theatres. Street performers held lively shows under streetlamps for small crowds. Rooftop restaurants clattered with porcelain as customers enjoyed views of the shimmering square. With bodies weaving under lamps, it was easier to trail him without notice. In this crowd, no one glanced twice at the First Colonel.

Was that his goal?

His huge form pivoted down a street between rows of tan mudbrick buildings with green doors. The lit lattice windows illuminated his figure and for the first time tonight, I observed the bag he carried. What was in there? It wasn't large enough to hold arms or documented information, but it was sizable enough to hold something just as bothersome.

A good amount of coin. A bribe, then? For whom?

My stomach twisted. The traitor could be Colonel Remmon. A soldier I'd striven to be like for years.

What hope did a kingdom have if its guardians were its own enemies?

He jogged up a building's verandah, flung the door open, and disappeared behind it. Some Baihan women in matching lace ambled past me, and from behind, I swiped one's embellished veil. It concealed my eyes and softened the daunting effect of my black ensemble.

Musky warmth and a syrupy tang clogged my lungs in the tavern. Blue-and-gold Irua fabrics covered the ceiling, gleaming with embroideries of stars. Customers awash in red light from painted lanterns guzzled spiced wine as lutes trilled. This tavern in the northern part of the city was far more sophisticated than the rowdy taverns my uncles frequented in the southern quarters.

Aziza lords occupied the leftmost table, the only neighbors not 'too grand' for human taverns, apparently. Then again, after the Treaty, the azizas *had* helped Thalesai find its footing, swapping their pillaging of our resources for a trade relationship. My chest skipped to spot Arno sitting with the other guards. But he was deep in conversation.

The dull lighting made blending in easier as I wove between tables. There the Colonel was. Kissing someone draped over him as if determined to suck their face off.

Who would've thought the great Colonel Remmon's vice was women? He patted her bottom, grinning as he went on, and I followed him down a corridor.

He made my work easier by stepping out onto a balcony with a small loge above it. Drawing from Nergal's training, I silently gripped the slender panels in the engraved wall and climbed them, into the loge that provided a view of his broad back.

There was someone else down there. Someone who stepped out of the shadows like he belonged within them. He lifted his head. And revealed my eyes.

Bells pealed in my head.

None of this was *normal* of a First Colonel of Thalesai! He was meeting with an Esan *smuggler*. The leeches who practiced dishonorable acts continued to worsen Esan's reputation!

"Where is it?" Colonel Remmon queried.

"You'll have to give me more time," the smuggler said in a sandpaper rasp. "And money. The item is proving more difficult to acquire than I'd expected."

What *item*? Why not state what it was if it was lawful?

Because it's not lawful.

"More money?" Colonel Remmon demanded. "Haven't I given you enough, azishit?"

Anger flickered in those gold-ringed eyes. "It's not enough until it's enough."

"For months, you've asked for more time and more money. Time and money are running out," Colonel Remmon gritted. "My Timekeeper has granted me no more than two weeks to conclude my business, and you've been chasing this item for months. You're supposed to be one of the best, you slime."

Timekeeper? And why two weeks?

"The item isn't easy to acquire," the smuggler snarled. "In all my years of smuggling, no one has ever asked from me what you are. The makers swing hot and cold, uncertain if to release it to me. I have to breathe down their necks and follow with bribes. I'm close now. So you have to decide. Would you conclude what we've already begun or give up now that we're so close to getting it?"

Colonel Remmon grabbed the smuggler's throat. "Don't think to give me ultimatums, azishit."

The smuggler shoved his hand off. "Take it or leave it."

The Colonel cursed bitterly. "How much?"

A quiet answer followed. Colonel Remmon tossed his bag at the smuggler. Although infuriated by it, he'd come here knowing more money would be demanded.

"Next time we meet, I *will* be the one taking. Don't think to test me," Remmon warned and left the balcony without giving the Esan his back.

The smuggler swiftly counted the *siyvas* in the bag, and anger simmered in me. Tribesmen like *him* made acceptance, a better future, impossible for the Esans.

He hooked the bag to his waistband and swept his cloak over it. His boots were as silent as my slippers with each step from the balcony.

I shifted deeper into the shadows, hoping the raucous laughter muted the scratchy noise.

The smuggler suddenly halted beneath my loge, as if jerked by some perceptive string. Despite the resounding laughter, his ear angled up in my direction. As if he could *sense* me.

Chances were that he could. More than the keener senses of the Esan, he was also a smuggler.

My anger yielded to self-preservation as his hand drifted to the hilt of his throwing knife. He knew I was here. My heart jerked and I held myself still.

If he confirmed he was being watched, he'd warn the Colonel that someone was on his tail. I might lose this lead entirely.

"Who's there?" he asked, scanning his surroundings with gold-ringed eyes.

My breaths grew shallow.

His head tilted upward to the loge.

Move. I flung myself over the loge's other edge and onto the balcony door resting against the wall. Weightless as an aziza, the door didn't move or squeak with my slippers balanced on it. I climbed down swiftly, quietly, onto the balcony, drawing inwardly on the dregs of my magic like a person scraping a pot for the last slurp of stew. A warm sensation swept weakly over my skin, the fluttering wings of a dying bird.

His repeated question, more hostile, drifted onto the balcony.

My feet met concrete with more noise than I'd intended. It was a soft sound, a whisper of a squish, yet those honed Esan senses would catch it.

He harnessed his Esan speed, too, as his footsteps quickened for the balcony. I shoved the door shut in his face and jumped over the railings, bolting into the night.

THE UNDERGROUND CELL WAS EMPTY.

I climbed out of the smell of ground wheat and blood into the sounds of the Secruvi Market. Wind whipped at my clothes as I ran for the main street, where the public carriages gathered. From the tavern, I had made my way to the cell of our capture. A long detour, but one I'd hoped would reveal clues that pointed to who sent our attackers.

If it would be the traitor. I had found the cell's lid open with dock workers carrying sacks into it. Head kept low, I'd asked one what was happening.

The butchers were no longer in the cell and a wheat merchant was wasting no time in renting it.

I'd gone inside, searched the horrible place, and found nothing beyond a burnt cell where the butchered bodies had been and sacks of wheat in the others.

Did it mean our soldiers had found and arrested the attackers? My heart leaped in hope—yet it could also mean that the bandits and their sponsors had escaped.

18

DATHAN

The Plateaus of Rahbat spread like giant tables to the east, and winds from their peaks howled along the palace's glowing walls. The Niger River wound its slender blue fingers through the plateaus' gorges, circling behind the legendary pyramids, to spread vastly for the Atlantic Ocean.

Leaning against the dining balcony's railings, I tried to find calm in the view. My hands hadn't stopped shaking for hours and a queasy spell unbalanced me.

Years ago, when I was younger and Ari'el was only a place my family traveled to visit in winter, my mother told my sister and I that the night winds were the plateaus panting after a day of hefting the scorching desert sky. I preferred her tale to the reasons we'd been taught at Gergesenes. I told Jaziah the tale one day, while we hiked through the plateaus to find a flower for his ladylove, and he'd said it was the explanation he also preferred.

Jaz and I were so alike that our schoolmates and neighbors often teased that we'd been twins in another life.

A strange presence slipped onto the balcony. I rotated, placing a shaking hand on my dagger.

Glowing in a white ensemble, his frozen eyes chilling me to my bones, the Spaeman inclined his head. "Dathan Issachar."

"Khosa Spaeman." Puzzled, I bowed while glancing behind him. I wouldn't be on the balcony, paying this much attention to the plateaus or the guards patrolling past our lounge, if Zair was in her chambers. I'd sighted her sneaking out right after entering her rooms, off chasing her quarry.

While it chafed that she could be making more headway than me, I was humbled enough today to accept that tonight wasn't a good time to trail my suspect. I swallowed against the sick whirl in my gut. My hands trembled uncontrollably. I'd managed to move around the palace with blurred vision days ago, but I couldn't use my tools or scale walls if needed with unsteady hands. *How can I save Jaziah when the past holds me captive?*

"How can I help you, Khosa Spaeman?" I asked him.

After today's capture, with parts of me shattered under the weight of old memories, I had no strength for evasion. I was tired to my soul.

White-blue eyes peered into me. "No, Issachar, I think *I* can help you."

In a streak of white, he was before me. His icy fingers touched my forehead, and I fell out of my body.

The world became a black canvas. And then, mammoth walls rose, blades clashed, and I appeared in the Gergesenes Military Academy.

Scrambling to my feet, my ribs clenched as a few steps away, I saw *me*.

In the watery memory, I sparred with my year-two mates in the wrestling pit. Exhilarated as I defeated them before our Commandant and teachers.

"Get them, Nath!" Jaziah cheered from outside the pit's bars. He grinned at our other friends. "I taught him that move."

Jaziah. My chest lightened with joy, drinking in those mischievous grey eyes and thick brown hair he barely let me trim. Despite knowing all this wasn't real, I hurried toward him. Wanting to crush him so tightly to my chest until neither of us could breathe.

But my classmate shoved younger-me from behind. In the memory, I crashed facedown and my classmate dived to pin me to the ground with his knee to my neck.

Bile filled my throat. It was the same position I'd been held down in the night my sister was dragged into the bush and violated. I watched year-two Dathan become that helpless ten-year-old boy again. Screaming at my holder to get off me, even though I could've maneuvered free and tackled him.

Jaziah jumped into the pit, alarmed as he yanked our classmate off me. Like overheated water, the memory evaporated just before I could reach Jaziah.

"Take me back!" I yelled into the emptiness.

The sky fell and bricks surged underfoot until I materialized on the Gergesenes Military Academy's windy ramparts. Walking before me were year-two Dathan and the Commandant.

"I watched today's challenge," he said, his voice grave. "I know you're strong and sharp enough to have broken free of that hold. But something beyond that moment restrained you, Issachar. Chains unseen."

His observation still made me feel naked. Thankfully, the Commandant didn't ask why I'd become a crazed weakling after displaying perfect control only seconds before.

Instead, he said, "Pay attention to your triggers, Issachar. Places, people, and things that pull you to that bleak place. Take a step back when faced with these things until you can prepare your mind, and then you tackle them."

Applying that insight was still a battle. It still made me feel deficient. Great soldiers didn't have such weaknesses. The Commandant didn't have them. My friends didn't have ghosts from the past incapacitating them. But I'd had no choice but to heed.

The Commandant taught me a lot of lessons that... I wished my father had.

The world evaporated once again, building around me a stuffy little room in the southern quarter's slums. My family's first house in the capital.

"You're a smart boy with gifted hands," my father said ardently to a twelve-year-old Dathan. "If you only give healing a *chance*, you'll thrive at it like your sister is."

"I'm not passionate about healing, father," young Dathan said desperately. "I want to be a soldier. To train to defend you all."

"No. If you choose soldiering, then you have no love for us. No care for our lives."

The bitter words were still a knife to my heart. I rubbed my chest.

"Soldiers can't hide. Your recognition will endanger us. Worse, if you're sent to the north!" He cupped my face. "Is *that* what you want?"

"Hiding has solved *nothing*, father. It only keeps us helpless with no skill to defend ourselves because you won't let us venture out to find one. There is only a small chance I'll be sent to the north as a Baihan. And even then, there are ways to disguise myself."

Nothing I ever achieved as a soldier-aspirant was good enough to make him understand that at heart, I was a defender. Not even my plan today that had freed us from capture would convince him.

"Stop it," I said. Wherever this place was, wherever the Spaeman was, I wanted out. "Stop it!"

The memory dissolved and—this new location clicking into place was unfamiliar.

I was submerged amid giant rocks. The odors of urine and blood clogged my nose. Torches barely illuminated the darkness, but this was a valley.

A few steps away, scores of youths around my age were clustered together, their ankles tied. Some sobbed weakly. Some lay unmoving on the cold ground, staring blankly like the fight was gone from them. Their clothes were filthy, ragged but... I stumbled forward... the Nergal's school badge gleamed on their chests.

The Nergal students. This was the *present*.

Agonized screams pierced my chest. In the hazy world, I stumbled into a run for the large rock the sounds tore from.

The sights behind it stole my breath. Cloaked men slammed rods onto male students who'd been tied up like animals. Beating the boys without mercy even as they cried and pleaded.

The battered face of one of them registered. The light brown skin. The grey eyes. The mouth that was once always grinning, now pressed together and trembling as he fought to keep from shouting.

"Jaziah," I rasped.

Two masked men lashed his back with rods. A sound of pain broke from him.

"*I will overcome*," he started to whisper.

"Leave him, you bastards!" I made to shove his assaulters but went right through them each time. Frustration and panic gripped me.

The rods came down hard as the boys coughed blood, as they vomited on themselves, as they dropped and lost consciousness. But unlike the other students, Jaziah was a soldier-in-training. He had stronger endurance so his beating continued, and soon he was shouting. *Pleading.*

Nausea sent me to my knees. I dry-heaved.

Jaziah's body finally dropped, unconscious, and I rushed over to him.

"Hang on, Jaz," I choked out to his battered form. I tried to touch his sweat-covered face, but touched only air. "I'll free you from this place and make these mercs pay."

The mercenaries weren't just breaking their bodies, but also their spirits. These students weren't guilty of any crime, yet were being tormented.

Why? What did the mercenaries want?

Shattered, I threw back my head and roared, "Stop!" At the brutalizers. At the Spaeman. At this vicious world we lived in! "*STOP!*"

The visions disintegrated and panting, I stood on the balcony with the Spaeman once more. Grief filled his eyes.

"Why?" I rasped. "Why did you show me that when I *couldn't* help them?"

"Why do you think?" he asked.

I didn't know. I could hardly think beyond what I'd seen. Could hardly be shocked that this being I'd believed was an impostor possessed the power to throw my mind across time. I slumped into a chair, and buried my head in my hands.

"Sometimes, when you can't find answers inside yourself, look outward and the world will give it to you," he said. I couldn't even rise as he turned and left.

He'd seen that inside me, with these persisting reactions to captivity, I'd felt unworthy of this mission to save Jaziah. So he had taken me to look outside instead and *see* why I needed to keep fighting.

I had to pull myself together and rescue Jaziah and the students fast.

My shredded thoughts zipped back to Zair. She still hadn't returned. Skies, could she have gotten into trouble?

I shouldn't care. She was like a cactus with me, prickly and tart. She kept the highest walls I'd ever seen of anyone so young.

I'd lowered my pride and expressed my admiration for her fighting skills today. She hadn't done the same for my plan that had freed us, or even given me the tired smile Lysias did when I'd praised her part in our escape. Rather, Zair barely nodded and swerved to follow some other route as if I was volatile.

Yet, here I was concerned.

Maybe it was because I didn't like how the First Advisor shunned her tonight. Seeing the tears glittering in her eyes awoke an urge to look out for her. Even if it was just this one time.

A figure of night and wind brushed into the lounge. Fast and wary, gone in a blink.

Zair.

The soldier in me said to go over and eavesdrop, see if I could glean what she'd discovered tonight. Use it, if helpful, for my mission. But I silenced it.

She was allowed so little dignity. I wouldn't take anything else from her.

I had to find my own answers.

"How are we dressed in the finest garments and jewels, yet look so... blah?" Lysias thumped her tumbler on the dining table.

The balcony was relatively quiet as we ate hungrily, as if yesterday's capture had sapped us. The Blessing of the King, the third ceremony, would be held at the HaMīqdaš Temple, and Lysias was right. We looked like we'd been chewed by camels and then stampeded by elephants. I hadn't slept and was drawing strength from my cocoa tea.

Even Ibhar, who wasn't abducted yesterday, looked like the nightmares that had haunted us four also kept him up. And even more interesting, he was too preoccupied in thought to prey on anyone with that careless mouth.

Why was he tired? *What* did he do last night? Why hadn't he ridden down that alley with us yesterday? He could easily be a spy too. But a spy for *whom* was what I couldn't figure out since Ahimoth Academies only cared about Ussi students.

Shadows fell over us. Winds rushed, flinging food over our clothes.

"Kai! Back away, you overfed horse-bird." Mishan waved his bandaged fist at the swerving tulpar—the whip had sliced his wrist open and cut into his ear.

I could've sworn Zair *laughed* as she caught her veil from flying off. But when I looked with more intrigue than I cared for, she was leaning over the railing, watching the flying creatures with wonder. Must've imagined that melodic sound.

"The shapeshifters unleash their winged horses to exercise them so the creatures won't destroy the stables from restlessness," I explained, dusting off breadcrumbs.

"Sure. They're just showing off their 'specialness'," Mishan drawled darkly. "Let them wait till I complete my invention."

"Someone is projecting," Lysias sang, glancing at Mishan's injuries.

Amusement twitched at my lips. "What is that Mizsab mantra again, Lysias? *'Fight everyone when you're angry'?*"

Mishan glared at me, adjusting his costly cufflinks. "*Together for greatness.*"

I waved. "Close enough."

Lysias laughed as he glowered at us. Zair resettled in her seat, traces of anger and sympathy on her face as she glanced at his bandaged wounds, but she didn't *speak* on it. I'd waited to hear her melodious voice all morning, told myself it was because she might blurt out what she gleaned last night.

"Now I wonder where that dragon egg could be," Ibhar murmured, adding dewy sugarcane cubes to his plate. The Ussis harvested the best sugarcanes, a plant that kept those of us living in Thalesai's hot regions hydrated. "I'd have had the dragon eat those damned tulpars."

"Even if the dragon egg is found, it'll go to His Majesty," Lysias muttered.

"*No*," Mishan protested playfully. "Finder's keepers."

Lysias wagged her finger under his nose. "There is no way a mere citizen would commandeer a dragon while the king rides a horse."

Ibhar shrugged. "Speak for yourself. We Ussis are entitled to keep what we find first."

"And if you found the egg right now, Ahimoth," I drawled, "would you know how to hatch it?"

"Obviously." His mouth quirked. "You put it in fire."

"You don't hatch dragon eggs with physical fire."

All heads turned to Zair with varying degrees of surprise that she would contribute.

Zair stirred her tea. "If a dragon senses your inner fire and deems it fierce, the dragon will be drawn to it and break out on its own. Otherwise, dragon eggs are kept with other dragons and hatch to join their kind."

Curious, I challenged, "How do you know this?"

The air sparked as she held my gaze.

"I like to read," she said simply and sipped her tea.

"Books about dragons?"

"Books about everything."

Mishan and Lysias raised intrigued brows as they looked from her to me.

Ibhar said icily, "If I found the dragon egg, I'd smash it against the wall first before following an Esan's instruction."

The curious sounds of footsteps from the window beneath our balcony silenced us.

"Two of the missing students' bodies were found last night," a heavy voice said. "The young ones. Captivity had been too much for them. Their uniforms were torn, skins sunburnt, feet raw and blistered. The mercenaries must've dumped them when they became too weak to drag along. Left them to die of exposure."

My chest caught fire. Zair's face twisted with such grief that it almost rivaled mine. We shouldn't be eavesdropping, but no one moved.

"That's sad. *For* the Baihans," another chamberman clarified. I knew that voice.

"It's Second Advisor Drake," Lysias mouthed.

The Second Advisor spoke on. "For *us*, Ussis, we now have more offspring in the elite academies than the other tribes. More of us to dominate the Al'Qtraz in the future."

My blood froze. *What the bleeding sheols?* Mishan's hands flew up in frustration, but they banged on the table. The voices below halted, and then footsteps clapped away.

I seethed. "And we say the foreigners are the problem."

Mishan laughed bitterly. "Thalesai's rulers, friends."

Zair looked crushed. "The students are dying already."

They were dying, and I was no closer to uncovering the mercenaries' enabler. I had to move faster.

As cutleries clinked over plates, I kept an eye on the ever-busy palace grounds. Zair's cutlery dropped and she briefly disappeared under the table.

Unlike yesterday, the retinue wouldn't ride out together for this ceremony. Some chambermen and their families were already leaving the palace for the HaMīqdaš Temple at the riverside. The king and queen, though, were yet to emerge. The five of us would accompany them and their guards when they did.

It was a privilege unlike any other to witness the Blessing of the King from the front row. One every student in the kingdom would covet... *No.* Everyone would be watching us. I had to focus on being inconspicuous. Honor should mean nothing if it was at my family's detriment.

As I sipped my coffee, appetite lost, I gave everyone on the grounds motive for treachery. Weighing who had the strongest.

Second Advisor Drake was there now, harried as he ordered guards and maids about in preparation for the event. Last night after we'd risked our necks to spare the king's reputation, the king had thanked us and the Second Advisor had been annoyed instead of equally relieved. He'd just shown *joy* over the missing students' plight. And he had the wealth and strings to sponsor mercenaries.

He was one to monitor.

A man in beige attire embellished with gold threads emerged from a doorway and my blood simmered to see Sarhedrin, the

Dynast of Bornoir's, shining bald head. The Royal Accountant strode beside him, a rangy, elegant man with a scar circling his eye.

There was nothing unusual about the sight, but Sarhedrin's easy movements made me restless. I itched to *shatter* that peace.

"I heard that the king almost canceled the Best of Ten competition after our capture yesterday," Lysias said quietly.

The comment dropped like a boulder.

"*What?*" the four of us exclaimed.

Lysias huffed. "Well, don't bite the informant! Calm down. The advisors were able to change his mind. Nothing can be amiss during the coronation ceremonies, and the Best of Ten is one of the most anticipated events."

The four of us relaxed in our chairs, even as that strain that often flowed between competitors gurgled onto the balcony.

"The king was an elite student once. He must also understand that nothing short of death would stop us from competing against other students in our fields," Lysias added. "He agreed to let the contest be held."

Ibhar glanced at me. "Good. I won't miss the chance to win Ahimoth the prize for best military student for the second contest in a row."

"That prize is Gergesenes'," I said distractedly, once again keeping Sarhedrin within my line of vision.

I thought Zair murmured, "The victory will be mine and Nergal's."

Rather than retort as usual, Ibhar snorted and returned his attention to his food.

"The Best of Ten is a *friendly* contest," Lysias reminded us half-heartedly.

"Is it *really?*" Mishan lifted his brows. "I can't wait to contest in the engineering category. And I know you're just thinking of *all* the ways you can beat nine other healers for the healing prize."

Lysias began to nod, but then straightened her back and insisted, "Friendly competition."

Mishan chuckled.

Silence fell and the other students ate but were alert. If I left to trail Sarhedrin, they'd wonder why I was leaving in the middle of breakfast. I couldn't do anything that would be considered odd if I was ever investigated. I looked to Mishan who sprinkled groundnuts into his bowl of rich yoghurt. The Felax student had a knack for analysis. I just had to provide a theory.

"You think we'll be updated on what's discovered about yesterday's attack?" I said. "I hope so."

"You mean will they let us know if the bandits have been executed?" Lysias arched a brow.

Despite the eye-bags, she resembled a dandelion in her yellow blouse and white-encrusted scarf. Worlds away from the rags Jaziah and the missing Nergal students wore in the Spaeman's vision.

Zair continued sipping her spearmint tea, her kajal-lined eyes focused on some distant point, yet I knew she listened. Little went past her. Besides... her movement was *too* calm. Did she know something about the bandits? Was that where she went off to last night?

I knew I'd get no answers from her. Hopefully, this distraction worked on her too.

Mishan tapped his porcelain bowl imported from Qing. "I doubt they would."

"Why not?" I prompted.

Mishan glanced at Ibhar—who scowled as if we were disturbing him—but spoke on in a lowered voice.

"The Majesties didn't mention it yesterday, but I suspect one thing the king was grateful for... was that we'd joined the procession *quietly*. Rather than announce to the people that we were taken right under his nose. As Lysias said, nothing can go amiss during this coronation. If the bandits are caught, I suspect they'd face private trials and our encounter with them would never be mentioned again."

Zair bit on her lip but didn't share whatever was on her mind. After the First Advisor's acidic dismissal last night, I suspected now that her quietness was from self-preservation, rather than a simple dislike of rival students.

And then I noticed it. Beneath the table, my boot laces had been tied together.

If I'd tried to sneak out, I'd have fallen on my face.

Zair.

She pretended not to notice my glower as I undid her handiwork, her tea-slick lips twitching. She reached for her tumbler. I snatched it before she could stop me and downed the rest of her tea—the liquid helping her wake up after a stressful night—in revenge. She huffed at my grin.

"*I'd* like to know if they've been caught," Lysias muttered, her eyes shadowing with memory. "I'd feel safer."

"I hate to admit this, but I'm almost afraid to ride out today," Mishan said glumly.

Ibhar barked for silence, Mishan snapped at him, and I escaped the lounge.

19

DATHAN

"You're the human who started a brawl with the wraith lord and wasn't punished by Thalesai's king for that insolence," a male voice cooed. "He'll listen to you."

I tautened at the male and female shapeshifters marching into step on either side of me. Half-beasts, half-people, with their savageness always close to the surface, they were born predators. Even in human form and resplendent in vermillion silk, their magic pulsed like errant heartbeats around us.

But finding Sarhedrin had my entire focus.

"There are royal servants to see to your needs, my lord," I said with careful courtesy.

"Another attractive human. I'd sworn there were only a handful of you," the female purred, her hand resting flirtatiously on my shoulder, her curves pressing to my side. "The servants can't persuade your king to allow us shapeshifters to fly our marvelous tulpars. He's insisted we only ride your horses here, and we find those creatures to be... lacking. He might listen to you if you asked him on our behalf."

Ah, because I was a *student* that His Majesty had spared, they thought I'd be easy to manipulate for their superiority whims. Annoyance filled me, but I wasn't callous enough to bait shapeshifters.

"Besides." The male *sniffed* me. "I sense a kindred spirit deep in your bones, human. A fearsome beast."

Something kicked against my ribs, the statement repelling. He was sorely mistaken.

Smiling grimly, I halted and removed the female's hand from my shoulder. She gasped.

"I don't know how things are done in Sarqi, but in Thalesai," I said, "we obey royals' orders. Excuse me."

The atmosphere pulsed thicker as I continued on, drumming with their anger.

"Pray you don't meet us again," the male's growl followed me. "Shapeshifters hold grudges long."

I brushed aside the discomfiting interaction as nobles patted my shoulders in greeting. I bowed, giving them my most disarming smile. Some male youths invited me to drinks and games on a rooftop. While it sounded fun, they confirmed it wouldn't be only Baihan youths present so I politely declined. Khosana Anesua and her mother reminded me of my promise to visit them.

Pretender, a voice hissed. *They wouldn't be so warm if they knew your truth.* I buried the thought.

Through one of the entryways, Sarhedrin was just returning into the palace. Thank skies, he moved alone. The Royal Accountant was now in a caleche with his family, riding out of the palace.

The ground floor was busy as frantic stewards ordered servants about in preparation for the event. The chaos allowed me to tail Sarhedrin with little risk of being noticed. But... he moved with complete calm. No sign of disquiet. Perhaps following him this morning might not be worth the risk. But only amateurs showed signs that they were about to commit evil. Sarhedrin was too clever for that.

We reached the office wing without incident, and he didn't move toward the rulers' offices under the king's second Chamber: the Chamber of Claws.

Instead, we advanced up the sweeping stairs leading to the Chamber of Wings. The level for the king's first and closest councilmen—a tightly guarded area.

Interesting.

Sarhedrin studied the area with the attention of an eagle, as if memorizing the layout. How many guards were there. Where they were positioned.

My fingers prickled. What was the connection between Sarhedrin, the king's brother Caiphas, and the Royal Accountant? Theirs was a powerful combination, but they were of different tribes. And Sarhedrin was a tribal bigot with unrepentant superiority. I couldn't quite believe they were *friends*.

He reached the top of the stairs and an armored guard politely but effectively stopped him. They exchanged words. The guard stepped aside. Blast it, I'd never get into the Chamber of Wings.

I jogged back downstairs, swiftly formulating an alternative plan.

On the Chamber of Claws' level, it could be possible to get past the guards with the right lie. Wearing an earnest facade, I told the soldiers that I needed a ruler's insight for a school project. The adults in Thalesai loved nothing more than the younger generation learning. I got in. In the busy level, I lingered around Sarhedrin's office until I glimpsed him through a doorway that led to a stairwell. Finished with his goal in the Chamber of Wings.

I calmly walked into the stairwell, pausing inside the threshold to slip off my dress shoes. Against the tiles, my bare feet were soundless as I moved to crouch by the waist-length banister. Unlike most of the palace's railings that had wide spaces between slender bars, these engraved wooden bars were thick with slim gaps between them. As long as I kept silent, the banisters were the perfect concealment. I peered down a thin gap.

On the flight of stairs just beneath mine, Sarhedrin wasn't alone anymore. Two other men had joined him. Ussis, judging from their embellished native ensemble. Their glinting jewels and proud bearings proclaimed their noble blood, perhaps sub-rulers of Bornoir.

Sarhedrin's Al'Qtraz allies. I silently descended the steps, maintaining a good distance.

"Was a decision made over who the land gifted to the Baihan king will be granted to?" one of them asked in Uhese, tilting his head back to survey the vacant stairwell.

What land?

"The dawn meeting was inconclusive," Sarhedrin answered in his collected and prideful manner, his Uhese fluent. "Every tribe in the Chambers argued, insisting the wraith king's gift should go to them. King Khasar has yet to decide who he'll appoint to build the land into a new Thalesai seaport town."

The *Wraith King*—a being that would much rather enslave us so he could feast on our blood—had gifted humans land?

"The land must go to the Ussis," the third nobleman blustered. "We provide more than thirty percent of the kingdom's funds. Ruling that land is our right."

Thirty percent? These men were either delusional or illiterate. Geography was taught to every year-one student in Thalesai's academies. Ussi's northern lands were the kingdom's desert lands. While it produced the most gold, iron, and spices, the Baihan and Kwali lands in the tropical west and south produced the agriculture traded for the most income. Esan lands, the southern rainforests, might've been one of our largest sources of revenue if they hadn't sold it to the Azizas.

The Baihans would riot if they heard this man's claims.

"Is it indeed?" the first questioned patronizingly. "I'm sure those self-righteous Baihans think ruling that land is *their* right too."

"It's ours," Sarhedrin flung. "The land is by the sea and will be marvelous for commerce. No other tribe but the Ussis will have it."

"And if the king dares give it to anyone else, we'll ensure he knows no peace!"

My jaw clenched at the blatant threat. They were willing to pull Thalesai backward if *they* wouldn't be leading it forward. Had they any clue it was what our former oppressors wanted?

Clearly, Sarhedrin had no issues with being a traitor.

And the way they spoke of King Khasar without respect or loyalty. It was this entitlement of the Ussis that made them the most despised of the tribes. What would Queen Yval do to them if she knew this?

If she didn't know already.

I frowned at the thought. She was a daughter of the Dynast of Kadnazi, a man who breathed ambition. Some rumors said he'd threatened the High Priest into ordaining his daughter as the Queen of Thalesai. Apparently, the High Priest hinted at the temple that the queen he was shown by the saints was from the Kwali tribe.

I hadn't believed the rumors then. The High Priest did no one's bidding but the great Osime's. Now though, I wondered.

Thalesai had never had a queen as its sole ruler. But if that was the scheme of the Ussis, they would destroy whatever stood in their path to make her the first, so that they wouldn't have to bow to the Baihan king.

The Baihans wouldn't submit to an Ussi queen, and the kingdom would crumble under the power struggle.

The men exited the stairwell, and I slowed my steps. Sarhedrin had been plotting with the king's brother only days ago. Now, here he was, threatening destruction that would shake the entire royal family.

The Sand Palace was naught but a pit of sidewinders.

My mood murkier than ink, I marched back to the scholar's lounge. A body with overly long limbs clad in perfect white robes swept in to block me. The atmosphere shifted into an icy kaleidoscope.

The Spaeman.

I instantly blanked my face, my heart increasing pace. Did he know I'd been spying on chambermen? He'd touched my mind last night. If he dug in too deeply now, it wasn't just my mission he could uncover. If he knew about my family, our truth... he could ruin us.

"Prosperity upon your day, Khosa Spaeman."

He just stared long at me until I looked away.

"Chase a scorpion to its pit *only* if you are willing to be poisoned," he said.

My brows lowered. What parable was he on about now? No, I couldn't stand here wondering and give him more time to read me.

"Yes, Khosa Spaeman," I said and made to leave.

He hindered me again, and lifted a brow. "We're not yet finished here, Scholar."

"I wasn't aware we were having a conversation," I said uneasily.

"Is there something you want me to know?" He peered at me with ancient eyes, like he could see my soul. "A weight your young shoulders struggle to bear?"

My mouth dried up. "No, Khosa Spaeman."

"There are many snakes slithering in the sands of the Al'Qtraz, Issachar," he said so quietly I almost didn't hear. "You and the Nergal girl are only two of them."

Shock rocked through me, breaking my grim facade. He knew. He knew what Zair and I were. But how?

Skies. He didn't just manipulate thoughts. He truly had the sight.

His mouth twitched, and I didn't dare imagine he was amused.

"Khosa Spaeman," I started. "It's not what—"

"The serpents here," he went on grimly, "are bigger. Older. Hungrier."

And with that, he made to walk away. I lunged forward and grabbed his arm before he could. Female gasps resounded in the landing. Grabbing the king's Spaeman was not something anyone who valued their lives did.

But the question bubbling up my throat would not be stopped.

"If you know so much, if you... Why aren't you doing anything?" I hissed. "Why aren't you telling us where the mercenaries are? You already showed me their temporary camp. Why not help us rescue our peers, the *children*, and rid Thalesai of these beasts?"

I couldn't *bear* it when people who could help watched passively while others suffered. It was the same way when my family went into hiding. We'd gone to friends' doorsteps for help. They'd told my parents they empathized before shutting their doors in our faces.

The Spaeman studied me now like one reading a book. Rather than smite me, something like sympathy dimmed those disturbingly arctic eyes. He swept my hand off his sleeve.

"*This* is beyond what you think, Issachar. The worst..." Ancient darkness brushed his eyes. "...is yet to come. Ari'el is a desert of bleeding sand. Terrible things must unfold for rifts to be sealed, for enemies eating through the land like worms to be exposed, and for the truly chosen to finally occupy ranks and battle to ensure no such evil ever comes upon Thalesai again."

The worst was *yet* to come?

No, I disagreed with his logic. Couldn't accept it. Students and poor borderland farmers were the scapegoats here. Students like Jaziah, who'd only wanted to learn so they could do great things for their land, were now in chains, raped, tortured, and starved. And no one could help them.

Rather, *he* could help them. But he hoarded knowledge because 'the worst was yet to come.'

Before these thoughts could erupt out of me, the Spaeman shook his head in firm warning and left.

20

ZAIR

Don't *look at Colonel Remmon. He can't suspect you know his hands are dirty.*
  I managed to avert my stare, replaying the memory of Remmon with the Esan smuggler as we trooped down the aisles in the HaMīqdaš Temple. It was a solid lead. My instincts hadn't steered me wrong. Now I had to probe deeper and find what Remmon was smuggling, why he watched the Admiral, and if he was the traitor.

Breeze from the sparkling river kept the ostentatious building mild, even as its rows and galleries brimmed with citizens from far and near. Ussis, Baihans, Mizsabs, and Kwalis mixed together on the long benches, some leaning forward to watch our advance and others adjusting their head coverings.

The wraith lords surveyed the soaring walls of gold-veined marble. The lofty alabaster pillars of the ten saints hefted the burgundy ceiling with diamond patterns. Their eyes betrayed their wonder.

"It was constructed in the year Ari'el was declared Thalesai's capital," the First Advisor told them.

"And is this temple where the priests see the saint-sent visions that tell them who would be ordained Thalesai's king?" the wraith ambassador asked, soft shadows whispering over his neck.

"I'm the First Advisor, not a priest," the candle said with courteous humor. "I won't claim to understand the intricacies of the priests and priestesses' link with the saints. However, our High Priest dwells here, which naturally means he sees his visions here. The other nine priests and priestesses live across the capital, and on the night the saints ordain Thalesai's rulers, they all see the same vision."

"I've heard of this," the wraith lord said, intrigued.

"A night after our last king passed, Thalesai's ten priests had a vision of King Khasar as the chosen of the saints. Not one had a vision of another person."

The wraith dignitaries nodded with understanding. The aziza and shifter lords exuded doubts.

I glanced at the dais where the queen's zenana encircled her. Sometimes, the queens were also saint-chosen, like Queen Yval, but there were periods in our history when the saints hadn't ordained a queen and the king chose who would sit on the throne beside him.

My older sister and I had asked my mother why once.

"I asked my mother the same question years ago, but no one can explain the ways of Osime," she'd said. *"One thing we can always be certain of is that the saints have a reason for everything."*

Ironteenth Fighters manning the loges kept eyes on the shapeshifter and aziza lords who cut through the crowds to lounge on the outer verandahs.

"Isn't it rude for the shifters and azizas to sit outside when such an important ceremony is held inside?" Mishan fumed.

"Remember, the wraithlands introduced the Crisdai divinity to us during the Invasion and erased our traditional worship," Dathan said. "Our saints are not that of the shifters or azizas."

Mishan grumbled that it was still rude. We formed long rows at the very front of the great dais with the advisors and other chambermen.

Dathan scrutinized the Spaeman, who stood on the dais with the Majesties and Priests. He'd restyled his hair, letting gleaming tendrils curl over his intense eyes, and I smiled smugly inside at his shock to finding his laces tied. I'd sensed his heightened focus toward something at breakfast, sensed he had been watching someone. But he'd been careful not to fixate wholly on a person, and I hadn't been able to tell who exactly he watched. Tying his shoelaces together had been to make him trip whenever he stood up and alert me to his movements. If he tried to leave before the rest of us, I could follow him and see who he watched.

As if reading my thoughts, Dathan moved suavely to stand beside me. "You tied my shoelaces together, Nergal."

I kept my face innocent. "You need proof to back that accusation, Gergesenes."

He lowered his brows, his eyes a deep green in the bright temple light. "I could've fallen on my face and bruised myself."

But we both knew that wasn't the outcome he dreaded.

"And have fewer women ogle you? How tragic," I murmured, struggling to keep my mouth from twitching as he growled in his throat.

"Whatever this is happening between us—" he gestured his hand in the space between us and his finger brushed my arm, igniting a hum in my skin, "—sabotage is against the rules."

I drew a soft breath and resisted the urge to leap away from his touch. "I can smell lies and you just lied to me."

The garlicky smell of falsity lingered near my nose. He had every intention to sabotage me if it suited his purposes.

"Perhaps I just wanted to... escort you and see who you'd been monitoring this morning."

He tautened, then tilted his head at me. "So that you could have a new suspect to spy on?"

Yes, but no way I would confirm his suspicions of my purpose in the palace. Along with my search, I had to know who he watched and why, in case he was after the palace's traitor and close to finding the person first. But Dathan was proving hard to trick. Despite my attempt to track his movement this morning, he had exited the dining balcony without my notice.

"If *theoretically* you and I have the same goal, like to win at the Best of Ten," he started but again, we both knew he was not talking about the Best of Ten, "forget winning. I'm not a soldier that loses."

Memories of Sarai in the mercenary's grip flashed in my head. I said with soft lethalness, "If theoretically you and I have the same goal, nothing—and I mean nothing—will stand in the way of my winning. I'll have what I'm after and nothing will stop me."

He gave a slow nod, but a sharp glint of challenge had entered his eyes. "May the best soldier win, then."

I lifted my chin, determination flooding me as I held his stare. "May the best soldier win."

Something powerful surged and rumbled between us, like the beginnings of a great thunderstorm. Dathan's eyes grew darker with intensity, his energy like a battering ram hurtling for that enforced barricade within me.

I straightened my back and moved to the space between Mishan and Lysias, keeping my focus away from Dathan's smirk.

The ceremony began as the High Priest, cloaked in a pewter-green robe, read passages from the hagiography: a sacred book of Osime and the saints. He poured saltwater over King Khasar, who knelt before the saints in a deep pool. The High Priest declared the message that the saints had given him when they ordained Khasar as the king.

I subtly watched Colonel Remmon. During the priests' chants, he was the epitome of a loyal subject, chanting too. The Dynasts of Caso and Irua talked in low, heated tones behind us, stirring up my curiosity. I inched closer and sharpened my hearing, but they only argued about the olive oil trade between their towns.

The Second Advisor soon moved to caution them. "Khosas, keep your dispute for the private halls of the Chambers."

The elderly men bristled at each other but fell quiet.

"The chosen head of the five tribes," the High Priest hailed, presenting the King of Thalesai his god-given *oriki*. "The one who roars and the desert answers!"

I and many others gasped at the powerful *oriki*.

"The one who roars and the desert answers!" the entire temple hailed.

Dathan's focus didn't drift once to Remmon. If we had the same orders as we both suspected, someone else was his target. Who was it?

The ceremony ended, and I noted that King Khasar had worn a plain white attire while in the pool. Now, he stood in a magnificent purple robe and gleaming circlet as his people cheered deafeningly.

"That was an experience," Mishan said, clapping.

"It was," I murmured, wincing guiltily. I had been distracted for most of it.

The hall remained crammed, but enough people proceeded to mingle on the shore outside that movement was possible. Some old women couldn't advance in the crowd. I helped create a path for them to reach the freer aisle. My head remained carefully bowed, concealing my eyes. The women smiled their thanks, and it felt... wrong that my help was only appreciated when people didn't know who I was.

"Zair?"

My heart jumped. A smile exploded on my face as I twirled.

"Papa!" I flung myself into my father's giant arms. "How is Sarai? Is she well? Safe?"

My heart raced in my throat.

"Ah, look at my little soldier at the king's coronation! Sarai is well and safe, *mihe*. She's... smiling again."

A sob rose in my throat. I hadn't realized the depth of my terror until his words eased it. Sarai was safe. For now.

"Thank Osime," I whispered thickly.

My father kissed my forehead.

"We were beside ourselves with worry when we didn't see you at the king's procession yesterday." He planted his hands on his hips. "Your mother was sure something was wrong. What happened?"

"We, ah, lost our way for some time," I hedged. "I'm fine."

I didn't ask why my mother and sisters didn't come too. My mother must've fretted that her presence would only ruin the occasion for me, so she'd made herself stay away.

"They miss you," he said. "We're so proud you're Nergal's representative, Zair."

My eyes burned. "I miss them so much too. Please tell them."

Eyes twinkling, he brought out a parcel from his satchel. "Your mother sent this."

The sweet, yeasty aroma wafted up. "Yellow buns!"

He laughed. "She woke up at dawn to prepare them for you."

I smiled as warmth filled me and teased, "You look like you've been helping yourself to a lot of the buns."

He patted his stomach. "You mean I look younger and stronger? I agree."

I chuckled and we talked about home and the coronation. I started to guide him to one of the empty benches, but a bell chimed in my head. I glanced around the temple. A sudden urgency fueled the royal guards' movements as they spoke in chambermen's ears. Trouble was coming.

My father's forehead grooved too.

Before he could fret, I said, "I should return to the king's retinue, papa."

"Wait, there's unease in the air." His concern grew stronger as the nobles slowly converged. "I don't want you around the palace if this coronation is about to cave in on itself."

"I'll be fine," I assured him and hurried away.

The danger remained just a ripple against my senses—subtle. A bit distant. But firm because it was surely coming. A small part of me hoped that whatever came would offer a valuable clue, yet the deeper part prayed that everyone would remain safe.

My gaze drifted to Dathan, drawn as if by an unseen force as he strolled through the crowd, his hair shielding parts of his face.

Trouble is coming, Dathan... something within me whispered to him.

The unexpected desire to go and warn him jolted me. He had all but raised the challenge between us moments ago. The soldiers pulling the nobles together would warn him. I tore my eyes away and squared my shoulders against the pull to go to him, but my father's voice stopped me.

I turned around. He bounded toward me, worry on his face as he stopped in front of me. "I know you're strong, but promise me you'll stay safe."

I stepped forward and hugged him tightly, his fear so tangible that I felt it in my own heart. I looked up at him. "I won't let anything take me away from you, papa."

21

DATHAN

Sarhedrin embodied loyalty as he moved to speak with the Majesties. He kept a hand against his chest, smiling mildly as his lips moved.

He won't hurt them here. Seek out other suspects.

I forced my glare away and spotted Zair hugging a giant of a man with an adasword sheathed on his hip. I rested against a pillar, tilting my head and taking in the man who had to be her father. Zair pulled back so I could see her face. Her smile, as bright as the moonlight, hit me like a rock to the chest.

Her smile transformed her ethereal beauty into something pure and renewing. My entire chest seemed to slide open under her beam.

She's exquisite.

Her father turned to survey the hall, and my heart kicked in my chest as I stared at his eyes. They were clear brown without gold rings circling them.

If Zair's father didn't have Esan eyes, then she had inherited them from her mother. Which meant...

Zair wasn't an Esan tribeswoman.

At least, not entirely. She was of her father's tribe, one of the four accepted tribes. Yet she was dealt the full hatred felt for the Esans because of how she looked.

My chest ached. Skies... Thalesai had failed Zair Nebah terribly.

Their smiles as they talked made me scan the rowdy temple for my family. I wanted to see my father. To see the light from Zair's father's eyes in his when he looked at me. At the same time, I hoped he hadn't come. It would be too risky for them. And even if it wasn't, it wouldn't be pride in his eyes when he looked at me. There would be love. There was always love, but anger and disappointment would quickly follow.

A complete scan confirmed my family wasn't in the temple. Relief and deep aching squeezed my chest in equal measure. Perhaps one day this existence that had been forced on my family would be easier to accept.

Subtly studying the nobles, I walked past Ibhar talking with his father, a chamberman every bit as arrogant as his son.

Three graceful women in rich caftans surrounded Mishan. They alternated cupping his face with tattooed fingers and kissing his cheeks as they fretted over his wounds. Based on their resemblance, they were three generations: his sister, mother, and grandmother.

"Having your boo-boo kissed better, Scholar Mishan?" I murmured in passing.

Mishan grimaced. "Shut up, Gergesenes."

I chuckled and stopped by another pillar as a group of Ussi elders ambled by.

Lysias stood alone too. Our eyes met and she hesitated, then sauntered to me like sunlight streaming through the temple.

I resisted the impulse to turn in another direction. I needed to be alone to focus but I couldn't be a rude cad and rebuff her. Standing with someone *would* be less conspicuous than standing alone, even with tendrils of hair fluttering over my eyes.

"Thank Osime *this* ceremony ended without us in shackles," she joked when she reached me.

"Let's not tempt fate," I said amusedly. "We still have four ceremonies left."

Skies, only four.

She chuckled, pleased that I was open to casual conversation. *My father would like her*. She was Kwali, the most peaceful of the tribes. She was friendly and intelligent enough to be a prime elite student. And as if those qualities weren't enough, she was a healer like him. Taking her home would put me in his good graces.

My focus drifted to Zair, an Esan-looking soldier aspirant who laced my boots together and vowed to beat me at our unspoken contest. Ah, my father would bite my head off if I dared. He couldn't accept his soldier son—he would never embrace a daughter-in-law who was also a military student and from a tribe no one trusted. It was one more reason I needed to sever this *simmering* pull to her.

"Only Ambassador Caiphas could make the king smile like that," Lysias remarked, observing the royals.

Ambassador Caiphas was gesticulating, and the king grinned wryly.

"Many were sure their closeness would die from envy," I said.

The younger brother was crowned king over the older, after all. People had shared the same belief about my friendship with Jaziah. Jaz, too, had been vying for an Ironteenth rank.

"It's been over a year now." I cleared my throat. "I'm glad they're proving the predictions wrong."

Lysias hummed as if impressed with my thinking. "*And* only the king's father could make our regal queen look so uncertain."

Indeed, Queen Yval's smile was nervous as she talked with her father-in-law, a Baihan elder with a weathered face. He glanced at his sons with pride.

"Thank you for yesterday, Dathan," Lysias said warmly. "Not just for a great plan, but you were patient with us in the cell. Not many men believe that strength and goodness go together."

I shifted on my feet. "Gergesenes' teachers are some of the best for a reason."

"So modest." She laughed, and then flapped her hands. "Ambassador Caiphas and his entourage are coming *our* way. Quick, smile."

"What?" I chuckled and her gaze lingered on my face for a moment.

"We all have goals here and mine is to gain sponsors for my project. I desperately need the nobles to take to me, so smile," she rushed out in a plea, moments before the king's older brother stood before us.

At only twenty three years old, Ambassador Caiphas's black

hair gleamed under his gilded cap, framing a youthful face that was darker and more handsome than his brother's. His exquisite seafoam-and-brown ensemble emphasized his lithe physique, carved bronze bracelets glinting on his hands.

Lysias and I bowed in greeting. "Khosa Caiphas."

His mouth curved, his stance easy. Despite being Thalesai's ambassador to the wraithlands, he was the jovial brother. "Scholar Issachar, yes?"

"*Si*, Khosa."

"Our Baihan brother," Caiphas said to his entourage of three men. They beamed at me. "We've heard impressive things of you."

Impressive. A thrill surged through me. Perhaps making it into the Ironteenth was a real possibility. "I'm glad, Khosa."

"You must make us proud at tomorrow's coronation event. The Best of Ten."

"That's my intention," I said, maybe a bit cockily. But I loved sports and competition and thrived at both.

Caiphas grinned now. "I see why my baby brother likes you. I'll be cheering for you too."

My smile grew. "That means more than I can say, Khosa."

Jaziah would *faint* when I told him—

My smile died as the Spaeman's vision fluttered into my mind.

Caiphas's gaze drifted to Lysias and interest flickered. "Quartus Academy?"

"Scholar Lysias, actually," Lysias corrected sweetly, a bit sassily.

Ambassador Caiphas's brows rose at her boldness, but he looked more intrigued than offended. "A pleasure to meet you, Scholar Lysias. So, you're an aspiring healer."

She radiated. "Year-five."

"Perhaps you would be open to sharing your research for the Best of Ten ceremony with me at tonight's feast?" He added with sudden seriousness, "My growing settlement could benefit from innovative ideas, especially in medicine."

I wondered at his seriousness while Lysias vibrated with joy. "I would be honored, Khosa."

He nodded, pleased. To us both, he said, "If you need anything, both in the palace and outside, don't hesitate to ask."

It was no small favor he was extending or humility he showed, coming to speak with us rather than summoning us.

Lysias smiled brightly. He lingered near her until his shorter friend coughed, "Close your mouth, Cai, you're drooling."

I coughed to hide my smile. Lysias giggled quietly. Caiphas, ever good-natured, made a farewell gesture and strode off with his party. What business could an easygoing young man like him have with an ancient viper like Sarhedrin? And why had his mien shifted when he'd spoken of his settlement?

"Your father didn't come?" Lysias idly surveyed the socializing crowd. A few steps ahead, some temple acolytes played with children.

My brows lifted. "You know my father?"

"What student in a healing academy doesn't know Med Luke Issachar?" she asked like I should know this. "He was invited to my academy a few times to teach his research on the *Sacred Steps of Herbal Experimentation*. He's an *icon* in our field."

"My father doesn't work in the royal infirmary," I pointed out slowly, confused.

"He's one of those lucky few who don't have to work with the rulers to hold exceptional status. Patients of his infirmary give sufficient testimony."

My father was going to lecture at Quartus, the biggest healing academy in Thalesai? It wasn't that he lacked the skill. Luke Issachar had enough charisma for three and was the most intelligent man I knew. *Life From Knowledge* was Quartus's slogan and in some ways, my father's. But nine years ago, his mantra became *keep your head down. No one must know about us.*

Lysias went on, "Contrary to misconception, I'm not a caregiving healer. My specialty is experimenting with herbs and creating medicine. Therefore, if you suspect I'm here talking to Luke Issachar's son just so I can win an introduction to him, you're absolutely right."

I placed a hand on my chest. "I'm wounded."

She rolled her eyes. "No, you're not. Not when your attention stays on a certain golden-eyed girl half the time we're all together."

If only she knew we were rivals likely after the same target.

"It's not what you think," I said, yet a voice that was poignant and deep and old hummed within me, '*Yes it is*'.

Lysias looked unconvinced. "*Is* your father coming?"

"My family isn't very... keen on large gatherings."

We had altered our appearances and last name to fit what we now claimed we were, yet that fear of recognition always pressed on their shoulders. The fear kept me up every night too, but the path I chose made living completely in the shadows impossible.

Lysias pouted. "That's disappointing."

I diverted the topic. "Is *your* family coming?"

She gave a sad smile. "I don't have a family. At least not in the way you four do." She gestured a be-ringed hand to encompass Mishan, Ibhar, and Zair, who were still surrounded by theirs. "The Headmistress of the Quartus Academies is my aunt, so the academy essentially is my whole world."

"I'm sorry."

She nodded with that sad smile. Was that why she was so friendly? Trying to fill that hole in her life with friendships?

Soft laughter yanked our attention like a hand to our collars. Because the musical sound, the *laughter*, came from Zair's direction.

"Hmm?" Lysias's brows surged to her hairline. "I didn't think she had the ability to make that sound."

Her tone wasn't malicious, still I found myself coming to Zair's defense.

"She hasn't exactly had reason to laugh around us."

"True," Lysias agreed. "If Ibhar isn't being a bastard to her, someone else is treating her as less than. You know, before I met her, with how people speak of Esan tribespeople I'd imagined they had horns along with their gold-lined eyes. But she's... just like us."

And she's not even Esan, I thought but didn't say. If Lysias hadn't already noticed it and Zair chose not to correct the assumption, it wasn't my place to.

"Scholars," a voice called.

Lysias and I turned to the grim guard.

"It's time to head back to the Al'Qtraz," he said.

The grimness seemed to have also fallen over King Khasar, Queen Yval, and every member of the Chamber of Wings.

Before the guard could bound over to Mishan and Ibhar to alert them to our abrupt departure, I asked quietly, "Sir, is something wrong?"

The guard hesitated, then glanced around before leaning closer to Lysias and me. "The Ironteenth encountered something disturbing."

"What?" Lysias asked.

"A threat," I said, reading the guard's face.

He nodded. "An armed group of Mizsab rebels tried to attack the temple. They've been arrested, but they got too close for comfort, and there could be more of them coming. We need to get the Majesties to safety now. Go to them."

Before I could ask if it was best that the entire temple was evacuated, the guard hurried off. Soldiers herded the royal procession together, flanking us as we proceeded to the entryway.

"What's wrong?" a familiar voice asked.

I looked behind us at Zair, who had caught up with us. Her face was guarded as if expecting us to ignore her.

I held her gaze to make a point clear and answered, "Armed Mizsabs tried to infiltrate the temple. The Ironteenth aren't waiting to see what happens next."

Our procession left the temple and rode hard for the palace.

22

ZAIR

We reached the palace in one piece, thank Osime, but after the breakneck ride, the foreign ambassadors were restless. They demanded answers. Tension vibrated through the sandstone walls up to the domes as I hurried into my room.

I closed my door and beside my balcony, a silhouette moved. I snatched the bow and arrow I'd propped up by the door and aimed.

"I would not advise that."

Arno! Dressed in his native dyed seasilk and aquamarine necklace, he perched high up on my balcony's door, weightless as the door waved in the breeze.

I squeezed my weapon. "You aren't allowed in this part of the palace, or in my *bedchamber*."

His jaw clenched. "There is a problem. It is why we were rushed out of the temple. The human councilors and soldiers won't tell us what is wrong." His wings beat once. "Tell me."

Blast it. The azizas couldn't know that some humans didn't want a Baihan king on the throne. Yet if I told him this, his hold on me would end. *Twice*. I'd be free to focus on my mission without feeling like a three-faced vixen.

"I could just release my arrow and kill you."

"Then the King of Dahomey will burn down Thalesai. Zair Nebah," he prompted tightly.

Drawing a breath, I threw back my shoulders and lowered my weapon. "There was a threat in the temple, but it has nothing to do with your party or any of the foreigners."

"If the threat is not against us, then who?" he demanded.

No, I couldn't bring myself to say it. To prove that, indeed, Dathan shouldn't have trusted me with an answer at the temple.

Those sharp instincts read my silence.

"The threat was against Thalesai's Majesties." His brows surged high. "From their own subjects."

"Yes." I swallowed back bile. "So as you can see, you have nothing to worry about."

Face softening, his wings fluttered until his boots met the carpet. "I will admit I was perturbed until now. Thank you for your honesty."

I scoffed a bitter laugh. "Unhappy to be of service. I'm free of your blackmail, Arno. Now, stay away from me."

His expression was unreadable for too long. "We will see."

We will... "No, we won't. No, we won't see anything!"

He streaked out of my *window*. I resisted the urge to go see if he had fallen. I couldn't be that lucky. Whatever happened, I was finished being his informant.

A careful knock came on my door. I'd barely opened it before Lysias tugged me into the lounge.

"We have two hours until tonight's feast," she said. "I thought we could play a game to unwind."

"A game," I repeated warily as my gaze cinched first on Dathan. His curly hair was brushed back again—why did he frequently restyle it? He reclined with Mishan by a window seat, both looking amused but interested in Lysias's invitation. Was this a ploy to make a spectacle out of me? Use me somehow as Arno Irmah did?

"Yes. 'Name of Things.' Do you know the game?" Lysias quizzed.

"Of course Zair knows the game," Dathan answered before I could. That quick mind had sensed that I'd just been about to feign ignorance of the game so that I could disappear back into my room. "We all played it as children."

"You don't know what games I played as a child," I said.

He shrugged broad shoulders. "Just admit that you are afraid of shaming Nergal by losing to the other elite academies."

"Oooh." Lysias giggled, encouraging him.

"Surely you are not afraid, Zair," Mishan chipped in, hopping over to gesture me to a chair.

"Gergesenes wishes I was afraid of it," I heard myself answer as I sat gamely. I knew he was provoking me, but I couldn't let Nergal slander go from a Gergesenes hawk.

Or you are curious to spend more time around the man who has provoked you but has yet to disrespect you.

No, I did not. Dathan Issachar was no saint. He had openly challenged my goal in the palace, and I'd be wise to remember that.

Dathan grinned and it almost knocked the air from my lungs.

Lysias, too, faced momentary distraction from his smile before she clapped and sat with a noblewoman's grace on the opposite chair.

"Alright. This is the rule. The winner's academy will be deemed the greatest for the day. If you lose, however, you have to dance at the center of the lounge. The first loser dances alone. The second loser dances with the first. And on until we have one winner."

Three of us passionately protested the rule. No one wanted to dance in front of everyone, much less without music.

"Then do not lose," Lysias said primly. "Now, let's begin."

The 'Name-of' game had been introduced to my sisters and me by our older cousins. It could be 'name of animals' or 'name of colors.' Everyone had only a second to think of and call out a name once it was their turn. If you took longer or repeated someone's answer, you lost. It seemed easy until the competition began and you started to sweat under the tight timeline and fear of losing first.

Lysias started with names of villages.

It went around four times, our brains working fast and shifting from the palace's tension, before we began to exhaust the names of popular villages. I was terrified of losing first, couldn't shake off the suspicion that they didn't really want me here to play but to mock me.

But *Dathan* lost first! To be fair, we had exhausted the known village names by his turn, but he still lost.

I stared victoriously at him.

To my surprise, he was not a mean loser. He sighed dramatically as Lysias and Mishan teased him but moved confidently to the center of the room. Mishan and Lysias made terrible music with the table, and Dathan gave a smooth Baihan dance that made me shift with reluctant admiration.

"Now, name of foods," Mishan declared.

The three of us went five rounds this time before the options began to dwindle. By the time Lysias and Mishan started to mention the exotic foods that their servants prepared at home, I ran out of names.

"I'm not dancing," I exclaimed in dismay.

This was it; they would snicker at me while I danced.

Dathan took my hand and tugged me to my feet. His grip was warm and steady in a way that sent a pulse of awareness through me. I shoved it down, couldn't dare acknowledge the unsettling rush moving through me.

"You have to. Losers are only pathetic when they don't lose gracefully."

"Dance! Dance!" Mishan and Lysias cheered, drumming a scattered beat.

"Fine," I said uncomfortably, readying myself to be mocked. "Beware, I don't know how to dance with a partner."

"Lucky for you, I know how to do everything," Dathan said.

"You need some serious humbling."

"Later. For now?"

He placed a hand on my waist. I startled as wild birds took flight in my chest, sparks igniting over my skin. A surprised look skirted his face too, just before he twirled me around in dance. I gasped with a heady sensation. I was back in his arms before I knew it, and he slanted me backward over his strong arm.

My heart slammed in my chest as he leaned in and curiously studied my face.

He murmured, "I suppose even loss can feel sweet sometimes."

"Save the honeyed tongue, Gergesenes," I breathed. Yet I wondered what he felt as we danced—if he, too, was struck by the same sharp awareness as our bodies moved together. Did he feel the heat between us, the charged energy in every brush of fabric and fleeting touch? Could he hear the frantic rhythm of my heartbeat or see the pulse fluttering at the hollow of my throat?

"Next round," Mishan called, already bored with the performance.

"Yes, before you both melt the lounge." Lysias's blue eyes twinkled as she stared at us.

I leaped away from Dathan and adjusted my blouse, my cheeks burning. I didn't know whether to be embarrassed or entertained.

Thankfully, Mishan plunged into the next round of the game. He spat out names as if his life depended on it. Still, I suspected Lysias let him win because she wanted to play.

"I lost!" she declared happily and stood up to dance with us.

Dathan ducked and tossed her over his shoulder as if she weighed nothing. She squealed in delight as he spun her around and tugged me into the swirl. I tried to pull back, but he wouldn't let go. That strange, giddy feeling fluttered in my ribs.

"It looks like I'm the winner of this game, Mishan," Dathan called.

This playful side of him captivated me.

Mishan laughed and continued to drum for us. Could I let myself believe these wealthy, renowned youths were sincerely playing *with* me and not at my expense?

It has to be because they are bored, not because they like you.

Dainty footsteps neared our archway, their voices loud and angry, reminding us of the palace's tension.

"Remember the Sosthenes' fate? That's how the king will make examples of the rebels if they continue to obstruct the coronation," an unknown voice, tight with tension snapped.

Dathan instantly settled Lysias on her feet and let go of me. I turned to him. All traces of his humor had vanished, his face an impenetrable mask. Even with my training, I couldn't glean any hint of what he was thinking.

"Dathan?" Lysias called, her smile fading.

"It was a pleasant game, Lysias. Thank you." He nodded politely to us, his body firmly angled away from the threshold. "I'll rest for a bit before the feast."

He walked briskly and disappeared behind his door just as the footsteps reached our lounge. I stared at the three women as they passed the threshold. They were middle-aged Ussi women. Harmless.

What had turned Dathan cold? And why did I so badly want to know?

A STEWARD ARRIVED, prompting us to prepare for the celebration of a successful Blessing of the King. Lysias and Mishan went into their suites with their servants. I hesitated by the door Dathan had walked behind and shut firmly. What was he thinking in there? Did our dance cross his mind?

I couldn't deny the consuming thrill I felt when he touched me anymore, but... it couldn't mean *anything*. He had all but made his determination to best me in the palace clear, and I wouldn't gamble with Sarai's life by letting him succeed if we shared the same goal. And even if he felt this *thing* between us, Dathan Issachar had too many wife prospects to choose to be with an Esan-eyed girl who would make him a pariah and cost him his aspirations.

I swallowed. I would be foolish to let myself feel tenderly for him.

Maids pulled me before my silvered mirror, and I disappeared into billows of fabrics.

I surfaced in a sleeveless aqua blouse encrusted in the palest pink stones. Delicate armbands glinted on my upper arms. A lush merlot wrapper wound around my waist, enhancing my hips. Ostentatious earrings sparkled as they grazed my shoulders, and thick kajal lined my eyes.

Satisfied with their work, they sashayed out. I *radiated*. It would be impossible to disappear into the shadows like this. Even in more fabric than ever, my skin tingled as though wholly exposed.

Twisting my snake rings, I stepped out of my bedroom. Dathan and Mishan were in the lounge with Dathan helping Mishan adjust his collar. The boys swiveled when my door clicked closed and promptly froze.

Dathan stared like he'd been kicked in the chest. Clad in merlot and sable finery, he was perhaps the most handsome man I'd ever seen. For a moment, I found myself caught in his gaze. I liked the stunned admiration in his eyes... especially as his gaze fell to my lips.... Heat rushed to my cheeks.

"Zair," Mishan said, as if to confirm it was indeed me.

"Yes?" I answered cautiously, dragging my gaze from Dathan.

"Saints. You look..."

I braced for the insults that I often received, yet also found myself hoping for a compliment.

Ibhar's door swung open. He scanned my finery and his eyes widened. But just as quickly, he sneered at me. "New clothes won't make azishit fine."

I flinched.

"Shut your mouth, Ahimoth," Dathan growled.

Surprised, Ibhar paused, then sneered at Dathan as he stomped off.

My hopeful confidence was already shattered. Worse, Dathan and Mishan continued to look at me and my neck burned.

"What are you both staring at?" I snapped and stalked off.

THE GREAT DINING hall was a staggering world of mosaics. Hues ranged from soft beige to the deepest brown. Clusters of copper lanterns dangled low over bone-inlaid tables. Plush mahogany carpets cushioned the expensive footwear traipsing over them. Sprawled on damascene chairs were nobles in exquisite gauze and brocades that instantly cast my attire in the shadows.

I released a relieved breath. Girls my age dripped in rubies with golden bracelets tinkling. Dathan and Mishan would forget me once they sighted their tasseled two-piece dresses. Ibhar already flirted with some Ussi girl, both gazing into each other's kohl-lined eyes by the entrance. Even Lysias looked more glamorous in her lavender attire and silver jewels. Two Kwali boys with their native piercings flanked her seat, seeming to hang on her every enthusiastic sentence.

Calmer, I moved down an aisle. Which table would set me closest to First Colonel Remmon?

"What did the Spaeman say to you?" a deep voice asked close by my ear.

Startled, I bumped into Dathan's towering form behind me. Moving with confident grace, he had to be the most riveting young man in the hall. I frowned at the tingle in my chest, worse when his scent urged me closer.

What was he doing walking with me? I needed privacy to focus. Besides, I couldn't be affiliated with him in any way. If his mission collapsed, suspicion could be cast on me too.

"It's no business of yours, Gergesenes," I said haughtily and quickly swerved to a random chair with people flanking it.

Dathan guessed my intention. If I took the seat, he'd be forced to leave me alone unless he wanted to be left standing behind me. Before I could pull out the chair, his foot shot out like a whip and wedged it. I tugged on the frame but his foot was annoyingly strong.

Glaring at his stubborn smirk, I released the chair and continued fast down the aisle, bodies weaving leisurely around me.

Dathan, curse him, kept easy stride. However, when he leaned in to speak again, there was nothing easy about his words.

"The Spaeman knows who you are, and what you're here for."

I halted as the statement registered. Dread churned in my stomach. *Ask first. Panic later.* I swung to face him. "How do you know that?"

Rather than answer, Dathan strode over to settle into a chair with empty seats beside it. He tipped his head at a spare chair; he wouldn't utter a word until I sat beside him.

I bit my lip. I was better off walking away and resuming my search for the closest seat to my target. Yet, I had to know what exactly the Spaeman said concerning me. Making my wooden legs move, I settled in the huge chair to his left. Different sizes of terracotta bowls sat on jute placemats before us, between dainty gold-and-glass lamps and brown-red garlands.

"Half the girls here would've jumped at the chance to sit with me," he said.

His tone was wry, but I glanced around. The glares of the girls sitting opposite us confirmed the statement. They didn't think I was worthy of Gergesenes' star student's attention.

Insecurity trickled into me and made me feel small. No, I didn't have to endure this. Whatever the Spaeman had said, I could find out myself later.

Horribly observant, Dathan's hand grabbed mine before I could rise, and that heat from dancing with him crackled where he touched.

"Zair."

I glowered at him, pushing down the reaction to his touch. But he peered at me, questions in his intense eyes. Tried to peel through my defenses.

"Why are you so guarded?" he murmured, speaking more to himself.

It was either the question or his discomfiting stare, but my defensiveness intensified.

"You wouldn't know, would you?" I flung in low tones. "When you fit in here, are accepted so easily by the nobles that one would insist you were born in the palace. When you're indisputably here because you're one of the best students in the kingdom and don't have to constantly fight to *prove* it. Why would you understand anything less?"

Defensiveness flashed on *his* face. Like my accusatory words had hit a sore spot. Had it?

Skies, I was like a stranger in my own skin. Lashing out was not like me, and I didn't like the direction this conversation was heading.

I pulled my hand from his, took a calming breath, and asked in a more collected voice, "What did the Spaeman say to you?"

He pinned me with an intense look for what felt like hours, then glanced away with a released breath. When he turned to me again, his face was shuttered. He leaned in until his breath brushed my ear, and I shivered from the warmth.

"He knows we're both here on espionage."

No no...

My heart rattled in my chest, throat tightening, but I forced an unconcerned demeanor and lifted a brow. "Espionage? Then his warning was *only* to you."

Impatience flashed in his eyes. "Don't do that. This is serious."

I swallowed thickly, my mask slipping, but I would never verbally confirm to him that I was a spy. "Was he warning you to leave the palace when he said this?"

Dathan's gaze fell to my lips at the slight tremble of my voice. Softness flickered there and his rigid mien eased.

"He *was* warning me. Warning us. But I got no sense that it was to stop what we're doing here."

My brows knitted. "I don't understand."

"I believe he's telling us that there are others with worse agendas than ours, and to know that we could get crushed locking horns with them."

The squeezing in my torso alleviated, yet my relief wasn't complete. The Spaeman knew we were breaking the law, and wasn't throwing us into the dungeons for our audacity? He had a reason. What was it?

Suspicion rose in me as I looked at Dathan. He still studied me.

"Why are you telling me this?" I queried. What did he stand to gain from keeping me informed? He could've easily told me the Spaeman was monitoring me to ensure I fled the palace, making *his* goal easier for him.

He tilted his head. "I thought you should know."

My forehead grooved. Could he really? Share information with *me* without ulterior motives? No one was that kind. What if he was lying? What if the Spaeman had said something else, warned me to get out of the palace, but Dathan wasn't telling me so I'd be caught and dragged out of his way?

It was possible, but—on this Dathan seemed open. And I didn't smell a lie.

Since he had given me this warning, I had to repay him in kind. Perhaps it was what he expected all along. Otherwise, I refused to be indebted to him.

"The morning of the King's Tour," I whispered into his ear. "The Spaeman warned me of our abduction. He didn't provide a clear context, so I didn't understand until after, but he'd said to beware."

Dathan's brows curved. I watched his mind work, trying to make sense of it all.

I hesitated on my next question because we weren't allies, but I made myself lean in and ask, "Do you think the Spaeman is giving us these warnings because he could..."

"Be in support of our goals?" Dathan completed my thought.

I gave a nod.

He tapped his placemat. "I don't know. On one hand, it seems like it, but we might also be misreading him entirely."

Gongs clanged in signal. Servants bustled into the hall with trolleys heaped with mouthwatering platters. They lined them on the aisles, lifting lids to reveal roasted fowls, golden abacha, spicy catfish pepper soup, garnished rice, and simmering foreign sauces for the visitors.

Dathan and I didn't speak after that. I was too busy monitoring First Colonel Remmon, who thankfully, while two tables away, was within my line of vision. He was oddly reserved tonight, mostly staring into his goblet as he swirled his wine. Wondering if his Esan smuggler would succeed in his secret errand?

The Second Advisor made a boisterous joke, and Mishan—who chattered with some Mizsab youths—glowered at the Second Advisor with surprising hostility. Ambassador Caiphas strode off the royal dais and sauntered over to Lysias. There was a youthful ease to him, but word was that he was a force to reckon with at his ambassadorial duties; his clever negotiations were a major reason the wraiths kept to the Treaty. He made his presence known with an arm tap, and Lysias's smile brightened. She didn't even blink at her fawners as he made them move so he could sit beside her. They conversed, barely breaking eye contact, their smiles unwavering. They looked spectacular together.

Some girls opposite me whispered about them while the others glanced beneath their lashes at Dathan.

Dathan's attention, however, was entirely elsewhere.

Each time I tried to trace it, to catch who he was monitoring, *targeting*, I found stenciled walls or the Kwali dancers. He was good.

I scooped steaming coconut rice into my mouth, not only to be less obvious about stalking the First Colonel, but because I was famished. I shut my eyes to savor the spicy flavors bursting on my tongue. *Delicious*. I took the serving fork and arranged two whole roasted plantains garnished with fried peppers on my plate too.

The roasted plantains—my favorite meal in the world—added charred sweetness to the creamy rice. I almost hummed in response.

"Sheols," Dathan suddenly swore under his breath.

My eyes popped open, but he'd already moved down the aisles amongst the maids and stewards.

His advance intrigued me. Dathan had a commandeering physique with his height and broad muscles, yet he calmly followed the rhythm of the hall, gave the impression that he was precisely where he ought to be, hence didn't draw second stares. I might have been fooled too if I hadn't heard his silent curse.

Girlish whispers drifted over to me across the table, but I couldn't look away.

His stealth was so fascinating, I almost missed that when he neared the edge of the third aisle, he wove amongst the throng of servers attending to the nobles there. Drifted even closer as servants' hands flew over plates and platters, and he swiped the Royal Accountant's goblet of wine.

Skies above. The guts. The *risk*. If he was seen...

"Ey, Esan girl."

Yanked out of my mind, I tilted my head to the girls opposite me.

"Scholar Issachar is beyond your status," the first bit out fiercely. They hadn't seen him all but disappear before them. They only stewed over the fact that he'd sat with me.

The other girl smirked. "Stop salivating over him, you desperate whore."

The words struck me like a blow and her friends snickered, but I held her gaze without giving them the pleasure of a single wince. Held her gaze with simmering anger until her smirk faltered. Her attention dropped at the table and the others shifted uneasily; I was Esan with magic after all.

But I knew a sharper way to strike back at them. Giving them a cool smile, I rose to my feet and walked away.

23

DATHAN

Poison.

As the son of a healer who specialized in herbal experimentation, I didn't miss the smell of *ddoro*, a herb that became poisonous when seeped in liquid.

The starlit Ari'el sky and windy night enveloped the balcony I stood on. The Royal Accountant's bronze goblet glittered on the railing before me.

From across tables, I'd watched Sarhedrin swipe a hand over three goblets, sprinkling some powder as the servers placed them before the Royal Accountant and his assistants. It was already odd that Sarhedrin chose to sit at the Royal Accountant's table rather than amongst his friends.

It was clear Sarhedrin wanted the financial office weakened to achieve some insidious goal. But *ddoro* only killed in large quantities. Did Sarhedrin want them dead? Or indisposed while he carried out his scheme? If he wanted them indisposed, his motive, while still criminal, might not be hideous. But if he was brash enough to want the Royal Accountant *dead*, then his scheme was something lethal.

A chill crawled up my torso. I needed to gauge the poison's potency.

Noises drew my attention to my balcony's threshold. The assistants Sarhedrin poisoned burst from the dining hall, hands clutching their stomachs, faces twisted in agony.

Heart picking up a beat, I slid back in the shadows. Was vomiting the effect?

Let it be the effect. Saints, please, don't let these men die.

Before reaching the privy door, the first nobleman slumped. Blood slipped from his nostrils, reddening the tiles. My breaths stalled. The other nobleman stumbled over his body and crashed, clawing desperately at his throat.

His eyes locked on mine. "Help. Me."

Blood pooled sickeningly fast around them. I rushed forward, forgetting the poisoned goblet I held, but the approaching maids saw the accountants and screamed. In seconds, guards flooded the scene.

They frantically inspected the bodies, and their sub-head growled, "They've been poisoned! Get into the hall, very subtly, and remove every jar and goblet now!"

The maids hurried off.

"The foreigners mustn't know what's happening," the sub-head said to three guards. "Make sure the maids gather the goblets table by table, and make a list of who sat where. We'll get to the root of this."

Blood roaring, I marched forward to expose who the poisoner was but forced my feet to stop. I burned to see Sarhedrin in chains. But if he was executed for this poisoning, his other atrocities would die with him. And if he was the mercenary spy, we would never uncover the mercenaries' secrets or find Jaziah.

Jaziah's life is more important than this burning for Sarhedrin's blood.

Four guards carefully carried the bodies away. As they approached my hiding place, the goblet of poison felt searing in my hand. Blast it.

I jumped back, poured the wine into a vase and dumped the goblet behind it. Once the guards passed, I returned to the hall.

Nobles grumbled as servants with shaky smiles retrieved jugs and goblets, apologizing profusely.

"We found out the liquids are stale," a maid was explaining as I reached my chair. "We'll bring something fresher soon."

The Royal Accountant chattered at his table, blissfully oblivious that if I'd been a second late, he'd be dead. His assistants' wives spoke gaily with him, clueless that their lives had just fallen apart.

And Sarhedrin. His face was a storm cloud as he watched the maids. His main target's goblet was missing, his plan mostly foiled.

My hands pulsed to wring that murderous neck, but a force tugged at me. Like unseen fingers steering my head until my eyes met with snowy ones.

My gut hardened. Had he seen everything? If so, why wasn't he exposing Sarhedrin?

From the royal table, the Spaeman shook his head slightly and then looked away. Like a cord snapped, I regained control of my neck. Was he warning me not to give in to the urge to attack Sarhedrin? This was no time for vagueness.

"One goblet of wine isn't enough to quench your thirst, Gergesenes?" Zair asked.

My stomach hardened. I veered to face her. She placed a delicate hand on my chest and my skin flashed like she held fire in her palm. She had never touched me so boldly before.

"You saw that," I bit out. I should've known she was paying as much attention to me as I'd been to her. I'd discarded the goblet, but here was a living witness to implicate me.

"We're taught spectacular things at Nergal too."

Blast. If I'd learned anything of Zair since our first meeting, it was that she had a tiger's drive. Eager to earn the respect she was deprived. She might not lose a wink of sleep from exposing me, not understanding how deep a grave her report would dig me into. Two noblemen were *dead*, and I'd been in possession of the last goblet of poison.

I covered the hand placed over my chest and squeezed, a warning gesture. "You cannot tell anyone of that."

She moved even closer until merely an inch of space separated us. Enraged feminine gasps echoed, but I was too focused on silencing a threat to care.

"Why did you take his wine?" she asked contemplatively. "Why are you after him?"

"I have nothing against the Royal Accountant." *I'd just saved his life.* But I couldn't say that to her because the next question on her quick mind would be 'Saved his life from whom?' She would begin to monitor who was after the Royal Accountant, and likely detect and intercept Sarhedrin as my target. I wouldn't risk that.

She parted her lips. To use my need for her silence as leverage to wring details out of me. I had to back her into a corner.

"You cannot tell anyone what you saw," I stated. "If you do, I'll deny it and tell them about *you*. And you know who they won't hesitate to believe."

They'll never take an Esan girl's words over the words of a Baihan prime student. I didn't have to say the words aloud; they hung in the small space between us like blades. Resounded in the way she flinched like I'd slapped her.

My mouth soured, but I needed her to back off. There were no longer clear lines on this field. "Alright?"

Fire blazed in her gold-ringed eyes. "I hate you so much right now I can barely breathe."

"I tend to leave girls breathless one way or another," I ground out.

I expected her to yank her hand back and storm off. But Zair leaned in, anger steaming from her. Then her lips pressed against mine, and lightning flashed through my blood.

A soft brush of her mouth against mine, a whisper of contact. Yet my blood went aflame. Heat blazed in the inch of space between us, threatening to set the hall afire.

With a gasp, she made to pull away. I clutched her hand tighter, blood rushing in my ears. Her face pinkened, and her mouth parted as she panted in rhythm to my heartbeat.

"Zair," I said hoarsely. Why did I crave another taste of her? "You infuriate me, say you hate me, and then kiss me. Why?"

She blinked as if drawn back to reality, and then leaned closer to my ear.

"Tell your silly ladyloves," she said indignantly, "that I'm nobody's whore."

With that, she pulled away, leaving her seat beside me to take another empty seat on the opposite table.

My forehead grooved at her statement. And then I noticed the girls opposite us staring daggers at Zair's back. Having grown up around a few entitled wealthy girls, it quickly came together. They hated that she'd had my attention tonight while I'd ignored them. They'd insulted her, and Zair decided to hit them where it would hurt most.

Whore. I clenched my fists in anger. The insult had cut her deeply. It was why she'd needed to retaliate. I turned to the young noblewomen, to the expectant smiles they sent me, and let disappointment and revulsion edge my face.

"Status alone doesn't show class," I said.

They gasped in affront, stunned that I would defend Zair. Cheeks flushing, they broke my stare and turned to the dais instead. I buried the impulse to look at Zair.

That kiss... while it had shaken me to my core, it had been nothing but a tool of vengeance for her. *Don't overthink it.*

Gritting my teeth, I forced my thoughts away from her. Now wasn't the time to be distracted.

The Royal Accountant stood from his table, and his assistants' bodies refilled my mind. Would Sarhedrin give up on his scheme now that this murder attempt had partly failed? Somehow I doubted it.

24

ZAIR

Through the strange uproar in the palace, I hurried to my rooms. My heart thundered in my ears, drowning out every sound and thought except one—I'd kissed Dathan Issachar. What had I been thinking? Yes, those girls had wounded me with their words and I'd had to strike back, to stand up for myself. But my choice of revenge still took me by surprise. I'd never acted that brazenly with a man before. My lips still tingled from the warmth of his, as if branded with his taste. Were all kisses this scorching and sweet at once?

Dozens of guards marched past with steely miens, snatching me from my thoughts. Ironteenth Fighters loomed over disgruntled chambermen in lounges, seeming to question them.

What was going on?

Did it have to do with the goblet of wine that Dathan stole from the Royal Accountant?

A familiar rumbling from the dunes began as I swerved onto a vacant passage and sighted sheer black wings.

Arno.

No doubt he'd intercepted my route, waiting to wring an explanation of the palace's climate from me. His golden eyes held mine and he tilted his head, beckoning me. I veered around fast. I would follow another passage—

Arms grabbed me. My back rammed against the wall of a dark alcove.

I'd barely registered the palace guards when the first woman demanded, "Tell me, just where did you get the poison from?"

My heart dropped to my feet.

They'd discovered the phial in my uniform and my mission to assassinate.

"Answer us!" The guard crushed my shoulder hard enough to pop the socket.

I stuttered, scrambling for calm. "Ma'am, I-I don't understand—"

"*Why* did you poison the accountants? What is your aim?" she barked.

What? Shivers worked through my body. "I've poisoned *no one*—"

She slammed me against the wall. "Tell me the truth!"

"I swear! I've poisoned no one!"

I expected more manhandling, but her barrage suddenly ceased.

Composed, she surveyed me shrewdly, and I understood. The barraging military tactic was to disorient and terrify until a culprit blurted out the truth.

They didn't *know* that I truly possessed deadly poison and weren't certain that *I* had killed anyone.

"Go ahead then. But beware." She held my gaze. "We'll be watching, aziza girl."

My limbs still trembled as I entered the students' lounge. I dropped into a settee facing a window. It was so calm that I knew they hadn't harassed my peers this way. Hadn't suspected them.

Dathan's threat replayed in my mind. His harsh reminder that I —my word—was inferior to his. To all of them.

We'll be watching.

Blast it. I had to do something to absolve myself as someone to watch. Something to remind them that I was merely a student and divert their attention from me.

An idea sparked. *The Best of Ten.*

Tomorrow, I had to win the Best of Ten contest for the protection it would bring. Thirty students from Thalesai's best academies would arrive at the Combat Arena near the plateaus from across the kingdom. Ten to compete for the prize of the best among the military academies, ten to compete among the healing academies, and another ten to compete among the engineering students.

Dathan and Ibhar's buff bodies flashed in my mind and the despair intensified. *Find the positives.* I had the same training they did, even without my Esan abilities that would be prohibited tomorrow. I could win tomorrow's contest and earn commendation, pulling myself out of this mire.

Stars shone over the city—I gazed at the heavens and prayed for miracles.

Mishan suddenly barged through the archway like a fox with fire on its tail. "There's trouble in Thalesai."

I jumped to my feet. "What is it?"

Lysias's door clicked behind me. She and Dathan stepped out.

My stomach plummeted. What were they doing together? Annoyed, I tamped down the strange feeling and the memory of our kiss. How he had responded to me, rather than pushed me away in disgust.

"Why are you yelling down the place, Mishan?" Lysias asked, her embroidered wrap fluttering in the dusty wind from the windows.

He glanced at the archway, moved further into the lounge and spoke lowly. "I was with the Third Councilor, trying to pick his brain over tea when a report came in."

"What report?" I pushed, growing impatient.

His throat bobbed, his eyes dark. "The mercenaries have struck again. Much worse this time."

My knees wobbled. Deafening roars heralded the sandstorm. Through the windows, a massive wave of dust and sand poured in from the dunes like a monstrous tide, drowning out Ari'el's lights.

Cries of panic echoed from visitors who must fear Armageddon had come. And didn't it feel like it?

Lysias and I hurried to shut the windows against the choking dust.

Dathan took an urgent step closer to Mishan. "Struck where? How?"

"Jalin Base." Mishan ran his hand through his ever-kempt

blonde hair. "*The* Jalin Base. They killed dozens of soldiers, abducted senior officers, stole lethal weaponry."

I fell a step backward as the words hit me like a rock. The military base in Jalin was one of the largest and strongest forts in the kingdom. It also had an experimentation site where engineers built deadly weaponry designed to ensure humans were formidable should the neighboring kingdoms break the Treaty and threaten war.

Now... now these *hideous* mercenaries were in possession of weapons of mass demolition.

"If we thought them volatile before..." I trailed off, as if not completing the statement that might make this nightmare disappear.

And my sister. Oh, Osime, had the mercenaries gone to take Sarai now? Blood drained from my face. No... no, if they had, my older sister would've come to get me.

Lysias slumped into a sofa and buried her face in her hands. "Saints."

"The situation is spiraling out of control," Mishan said. "But one thing is for certain, they didn't abduct officers or take those weapons incidentally."

No, these errant humans were preparing for more destruction of Thalesai.

"Did the Third Councilman say what the mercenaries' goal could be?" Dathan queried.

"The Third Councilman asked me to excuse them before the conversation got that far, said I couldn't tell anyone what I'd heard." He didn't look guilty for telling us, though.

"So the chambermen are still prioritizing the foreign ambassadors at a time like this," I spat with frustration.

In their bid to keep the foreigners in the dark, they won't sound the alarms and use every means to dig out the mercenaries. They won't look deeply into *how* the mercenaries acquired information that helped them penetrate one of our strongest military bases. Rather, they would keep their approach mild so the foreigners wouldn't sense that something was wrong.

Then, the mercenaries would get away. Again.

Could the mercenaries—and their palace enabler—have chosen

the coronation to land such an audacious attack because they knew the king would prioritize the foreigners' ignorance over the mercenaries?

"I can't imagine the might they have to break into Jalin Base," Lysias exclaimed.

"It must've been an ambush," Dathan decided, pacing.

I bit on my inner lip until it bled. My time was running out.

As if thinking the same, Dathan looked at me. The words rang silently between us. The mercenaries had been targeting schools and farming villages so far, but with these advanced weapons, greater institutions like Jalin Base would begin to fall.

The time to find the traitor in the Al'Qtraz just shortened.

25

DATHAN

Your family is here.

The words echoed in my head as I armored up. It had been too long since I last saw them. After the news about Jalin Base, after witnessing Sarhedrin's murders, I needed to ascertain they were alright.

"It's barely nine o'clock and we've filled up the Combat Arena," Ibhar said, vibrating with enthusiasm in the rooms on the arena's ground floor. It was serving as the kitting room for the ten military students contesting in today's Best of Ten.

The Combat Arena, with the Plateaus of Rahbat rising behind it, brimmed to its two-thousand people capacity.

"Don't forget it's a *friendly* competition between the top ten academies in Thalesai. A platform to celebrate the progress of education in Thalesai while displaying to the foreigners that Thalesai's future is bright," I muttered.

Ibhar grinned as he buckled his boots. "Only on the surface. We all know it's really a contest between the tribes. I'll prove today that yes, the Ussis have the best youths to occupy Chamber seats."

"It's *also* an opening for us to beat you elite slugs and claim your ranks," the Eladah Academy student said with a glower.

Ibhar howled in laughter and the medley of top military students—stocky, lithe, short, tall, fair and dark young men—from the non-elite schools bristled.

While Ahimoth, Gergesenes, and Nergal had the prime military academies in Thalesai, Eladah Military Academy, Bethel, and the other five were impressive military academies also worthy of recognition. Their students had traveled across the kingdom to contest in today's military challenge against Zair, Ibhar, and me.

I scanned them. None looked tired from their travels, only ravenous to win.

Nine of the best engineering schools—including Gergesenes, Nergal, and Ahimoth Engineering Academies—had also sent their reps to compete, along with Mishan, for the engineering scholars' category. And nine had come to join Lysias in contesting for the best healing student's prize.

"I heard the philosophy and general studies' scholars are still crying about their exclusion from the Best of Ten," Ibhar said with a grin.

The philosophy and general studies academies had their own contests and accolades, but weren't included in the Best of Ten. In Thalesai—a kingdom built on the foundation of warfare—military might and soldiers were its utmost priority. Followed by the engineers who crafted inventions to level the playing field with our neighbors and the healers who kept the soldiers alive. Philosophy and general studies were respected, but not prioritized fields.

Eladah rolled his eyes. "What could the philosophy and general studies students possibly have to show us at the coronation?"

Their school heads and tutors often protested their exclusion, but it hadn't changed anything.

I snorted at the Eladah student. "And you say *we* are arrogant."

"Oh, you are."

Eladah and Bethel Military Academies especially had always been hungry for our elite status, constantly looking for ways to outdo us in the field.

Lucky for me, Zair had not let the inter-school rivalry push her to expose my theft of the Royal Accountant's goblet.

Last night proved that Sarhedrin was a person to tail; he could be the key to finally rescuing Jaziah. It also confirmed that Zair *was* after the traitor in the palace. I'd seen it in her eyes when Mishan announced the attack on Jalin Base, just as she saw it in mine.

Part of me wanted to blast it to the sheols and offer that we allied, share what we'd uncovered so far and end the traitor before the mercenaries and their newly acquired weapons completely destroyed Thalesai.

But I'd vowed to Gergesenes' Commandant that I'd tell no soul of my mission. Besides, I still didn't know what Zair's end goal was. If she had a different agenda, anything that might spare the traitor the full weight of justice he deserved or cost Jaziah's freedom, I couldn't let her have him. I meant what I'd said at the temple. I had no intention of losing the traitor to her.

"Ey, Gergesenes," a deep voice called behind me.

My leather armor in Gergesenes' colors gleamed as I rounded on the Bethel student. He was Baihan too, but challenge blazed in his eyes. Today, we were only contenders.

"Bethel," I said.

He brushed invisible lint off my shoulder. "Watch your back in the pit today."

I scoffed, strapping on my double scabbards as I glanced behind him. "Watch for who?"

A laugh burst from a tall student. Ibhar gave a bear's bark.

Bethel flushed red as he moved for the exit behind the five other scholars in crisp uniforms and their weapons of choice.

"Pompous jerks," he muttered. "Don't say I didn't warn you."

I wasn't trying to be a pompous jerk—or maybe I was—but Ahimoth, Gergesenes, and Nergal were the elite military academies for a reason. I wasn't letting any of these young men steal Gergesenes' honor. Even more, the Commandant had sent a note that my family was here.

It was the first time my father would see me in my element. This was my chance to show him I was good at what I did. That this was my right path.

Ibhar frowned as he surveyed me. "What is with the new hairstyle?"

I brushed the hair hanging around my face, lessening the chances of unwanted recognition. "Like to keep the women intrigued."

I stepped into the overwarm morning and lingering dust from the sandstorm tickled my nose. The Combat Arena was a tiered, crescent-shaped structure with an open roof. The royal dais marched down in stenciled tiers at its apex, allowing the royals a perfect view of the pit. Students from different academies, along with families and excited citizens, filled hundreds of stone benches on either side of the dais.

Gergesenes' students stood out in rows of evening blue on the highest tier to the right. For a tick, I eagerly surveyed their rows for Jaziah. To wave at him. But reality quickly dawned, bringing with it an agonizing throb in my chest. *Hang on, Jaz.*

My schoolmates cheered, waving our banners of the hawk. "Issachar! Issachar!"

Their enthusiasm caught the arena like wildfire. Cheers broke out.

It hit me again. *I'd* been chosen over two hundred of my peers to represent the academy. Regardless of everything happening, I had to be present in this moment. To ignore for once the voice that reminded me I was a bad son for working so hard for any of this. Even though my ultimate goal was to protect my family.

"Can't believe we're performing before the king," the Eladah boy said with awe as he stood next to me, his weapons strapped onto his dark-orange leather.

Cheers from his schoolmates resounded in the steaming afternoon. He tried to contain it, but a happy grin curved his mouth.

"Feels like a dream," I agreed.

On the dais, the First Advisor leaned in to speak to the king. King Khasar's calm expression fell, replaced with dismay. He quickly concealed his alarm and nodded.

What was happening?

My stomach hardened as I noticed the heaviness hanging over the dais.

Eyes were the portals to a man's truth, and behind the calm smiles worn for the public, bleak emotions peeked. Military officers' noses flared with anger; dread dimmed councilors' faces; advisors' mouths quivered as they joined heads to discuss. And each time they glanced at the king, their faces filled with doubt.

Blast. With the successful attack on the Jalin Military Base, it had to be because they didn't trust the king to take the right steps that would crush the mercenaries—who were now as well-armed as our soldiers.

"Part of me feels guilty," Eladah muttered. "Our mates are in captivity, and the king is celebrating a coronation."

I might've shared that thought if anything about King Khasar struck me as selfish. All I saw when I looked at him was a young man trying to find his footing on a field that was bigger and more volatile than anything he'd ever walked. He was trying to keep his court from falling apart, especially with this new land Sarhedrin had said the tribes were hungry for, while also trying to keep the rest of his kingdom from destruction.

"I want to trust that he's doing the best he can," I said, "and that the rest of us must rise, too, to save Thalesai."

"And where's the queen in all this?" Eladah pushed.

"She likely had other matters to see to." I shrugged, but my thoughts were jumping to the pieces scattered across my mind. A queen shouldn't miss any event of the coronation. Why was she suddenly absent the morning after Jalin Base was taken down? Away... when every member of the three Chambers was here. What was she up to?

"Would she also miss her *vyji* tomorrow for those 'matters'?" Eladah murmured. "Typical Ussi arrogance."

I stiffened. "Don't slander the queen."

Eladah bristled but had the grace to blush.

Ibhar stepped out of the kitting room and Ahimoth erupted, chanting his name so loudly it likely echoed across Ari'el. He grinned and lifted his bent fingers like bear claws.

"The military students will contest in two challenges. Their challenges have been chosen to display their aim, persistence, quick wit, and strength," the First Advisor explained to the arena, but focused on the foreigners. "The first is an archery challenge, and the second is an open battle."

People cheered because the military students in action was what many came to witness today.

"Once the military students conclude their challenges, our young healers and engineers will hold their contests next. Theirs will be presentations of their personal projects to improve Thalesai in their various fields. Whoever has the most innovative project from the healing and engineering categories will have it sponsored by the Majesties."

Cheers arose from the students of the healing and engineering schools.

Mishan, Lysias, and eighteen other students in their fields filled the canopied bench to our left. Despite the dust, their uniforms were spotless, their boots tapping eagerly. The prizes were a great privilege *and* a career boost they were ravenous for. I was growing fond of Mishan and Lysias, but my loyalties were to the hawks first. I gave the Gergesenes' students who sat side-by-side nods.

"Let's make today Gergesenes' day," I called to them. "For honor."

With grins, they nodded back and repeated our slogan, "For honor!"

Zair stepped out of the kitting room in sleek black leather with Nergal's silver emblem embroidered over her heart. As the only girl amongst nine boys, she'd been given a separate room to armor up. The students of Nergal didn't cheer for her, but despite their reservations, they leaned forward in their seats with wide-eyed expectation. No academy wanted to lose any of the categories.

Zair cast a sweeping but brief stare in the direction of her schoolmates. She didn't look at all in the direction of the Nergal's healing and engineering students, and they sternly kept their faces away from her.

She already wasn't expecting any acknowledgment from them, I realized.

I surveyed her determined expression. "Still hating me today, Nergal?"

Her stare perched on my lips and quickly darted away. "Very much."

I leaned close to whisper into her ear. "Mutual. Very mutual."

She glowered and fled over to Bethel's end. I grinned. Two soldiers led the ten of us into the wide, sandy pit at the center of the arena. There, a white line had been painted seventy meters from the five targets with four colors. A white round board with a black outermost ring, a yellow middle ring, and a red dot at the very center. I honed in on the red dot, pulling on every archery lesson since year-one.

Bow and arrows weren't my weapons of choice—swords were—but archery was one of the main skills Gergesenes honed in us.

Zair, however... she had stepped out of that kitting room with a bow as her weapon of choice.

The arena hummed and rustled with the crowd's eagerness. The arena soldiers gave us instructions, facilitating the challenge. King Khasar conversed with his brother, pointing at us and nodding as they talked.

"The archery contest will proceed in two sets," the Kwali corporal explained to us. "The first five of you, stand here on the white line."

"Many of you have worked hard for years to be here," the Mizsab corporal said as we arranged ourselves smartly. "Even if you don't win, let your skill reflect your years of training. Do not embarrass the military field."

"Yes, sir," echoed eagerly among us.

Ibhar stood with the first set of competitors, in the middle of the four other students. Zair, myself, Eladah, Bethel, and Xei stood to the side, observing our competitors as we waited. More soldiers came and armed the five students. They gave them strong teakwood bows and quivers with three arrows each sticking out.

"Each target has three rings," the First Advisor modulated, gesturing his hand to the targets. The arena listened raptly. "The five students who shoot all three arrows closest to the red dot—the *center*—will win this round and proceed to the next challenge. The students whose arrows are farthest from the target's center, however, will be eliminated from the challenge."

I shifted on my foot, noticing that almost all the military contestants did the same. Elimination after the first round? Absolutely not.

Zair glanced at me, then at Ibhar, like we were the competition that mattered most to her. I smiled. Wouldn't let them know they were my main threats too.

"Ready your bows! Nock!" the Kwali corporal instructed.

Ibhar kept his chin up as he reached over his shoulder for an arrow and nocked it. The bear could be silent and focused when victory was on the line, it seemed. The other students took solid postures and nocked their arrows, except the rangy Novana student whose shoulders were bent.

"Aim. Shoot!"

The audience held their breaths. Arrows flew and stabbed the targets, over and again until all the five quivers were exhausted. I stepped forward, surveying each target. Yells of rejoicing and disappointment erupted as everyone gauged the results.

Ibhar was the only student with two arrows piercing the edges of the red dot on his target. The last arrow had thrust the outermost ring.

Ahimoth whooped in joy. Ibhar threw up his fist in the air with a grin, then looked hopefully at the royal dais.

"His victory and procession into the last challenge is as good as sealed," Zair murmured.

I didn't like Ibhar, but I had to admit he had earned it.

The others' shots varied from only one arrow on the innermost ring to all three on the outermost ring. None had gotten as close as Ibhar's and left the white line with frowns, shamed flushes, or hopeful smiles.

"He's good," Bethel murmured.

"Maybe to *you*, slacker," the Xei student grinned. Like Zair, his weapon of choice was a bow and arrow. "My father is the head of the archers at the palace's gates. I would have to change my last name if I don't win this archery round, and I like my last name very much."

I wore a grieved expression. "Then I apologize in advance for stripping you of your last name. No hard feelings."

"Me too," Bethel chirped.

"And me too," Eladah added somberly with a hand to his chest.

Xei grinned, completely unfazed. "Prepare to weep, boys."

The excitement rose again as our set walked up to the white line. Students from our schools cupped their mouths and yelled at us not to fail them. They shouted our slogans down to us.

"For honor!" "Onward always!" "Triumphing together!"

A rush went over my skin as the arena soldiers armed three of us. Zair and the Xei student already had bows and arrows that, after a brief inspection of the Xei student's and a longer inspection of Zair's, were confirmed fit to use.

The arena's noise lowered to a hum. The military head on the dais watched with intimidating concentration, especially the archers. I placed my feet shoulder-width apart, flattened my back, and tightened my core—a technique that began a throb in my stomach but could make all the difference. I took a steadying breath as I nocked my first arrow. To my right, Zair nocked her arrow, too, her body calm with focus. No one in this set had poor stance, not even feet placed too far apart or bent knees. Determination surged higher in me.

"Ready your bows! Nock!"

I drew my bowstring, aware of all the expectations resting on me from Gergesenes, of the soldiers gauging our stances, but I closed them out. Shut out the noise and everything but that red bull's eye seventy meters ahead.

"Aim. Shoot!"

I released the bowstring with a snap and arrows zinged through the air for the targets. I nocked my second arrow and fired, then the last one.

I loosened the tautness in my stomach, releasing a bracing breath as I took in my target. Two arrows protruded from the red dot at the center and the last arrow stabbed just outside it. *Yes!* Elation surged in my chest. With a wide grin, I looked to my schoolmates. Gergesenes' students were on their feet, jumping and howling in joy. I lifted a hand in a wave.

Other schools screamed or groaned as they gauged which schools would be leaving the contest and which would make it to the next round. Eladah and Bethel students looked moments away from ripping off their uniforms and dancing around the arena in their undergarments.

I looked back at the other targets and Xei had two of his arrows on the outermost ring and the last on the ground. Eladah and Bethel each scored an arrow in the red dot and the others close on the yellow middle rings. And Zair... had three arrows crammed into the red dot.

All three hit bull's eyes.

Stomach knotting, I turned and stared at her.

Deep relief softened the lines of her body more than joy as she strapped her bow back on. Nergal's students appeared torn on their rows as they joined heads and jerked their chins at Zair; reluctantly joyful. Unwilling to openly celebrate their Esan schoolmate.

"You... won," I said in disbelief, sprouts of light unfurling in my gut.

"*Three* arrows in the target's center!" Xei exclaimed, only just deigning to look at Zair's target.

Eladah, Bethel, and Xei's expressions alternated from shock to affront. High-ranked soldiers' on the dais had their eyebrows either joined to their hairlines or lowered as they absorbed her flawless accuracy. The aziza dignitaries discussed, pointing at Zair's target and frowning, while the shapeshifters and wraith lords appeared grudgingly impressed.

Swallowing, she turned from the dais and gave the three of us a smug little bow. "Don't look so surprised. Bows and arrows are my weapons of choice."

Xei's shoulders slumped even lower. He gripped his bow, seeming like he wanted the ground to open up and swallow him.

"I'm sorry you have to change your last name," Bethel said with a sniff, ruthless.

Zair's focus was on me. She glanced at my target again. "Impressive, Gergesenes. Really impressive, but Nergal is taking the prize home today."

I straightened my back, flicking up a brow as resolve burned in my chest. To honor my academy and win my father's approval. "Not a chance, Nergal. This is Gergesenes' win."

26

DATHAN

The eliminated military students left the fighting pit with low gazes, even as the First Advisor commended them for their efforts. It left Gergesenes, Nergal, Ahimoth, Bethel, and Eladah in the last round of the contest.

The three elite academies had made it to the final round.

The steep competition delighted the people, but it irritated Ibhar to no end that he had come third place after Zair and me. His smile was gone. He looked ready to pounce on us. I returned the look, but with a grin, as the five of us returned to the gate of the fighting pit.

"I'll wipe the ground with that grin of yours," Ibhar muttered. He halted as if recalling something and turned back to the kitting room.

"You never managed to at butteball," I said as he jogged past me. "What makes you think you will now?"

Bethel snickered. The five of us had been allowed a brief break as the arena workers prepared the pit for the next contest. While we'd mingled with our mates in the other category, Zair had kept to herself and others had given her wide berths. No celebrations for the student who won the first round.

I wiped the sweat off my forehead with my sleeve, recalling her smug bow to me. It bothered me that she didn't receive praise for her win, but I didn't sympathize enough to let her take the overall victory for the once-in-decades contest.

The First Advisor introduced the next challenge to the quiet arena. "The final competition for our military students will further test their strength, skill, and perseverance."

"Demonic displays are against the rules, Esan girl," Bethel mocked.

She flinched and I barely held back from hitting him.

"I didn't need demons to beat you in the first round, and I don't need them to now," she said.

"Ha. Who are you deceiving? You used your Esan spells in that round," he retorted.

Zair's eyes widened. She wasn't allowed to use magic today, when none of her fellow contestants possessed magic. If any of the officials overheard Bethel's accusation, it wouldn't be hard for them to choose to believe she won by cheating.

"You didn't win the first round," I snapped at him. "Take it like a combatant and stop whining like a baby about it, or wear my fist's print on your face."

Bethel, Eladah, and Zair stared with shock at my defense of her.

Bethel's mouth tightened. He glowered at me and I growled low in my throat.

He decided Zair was a better mark for his frustration. "You think having Gergesenes defend you will make you win again?"

"I don't need anyone to defend me. And my drive, what I stand to lose and gain today, will make me win."

Bethel fumed, completely missing Zair's real answer. The tension in my shoulders loosened. She wasn't fighting to win only for Nergal's honor. Like me, she also needed to win... for approval. If my father could see today that I was a skilled soldier, he might finally approve of my direction to become a protector for our family.

"You will not win," Bethel said firmly. "I'm tired of being the best in my academy only for it to mean nothing, really, because I have no chance at an Ironteenth rank or becoming a military leader like you elite slugs."

Eladah gave a somber nod, but after his callous comments to Zair, Bethel's speech didn't move me.

"Then win fair and square," I said. "I doubt the Ironteenth Fighters are looking for pathetic people who can't lose gracefully, anyhow."

Ibhar returned to join us in front of the pit's waist-high gate. His new weapon of choice was a morning-star. He let it dangle menacingly as he squared his shoulders. Eladah turned grim.

Images of Zair falling victim to the thing hardened my stomach.

From butteball, I'd studied Ibhar's tactics. He ruthlessly preyed on those he considered weakest first and worked his way up to the toughest, eliminating all in his path until he won. While the rules said we couldn't kill our opponents, there was no rule against inflicting harm. If you didn't want to be harmed, fight better than your opponents. The students needed to display might and resilience, and if there was one thing Ibhar liked, it was inflicting harm on people he felt threatened by.

Zair isn't weak.

Indeed. I shook off the thoughts. If there was anything I should worry about today, it was impressing my father. I scanned the tiered seats for my family, although it was futile. Their faces would be covered with veils, presumed to be protection from the sun.

The First Advisor continued to moderate. "Our aziza neighbors from the south have generously provided the ball for the first contest." He gestured to the glowing, magical object darting in swift circles around the pit.

The aziza nobles accepted the applause gracefully, imperial wings fluttering.

"The first student to catch the ball wins."

The *ball* resembled head-sized ice, white and floating with an unnatural alertness. Like a soul was trapped inside and scared of being caught.

"*Eish*, that thing looks disturbing," Eladah said, rubbing his hands in anticipation.

My attention shifted as someone walked up to Zair. He was tall, lithe, and moved with a sleek gracefulness that bordered on surreal.

A shimmering scarf draped his head, concealing his face, but his wings gave away his aziza nationality.

Ibhar spat. "The azishit seeking magic from her spawns to help her win, huh? We'll see."

I shot him a glare but his determined attention had returned to the prize.

The aziza male spoke softly to Zair as he drew her quiver off her shoulder. He held out a black quiver with longer, carved arrows and steel arrowheads so sharp they could cut one's eyes if they stared too long. Zair replied and his mouth curved. She surveyed the quiver suspiciously yet intrigued. To my surprise, she accepted it.

She looked up at his glowing face and, was she... *blushing*?

My mood instantly soured. Why would she let this foreigner switch her weapons? Zair didn't trust people. She didn't let people into her space, least of all azizas. Yet there she was, standing only a few inches away from Lord I'm-So-Intense-Look-At-My-Shiny-Arrows.

My thoughts drifted to our kiss last night, her softness as her heart pounded against mine, and my jaw stiffened. The kiss was nothing but a point made. She thought those girls at our table were snobs? She was the one who never let anyone close.

The aziza male ambled away. I seethed with an emotion I didn't care to place.

Three arena soldiers went to Zair and inspected the new weapons for the telltale scent and sheen of aziza magic. Finding nothing concerning, they handed them back to her. Reluctant amazement lingered on their faces over the immaculate design of the weapons as they left.

King Khasar stood, drawing everyone's attention. "Scholars. Remember that while you wear different academy badges, you are one people under one banner. May the best Scholar win." He smiled and gave the signal.

Cheering abounded. The half-gate swung open and we swarmed into the pit. The ball zipped away, weaving around boulders scattered across the pit in streaks of frosty white.

Zair ran after it with surprising speed, her weapons untouched on her back, her aim clearly to get to the ball first.

I ran atop a boulder that was close to the ball, leaving my competitors behind as I lunged into the air and somersaulted over a vertical rock. The ball jerked from my reach and streaked faster as if in panic. My strategy was to pursue the ball while clearing out the competition—also known as Bethel. He rammed his shoulder into mine, nearly overtaking me. I rammed back into him, putting my entire body into it.

With a shocked grunt, he flew and collided with a curved rock.

"Curse you, Gergesenes!" he cried, clutching his torso.

Why, that was... extremely easy. I flashed him a grin and swerved around a rock for the frantic ball.

Zair ran past Bethel and ducked briefly beside him. A blade glinted in her hand as stood and she charged for me.

People gasped. "She took his sword!"

Bethel screamed at her, his face red with humiliation. Few things were more shameful to a soldier than losing his sword to his opponent.

But his wounded ego was the last thing on Zair's mind, and mine, as she swung the adasword at me. I whirled on my heels, spinning out of range, and pulled one of my adaswords. Boots gnashed on the sand as I blocked her next slash. Steel clashed against steel. She gritted her teeth from the impact, but after weeks away from school training, the familiar reverberation up my arms lit a rush under my skin.

She charged again and I parried the strike and the next, slipping into the exhilarating dance of swordplay.

"I thought bows and arrows are your weapon of choice," I called as I lunged and steel crashed together. "Or did you just want to humiliate Bethel?"

"You all had chances to showcase your archery skills in the first round," she said, her breaths fast as she blocked my next thrust. "Now you're showcasing your swordsmanship."

"You plan to show that you're a dynamic warrior too. Using me," I said drily through my teeth.

"Oblige me."

Our swords met in a slam, the sharp edges scraping against each other.

"Not today," I said.

My feet braced, I pushed against her sword. She stumbled two steps back, then dug her heels in the sand. Her hands trembled against my strength. She gritted her teeth, golden eyes of determination locked against mine, sweat slipping down our faces. Fire crackled between us. The arena shouted in intrigue.

I increased my force, pushed my sword harder, a smile growing on my face as her sword went lower.

"Perhaps, you should've stuck with your arrows."

Zair withdrew.

Rather than risk defeat too soon, she had the sense to swerve to my left and bolt for the ball.

"Smart choice," I murmured, sheathed my sword, and took off after her.

Swinging around, she grabbed an arrow from her quiver, aligned her body, and fired at me. I veered from her shot and dashed after the ball from another route. We could have a rematch another time.

Ibhar concentrated on eliminating competition as I'd expected. A few paces behind, he swung his morning-star at Eladah. The Mizsab boy ducked in time, avoiding a dent to his skull. Before he could recover, Ibhar charged forward and rammed his shoulder into his stomach. The crowd gasped as Eladah slammed against a boulder and crumpled almost lifelessly.

With only three of us standing, Ibhar lanced like a hungry bear for Zair.

Zair spotted him, unhooked her weapon and oriented herself to his form. She fired two arrows at once, forcing Ibhar to halt. Each arrow landed exactly an inch from his boots, close enough to warn him off but not too close that it impaled him.

Not many soldiers could pull off the flawless precision. No student I knew could.

As her shiny new arrows flew in twos and formed a perfect cage around Ibhar, high-ranked soldiers on the dais watched with increasing admiration.

Ibhar changed course, dipping between slanting rocks to dodge the arrows flying at him. He sighted me. I'd advanced far past them, running at full speed for the drifting ball.

"Remember butteball?" I flashed him a grin and increased my pace.

I reached out for the ball. A body jammed into me from behind, flinging me off my feet. My chest met with the hard ground and I grunted. *No time to dally*. I flipped onto my back, just as a morning-star swung for my face.

"This *isn't* butteball, Issachar," Ibhar crowed with triumph.

Dust sprayed as I rolled away from impact. The spiked ball crashed into the ground beside me like Ibhar would've happily buried my face in the earth.

Excitable gasps rushed over the arena.

I jumped to my feet, yanking out my two adaswords from their scabbards with a flourish. "Let's dance, Ahimoth."

Anger at my swift recovery reddened his face. "Prepare to lose, ricemaggot!"

The slur ignited a burst of flames behind my eyes. He attacked.

The ball zapped from us as if to save itself.

Ibhar expertly dodged my strikes and moved in, primed to crush the Baihan boy and show the world that, in all things, Ussis were superior.

If only he knew.

Our weapons clanged and tangled. I feinted a low attack but quickly changed to a high slice that could've removed his head if I'd wanted to kill him. He growled as I lifted my strike at the last second. The crowds moved to the edge of their seats as Ibhar slung his morning star for my legs. I leaped like a lizard and used his bent shoulder as a step before I flipped over his back. Landing gracefully behind him, I struck his armed hand with my hilt. He yelped, barely kept his grip on his weapon as he swung around

Ibhar was doubtlessly skilled, but he relied too much on force. I knew how to use force, but also when to be nimble. I parried his strikes, sidestepping deftly, then launched into a relentless thrust. I closed in on him and forced him on the defense.

The audience started screaming their heads off. Ibhar and I swung *our* heads. While we were busy dueling in a racing contest, Zair had closed in on the errant ball.

The little fox.

At once, we sheathed our weapons and bolted for her.

On the first tier of benches closest to the pit, some people jumped, cheering at the top of their lungs for Zair. Her family?

Ibhar tackled Zair, threw her roughly to the ground, and straddled her. Dirt sprayed. Ahimoth students whooped. The audience cheered good-naturedly as Zair's cunning plan to exploit our distraction was foiled.

But the hair on my skin stood because when it came to competitions, Ibhar did nothing good-naturedly.

He threw fierce punches. Zair blocked most with her joined arms. Digging her back into the ground like a worm, she wriggled her hips to create space and broke free of him.

Unbalanced, Ibhar landed on his backside, clearly caught off his guard. Nergal's students laughed.

The crowd seemed grudgingly impressed by the Esan girl.

Nergal cheered louder now, raising their fox banners. Their Commandant was noticeably absent, surely covered for by teachers. Zair wiped the blood off her mouth and looked at her hooting schoolmates. Happiness lit her eyes to have people cheer passionately for her.

Alright. She was safe from Ibhar. *I* had no intention of losing to her.

I scanned the dusty pit for the ball. There it was. Buzzing above three mighty boulders stacked up like stairs.

I bounced on my heels in anticipation of victory. Challenge filled Zair's face. "Hail my name when I get that medal, Gergesenes!"

"Kiss me again when I win it, Nergal!" I winked and broke into a run for the ball.

Zair followed beside me. Voices squealed over our race. We snaked around, jumped over, and ran atop boulders, seeking advantageous trails to overtake the other. I outpaced her by a few feet.

One moment, she was gaining on me. In the next, she flew off the ground with a startled cry. Her head made contact with a boulder.

Ibhar was on her in a heartbeat. Sweating, his knees straddled and caged her. His fists rained blows as dust flared.

They weren't the blows of a boy temporarily disarming his

opponent. Each blow carried the force of an enraged animal trying to break its prey.

Ibhar was furious that Zair had made a fool of him when she'd displaced him. Now, he wanted to disgrace her. It was why he chose to pin her down rather than spar one-on-one. Nothing killed a soldier more than helplessness.

With each blow Zair didn't manage to dodge, the cheering dwindled into gasps and, soon, a protest against Ibhar's outright brutality. Ahimoth students, though, were like rabid dogs, hailing Ibhar on.

I slowed to a halt as my mind zapped back to the worst night of my life nine years ago. My sister and I held hands, running through the darkness to lose the armed men chasing us. One of them plucked Asahel from beside me, flinging her so hard her head rammed into a rock. She howled in pain and terror. He'd straddled her as Ibhar now straddled Zair, while his accomplice dragged me away screaming. Hating myself for being too weak to save my sister.

A harsh cry ripped from Zair as Ibhar landed a blow to her chest. Like it was a drum he wanted to burst his fist through.

A leash snapped in me. I lunged for Ibhar, throwing him off her.

He'd barely hit the ground before my own fist flew at his face. Blood and spittle sprayed.

Face bloody, he flipped me over. I scrambled to my feet and dived for him, shoving him against a rock. The rock tumbled over from the force of the collision. He grunted in pain. Satisfaction eased bits of my anger over his assault on Zair. Over what was done to my sister years ago.

We both caught a figure moving—more like staggering—across the pit.

Zair. She was close to the ball, climbing up to it. Sheols, the girl was relentless.

Ibhar growled, "No way!"

He ran after her. I tackled him, throwing my might into pinning him down. He screamed at me to get off him. Clawed at my face until blood spilled down my brows. I held firm. Zair caught and restrained the ball.

First Advisor Maachah jumped up from his chair. "We have a winner!"

Unlike the archery round, the arena exploded in cheers for Zair.

Dirt and blood covered Zair's face, yet as she watched thousands of people jubilating for her, her smile was the brightest I'd ever seen it.

That smile. Something gentle swelled in my chest.

Torso heaving, I pushed off from a raging Ibhar.

At the movement, Zair's head snapped to me. Ibhar shoved at my shoulders until I stumbled backward, cursing at me.

"You let her win! You let her win, you bastard hawk!"

Understanding dawned. Her smile died and her face shuttered in that way I was starting to detest. She turned, back to the applause, but the happiness had left her face.

I moved to seek my family out in the loud crowd. Why on earth did I give up the chance to win, to impress my father and bring honor to Gergesenes, for a girl who had declared she hated me? I must've lost my blasted mind.

Their faces partly revealed so I could see them, my mother and sister waved heartily. Warmth filled my chest, and a grin broke free as Asahel placed her fingers to her mouth and whistled a celebratory sound. My mother and sister apparently didn't get the gist that I had lost. My grin faded, though, at the sight of my father seated beside my mother, his face grim.

THE NEXT HALF hour flew by. Zair received the medal from the Magistrate and won the Nergal Military Academy the funds for a major school project of the Commandant's choice. Nergal students and their parents went crazy in jubilation. It was the Nergal Military Academy's first win at the Best of Ten in the three categories. And while people presumed Zair was Esan, Nergal was Baihan-dominated so the Baihans, too, were having a jolly time over the win.

The other academies cheered with good sportsmanship, all except Ahimoth. In their red and black, they appeared mutinous over Ibhar's loss.

Shortly after, Mishan took to the pit for his presentation. A platform had been set before the dais so the royals, chambermen, and foreigners could clearly hear the students' innovative ideas to change the world.

I waited outside the kitting room, in no mood to share it with Ibhar. He'd want to rage at me for letting Zair win, and my Ibhar-tolerance cup was at dregs-level.

The arena calmed its noise as Mishan spoke about the device he was designing. "The goal of this project is to build humans a vehicle that navigates the skies as easily as we navigate the ground."

I lifted my brows. He addressed thousands with admirable self-assurance. Faces filled with wonder, intrigue, pride—from his schoolmates—and disconcertment, especially from the azizas. The only beings built to fly amongst us.

"Impossible," the aziza ambassador decided.

Mishan just smiled at the challenge. The nine other engineering students who waited to give their presentations—including Gergesenes' Engineering Academy—tilted their heads or knitted their foreheads as they listened closely to him. His invention intrigued me enough to shift my staunch loyalties a little from my Gergesenes' peer to him.

Imagine if humans could... fly. It would strengthen us in ways I couldn't even explain.

Royal attendants shared his sketches of the vehicle on the dais. He had been sketching those for days in our lounge, not allowing us to see even a glimpse of it. The azizas surveyed the sketch. Displeasure hardened their perfect faces.

Can't stand the idea of humans sharing your unique ability, can you?

Shifters who could shift into winged animals snarled at the sketches, hissing to each other. King Khasar and Ambassador Caiphas leaned forward in their ornate chairs, intrigued as Mishan explained his progress so far.

Ibhar stepped out of the kitting room in a clean mufti. We didn't exchange a glance as I left the arena and went in.

I washed fast in the tub, bruises and cuts stinging in the hot water. My family wouldn't stay until the end of the event. They'd seen my performance. They would rather leave while most people were still seated. It left no time to chat with the Eladah and Bethel students as I flung on my breezy trousers and embroidered tunic, or remain for the rest of the engineering students' presentations.

They hung their heads as they drew on their clothes.

"Can't believe a *girl* won the Best of Ten," Bethel muttered as I exited the kitting room.

A small laugh left me. He'd been busy marking me, when the real threat was a slip of a girl who never let anyone get away with underestimating her.

My family waited in one of the three passages leading out of the arena. My mother beamed, a silver veil concealing most of her styled, curly hair that was as golden-brown as the dunes. "Dathan!"

A daughter of gentry, my mother was a graceful beauty. The first time my friends saw her, they'd gone slack-jawed, convinced themselves that she was my aunt and insisted that I told them she was unmarried. Her height, combined with my father's, was the reason they had such tall children.

"It's been too long, *mihe*." She hugged me and my very soul calmed. Her presence felt like coming home.

"I've missed you too, ma."

Safe. They were all safe.

Her silvery brocade skirts glimmered as she leaned back to survey me. "You've grown even taller." Her voice wobbled.

"Ma, don't cry," I groaned as I brushed a finger over her cheek. She had a tendency to cry every time she saw me after long semesters.

"I won't," she promised, smiling instead. "You were so fierce in the pit. Did you hear my cheering? I said, 'Get them, Dathan, get them!'"

I laughed. She was the light in our home. The spark that turned sorrows to smiles.

"She's not joking. Even when I told her you were trying to win a ball, *not* start a brawl."

A grin splayed across my face. "Prosperity, Asa..."

My older sister collided into me, her amethyst veil slipping off her sandy-brown hair. "Look at my baby brother representing the whole of Gergesenes at the king's coronation!"

I started grinning, then grimaced when *all* of her words sank in. "'Baby brother' who's a foot taller."

Our mother chuckled. Our father remained where he stood, watching. Not saying a word.

Asahel rolled her eyes as she pulled away, ruffling my damp hair to disarm me. "You can never outgrow your *jidi*, baby brother."

Her eyes, the same hazel as mine, sparkled with life and excitement. So much more than the last time I saw her months ago. Each time I saw my sister, she seemed less controlled by the fear of being found by her assaulter. Each time, it eased bits of the wound in my heart.

As if sensing the direction of my thoughts, she smiled softly. "I'm fine," she whispered. "And did that Ahimoth boy have to get pummeled that hard?"

She'd known. When I threw Ibhar off Zair. She'd known what I'd been reliving in that moment. Why I snapped as I did.

"Oh, he's a worm," I assured her.

"Nath..." She hesitated, her eyes sorrowful. "You've heard about Jaziah?"

I swallowed and gave a nod, unable to speak.

Despair filled her face. "His father's agony worsens with each day that he and papa's efforts to find Jaziah fail."

I forced my throat to work, forced optimism into my voice. "Jaziah is strong. He'll fight to survive and we'll find him."

I'll make sure of it.

"Asahel, let Dathan greet your father," my mother chided softly.

The moment I'd been dreading.

I stepped away from Asahel and faced my father, Luke Issachar. His sable boubou rippled in the warm breeze sweeping through the passage. A scarf hung over his head, partly concealing his chiseled features. The last time I saw him I'd been an inch shorter than he was. Now, I stood at the same height as him, essentially his replica.

My mother remarked as much, her smile hopeful and worried. The strain between my father and I always ate at her.

I leaned over to place both hands on my father's feet and then to my chest in greeting. "Father."

He took my hands in his, surveying my split knuckles. "These need to be bandaged. They could get infected otherwise."

My father was a healer through and through, so it was natural that he'd be concerned about the beating I'd taken. But I didn't want the healer today. I wanted my father. Even if I didn't win, I wanted him to commend me for being *here*. For being chosen amongst hundreds for the king's coronation.

My throat tightened, and I retrieved my hands. "I'll have it seen to at the palace," I said, quietly prompting him to say something *more*.

He knew this. In his eyes, I could see that he knew how much I wanted to hear him say that he understood. That he supported me. Was proud of me.

He looked away, and something splintered in my chest.

Blinking, as if to hold back whatever emotions ran through him, he cleared his throat and said to my mother, "You've seen your son in action. We should leave now."

I'd suspected, but the confirmation that my mother was the reason he was here—not me—pierced my chest. I kept my gaze on the ground.

My mother drifted over and kissed my cheek. She said staunchly, "I'm very proud of you, *mihe*."

I forced my mouth to curve and gave a nod. With a gentle squeeze on my hand, she went over to my father.

"I'll meet you by the carriage," Asahel said to them.

My father glanced worriedly at my knuckles, and with a nod at me, he led my mother down the passage.

The moment they were gone, Asahel said, "It's been five months since we last saw you, with Gergesenes allowing you students only two breaks a year. He constantly asked us about our letters to you. How you were doing? I'd hoped the distance would thaw him when we saw you today."

I scoffed at the idea of my father missing me. "I'm sure he was just worried I was doing something that would bring problems to him."

Asahel sighed. "Saints, you Sosthene men. He misses you but is too bullheaded to show it. And it wouldn't have killed *you* to tell him you missed him."

I pressed my lips together.

Asahel sighed exasperatedly this time. "For what it's worth, mother is going to give him five sheols for his behavior when we reach home."

My mouth quirked at the image of my mother ragging him out, but then I shook my head. "I don't want them fighting because of me. I've brought enough trouble to our family."

Asahel smacked my arm. "*Do not* think like that!"

I was rubbing my assaulted arm when heels clicked against the concrete floor. Over my shoulder, I spotted Zair coming from the arena's end. From the entryway, four people hurried in. A small girl ran down and flung herself into Zair's arms with a happy cry.

Following closely behind, two females soon gathered Zair. Zair smiled broadly, surrounded by people who had to be her family. Their veils slid off with exchanged hugs, revealing midnight hair and a resemblance so uncanny they would be quadruplets if they were the same age.

"Ah, the girl my baby brother sacrificed victory for," Asahel said beside me.

I glanced briefly at my sister. "She won by her own merit."

Zair's mother's hands fluttered over Zair's face and the bruises already forming there.

Asahel shrugged. "I'm not contesting that. She was as relentless as a tiger. But I know how competitive *you* can be, especially when it comes to all things Gergesenes. Toward the end, it hadn't seemed like you'd been fighting to win as much as you'd been keeping that Ahimoth brute away from her."

"If she heard you say that, she'd never speak to me again," I said drily.

"Considering she has Esan eyes, chances are she can already hear me, right, Dathan?" Asahel asked.

A loaded question. I glanced at my sister again, gauging if she was hateful of Zair.

Asahel only cautioned, "Our parents would never approve. Our family can't afford that kind of attention."

My gut tightened. "It's *nothing* like that. She'd like nothing more than to knock me on my behind."

"A girl who holds her own against your notorious charms," Asahel said, impressed. "I respect that."

"I knew you would," I mumbled.

Asahel held my arm, making me turn to her. "Have there been any incidents while staying in the palace? Any risks of recognition?"

My heart softened. "A few close calls, but I'm careful, Asahel. I would never let harm come to our family."

"I trust you. I should go." She planted a kiss on my cheek. "Don't stay away too long, Dathan. We miss you."

I nodded. With a smile, she left to find our parents.

I released a long breath as dust blew across the vacant entryway. Their visit eased some of my anxiety over the tragedy at Jalin Base. The mercenaries would be plotting another attack, but for now my family was safe.

I pivoted to where Zair's father had joined their hugging group. I couldn't have any feelings for Zair Nebah. Being at this coronation ceremony was for *Jaziah* and the other students suffering out there. Not to be distracted by a woman who pursued the same goal I did.

Yet I couldn't quite say what urged my steps in their direction. Maybe it was the way Zair smiled at them. A smile she never gave anyone else, and the sudden need in me to experience it. Or maybe after meeting my father, I wanted to be around a parent who was proud of his child's choices. Whichever the reason was, I soon found myself behind Zair with her family staring wide-eyed at me.

27

ZAIR

"Prosperity upon your day, Nebah family."

Dathan's rich voice rolled over my shoulder to my family and I froze.

Even with our constant dread over Sarai's marking, they gave Dathan surprised but welcoming smiles. My mother's hands had cupped my face as she'd fretted over my bruises—which hurt like the sheols. On seeing Dathan, she brought them to her chest.

Their surprise to see someone my age around me was almost embarrassing, but then again, I'd never introduced them to any friends before. I'd never had one.

"Prosperity to you too. How are you?" my mother responded to Dathan, sliding me an intrigued look.

"As fine as I can be after your daughter ruthlessly punctured my ego in the pit, ma'am," Dathan joked respectfully.

My mother chuckled. My father surveyed Dathan with raised brows, a protective strain in his shoulders.

Of everyone, my mother wanted the most for me to make friends at school. When I told her I'd given up trying because no one responded kindly, she countered that I was no quitter.

Now, she thought I'd finally made that attempt with Dathan, which wasn't true. I glowered at Dathan to scare him away.

He ignored me, observing my sisters with surprise. If he

noticed the gruesome scar that roped up Sarai's neck to her chin, he didn't show it.

"I didn't know Zair had sisters."

Sarai, who'd shrunk against my father at Dathan's approach, now stepped forward and gasped. "She didn't tell you of us!"

Niah, my older sister, shook her head at me. "*Tsk*. Forgive my little sister's poor manners, Scholar ...?"

"Dathan," he filled in with a grin.

"Scholar Dathan," Niah continued. "I'm sure she was merely overcome by her love for us each time she tried to tell you. Sarai and I are the *most* important things in Zair's life, you see."

I bit back a smile. Skies, it was bad enough that they were so glad about my win, unaware that my drive was avoiding arrest.

"I have no doubt about that," Dathan said, giving me a searching glance.

"I'm Sarai!" my sister introduced, reaching out to shake his hand. "Did you know rice is one of the components that hold up The Great Wall?"

"I did not know that, Sarai. Thank you for enlightening me."

Sarai glowed. Despite the shadows in her irises, her smiling again made my throat lump. I had to protect that smile.

"I'm Niah," Niah said. "And these are our parents. The entire Nebah brood here to support our young soldier."

She pinched my cheek, and I cringed. "*Niah*."

"*And* our medal winner," my father added, his chest puffed out with pride. My mother beamed, immense joy radiating from her. My chest warmed.

"Zair was the very best today, but you were *also* good in the pit," Sarai enthused to Dathan.

Dathan chuckled. "How generous of you."

"You stopped that bully who... who was hitting my sister." Her mouth wobbled.

I pulled her into a hug, giving her my reassuring smile. "I'm alright, Sarai."

"And thank you," Dathan said to her. "My ego has recovered after that effusive praise."

The females in my family giggled.

Dathan Issachar was conversing with a group of Esan women.

Charming them. How? All my life, people turned cold the moment my family came around. It was one of the reasons I stopped attempting friendships. His open kindness made my heart beat a little faster.

My father patted Dathan's shoulder. "You did well too, son. Winning isn't always about the trophy. Sometimes it's still standing in the end."

Dathan smiled abashedly, glancing away as if touched more than we could tell by the words. So my mother chimed in with more praise.

It was irrational, but a sense crept up on me as they gathered around him. The same feeling I had when I'd been about to speak to the Majesties and the First Advisor silenced me, prompting Dathan to speak over me.

My family were the only people who made me feel seen. Wanted. Right now, they were only smiling at Dathan. And I couldn't stop the defensiveness rising. He was my rival in many ways. It constantly felt like I was steps behind him, trying to catch up.

If he hadn't tackled Ibhar or held him down while I'd chased the ball, I wouldn't have won. My win didn't feel very much like a victory but more like his charity. My pride was stung, overpowering the warmth of his kindness.

"We packed a picnic if you would like to join us," my mother offered him.

The thoughts churned in my mind, and before I knew what I was doing, I said to him, "Would you leave?"

The sudden request silenced everyone. Dathan blinked and then made to speak as if to soften the tension.

"I don't have much time to spend with my family before we leave," I said. "I'd like to do so without you here interrupting."

The second the statement left my mouth, an acrid taste filled it. *Saints, I was being unfair.* My father lifted his brows at me in silent question.

Dathan gave a nod. He looked at my family, gave a respectful bow, and his tall form strolled away, his hands in his pockets.

That was awful.

"Zair," my mother called in surprise. "What's going on?"

I really did want to soak in this time with them before returning to the tensions of the Al'Qtraz. I would face Dathan later.

Rather than answer the question, I asked, "Did you bring *sinka* soup?"

Alert and wary of strangers, we trooped out of the arena to my father's wagon. He had parked it underneath a tree and reined his horses to the branches. Dozens of finer carriages spread out around us, surrounding the arena. The great plateaus rose along the east, the briny scent of the Niger River tinting the dusty air.

"Is it safe to stay outside for long?" I asked apprehensively as we set up the picnic under the tree.

"You've achieved an extraordinary feat today, Zair," my father said, Sarai keeping close to him as they spread the mat. "Nothing will keep our family from celebrating it."

I tried to appear calm as we ate my mother's modest but delicious Esan dishes, and chatted about our cousins and the palace. I gave our leftovers to the beggars lingering outside the arena.

As we packed up, splitting the chores, my mother gestured for me to sit on the wagon beside her and asked, "Who is Dathan Issachar?"

"He's no one, mama," I said, placing the next basket Niah handed me by a pile of folded *adire* fabrics. "We aren't friends, or anything at all."

"To just you?" My mother folded her arms. "Or to him too?"

When I furrowed my brows, she said, "Why would he take the time to greet your family if he didn't consider you a friend? Or even something more?"

Oh no. There could never be more between Dathan and me, even if he wasn't a barrier to me saving my sister. He was Gergesenes' golden boy with a blinding future ahead of him. He might not have won the medal today, but I'd seen interest illuminate many officers' faces as he'd battled.

He was the star.

I, on the other hand, was just an outcast clawing for scraps of acknowledgement so that maybe I could have a bright future, too, that would finally help my family belong.

"I don't know about any of that, but your *sinka* was delicious," I said brightly.

She gave me a knowing look. It was hard enough that her maternal instincts kept her attuned to her daughters' feelings. Throw in her Esan instincts, and my mother missed nothing.

"Do you remember when I first started my teabag business ten years ago?" she asked in Esh.

My hands quavered as I retrieved a tea-tray from Niah. "Our neighbors were horrible to you, refusing to patronize you for being Esan."

She smiled sadly. "Things were hard, especially on your father with him solely providing for our growing family. Yet for the first ten years of our marriage I'd been *terrified* to even attempt a business. He understood my fear, was never cruel or bitter about it. Even though he hated that I wasn't free to practice what I was passionate about. A skill taught to me by my mother. Then Sarai came and I couldn't leave him with the burden of supporting us alone anymore. I found courage and started making teabags."

I was eight then, but I still remembered the derision in stall owners' eyes as my mother went around our quarters, advertising her teabags.

They'd refused to buy her 'poison'. She wore smiles but tears glittered in her eyes each time she assured Niah and me that someone would accept her goods soon. Around that time, my father hadn't been getting many customers. Meals were infrequent and my parents had to sell their bed to buy medicine when Niah and I both fell ill that winter.

"Then your father stepped in. Rather, *barged* in." A real smile played on her mouth.

On mine too.

"He gifted his customers your bags of mixed tea leaves, not telling them the source. The tea was so good that they'd swarm his wagon to buy more fabrics than they needed just for more teabags. Soon, they started asking where they could buy it for themselves."

She nodded. "He told them his wife made it, and good tea eventually overcame their derision of my tribe."

Now, most people in our quarters bought teabags from my

mother. Niah inherited her passion for teamaking, and she and my mother were in business together.

"Courage makes the difference, Zair. If I hadn't scrambled for courage to try in spite of people's scorn, who knows what would've befallen our family at that dire time. Your dreams of attending an elite academy and that you made that dream a reality will *always* awe me. You're *Zaisa*, my *'little miracle'*. But more than with ambition, there are aspects of your life I ache for you to channel that courage."

"It's not as if I enjoy being without friends, mama. It's just... None of my mates see me as good enough. Maybe someday when I have a rank people respect..."

"Stop selling yourself short," she interrupted softly. "Look at them." She gestured to the beggars hungrily eating our leftovers. "You have a good heart. Even without a rank, that is worth loving. Anyone would be *lucky* to have you in their life."

"My own sister wasn't lucky to have me. Despite being a military student, I couldn't protect her," I blurted.

Shock contorted her face. "Zair. Don't blame yourself for this. The only ones to blame for evil are the evildoers. But together, our family *will* save Sarai from their clutches," she assured me, even as her fierce words trembled with fear.

I swallowed and gave a firm nod. *I would save Sarai.*

"The queen's *vyji* is tomorrow," she said. "Since you students can't attend, why not use the break to get to know the others?"

"I'll try."

They climbed into the wagon, and I reminded them to write to me if *anything* happened. Heart in my mouth, I waved until they disappeared down the road, and then I headed back into the arena.

Lysias was rounding up her presentation. Standing before the attentive audience and the nine other healing students, she shared her research. A tool that would help healers insert cures into patients who were too ill to swallow the medicine, or unconscious. This perplexing idea tilted heads, including mine. To pair with this medical tool, she was also creating an herbal formula, a general cure that would be affordable to all. Her focus was the common ailments the poor endured rather than treated because they couldn't afford the cures. Fevers and aches.

Her clear passion and thoughtfulness planted a seed of admiration within me.

It forced me to acknowledge Dathan's own thoughtfulness. He had dragged Ibhar off me and sacrificed his victory for Gergesenes Military Academy, along with the advantages, for my sake. My throat lumped, and I rubbed a thumb over my neck.

No one had ever made such a sacrifice for me.

I scanned the arena and found him within Gergesenes' row, sitting with his Commandant. A bright fullness swept around my chest—and the problem was that I didn't know if I wanted to quiet it.

28

DATHAN

The ceremonies were flying by quickly. After the queen's *vyji* tomorrow, the Crowning and the Gifting would round up the coronation in six days. My chance to save Jaziah was slipping from my fingers.

An ache still pulsed in my chest, the defensive look on Zair's face as she told me to leave her family imprinted in my mind. It had been all I could do not to wince as her rejection cut between my ribs.

I silenced the flow of thoughts. Zair's rebuff today was the last thing I should be thinking about.

After I'd been dismissed from her family's presence, I'd joined my Commandant in the main arena. He'd congratulated me, not for winning—because I hadn't—but for a choice that I had already started regretting.

"It's not a thing one can be taught at any academy, that honor isn't merely in winning but in sacrifice too. You didn't win the medal, but you won the admiration of many senior officers today, Issachar. Be proud of that."

His accolade had moved me, especially with my father's aloofness to everything I'd done. Before the Commandant left, he'd slipped me a note. Throughout the ride back to the palace, the note had burned under my tunic.

My bedroom door locked, I'd unfolded the paper written in a

random scrawl that couldn't lead back to the Commandant. The message followed a coded pattern we were only taught to discern in year-five.

'A white scorpion wandered into GGSA.'

'White scorpion' was Gergesenes-speak for intel. The Gergesenes General Studies Academy had received intel.

'It bears news of Kurje and Irua, and the black feathers littering through.'

Kurje and Irua, two Baihan towns, were discovered to be on the mercenary's radar, it meant. Gergesenes General Studies Academy straddled the border of these towns. My nerves spiked.

'Hawks have been freed, streaking for the valley to scare ravens away.'

We are sending soldiers and increasing our defenses around GGSA.

'But only foolish ravens would confront fierce hawks.'

But the mercenaries were known to avoid head-on collision. Rather they attacked by exploiting weaknesses they shouldn't know about.

'What black feather floats over sandstone? Pluck it so we may meet the ravens in the sky.'

You need to find the traitor in the palace soon, so we can protect our students.

My mission to find the traitor had always been urgent with Jaziah's life on the line. Now, with Gergesenes right on the trail of a planned attack, it was dire. The Commandant wouldn't have told me of the feared attack, knowing the pressure it would cause, if he'd had another option.

I'd timed my exit of the students' lounge and joined the women celebrating the Gergesenes' student who won the healing prize at the Best of Ten. The wife of a royal healer had invited Scholar Aisosa to the palace to celebrate her. They had eagerly welcomed my presence in the group of twelve heading upstairs to the royal healer's suite. None had noticed the soft-soled shoes that made no sounds with my treads. I'd accompanied them up to Sarhedrin's residential floor on the fourth level, past the guards who manned the stairs. Then I'd snatched the first opportunity to slip into a washroom I'd marked during my study of the palace.

In the quiet washroom, I'd swapped my clothing. Donned my spy blacks on top of my regular tunic and trousers. My espionage tools were distributed in my sleeves and strapped to my calves.

Now wind rippled through my black garment as I curved like a centipede above the arched window on the passageway to Sarhedrin's rooms. I kept my breathing shallow, silent in the empty corridor. Unlike the other visiting nobles, he had chosen a secluded lounge at the northern end of the level. Could be for nefarious reasons, but for now it worked in my favor.

He emerged and old anger sparked to life at the sight of his unadorned form. He wore simple brown clothes.

Odd. Ussi lands were slabs of gemstones, and a pride of their culture was in displaying their wealth.

Odder than his clothes, however, were the two armed men flanking him. A murky aura clung to them. Their black fabric was coarse and old, not the quality livery of a Dynast's guards. Their faces were even more concealed than mine.

The arch's shadows engulfed me as I trailed them silently from above.

Their brisk, purposeful strides formed a daunting rhythm. Soon, the layout of our route morphed until mosaic walls formed a snaky passage. I hopped down and zigzagged around the curving walls, chasing glimpses of clothes.

The three men disappeared, and a dark threshold rose before me.

A carefully hidden doorway. I hadn't encountered it during my survey of the palace.

"Light." The Dynast of Bornoir's voice echoed from the threshold.

I counted to ten before treading softly after them. The candlelight below faintly illuminated a cavernous stairwell of stone.

The crisp space could be a secret exit, but also... more. It was exquisite.

Cleanly cut, baroque steps. Plasterwork walls depicted the decapitated. Shackled men being whipped. Weeping women cradling headless babies. Under the power of the night magic they *moved*, creating bleak, grating sounds as if rejecting our presence here.

Grotesque.

With each quiet step down, I decided the hidden route was built for the Majesties. The Al'Qtraz was a city of stairwells and passages. It was a standard measure that should the palace ever be invaded, the king and queen would have their own secret way out.

Why was *Sarhedrin* using it? And with these strange men?

"The Admiral uncovered one of the mercenary caves today. He led an ambush on the hideout," Sarhedrin informed curtly.

Skies above.

The armed men cursed.

My heart leaped with joy. Since their reign of terror began, this was the first time a hideout had been found. After Jalin Base, I imagined the Admiral would settle for no less.

"Did they execute the mercenaries?" an armed man asked tensely.

"That isn't the Admiral's style. He has other plans for them," Sarhedrin murmured. "His soldiers took them captive."

Sarhedrin's grimness over this progress showed just where the bastard stood. Against Thalesai. I only needed to find a little more evidence, something concrete, and I would rush at him in a blink. Drag him off to the Admiral and Commandant before he realized what hit him.

"The Admiral will try to force answers out of the mercs. If he succeeds, he'll be returning to the palace soon to report to the king. So no hesitation." Sarhedrin's golden earrings glinted. "We won't find other chances like this. *He* gave me two weeks and in a few days, he'll close every opening."

He. The mercenary leader? An accomplice senior to him?

Too many questions. I needed *answers*. Why was two weeks the deadline? Was it because the king's coronation spanned these two weeks? After which Sarhedrin and the other Dynasts would be returning to their towns?

They exited the stairway, throwing it into inky blackness. Sliding a hand over the railing to guide my movements, I quickened my pace.

The darkness kept me covered with its transient wall once I reached the threshold they had exited. A window opened in the secret stairway beside me but the passage they entered had no windows.

The entryway opposite my position was carved like broad white wings. We had followed a back way to the Chamber of Wings office. Judging from the plaque above the door they approached, they were targeting the Royal Accountant's string of offices.

A ticking began in my head. The reason he tried to poison the Royal Accountant, that he'd been monitoring this area, I would discover soon.

On sighting the Dynast of Bornoir, the four palace guards manning the offices saluted, but their faces held unease. They weren't expecting him. They were wondering why he'd taken the secret path relegated to the royals.

Their gazes swiftly moved to the scythed men, and their arms tautened.

"Khosa Sarhedrin..."

The guard never completed his statement. The scythed men flung throwing knives, impaling the two rear guards. Blood gushed from their unarmored necks as they crumpled.

Cold ran the full length of my body. *Bleeding skies*.

The nearer guards drew their adaswords but the bandits streaked forward with shocking speed. They slit the guards' throats with their scythes, kicking their dead bodies aside... as Sarhedrin strode up to the door barring the Royal Accountant's office.

29

ZAIR

Night magic beamed in the walls as I hurried to my rooms. Hopefully, the palace would leave me alone while I tailed Colonel Remmon.

I closed my door, my chest still throbbing from Ibhar's jarring blow in the arena. I tried to focus on that. Not on Dathan's coldness during the ride back to the palace. He hadn't looked my way, much less said a word to me. I shouldn't care, but his distance left a yawning hollowness in my stomach.

No, it is better this way.

My new bow and arrow glinted as I propped them by my bed. Arno had ignored my request to be left alone, instead giving me the beautiful weapons as a 'peace offering.' Weapons no sane archer could resist.

"Accepting your gift doesn't mean I want to remain acquainted," I'd told him.

He'd just given me an unreadable smile and sauntered off.

I scoffed and opened my wardrobe. I swiftly scanned through the Admiral's schedule that I had copied from Remmon's office. Pain seized my chest and I doubled over. A wet cough racked through my torso, and blood stained the rug.

Don't panic. It's just blood, expected after Ibhar's hits.

A royal healer had intercepted me the moment we rode onto the palace grounds, sent to lead me to the infirmary. I'd had to convince the healer that I was alright so I could hurry up to my rooms.

Knocks came on my door. Skies, who was it? I swiped an arm over my mouth, harried as I hobbled to open the door.

"Lysias," I said in surprise.

Lysias smiled tentatively. "I wanted to congratulate you on your win. You were remarkable in the pit!"

"Thank you." I gave a small grin, but when she surveyed me quietly, I asked, "Is there anything else?"

"Are you alright? The way Ibhar hit you... I'm surprised you're standing rather than lying in bed."

I swallowed. "It's the kind of thing we're trained to withstand at Nergal." Although, I'd never quite received a direct blow to the chest before. Or one so hard that it was starting to hurt to breathe.

Lysias didn't look convinced. "Are you sure you don't want to visit the palace's infirmary? I could go with you. They have great healers, and their services are free for us guests."

"No, I'm fine." *I ache all over, but I have a mission that can't wait.*

"Alright," she conceded. Her face slowly brightened. "I didn't win the prize like you and Mishan in my category. Scholar Aisosa from the Gergesenes Healing Academy did. But I had nobles volunteer to sponsor my project, the injector."

"Lysias, congratulations!" I said, genuinely happy for her.

"Thank you." Smiling, she glanced at our lounge's exit. "Would you like to visit the east-wing natatorium? The Dynast of Caso's daughters invited me for a soiree there. I thought—well, I thought it would be nice to go together."

My smile slowly faded. "I, um, planned to do some reading tonight. To prepare for our final exams."

"Oh," Lysias said with downturned lips. "Alright. Maybe we could do something together some other time."

As I closed my door, my mother's insistence that I was worthy of friendships, even without a great rank, filled my mind. Lysias had been kind so far, had even invited me to play a game days ago with no ulterior motive. Part of me wished I could've accepted her invitation. But even if I wasn't planning to tail the First Colonel, going to the natatorium would've only ruined the experience for Lysias.

I hurried to my bath chamber, soaked a towel in soap and scrubbed the blood off the rug. If the maids saw it, I'd be hustled to the infirmary and there really was no time for that.

Dressed in spying attire, I placed my ear against the door and listened with my sharper hearing. No sounds. The air felt still. Undisturbed. In five long strides, I would be out of the lounge and in the servants' stairs. I stepped out of my rooms, and bumped into a broad back.

"Watch it!" Ibhar snarled.

My heart stopped beating. Nobody should've been out here. Unless... he'd been moving and *breathing* very silently. Why would Ibhar do so in our lounge? I backed away as he gobbled up my unusual ensemble—black trousers, tunic, and a face covering—with a puzzled frown.

Oh saints, oh saints, oh saints.

His nostrils flared. "Disobeying His Majesty's orders, are we?"

I ripped off my face covering and placed it behind me.

"Leave me alone," I snapped in a low, hard voice despite the pounding in my chest.

Goosebumps rose over my skin as Ibhar closed in, peering down at my face as if to *see* what my motive was.

Skies, the king wouldn't forgive an Esan person sneaking about his home. Worse, any accusation I made against the First Colonel from that point would never be believed.

"Are you planning to rob the nobles? Is that why you're dressed so?" he sneered.

"Why were *you* moving as silently as a thief in your own lounge?" I hissed.

His eyes bulged like I had hit him. "I'll shut that snaky mouth of yours."

He pushed me and my head hit my door. He grabbed my shoulders, but I put all my strength into shoving his big form off me. "Get away from me, Ibhar!"

He stumbled backward, then lunged angrily just as a door popped open. I dodged his grip. My head spun from the fast movement, after the battering my body took in the arena. I didn't swing my fist fast enough. He grabbed and twisted my arm behind me.

Lysias stepped out of her room, dressed in an embroidered ochre gown, and gasped.

Seeming to decipher the situation, she hurried to me. "I didn't hear you knock, did I? Sorry. These doors are *so* thick. I've laid out the gown I wanted you to try. Come on."

"The azishit has a mask," Ibhar spat.

"We were playing a game," I snapped and pushed him off me.

Lysias took my hand, but she didn't have to pull me along. I followed after her like a raft as we gushed into her bedroom.

I shut the door and pressed my forehead to it, drawing deep breaths to calm my erratic heart. *That was close.* If Ibhar had known... If he'd exposed my sneaking even on suspicion alone, I'd have been damned.

I swallowed back nausea before turning to Lysias. She watched from the center of her bedchamber. It was an elegant merge of amber and rosewood. She fit within it better than I did in mine.

"Thank you," I said sincerely, adding in Walhese, *"Lahr kenan."*
I owe you.

Her bangles jingled with her wave. "No need for that. And don't worry," she added softly when I fiddled with my hem. "I won't pry."

Suspicion trickled through me. She spared me from Ibhar just like that? Without wanting anything in return?

"Why?" I asked her. Wasn't she at least bothered that whatever I was up to could affect her?

Lysias shrugged as she drifted to her mirror to adjust her bangles. "It's my duty as a healer to protect Thalesains by creating medicine to heal them. As a soldier, you're trying to protect our people too, aren't you? By... well, whatever it is you're about to do. Since we have the same goal—to protect the people and land we care about—we might as well help each other out in the process, I think."

I shifted my watering eyes to the curtains. She didn't help me for an unknown gain, but because she trusted that whatever I was pursuing was for the good of Thalesai. What had I done to deserve it?

"I still remember your patience in the Secruvi Market's cell, Zair," she said softly.

"If you need help in any way," I promised, "a guard, an experiment for your medicine, anything, just ask me, and I'll help."

She laughed. "You'll let me experiment on you?"

"As a return of trust," I joked tentatively.

Lysias grinned, but then she moved in on me. "Your nose is bleeding, Zair!"

Reaching up, the thick liquid slicked over my knuckles. I quickly wiped it off. "It's nothing serious." But my voice shook with panic.

"You need treatment," she said firmly. "I watched the fight with Ibhar. He'd aimed his blows to maim you."

And I wouldn't let him win. It was most likely part of the reason he'd been so feral moments ago. I'd beaten him and was still standing rather than bedridden after his assault.

"I'll be alright," I said to Lysias, gave her another grateful nod, and sidled out of her bedchamber. Once out of the lounge, I covered my face with my veil and carefully went down the servants' stairwell to a certain lounge.

BREATHING FELT like razors were cutting my throat as I lay in wait for the First Colonel. He emerged from eating his dinner, and I became his shadow. The palace was somber. As if the pretend smiles at the arena today after the Jalin Base attack had drained everyone.

Everyone but those utilizing despair to meet their own ends.

As if sensing me, the Colonel glanced over his shoulder. I had no choice; I wrung out magic from my veins to flow like air outside my pores and paint me the colors of the walls to external eyes. Fully camouflaged, Remmon saw naught but a vibrant hallway.

He pivoted right and as I ceased the camouflage, exhaustion dropped me to my knees. My bones felt liquefied.

Need to keep moving.

I trudged after him just as he disappeared behind an unusual oval door. Tamping down uncertainty, I dipped after him into a stairwell. He jogged up, up, up the stairwell, until he escaped the stairwell's darkness.

Straight into the Admiral's office in the Chamber of Fangs' area.

Why in the skies was the area vacant? Where were the guards? The beasts? The guards would not leave the Admiral's office unguarded merely because he was away.

Realization hit. Whatever reason Colonel Remmon was here tonight, he'd made sure to dispose of the guards and creatures first.

Colonel Remmon walked to the grand doors at the center of the right wall. In the silent hall, Colonel Remmon drew lock picks from his pocket and expertly vandalized the Admiral's doors.

Skies!

He shut the door behind him, but I couldn't end my investigation here. *When doors are shut, use windows.*

I raced to a window and scanned its exterior. There were no ledges that connected the window straight to the Admiral's office. Instead, the wall slid smoothly and the thin ledges only appeared in front of the office's windows twenty feet away. Unless I wanted to violently test if I had aziza wings hidden somewhere—I *didn't*—I had to quit. Not an option.

My gaze skittered to a tapestry hanging down a wall and an idea formed. Yes, I'd made no connections with the palace's magic after my second night here. Yet—yet it was worth a try.

Surprisingly, guilt weighed on my back as I unhooked the tapestry and crouched on it. I treated my aziza abilities like they were an extra, freakish limb to hide so people would accept me. And yet, the abilities had done nothing but help me in the palace.

Still, how could I accept them when they made me more bizarre?

"You know my intentions are good," I whispered urgently to the magic shining in the walls. "I want nothing but to rid the palace of threats, as you do. Please, help me."

The carpet remained flat.

Desperation churned. "*Please.*"

Silent seconds passed. My face burned from the ridiculousness of kneeling on the floor, talking to myself. Here was a great lead and I'd lose it because—

A shimmering sensation shocked over my skin as the palace

magic flowed over, moving like a glowing stream up my feet. It wove with the bits of magic in my blood until the night magic became a fuel to mine. My hands warmed as they glowed white, just like that first night. The tapestry stretched taut and my stomach pitched as it levitated.

Skies.

The tapestry swerved, carrying me swiftly out the window.

With a gasp, I clung tight as cold winds blew my clothes in the starless night. Dust and spices tickled my nose. I glanced down to gauge the drop. My stomach tightened. Four levels from the ground felt like a hundred when held up only by a scrap of cloth.

In a swift few seconds, the makeshift carpet halted just below a thin ledge under the Admiral's windows. I gingerly transferred onto it, clinging on my toes, almost moaning as the carpet flew away.

The window had been pushed open a crack, to allow air in perhaps, and I was thankful for that poor decision. Some soldiers were the most efficient in their earlier years. The more medals they received, however, the faster arrogance made them dismiss their training.

Once I had enough information, I would climb down the sills and ledges beneath me to the dark courtyard below.

An oil lamp illuminated Colonel Remmon writing furiously at the Admiral's desk.

What did he have to write in here *that no one could know about?*

Gripping the window tightly, I used my other hand to pull my little spyglass from my many pockets.

He was creating... records?

The page was divided with four lines and numbers poured between them in rough sprawls, he was writing so fast. Perhaps it was his intention? So no one could tell the handwriting was his?

At the end of the page, his red-tattooed fingers moved slowly. The Admiral was a major sponsor of the Nergal Military Academy, and I'd seen his signature on documents enough times to recognize that Remmon was *forging* it.

Hair stood on my freezing nape when he raised a stack of files from the desk—and slid his documents within them.

He pulled out fresh papers and repeated the process.

The words and precise numbers were too far away to read

clearly, but he was forging documents. Creating data that would likely implicate the Admiral for some reason.

Was this related to the forbidden item he was smuggling? Could it be that whatever it was, he was forging data to incriminate the Admiral as the smuggler so *he* would go unscathed if the item was discovered?

Oh skies.

Out of nowhere, a bird landed on the perch above me and flapped loudly. Colonel Remmon swung sharply in his chair. So unexpectedly that I gasped behind my face mask.

He barked a curse and jumped to his feet. He rushed and grabbed my shoulders just as I started to climb down.

Clutched in his grip, I could only shut my eyes. Hide the telling rings in them.

Fingers dug into my shoulders. "You'll die for this!"

Please don't!

He shoved me. I lost grip of the ledge and cried out in horror.

Screeching winds whipped through my hair and clothes. I flung open my eyes to find his form shrinking fast above me. I screamed and threw out what sputter of magic was inside me in a plea.

The palace magic didn't answer.

30

DATHAN

Orcus Sarhedrin, the Demon of Bornoir, kept attempting to break into the Royal Accountant's office. And failing.

What had he expected? This was the office of a chamberman who controlled the flow of money across the entire kingdom! The lock had to be more advanced than anything we were taught to pick at school.

From the windowless passage, blood from the murdered guards rolled down the tiles to my shoes. My chest ached from the depth of his betrayal.

These were men who'd worked hard for *years* to earn the honor of serving in the palace. What Sarhedrin did to my family, he did because, with his warped logic, he'd believed us to be traitors. Tonight, the Dynast of Bornoir just soullessly murdered men who vowed to protect him.

My blood simmered to barge in and take down the bandits in the same way they took down the guards. Without honor.

Hatred burned out thoughts of my mission. Of how lashing out would ruin it.

I just wanted Sarhedrin gone.

My fingers closed around my daggers. A flash of black plunged down the window beside me with a horrified cry. The sound cut through the red haze of my mind.

That cry. I'd heard it in the Combat Arena's pit. When Ibhar had hit...

Sheols.

I shoved my head through the window just as the figure slammed into the ground with an impact that filled my throat with bile.

It was too dark to make the figure out, yet my lungs seized.

It couldn't be her.

But what if? A wave of cold stole my breath. I looked to the doorway where Sarhedrin and his bandits perpetrated their evil. My mission or Zair?

Zair. It had to be her down there.

She's your rival. You need her out of the way to succeed. But I didn't want her *dead*.

The Dynast of Bornoir made the choice easier. He cursed vilely at the door and stormed off toward the main exit.

"Dispose of the bodies and leave no trace of our presence," he ordered over his shoulder. He'd given up. For now.

The smoldering bandits moved to fulfill his orders. My feet flew down the stairs. *Let this path lead to the chess yard.*

The saints answered.

In the windswept night, I scanned the dim yard built like a giant chessboard. A figure lay in a lump of tousled hair and black fabric by a queen sculpture. Blood pounded in my ears. *Please let her be alive.*

I lowered myself to my knees. "Zair?"

She didn't move. I peeled back her face mask.

"Zair." I shook her shoulder slightly. No sign of breathing. My stomach clenched.

I needed to get help.

Carefully, I gathered her up. She felt so small, so *broken*, in my arms that my throat ached. "I have you."

My feet ate the distance for the secret stairway. A step in, and boots slapped against the chessboard floor. An impatient glance over my shoulder revealed a man jogging past the rook sculptures. His head swiveled as he scanned the yard. A flicker of light caught his face.

First Colonel Remmon?

He tore about like a desperate Andes cougar. Benches screeched as he kicked them aside. Sculptures tumbled with his shoves. He was looking for someone.

Was he the lead Zair tailed? Was *he* the bastard who pushed her?

My jaw locked, but stronger was the need to get Zair out of there. I took off in a jog up the stairway of grating carvings and crisp blackness. Footsteps approached from behind us.

Remmon was on to us. I held Zair closer to my chest, running as fast as I dared around spiral steps and without visuals.

Remmon's presence in the stairwell was as poignant as a fuming volcano.

"You won't escape me, snoop!"

The stairs began to undulate like angry waves. I stumbled backward and then forward. *What in the skies?*

The figures in the walls grated deafeningly, releasing choking noises that made me gnash my teeth. The night magic was rejecting us from the Majesties' stairwell, Remmon's chase the proof that we were trespassing.

The stone beneath my feet suddenly swelled up, up, up. A stormy sea in a room. I lost my balance and slipped far down, spinning at the last moment so my back hit the end and not Zair's. My groan echoed.

The footsteps halted, but then scrambled for us with renewed fervor. "Found you!"

My harsh breathing and his stumbling progress resounded in the blackness.

I couldn't escape him while carrying Zair. Concealment was the next best tactic. But where?

Over here, a wispy voice evoked.

Who was that?

She cried for help. Bring her into my bosom.

A thin line of light cut across the air. Hoping against hope that it led to some sort of escape, I rose and carried her toward the lit line in the wall. I shoved my shoulder hard at the surface around the light. The stone caved in only slightly.

The stumbling footsteps grew nearer. "Show yourself and I might let you live!"

I shoved harder. The surface gave a slight bit again, enough to squeeze Zair in. The desperate merge of footsteps and panting came right behind us.

I flung my body in and pushed the stone closed.

Dull pain throbbed in my shoulder. I panted raggedly, half-waiting for the Colonel to barge in, primed to fight.

Wherever we were was musty, cramped, and dark, save for the gently glowing walls. The place was camouflaged, but the night magic had opened it to us. To Zair.

"The Al'Qtraz has so many pockets that one would think the first King of Thalesai was frightened of his own shadow," I panted to an unconscious Zair. "Yet with chambermen like Sarhedrin and Remmon, who could fault him?"

The glowing walls pulsed. Agitation and intrigue gripped me as the glow rolled like spilled water to Zair. Her honey-gold skin glazed with its magic, shining brighter and brighter until all the light winked out at once.

I leaned down to scan her face. What else had the palace magic done for her? If it was good, why was she not waking up?

I counted the seconds and Zair's unmoving body grew colder against me. Unable to bear it anymore, I pushed out of the alcove. The stairs were still; no sounds. Even if there were, I'd risk taking Colonel Remmon down over letting Zair fade.

I held her, covered her with my body, and took long strides up the steps. *Wait.* With each step, the ground beat gently a foot ahead of me, like a heart, only of stone. Frowning, I stepped consciously on the pulsing circle. Soft light swept under my feet like an approval. Pausing, I stepped outside of the pulsing circle. Beside me, the circle beat faster. *Warning. Warning. Warning.*

The palace was guiding us, guiding Zair, to keep protecting her.

Trusting my instinct, I walked within the pulsing guide. Step by step up the stairway, but I paused a moment before I carried Zair out of the stairwell's safety. If anyone appeared in our path, knocking them out or scaling outside the windows wasn't an option. Hiding behind the elephant-tusk statues along the left wall was the best chance at concealment, and with Zair, I needed to be ready to move fast.

I stepped out and stayed close to the statues, senses alert. But the pulsing bit of the palace led us down three *quiet* corridors, even as the rest of the palace buzzed. Almost like... the magic steered her from trouble. *Amazing.*

I had never been gladder to see the students' lounge. The ground stopped pulsing the moment I crossed the threshold, but there wasn't time to dwell on what the palace was doing and why it did it for Zair.

Carefully, I lowered her onto a settee in the lounge, drew out picks, and went to work on her lock. Her door gave and I carried her into her bedroom.

I reached her bed and suddenly... didn't want to let go of her.

It made no sense, yet she was cold and I was the source of her warmth. Of our joined bodies, she was still and I was the moving part. What if I was the one willing her to live? What if I let go of her for one moment and she breathed her last? Then this brave, fighter of a girl would be lost to this world.

Her torso suddenly trembled. A wet cough racked her body. Blood dampened my neck and shoulder, but relief overcame me.

It was a bloody cough, but it *was* sign of life.

I made myself lower her onto the bed but my relief quickly dwindled. She was in bad shape. The bruises from battling Ibhar had darkened on her swollen face. Her breaths rattled, as if she was struggling to draw air.

I strode out to find Lysias.

Yes, Zair wouldn't want to involve anyone, to risk sabotaging her mission. Skies, she wouldn't even want *me* involved.

But her secrets were not worth her life.

Closing her door, my joints locked as dozens of guards bounded past the hallways. They interrogated stewards and barged into suites.

Remmon had declared a breach of security. They were searching for a spy.

I yanked off my mask and outer black tunic, tossed them under the settee and dropped atop it just as a guard burst into our lounge. His barghests charged in like rolling boulders and began to sniff around.

Would their senses lead the search straight to Zair?

I masked my face into the appropriate level of bewilderment. "Prosperity, sir."

The beasts prowled over with fuming nostrils, hungry to sense evil.

My heart beat faster. Blast it, I couldn't afford to be bitten again. Zair needed me.

The guard grunted a response, tossing cabinets open and searching the balcony. "There's report of breached security. Have you seen anything odd tonight?"

I frowned. "Define *odd*, sir."

A vicious snarl vibrated into my ear. Hot canine pants burned against my neck.

The guard faced me and the beasts, and his eyes narrowed. Would they bite me? Point me out as the culprit? My heart raged against my ribs, but I kept still.

Moments passed and the fangs still didn't pierce my skin.

Impatient, the guard ordered the barghests out. "The search will not cease until we find the culprit. Make a report if you see anything."

I sat up, took a moment to breathe deeply, and tucked my extra tunic into my waistband. We weren't out of the woods just yet.

I banged on Lysias's door. Paced a bit. Banged. Paced some more. After the third knock, she opened, wrapped in a lilac sleeping robe. "Saints, Dathan. Where's the fire?"

"I'm sorry, but..." I ran my fingers through my hair. "Zair needs help."

"Where is she?" she asked, and I led her into Zair's room.

"What happened?" Lysias exclaimed, her ear lowered to Zair's trembling chest.

"She fell," I said.

"*Fell?*"

"Down a balcony. Or a window." I grappled for calm. "I don't know which or how far from the ground it was, but I saw the impact and it was bad."

Horror twisted Lysias's face. But only for a second. She sat beside Zair, running her hands over her limbs. "I need to know if she's broken anything."

Lying there, an acute loneliness clung to Zair. Something I now recognized always lingered underneath that shuttered surface.

Why are you so guarded? I'd asked.

But Zair wasn't guarded and arrogant... She was guarded and lonely. Seeing her this way stoked that fire in me to protect her. Take care of her in a way I realized now that no one else did. More and more my resolve to stay away from her crumbled against this powerful draw to her. Like a gale propelling me closer with a force I'd never felt before.

If she makes it through this, I vowed silently to the saints, *I'll protect her. Please let her make it through.*

I'd just watched four innocent men murdered. I couldn't stomach another death I was too late to stop.

Lysias finally let herself breathe. "Nothing is broken."

"How is that possible? I saw her fall."

The night magic. It healed her bones.

"She *is* in bad shape, Dathan. Her breathing is labored. I'm worried there might be an internal damage."

"Will she wake up?"

She was feeling Zair's pulse. "I believe so."

My heartbeat calmed a bit, even as the ground throbbed with the angry footsteps of guards.

"She still needs treatment," Lysias insisted. "The royal healers will have all the tools."

"She wouldn't want to be taken to the infirmary." Questions would be asked. Questions Zair couldn't afford to answer. And there was Colonel Remmon. For whatever reason, he was after her. If he'd pushed her, he surely had guards watching the infirmary.

Lysias stamped a foot and started to chide me on priorities, but then she paused. "I'll be back."

The door swung closed. I moved nearer to Zair. Her breathing was still so choppy it retained my alarm. I swept tendrils back from her face, this girl I felt the overwhelming need to protect.

What were you doing, Zair? How did you fall?

The swinging door announced Lysias's return.

I stepped back, but she waved me closer. "I need those muscles, Dathan. Prop her up so I can make her drink this."

She held a half-full tumbler, placing a salve and an unfamiliar object on the bed. I sat by Zair, carefully tugging her so her back rested against my chest. If she was conscious, she'd feel my heart pounding as if to exit my chest. Unlike the resilient girl I went head to head with daily, she now felt like glass. Like my hands could shatter her.

"Alright." Lysias tipped Zair's head back so it fell over my shoulder and pulled her jaw open. She poured in the tumbler's content and held Zair's mouth closed. Zair didn't swallow. She clamped Zair's nostrils shut. Zair coughed out the liquid.

"Ach, she's such a fighter," Lysias exclaimed.

Indeed, Zair was. A small smile curved my mouth. I noted the tomes stacked neatly on her table. As was the school practice, her full name and home address were scribbled neatly on the bottom left of a book cover:

Scholar Zaisa Eniye Nebah.
House 16, Esodi Lane, the Southern Quarters of Ari'el.

Even here, she was studying for upcoming exams. No one believed an Esan would be recruited in the Ironteenth unit or even allowed to serve in the palace. Still, Zair hoped, working toward that future. One that could've been snatched from her tonight. My throat tightened.

Conflict edged Lysias's eyes. "We need this remedy in her body."

Resolvedly, she reached for the unfamiliar tool. A metal tube with a wide needle protruding from an end.

"The invention you presented in the arena?" I asked, my defensive instincts rising.

"You summoned me here. You're going to have to trust me," Lysias said. She opened the bottom of the metal tube, checking the liquid content. Satisfied, Lysias took Zair's hand and studied her wrist.

"What are you searching for?"

"A vein. I need to inject the formula into a vein to make sure it passes through her bloodstream." She looked at me and explained,

"My injector is like... a pump. I need to pump the formula into her body since she can't swallow remedies."

"Have you tested this before?"

"On camels and dogs, yes."

I ground my teeth against my protest as Lysias gently sank the wide needle into Zair's wrist and pushed the bottom of the metal tube. Zair's body stiffened. The tube moved and moved to half the size before Lysias carefully pulled the needle out of Zair's wrist.

Zair's body slackened as blood dotted the needled area. Lysias and I released soft breaths, and Lysias dabbed the blood away.

Picking up the salve, she answered my question. "And yes. The medicine's not yet as effective as I plan to make it, but it should relieve her pain. Since you're determined not to let the royal healers take charge."

I wanted nothing *but* to let the healers take charge. Yet I knew the risks and was painfully aware of how quick people would be to persecute Zair if she landed in trouble.

"It has to be Zair's choice," was all I said. I didn't want to, but Lysias was watching me as she applied salve on Zair's bruises, so I pulled away.

Guilt shadowed Lysias's face as she went to shut two of the windows. "She's already cold. She doesn't need the breeze."

"What is it, Lysias?"

She fidgeted and sighed. "I shouldn't have helped her escape our wing tonight."

"You knew Zair was... heading out?" I picked my words, surprised.

"I'd invited her to accompany me to a soiree after we'd returned."

"...and she declined," I surmised.

Lysias nodded, breathing faster now. "I was leaving when I saw her with Ibhar. Look how she's dressed. Sneaky, right? Ibhar seemed to notice too. I made excuses for her so she could escape him. I thought I was... I was being a friend. But if I hadn't, she wouldn't be in this state."

I shook my head, taking a step closer. "You protected her and now you're taking care of her. That *is* a friend."

My stomach suddenly hardened with memories of my own missing friend.

Questions flooded Lysias's distraught eyes. Questions she sensed I couldn't answer. Regret pricked at me. I'd dragged her from her bedroom, and she didn't hesitate to help me or Zair. I felt like a bastard keeping her in the dark.

She gave a weak but kind smile. "Just make sure you take care of her, alright? She doesn't receive a lot of care around here."

I gave a tense nod and the door closed behind her.

I went to work pulling off Zair's slippers—soundless slippers, clever—and tucking her beneath her blankets. I needed her to be warm. To feel alive.

"Before my father made wealth as owner of one of the best infirmaries in the Baihan quarters," I said quietly, "when my family first settled in Ari'el after long months of fleeing for our lives, I found it hard to sleep. So I'd roam the tiny rooms of our first apartment in the southern quarters. Most nights, I'd find my sister dozing on the couch. Ari'el's nights are icy in the winter and although she had been too numb with sorrow to notice the cold, I'd take blankets and tuck her in. She had looked then just like you do now. Unwilling to ask, but in need of someone to look out for her."

I ran my finger beneath a bruise. *I can't leave her*. I didn't want her to wake up at midnight alone and afraid. She might've been prickly today when I'd gone close to her family, but my anger had long faded. I wanted to listen to her breaths until they were normal again. If whoever pushed her came after her, I'd be here to face them.

And... I didn't want to sleep alone either.

Not when it was guaranteed to be rife with nightmares after seeing Sarhedrin's men murder soldiers.

Perhaps, I needed her as much as she needed me.

I kicked off my shoes and climbed into the bed, maintaining a good distance.

The wry part of me half-expected that even unconscious, her fist would fly up to connect with my jaw for daring to breach her personal space. But the moment I brushed her hair from her face, Zair reacted. For the first time since I found her, she moved on her own. Closing the gap between us, like mine was a warmth she craved in the iciness of her mind.

As she turned into me, her raspy breath tickling my skin, something unfurled deep in me. A sense of... completion. Rightness in my crooked world.

I held my breath as I gently pulled away. She wriggled back like a little worm, and my heart beat faster as she buried her face into my neck.

She mumbled meaningless words. "I've waited for you."

The palace magic flashed brighter, as if in response, before it settled into a beam. Zair had deeper connections to the Al'Qtraz's magic than she'd told me. A peculiar connection that I had never heard of before. For now though, my concentration was on her waking up again.

Snuggled like two parts of a whole, I closed my eyes and listened to her breathe.

31

ZAIR

P ain rushed through my body like an acid pool, gnawing until I tried to cry out. It ate into my chest. I couldn't draw air.

"It's okay," a deep voice called from a distance. "Breathe with me."

Breathing hurts, I wanted to say, but the agony was paralyzing. Visions flashed in my mind: Blood everywhere. Hands covered in red and blue flames. Shooting stars. Explosions. Rotting piles of bodies. And there I stood, translucent and levitating. A huge piece of my chest was missing. It was hollow, and cold, and dark. An emptiness I had carried my entire life.

"Breathe with me."

Light pressure warmed my back. It moved in a comforting rhythm. A broad chest, a heart beating against my struggling one.

"Just like this, Zair."

My panic abated as my heart imitated the rhythm, syncing with his.

My head pounded, and for a moment all I could do was breathe.

I slowly surfaced into myself. I made to move my limbs but failed. My mouth was parched, like I'd traded my tongue for the scorching dunes.

I forced my eyes open, shutting them quickly when blurry light jarred through my head. What was happening to me? My chest burned. A wet cough dragged through my body. *Saints, I don't feel well.*

I opened my eyes again, angling my head downward. Blood stains streaked a crumpled white sheet. The sight tossed bits of memories at me.

Blood on my rug. On my knees scrubbing it off.

I made to move my limbs again, but a sturdy warmth surrounded me. Completely lost, like a leaf drifting across the Niger, I burrowed into this solid presence. *Safe.*

The presence wrapped muscled arms tighter around me, and I turned to stone.

My body lay swaddled in blankets... and stretched out beside me was a person. A *male*.

The bed bounced as I jerked upright and snatched my weapons from the corner. The motion was second nature, yet my very bones protested the speed.

My peach-and-green chamber glittered in the morning light. Perfectly in order, like the world was right. But over the mess of blankets, I straddled the legs of a muscled body stretched out on my *bed* and angled my nocked arrow at the invader's neck.

I released a strangled cry. *Dathan.*

Dathan's hazel eyes fluttered open, more green and gold this morning. He lifted a hand to rub back the tousled hair falling around his chiseled face. His face was tired yet somehow relaxed as psalms from the palace's temple trickled into the room.

"You woke up." He smiled dreamily, and my toes tingled. And then he registered my horror, my arrow set to kill him. "Blast it to the sheols. Set that arrow away, Zair, it's not what it looks like!"

"I'll rip your neck open if you don't start talking! Why are you in my bed—"

It happened in a blink. Dathan grabbed my wrists and shoved my weapons upward. My arrow released and slung for the wall. He yanked my bow and flung it from the bed. And then he twirled us until he pinned me beneath him, his face furious.

"That's no way to greet your savior, you murderous woman."

"Get off me!" I pushed at his shoulder and he instantly let me loose.

I sat up and yanked a blanket to my chest, although I was *thankfully* clothed. *What is this stinging pain on my left wrist?*

"I can explain," he said, swinging to a sitting position.

"Saints." Even through my alarm, heat sped over me to be this close to him. "*Did* we...?"

He pressed his lips together. "My intentions were completely honorable. It was you groping innocent me in your sleep."

"Don't laugh at me, you... you *rogue*! Explain!"

"Alright. I promise, nothing happened," he started somberly, but then his focus found the blood stains on the sheets. His face grew grim.

I grabbed a pillow and threw it over the stains. "That is *not* the point right now."

He yanked the pillow off and pointed at the stain. "You need a healer."

"How about we begin with *this* incriminating situation..."

Clattering noise from outside interrupted us. What was happening out there?

Dathan swung his long legs off my bed to investigate.

My door opened and a stream of cobalt, emerald-green, coral, and vermillion glistened into my room. In the dazzle, it took a long second to recognize the queen's zenana, led by the queen's sister, Khosana Meah Tedath.

My head spun. This could not be my luck.

The women sighted us. Their prim facades shattered into horrified masks. Collective gasps drained the air from the room.

"Fornicators!" a woman wailed, and I heard the glass walls of my future—every dream of joining the Ironteenth, of ever being accepted—shatter.

With five starkly different tribes constituting Thalesai, there were only three customs we'd collectively shared as individual kingdoms. Chastity was a third of those.

Kissing in public was one thing. Youths had to court, after all. But Dathan and I had no business even sitting on the edge of a bed together, much less be by ourselves on rumpled sheets.

My ragged breathing accelerated under their condemning glares. How could I fix this? Their hatred wouldn't just be over my tribe anymore. It would intensify now they believed I was tarnished.

"You would behave this shamelessly under the queen's roof?" the oldest noblewoman demanded.

I held out a beseeching hand. "Khosanas, it's not what it looks like, I promise."

Dathan walked from the bed with such controlled movements that eight pairs of eyes swiveled toward him. Those eyes surveyed his tousled appearance appreciatively.

"I can explain," he assured.

That seemed to be his mantra this morning! I wanted to fling a pillow at his *head*.

The queen's sister didn't glare with condemnation like the others, but she was perplexed. "Please do so immediately, Scholar Dathan."

Dathan braced himself. Would he heap the blame on me to save himself? To get me out of the palace and out of his way?

"Yes," a blonde Mizsab noblewoman said sympathetically, starry-eyed as she sashayed to touch Dathan's arm, almost molding herself to his chest. Queen Yval's distant cousin. "I'm sure you can explain how this *Esan* roped you into this... situation." She scowled at me, then smiled up at Dathan. "You innocent man."

My chest roiled. *Please, Dathan.*

Dathan gave the blonde a tight smile, then said to the zenana, "Khosanas, Zair Nebah and I are betrothed."

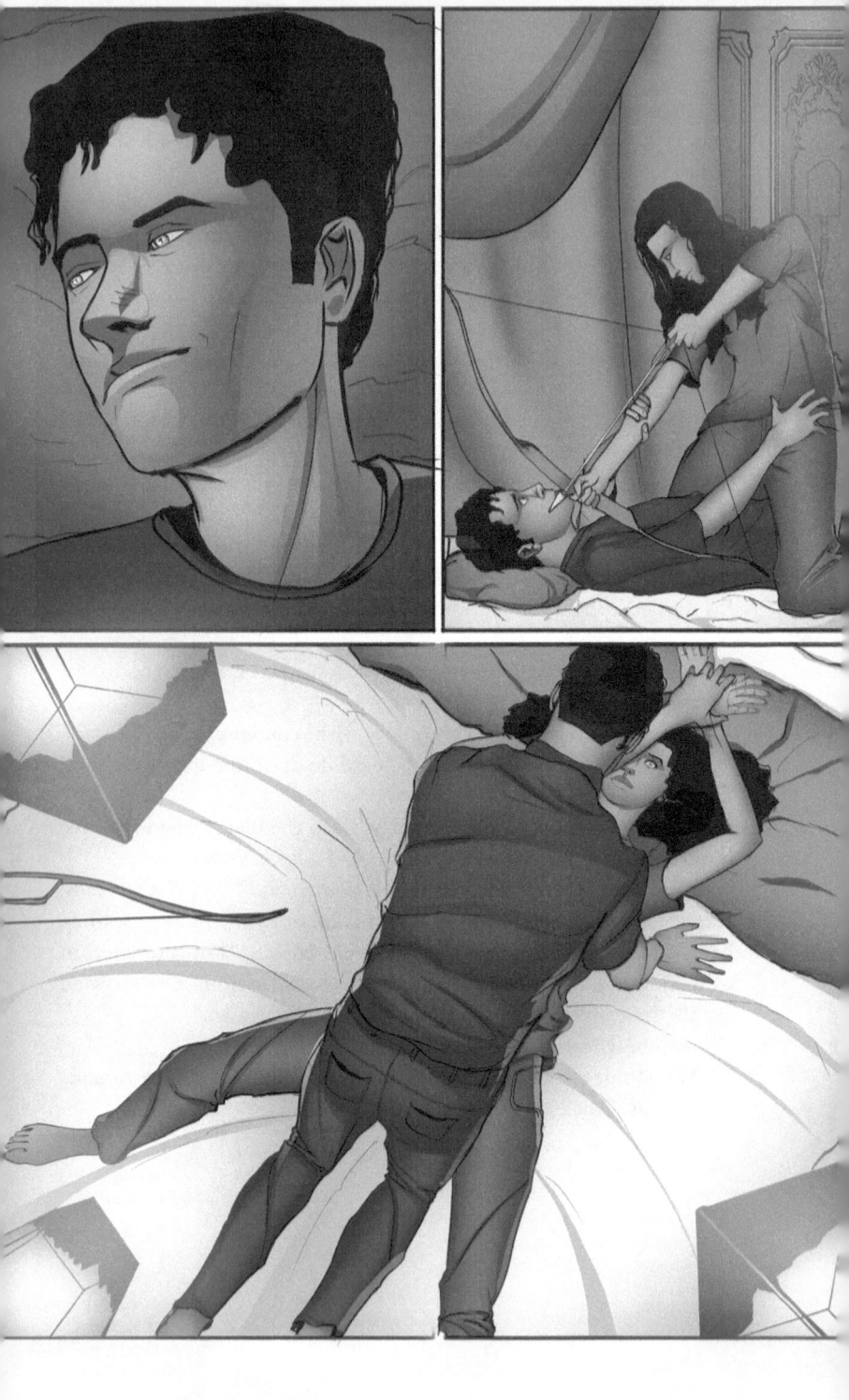

32

ZAIR

Another shocked gasp resounded in the room, this time from me too. Thankfully, no one noticed. Not even Mishan and Lysias, whose mouths fell open by my door.

"You're *what*?" the queen's cousin shrieked, her gold-tattooed hands jumping to her lush bosom.

"Betrothed," Dathan repeated, and she looked set to weep. "Zair and I had a private betrothal at the temple. After the Blessing of the King."

"No," the blonde refused. "No, you can't be betrothed to *her*."

I flinched. Yet at the mention of the king's Blessing, my mind recovered.

I couldn't allow these women to leave believing I was besmirched. Once the news spread, Queen Yval would throw me out of the palace. That wouldn't only damn me and bring the worst kind of shame to my family—my stomach cramped—but it would end my mission. Any chance to find the traitor, to ruin my sister's tyrants and help the missing students, would be gone. And if, by some luck, Queen Yval didn't throw me out, then *everyone* would be watching me, condemning and gossiping, and my goal would be harder.

Bits and pieces of last night returned to me.

Colonel Remmon had shoved me from the window after I'd caught him forging documents in the Admiral's office. My throat squeezed as I relived the agony that erupted in me as I slammed into concrete.

That I didn't wake up in a dungeon had to mean that somehow Dathan had found me before the Colonel did. Dathan had brought me back to my room.

He'd lied for me, tying himself to me, rather than denouncing me to spare himself. Someone who would show such selflessness... wouldn't deposit me in my bed and leave after finding me unconscious. My anger at him melted completely, replaced with a well of surprised gratitude.

The Colonel had caught me, but my chance to expose his schemes wasn't lost.

And this lie Dathan spun while stupefying, could save me in more ways than one.

The women stuttered, shocked that we'd been betrothed in the temple. Suddenly, their mouths pinched. They knew we'd say anything at this moment to escape a scandal. And they *wanted* to be correct so they could have scintillating gossip.

So I swallowed hard—and lied. "He's telling the truth, Khosanas. Dathan and I have been... interested in each other for some time. After a few days together in the Al'Qtraz, we knew... we knew..."

"That we have a persistent connection." He stared at me as he spoke. Almost musing. "So on the eve of the king's Blessing, I asked Zair to be my wife."

The queen's cousin made a choked noise.

The words, the intense way he spoke them, made me flush from head to toe.

"With the king's coronation ongoing," I scrambled, "now didn't seem like the right time to throw our betrothal ceremony."

"I proposed we have a private one," he said and his lips quirked in a soft smile, making my stomach flip. "I bound myself to Zair in heart until we could tell our families and throw a proper ceremony."

A few of the women softened from the romantic tale we were spinning. The other five, Khosana Meah included, still had creased brows.

I blurted, "And the king's Spaeman was there. He was kind enough to do our binding."

"The *Spaeman?*" voices exclaimed.

Why did I say that? Skies, this was why I avoided lying. When I was desperate to be believed, the strangest things came out of my mouth!

But if by some great favor the Spaeman vouched for us, no one would question our 'private betrothal'. We'd both suspected the Spaeman could be on our side. There was no better time to test that supposition than now.

The zenana's quizzing ceased. Any further confirmation they needed, they would have to get from the Spaeman.

Ibhar was also at the door now, his brows touching his hairline.

"By the by," Khosana Meah finally said, "being betrothed is no reason to be sharing a bed yet."

"Yes, Khosana Meah, but it *does* make it excusable since Zair and Dathan are to marry," Lysias piped in respectfully. "In the Kwali tribe, with our culture centered on family, couples are encouraged to share a bed after the betrothal so the bride can conceive before the wedding to be assured of her fertility, growing our modest tribe."

No one could contest *now* and dare insult the Kwali culture. I could've kissed Lysias's feet. She gave me a subtle wink, and I managed a wobbly smile of gratitude.

Wrung from the extremes of emotions I'd been jerked through between last night and this morning, I squeezed the blanket at my chest. "Did you all need something from me, Khosanas?"

Khosana Meah seemed to understand my thorough discomfort. Mercifully, she allowed the topic to change. "Today is Her Majesty's *vyji.*"

"She will be washed by the priestesses, anointed, and adorned in the jewels of the Queen of Thalesai," the cousin said stiffly.

The *vyji* was like the Blessing of the King, for the queen. But her blessing was attended only by women, and not just any but only the fifteen the queen wanted to witness her honorary moment. When she decided on her fifteen witnesses, she sent her zenana to invite them, bearing gifts.

I gawked. Being invited was an honor noblewomen would kill for. Queen Yval couldn't want *me* to attend.

Khosana Meah made a hand gesture. The youngest noblewoman stepped toward me with a heap of folded fabrics. I had no choice but to lower my blanket, my flimsy defense, and retrieve the twinkling deep-blue fabrics. An open box of jewelry sat on top.

"Queen Yval Izrymia Nogbaisi has invited you to witness her *vyji*, Scholar Zair," Khosana Meah said.

My eyes almost fell from my head. Dathan's brows flicked up and Lysias's hands flew to her mouth.

"Will you be there?" Khosana Meah asked as was customary.

I managed a nod. "I would be... *honored*."

Light danced in Khosana Meah's eyes as she gestured for the women to sashay out.

"Scholar Dathan," the blonde said. "You truly are vowed to this Esan?"

Every head tilted to Dathan.

"To Scholar Zair," Dathan corrected courteously. "Yes, I am, Khosana."

"Come along, Asha." The oldest noblewoman pulled the distraught blonde out.

We waited for the room to empty, but Khosana Meah cleared her throat delicately and narrowed her gaze at Dathan.

Dathan played oblivious.

"*Scholar Dathan*," she called.

He sighed with annoyance. "I'm leaving."

As he strode around my bed, he pinned *me* with a look that said '*you and me are going to talk.*'

I squirmed yet somehow, everything in me felt heated.

"The queen's *vyji*? Congratulations!" Lysias grinned before closing my door.

My bed rippled as I fell into it, staring at the ceiling. What had just happened?

Dathan saved me. I'd done nothing to deserve it or to show I'd ever needed his help. I'd needed to prove to the Commandant that I could be an independent soldier. Worthy of her approval. Yet... if Dathan hadn't come to my aid, I would've been in a damning situation.

What if... doing everything alone wasn't the best strategy? Not just with this mission, but with *life,* the way my schoolmates' rejection at Nergal had led me to believe?

I quickly shook off the thought. I was grateful, but Dathan was still my opponent. He was still after my target. I couldn't show him further weaknesses by seeming incompetent. I had too much to lose.

My chest seized. When I coughed into my hands, it was no longer just drops of blood but a pool of it.

"Such an inauspicious day for a *vyji*," my maid murmured, clipping silver jewelry to my ears. "After waking up to a threat in the palace, who knows what other dooms the day might bring?"

I bit my tongue, terrified to say or do anything that might stir her suspicion too. Thankfully, the hot bath she'd prepared eased the soreness in my body so I wasn't limping about, indeed, like a person who fell from a window. I could hardly fathom how I was standing at all. Or where the piercing on my wrist, like something punctured it, came from. My face was bruised but not as badly as it should be.

She smiled teasingly. "Do you need me to help you apply the betrothal symbol?"

Betrothal. I gulped and reached for the kohl. "I'll do it myself."

She batted my hand away. "*Kai!* It's your first *majja* application. It's a taboo to do it yourself the first time."

"My mother and older sister aren't here to apply it," I protested.

"Which means it's up to me."

I was too surprised that she wanted to do it, apply my *majja*, to say it wouldn't be a taboo because the betrothal was a lie.

"Thank you," I said quietly.

"Ah. So you *can* smile. It might be a day of miracles after all!"

I chuckled. She dipped the liner in the kohl and created three black dots above the golden-brown skin of my right brow.

"There. You look like a woman vowed," she smiled.

For a moment, the burdens on my shoulders fell away. An unfamiliar feeling filled me as I surveyed the result. I'd resigned myself to not marrying years ago. While it was a dream of my mother to see her daughters wed to people who treasured us, Niah and I knew better than to hope we'd be as lucky as my mother had been, meeting my father who accepted her, Esan and all. So I'd poured everything into soldiering. Burying the young dreamer who longed for love someday.

Now Dathan Issachar, my nemesis, was my first kiss.

I ran my fingers beneath my rouge-reddened lips. Dressed like a girl betrothed, like a woman a man desired regardless of my tribe, it nudged the dreamer awake.

Smiling at my expression, the maid gave me a gentle push toward the door. "It's wrong to keep the queen waiting."

The queen. My mission. My bubble popped.

Can I trust you to let no one and nothing stand in your way?

Giddiness morphed into dread. Saints. My Commandant would ruin me if she learned the boy threatening her goal of catching the traitor was now my *airran*.

THE QUEEN HAD carriages prepared for the witnesses of her *vyji*. As if secretly concerned that today was inauspicious too, she'd prepared guards for us. We rode through the city's quickest routes, encountering light traffic, but reached the outer gates in an hour.

I opened my book and escaped into the hoary pages as we cut through overlapping sand dunes. Eventually, the turquoise oasis of Saint Ame flattened out a slice of the golden landscape, and I shut my book.

"It's vacant," I observed with surprise.

Its waters were believed to be fed by Saint Ame's sweat as she toiled to keep women strong through life's challenges. After the healer had treated Sarai's slash from the mercenary's blade, my distraught mother brought us here to pray for Sarai's safety. It had been crammed with women from the nearby settlements that day.

"For the queen's *vyji*," the guard muttered.

I disembarked from the carriage. Tall palm trees created an umbrella as I ambled through a path to the oasis.

The turquoise pool rippled in the sunlight. Plush trees formed a thick crown, branches dancing almost eerily with the desert breeze. The women present were dressed in the same midnight blue as I, but in different styles and jewels.

I took quiet steps closer to the beginning ceremony. All present here were wives of Generals, wives to Dynasts, and Councilwomen. The enormity of the queen's invitation to witness struck me again.

Why did she want a mere year-five Esan student here?

Queen Yval stepped forward. She shrugged her thick robe off her shoulders until she stood bare. I averted my gaze until she waded into the oasis to waist level, halting where the High Priestess awaited her with a golden jar.

We sang the chorus praising the young queen, clapping along as the High Priestess poured oils over her head. Water shivered from the droplets, and Queen Yval stood with squared shoulders as thick steam drifted from the water.

I gasped at the sign of Saint Ame's acceptance.

If this was indeed the saint's abode, could she have heard my mother's pleas for Sarai's safety? *Please help us, Saint Ame.*

Voices grew louder with our song, the clapping merrier.

Experiencing the making of a queen... it was an ethereal experience I'd never forget.

The High Priestess declared, "You entered the pool of Saint Ame, a commoner, Yval Nogbaisi. Now, you emerge Her Royal Majesty, the Queen of Thalesai."

Queen Yval swam through the oasis, cleansing herself of the oils in a symbol of newness.

Her older sister, Khosana Meah, wrapped a towel around her and dried her. With the assistance of two zenanas, Khosana Meah dressed the queen in gilded lace and a circlet of diamonds.

She looked surreally transformed, yet so young.

What a time to be queen. When Thalesai, still seeking its footing as a kingdom, seemed to be falling apart around us. Yet there was both strength and vulnerability to her. And it made me want even more to be one of her archers. To defend my queen.

Queen Yval glided beneath the palm trees, thanking the women for bearing witness. How many of them were genuinely happy? How many harbored scorn against an Ussi queen behind their smiles?

As the queen approached me, I shifted on my feet. The queen shouldn't be thanking me; I shouldn't even be here.

I wore a tentative smile. "Your Majesty. Thank you for inviting me to witness."

A surprised smile lit up her face as she gestured to my right brow. "Is it to who I suspect?"

I tried to answer but my throat wouldn't work. *Who she suspected?* Queen Yval paid attention to me?

"Indeed, it *is* to Scholar Issachar," Khosana Meah answered beside the queen. "We found out in the most... interesting manner."

My face caught afire.

Queen Yval gave a wave. "The king and I weren't exactly modest while *we* were courting."

I blinked. The king and queen were ordained from different tribes for the sake of balance and peace. I hadn't known there was a courtship.

"Has there been a betrothal ceremony?" Queen Yval asked with baffling enthusiasm.

"We are... still planning one," I hedged.

Heads swiveled in our direction, noblewomen wondering what the queen could possibly be saying to me for this long.

"They were vowed in secret and are postponing an official celebration until after the coronation," Khosana Meah said.

"Is that so?" Queen Yval tapped her chin. "Well, then, I suppose it falls to me to throw you both a ceremony in the Al'Qtraz."

What?

"Your Majesty, please, that is unnecessary," I exclaimed. Bells started *tinkling* in my head, and I rubbed my temple absently.

"Nonsense." She waved, her smile excited. "You became betrothed while being my guests. Your families aren't here to celebrate because you're both here for me and the king. What kind of hostess would I be if I didn't throw you a befitting celebration in their stead..."

The bells in my head shrieked.

Boom! The earth quaked, the impact hurling some noblewoman to their knees. Above, the sky darkened and churned like a grey and black soup.

Oh no! It was *them*.

Queen Yval looked to her Ironteenth Archers charging in on kiniuns. "What's happening..."

White light flashed in the sky and plunged down in a thin streak.

"Your Majesty!" I grabbed her arms and threw us both to the ground. Lightning struck the exact spot she'd stood and fire exploded.

Screams split the air. Black smoke fogged the oasis, and ugly memories surged. Sarai dragged away. Failing to save her. I trembled uncontrollably as people ran around me.

Sarai is safe at home. Protect your queen. Arrows flew at the sky.

"*Where is Her Majesty?*" a deep voice yelled.

Forcing my body to obey, I flipped over to shield the queen with my back. "Your Majesty, are you alright?"

She panted. "I... I think so."

"We need to find cover!"

I rose and helped her stand. But lightning blackened my vision, and I lost hold of the queen as an explosion flung me against a tree. The world spun, pain barking up my body. A bloody cough stained my hands as I crawled through mud.

I've lost the queen. In the chaos, I scrambled around in a panic. They'd taken the queen. They'd... There, by the murky water, her diamond circlet shone. I crawled faster for it, heart in my throat.

On the side of a log, she lay unmoving in the shallow end of the water. Fire blasted and sand poured like rain, almost burying us underneath the slush.

Grabbing her shoulder, I shook frantically. "Please wake up. Please!"

She heaved in a breath and coughed water onto my hands. Her eyes opened, terrified.

"Thank the saints!"

"Zair. Are these the...?"

"Mercenaries. Yes. We must go!" I took her arm and we staggered up together, stumbling over shattered trees in the smoke. We found our way to some wailing women the guards herded to the carriages. Their relief abounded at the sight of the queen.

"The dove still flies!" an Ironteenth Archer called.

And as we made it to the carriages, the lightning and booming slowly ceased. The lingering smell of sulfur filled my lungs.

Minutes flew as the Ironteenth tore the oasis apart for the attackers. I moved to check on the women—nobles who were too shaken to reject my concern. Many were bruised, some in shock, but none were lost.

"What sort of people would attack their own queen?" Khosana Meah fumed.

Soon, the Ironteenth affirmed that the bandits had fled when the arrows began to fly. They were gone.

Queen Yval was filthy and shaken. Still, she stepped forward, looked at each of us, and said quietly, "Word of this must not leave this place. We came and held my *vyji*. That was all that happened here today. Is that clear?"

33

DATHAN

Tension was a breathing beast in the palace over the Jalin Base attack. News had quickly circulated around the capital and the kingdom beyond that the Admiral had apprehended twelve mercenaries.

Within the palace, however, additional reports had arrived.

Spotting the emissary from my balcony, I made my way outside the palace and followed him from a distance. I kept my demeanor casual, greeting some of the passing Baihan dignitaries. They responded absently. All the unwanted attention—the shock and indignation especially—over my surprise betrothal to an Esan girl had been redirected to the Admiral's successful capture of mercenaries.

Skies above, I was a betrothed man.

It's not real.

It *was* real enough in the eyes of the most important women in court. When the queen's zenana had barged into Zair's room and given her those condemning stares, I'd known it would only either take an act of Osime himself to draw back the claws they'd been ready to sink into Zair or a betrothal.

The protector within me had reared. I had just risked my life to save Zair's last night and had spent half of the night coaxing breaths from her. I'd had no intention of letting the women shred her apart. It had made spinning the tale flow as fluidly as swordplay with Jaziah. A part of me had enjoyed seeing her squirm a little as I held her gaze and purred the story of our secret betrothal.

Now that it was done, reality barreled down.

Big lies had big penalties. My breathing slowed in the hum of the ground floor. If the zenana found out we lied... I didn't want to contemplate the terrible consequences that would follow. And despite the insistent flames flashing through my chest each time I thought of her, I needed to keep holding her at arm's length. Far away from my suspects and mission. But this false betrothal had just placed her right in my arms.

If we were lucky, the zenana would leave it all as it was, and we would leave the palace with the ruse in place. With the internal clash between good logic and impossible feelings, that was as far ahead as I could plan.

The emissary entered the royal orchard. I drew a steadying breath, settled my mind, and followed silently. Orderly rows of trees hid me, the scent of sweet clover soothing my clenched chest. Many yards away, smilodons—the king's two wild pets—wrestled with long fangs and vicious claws, their growls scaring birds off trees.

Through the rows of trees, I spotted the king's closest circle in the velvet chairs surrounding a stone table. I lithely pulled myself onto a high branch and vanished behind the leaves as I listened.

"The apprehended mercenaries won't break," the emissary said gravely to King Khasar, Ambassador Caiphas, and the two Royal Advisors. "Eight are dead after secretly ingesting poison. The rest were forced to vomit the poison before it could claim their lives. Their leader is close to death."

Curse it. This could be another dead end.

Ambassador Caiphas swore, jerking upright to kick a cluster of leaves. "We *finally* have captives that include some of the mercenary leaders, and they plan to die rather than give us what we need to end this threat!"

Disappointment gripped King Khasar until he seemed like he might snap in two on his ornate chair. He looked... lost.

Second Advisor Drake's eyes gleamed to see the Baihan king he had to serve appear overwhelmed. My jaw clenched protectively.

Ambassador Caiphas saw that gleam too. He moved protectively before his brother, held the king's shoulder, and their resemblance shone.

"The news is destabilizing, yes, but you *can* handle this. Give the orders. What do you need us to do, Your Majesty?"

King Khasar seemed to draw strength from his brother's faith. He rose. "Gather my Generals in the Chambers. We need to change tactics."

"Alright." Caiphas squeezed the king's shoulder. "You have this, Khasar."

First Advisor Maachah paced, stroking his candle-white beard in thought. "The foreign guests should be kept busy while we hold this meeting. The councilors can give them a tour of the history gallery. They're sensing the city's tensions and growing intrigued. We need to keep them as far from all of this as possible."

"Good thinking." The king tapped the table. "See that handled, Maachah."

"You know my history, Your Majesty." The First Advisor's temple ticked. "How bandits captured me, my first wife, and our children. How they... tortured me and murdered them."

I frowned with surprise.

"You felt helpless," the king said grimly. "And it made you aspire to become a leader and protect those you care for."

First Advisor Maachah swallowed. "You're the leader of all. Now, let's protect our interests."

The king gave a resolved nod. The Second Advisor bristled like the rustling leaves, envious. I half-expected him to launch into his own tragic history.

As they dispersed from the orchard, I wondered if the foreign ambassadors knew more about Thalesai's unsteadiness than they admitted to. If we couldn't keep Thalesai from falling apart under treachery, what the foreigners knew would ultimately not matter.

I had already decided to use the exclusivity of the queen's *vyji* today to my advantage. The Crowning, the sixth event, would be held tomorrow. I needed to use this eventless day to travel to Gergesenes and speak with my Commandant.

After charming an elderly secretary in the Chamber of Hoofs, I was granted a day's pass.

Ibhar strolled into the busy ground floor just as I exited. He was windblown, as if he'd ridden hard from somewhere. He moved as I did sometimes, as if taking advantage of the crowd. Blending in.

What was the blackguard up to?

Two weeks, Sarhedrin said. Just before he'd killed four men.

Pushing Ibhar from my thoughts, I rode hard, out of the city's grand southern gates and into the Geidam Dunes. A long hour filled with glimmering sand and rattlesnakes passed. Finally, the Gergesenes Military Academy sprawled imposingly in the Dades Valley, to the east of the dunes. I traveled through the flat-roofed buildings of the settlement and the spring where Jaziah and I had our last conversation. Familiar faces called out greetings. I wore a smile, but inside memories of the Spaeman's vision of Jaziah cut me to pieces.

Clad in my uniform, I passed Gergesenes' elaborate gates without hassle from the sentries and trotted down the broad road for the administration block. Hot air ruffled through my cape as I slid off my horse and drank in the school.

Clashing weapons echoed from the training fields, classrooms buzzed with our tutors' no-nonsense voices, and I greeted military staff weaving across the staff blocks.

Back in the familiarity of my second home, Jaziah's absence threatened to overwhelm me. He should be here. I would've gone to tell him about the jarring events at the palace. I could envision him choking on his water canteen as I told him I happened to be betrothed.

But he wasn't here. And he would never be here again if I failed. I turned and strode to the Commandant's office.

"Sir, has there been news on Jaziah?" I asked the moment I closed the Commandant's door behind me.

"None for now," he said grimly. My spirit plummeted.

With the threat hanging over the GGSA and one of his best

students still missing, the Commandant seemed to have aged a decade since I last saw him.

"Sit, Issachar," he ordered and I obeyed. "The Admiral informed me that you students were taken captive during the Tour." His fist tightened. "How are you recovering?"

I stiffened. The Commandant knew that being restrained was my trigger. That this man I only wanted to impress knew my weakness would never be easy to swallow.

"Perfectly, sir. Have the Secruvi bandits been punished?"

His temple pulsed. "The Admiral and his soldiers searched the storage you described in Secruvi."

I leaned forward, nodding.

"The place was cleaned out, with one cell burnt. They left no sign of usage, which is enough to suspect that it *had* been a base for insidious dealings."

Heat flushed through me. So they had gone unpunished.

"I'm sorry they weren't brought to justice." He shook his head. "That seems to be Thalesai's new tune. To be barraged by criminals we can't punish." He sighed bitterly. "Tell me everything you've found from the palace."

I laid before him the pieces. Pieces I turned over every night while I battled sleep, yet were still not adding up. The Dynast of Bornoir schemed with Ambassador Caiphas—the king's own brother, while preying on the Royal Accountant. How he poisoned the Royal Accountant's drinks and killed his assistants, was restless about the Admiral capturing mercs, murdered the Royal Accountant's guards with men who resembled bandits, and attempted to break into the Royal Accountant's offices.

Commandant gave a thoughtful nod. "Did he succeed?"

I lowered my brows over the Commandant's lack of shock. He was grim. His eyes flashed when I mentioned the murdered guards, but he wasn't half as shocked as I still felt.

"He couldn't break the lock, but I know the Dynast of Bornoir. He won't give up trying until he's in that office." Bitterness slipped into my voice.

Commandant rubbed his jaw. "A lot of dirty games are played in the palace," he finally said. "Outside, the Al'Qtraz is a riveting beauty, but within is a festering rot caused by the hunger for power. I know you aspire to serve there in the Ironteenth unit. If you are recruited, it won't be just bandits or external forces you'll protect the Majesties from, but also those who are supposed to love them. Right now, our target is the traitor sponsoring the mercenaries. No one else."

In other words, he hadn't sent me to monitor Sarhedrin, even if Sarhedrin had proven to be a cold-blooded murderer. It enraged him, but his foremost priority was getting his hands on the person who threatened his students, Thalesai's next generation of leaders.

I needed to convince him that I wasn't chasing wind. Convince myself I wasn't driven by the need for revenge.

"One way the traitor supports the mercenaries is through funding," I stated. "The Dynast of Bornoir is wealthy. Yet he's been doggedly after the Royal Accountant, a man whose duty revolves around managing Thalesai's wealth. I believe he is after a great sum of money that only the Royal Accountant has access to. Why? For nefarious purposes."

Even though I had yet to uncover *how* he intended to get the money. I doubted the Royal Accountant stacked his offices with gold like a trove. Still, I could see the Commandant was considering my argument.

"And there's also the secret meeting I saw Sarhe... the Dynast of Bornoir have with the king's brother Caiphas."

The Commandant frowned. "I can't argue that it's puzzling. Ambassador Caiphas is loyal to the king and fiercely protective of him, so why confer with an Ussi fanatic like Sarhedrin?"

His confirmation of my suspicions lightened my joints. While I loathed Sarhedrin, I wanted to believe I was putting Jaziah, my kingdom, and academy first.

"Investigate there," he ordered. "But remember, we don't have time for misjudgments, Issachar. Cast a wide net and let nothing slip past you."

I nodded, opened my mouth, but hesitated.

The Commandant spoke watchfully. "Tell me everything you know. Even the smallest detail could be the clue that helps us save hundreds of lives."

"Nergal Academy also has a spy in the palace."

The Commandant's face tightened. "I suspected that might

happen; their academy has taken all the hits so far. And Nergal's Commandant is keen. She must've pieced together that there's a traitor pulling the strings in the palace."

I frowned, sensed there was more he wasn't sharing.

"Colonel Remmon tried to kill the Nergal spy last night." I fisted my hands at the image of Zair unmoving on the ground. "I believe the spy was tailing him and got caught."

At the mention of Colonel Remmon, the Commandant jumped to his feet, knocking his chair over. "You are *certain* the spy is after the First Colonel?"

"I saw his face." My fingernails dug crescents into my palm.

A vein in the Commandant's forehead throbbed. "So you two spies are for the same cause yet following different leads."

"Yes, sir."

"Do you know what information the Nergal spy has on the Colonel?" he asked urgently.

"Neither of us is opening up with what we know."

"Good. Keep your lead close and *away* from the other spy, but find out Nergal's lead. I've served with the Commandant of Nergal. The woman is merciless with traitors. If she wants the traitor in the palace in her grip, it would not be to interrogate him."

A ticking began in my head like the clock on Gergesenes' watchtower.

"Why then would Nergal's Commandant want the traitor?" I asked carefully.

"To kill him. Ensure he never aids the mercenaries in tormenting her students again."

The air left my lungs. That was Zair's mission. To *assassinate* a chamberman.

She wasn't just my opponent in finding the traitor. While I had to capture the traitor alive, Zair's mission was to kill them. She was a lethal opponent, and I'd just tied myself to her with a fake betrothal. My muscles tightened. I knew her end goal. Now more than before, I had to sever this tenacious pull between us. I couldn't let my guard down.

"But the Nergal Commandant's approach would waste good intel," my Commandant said crucially. "If she kills the spy, our strongest link to the mercenaries dies. Do you understand?"

I did. I had to block Zair's mission.

"Why don't we take these suspicions to the king?" I asked with some frustration. "After the attack on Jalin Base, shouldn't he be hungry for every lead on the mercenaries?"

"Thalesai is a house on fire, and the king is throwing a blanket over it to keep the neighbors from finding out. If we go to the king with these suspicions, he won't only treat it as one more secret to hide. He'll pour his anger on us for pointing fingers within his court and causing dissent. He's determined to trust his chambermen because he believes that will unify Thalesai. We have no choice but to take matters into our hands."

The weight on my shoulders increased. I was only one person, a student, going against the king's rules and a network of traitors. My failure meant the missing students would never be rescued, that the kingdom could fall apart.

That I could lose my friend forever.

It was too much load for one person.

"I know this is a heavy burden to bear, Issachar," the Commandant said gravely. "But now isn't the time to waver under it. Can you go on, or do I have to send another in your place?"

No way. My boots snapped at attention. "I am capable, sir."

34

DATHAN

Zair was an assassin. Her mission would destroy mine.
I won't let her do that.

Evening was spinning blue webs around the world when my mount reached the palace. My boots barely met the ground before courtiers surrounded me. They talked over my baffled questions, draping garlands over my neck and pulling me up the stairs.

"*It's time, Scholar Dathan!*"

"*...the Majesties are waiting.*"

At the students' lounge, Mishan strode out of his room, dressed lavishly as if attending some celebration.

"Mishan, what's happening?" I called over the relentless wave of bodies.

Mishan grinned. "Your betrothal party, Gergesenes!"

I could not have heard him right. "*What?*"

"Queen Yval is throwing you and Zair an official vowing tonight."

Blood drained from my face. The servants draped thick clothes on my shoulders, and hands nudged me into my chambers.

Bleeding sheols. I'd ridden hard to the palace to latch myself to Sanhedrin tonight, expose and cart off the culprit long before Zair found him. There was no time for a betrothal ceremony, one that would cram Zair and I in the *same* room for hours.

I slipped out of my jacket, impulse pushing me to dodge the ceremony. I shook my head and let the soldier's voice of reason prevail. I couldn't ignore Her Majesty's summons, or even keep her waiting if I didn't want to worsen the situation. I donned the embroidered knee-length tunic of ivory and silver, and the slender silver trousers. The hems and high collar gleamed with quartz: because the attire was a royal gift. *Curse this*. I donned the white velvet cap, the ivory-beaded necklace, and bracelets.

My image stared back in the mirror and the ramification of my lies hit me like a fist to the gut.

I looked... like a man about to be betrothed before the world.

What had we done?

Lying that we were betrothed was one thing—having a ceremony with a priestess present and all the customs fulfilled would truly bind Zair and me. There would be no leaving the palace and being free of our lies. Zair and I, two students from rival schools and very different tribes, would be locked together. My door flung open. The wave of courtiers swept me back downstairs into two rectangular halls connected by an archway.

"My daughter had eyes for you, Scholar, but alas life will go on," the mother of Khosana Anesua said with a tense smile and guilt pricked my gut.

Courtiers peeled off into the celebration, swiping goblets and small cakes from the buffets.

A tattooed hand landed on my shoulder, and Mishan came up beside me. "You could've told me it was like that between you and Zair. I would've given you tips on satisfying women. Zair looked very... tense this morning."

"Save your tips, rooster, it's nothing like you think," I countered testily and tugged at my neck scarf. "How are there so many courtiers here?"

Mishan winked at a girl who giggled. "Two elite students under the king's roof engaged? One of them *Dathan Issachar*, the pride of Gergesenes and the Baihans? Who'd want to miss this historic moment?"

"Hilarious. You should have gone to theater school."

"You know it's the truth."

An Ironteenth guard appeared in front of us. Mishan excused himself, congratulating me with a grin.

My stomach hardened. "Sir."

The doors whipped open. We both angled our heads as a flustered Zair walked in. My chest constricted.

My exquisite adversary.

A gilded caftan of ivory and silver cascaded down her slender body—a tense body that had felt soft last night, snuggled into me in sleep. Even the bruises on her face took nothing from her allure.

Zair, though, the *aiyena*, looked like she'd been thrown into a battlefield.

Her harried gaze found mine and widened slightly. Her cheeks lightened as she took in my identical ensemble, and I corked my head. Not the reaction of a girl who had once declared hatred of me. I reveled mercilessly in her shy fidgeting, finding that the three dots of kohl above her brows didn't make me want to bolt for the dunes like some neighbors had said they'd wanted to at their betrothals. I appreciated the symbol that declared to the world, to all the ogling males in this room, that this brave, fighting girl was *mine*.

The powerful tug, the intense possessiveness, shocked me. But it had taken root. Our rivalry could continue tomorrow. Even if it was all fake, I now needed to perform—and the idea didn't seem daunting at all.

"The king will meet with you, Scholar Dathan," the Ironteenth Fighter said.

I'd forgotten he was there. Shaking my head to gather my wits, I said, "Of course."

Wait, did he say the *king*?

He smirked as if saying he understood being besotted with a woman, and then his broad form preceded me to the second hall.

We would have to lie to the Majesties too. We were so damned.

Hands clapped my shoulders, wishing me curious congratulations while I braced for my reckoning. In the second hall, everyone gravitated toward the king and queen who sat on bronze thrones at the center. Blood rumbled in my ears.

"Your Majesties." I went on a knee before the dazzling royals, stunned that they were present here.

Their amber damask regalia flowed around them, glimmering with obsidian studs and casting every other guest into the shadows. The queen's dawn-red hair rippled in braids and twirls, adorned with a delicate crown of cowries.

The king especially hated deceit; our missions would end, any dream of joining the Ironteenth ruined, if they had learned that Zair and I were lying snakes. Our motives would not matter.

"Rise, Scholar," King Khasar ordered me. His sharp coffee eyes ran over my face and his voice softened. "Tonight, we're here for you."

Wait. Queen Yval was *smiling* at me.

I slowly obeyed, betraying no hint of my unease. What was happening?

The king tilted his head. "The Spaeman told us that you and Scholar Nebah have been joined for some time."

I choked on air, accepted the goblet of water a servant held out, and tried to keep up with what was going on here. The Spaeman had lied for us? It took powerful discipline not to gawk at the intimidating being standing beside the Majesties' seats.

"How sneaky of you to also use the Blessing of the King for your vowing," King Khasar said.

No hostility in his tone. If anything, he seemed... amused.

"They *are* military students, taught to optimize opportunities," Queen Yval said in her lilting voice.

"I... we..." I couldn't complete the statement. My brain was a shattered vase.

Queen Yval chuckled delightedly. Her glowing tresses rippled aside, revealing a bruise on her jaw. "I adore seeing how strong men react to love."

King Khasar gave my blanched face a wave. "The queen and Spaeman believed you deserve a real ceremony as the prime students of your academies and guests at the palace. And I agree."

Not just the queen, but the *Spaeman* had pushed for Zair and I to be betrothed in truth? Why? He knew we were lying.

"I cannot stay long." Grimness passed over the king's face. *What had been decided at his strategy meeting with his chambermen over the mercenaries?* "I have matters to attend to, but I came to give your union my blessing."

The queen smiled softly at him and he smiled back, something tender and deep passing between them.

I cleared my throat, forced my thoughts to correlate. "I'm honored, Your Majesties. For your blessing and presence here."

"It's our pleasure," the king said.

I dared shift my gaze to the Spaeman.

For once, the Spaeman's thoughts were clear in his glower.

If you two fools want me to vouch for you, you might as well make your betrothal real and not make me a liar and accomplice!

I stifled a cringe.

King Khasar clapped and ordered the vowing to begin.

Bodies surrounded me. Zair and I were thrown together on a low dais at the center of the first hall. A priestess sat opposite us on the ottoman with silk ribbons and jars of frankincense before her. Lysias and Mishan pushed their way to the front of the nobles on Zair's end, calling themselves "friends of the couple." Lysias beamed at us, then inched up on her toes to speak in Mishan's ear.

"You just had to call the Spaeman's name, didn't you?" I leaned close to accuse in Zair's ear.

Her scent of spiced honey could make a man sell his house for just another whiff.

Pink tinted Zair's bruised cheeks, but she whispered back, "*You* had to use a betrothal as an excuse. Of all things."

The priestess gestured for us to place our hands in her open palms. A chorus rose in the halls with the chiming of cymbals, a song about the life journey we were beginning together. The Majesties had taken new seats in the first hall, and Queen Yval sang too, laughing softly at whatever the king whispered in her ear. Lysias looked happier than the *aiyena*, swinging her hips as she sang.

"Well forgive me for not realizing I had many excuses to choose from," I began drily in the din, just as the women beside me shook their heads with pitying looks.

"Too bad," one's words carried to me. "One of the best students that Gergesenes has seen, being tied down to an Esan girl. He could do so much better."

My shoulders tensed, but I tried to ignore them, to avoid interacting with Ussis.

"Do you think she's with child? She might've used that to trap him," the other whispered.

"That would explain the secret betrothal! Esans have no honor after all."

"None at all."

That was it. I stared at the Ussi noblewomen, and they gasped when they caught my message. *Back off*. They lifted their chins in affront and murmured in lower tones about how they shouldn't have been concerned for me.

Zair did not deserve to be spoken about disrespectfully. Fake vowing or not. If she had heard them, she gave no indication, and I prayed she hadn't.

"Being betrothed to the man you hate must be hard," I murmured to her.

"Sheer agony," Zair parried.

The priestess joined our hands together. My skin sizzled at the contact. Zair sucked in a quiet breath and although she avoided my gaze, I knew she'd felt it too.

If fate was not full of tricks. The girl who was determined to kill the person I needed alive was who my chest pounded hard for.

The priestess gave an amazed cry. "What a union! *Siele mhueli uyeme e!*"

Souls bound beyond lifetimes in Binhese.

Zair gaped. My ribs locked. Not possible. No. This priestess must be playing along with our ruse. The Spaeman must've involved her somehow.

"*Soulmates?*" Lysias gasped gleefully.

Mishan snorted. "There's been no human soulmates recorded since Thalesai's first king and queen, Lili-girl. Your Binhese must be terrible."

Lysias stuck out her tongue at him.

The priestess wrapped red silk ribbons around our joined hands. A binding symbol that made the singing louder and more cheerful. *One*. It meant. *Two to become one*.

As if having the same thoughts, as if desperate to fight it, Zair whispered, or wailed, to me, "You could've told them that I was ill. That you'd stopped by my rooms to check on me."

I didn't say that in addition to making certain she was well, last night... had been for me too. I couldn't explain how, but I'd slept better than I had in years with her beside me.

"If I'd given the zenana that excuse, then the bastard who'd pushed you down saints-know-how-many-feet," I said with a burst of rage at the thought, "might've heard and pried into what happened to you."

The snarled answer seemed to sink in. That this betrothal, while extreme and destabilizing, had spared her in more ways than one.

She swallowed but kept her chin stubbornly tilted. "Thank you."

"You also owe me an apology," I said.

She squished her brows. "For what? And do not say it's because I said I hated you. I did hate you that night."

"I could think of a dozen ways you've been... inhospitable since we met. But," I said before she could interrupt, "for being rude to me in front of your family."

Her eyes darted away. "You shouldn't have come to join us."

"Why is that such a crime? Students greet each other's parents during visitations. It's a friendly gesture."

"You know we could *never* be friends. I can't have my family thinking otherwise."

I stifled a flinch, then clenched my jaw. "Indeed?"

"Yes, because then they'd like you and expect you to always come around. And we both know you wouldn't want that."

"Because your Esan instincts are so omniscient that you know everything about me."

She bit on her lip, and then released a breath. "You're right. I was rude, while you were... respectful. I'm sorry."

My jaw almost dropped, and yet she was so sincere that I heard myself say, "You look wonderful tonight."

Flustered, her cheeks brightened as she searched for a retort. Finding none, she settled on, "Hush, Gergesenes."

I chuckled at her lovely face, mumbled, "You're a heartbreaker, and somehow you don't know it."

She fell silent as we were officially declared betrothed, *airran* and *aiyena*.

We were immediately pulled apart and married folks pelted us with advice until I never wanted to hear the words 'marriage' and 'betrothal' again. Each time I glanced at Zair, she was surrounded by courtiers' fake smiles and sharp eyes.

This isn't how it should be.

The Royal Accountant entered the halls, light playing on his scar, and I released a pent-up breath. I'd been toying with a plan during my ride back from Gergesenes. It was risky, but now that Sarhedrin's prey was right here, I couldn't miss the opportunity.

The Royal Accountant made for Queen Yval. I quickly excused myself and wove through bodies.

"Khosa." I moved before the elegant man. I took his hand, wrapping my hands all the way up to his wrist. His embroidered sleeve concealed it. "I'm *honored* to have you at my vowing."

The Royal Accountant's return smile held guilt, because the vowing was not why he was here. But with courtesy, he said, "Of course. Congratulations, Scholar."

"Thank you, Khosa," I grinned, already in contact with what I sought. I made sure to brush closely past him as we separated. The excess body contact made it easier to snatch the object without notice.

What I'd just taken was no small thing. But the Royal Accountant moved along, oblivious.

A silent sigh escaped me as I scanned the halls for Zair. She stood with the queen now and my shoulders went rigid with a memory. The queen's icy dismissal of Zair at the student's first introduction. But Zair was smiling lightly, and the queen did not regard her haughtily.

Why would Queen Yval, a gently-bred Ussi woman likely indoctrinated to feel superior like most of the tribespeople, take interest in an Esan girl? Was she suddenly having a change of heart, or was there a motive?

The Royal Accountant stepped into their space, and Zair excused herself—but she didn't come to me.

The lie and emptiness of the ceremony reverberated through my chest. Zair deserved better than this. Her family should be present at her betrothal ceremony, giving their blessings, and to a man that she chose.

A man that was clearly not me. After the vowing, she hadn't glanced once in my direction, much less walked along my path.

And I wanted her to.

Sheols, I was losing my mind.

I considered draining one of the goblets constantly being thrust at me, when a hand tentatively touched my arm. Just a simple touch and my skin thrummed.

Finally. I turned to my *aiyena* and frowned over the deep sadness unchecked in her eyes. "Zair?"

She quickly squared her shoulders. "I owe you another apology."

Curious glances flicked toward us. We were finally talking after dancing around each other all night.

I ignored them and teased halfheartedly, "Two apologies in one night? Is this Yuletide?"

"To help me, you've had to tie yourself down to an Esan girl..."

"You're Baihan."

She swallowed but went on seriously, "Yes, but when people look at me, my Esan side is all they see. After tonight you'll be saddled with pitying remarks or alienated."

I folded my arms, staring down at her.

She drew in a breath. "So as soon as we leave the palace, I promise to go to the temple and process a severance to the betrothal. You won't have to be tied to me any longer than necessary. I know it's a ruse."

If she'd intended the promise to bring me relief, it didn't. It should have. But tomorrow we could be competing students again. Tonight, I wanted the sweet girl I'd held to my chest last night, who thawed when I called her wonderful.

"How about we focus on leaving the palace in one piece first?" I muttered. She started to go and I held her arm. "Will you tell me about your magic?"

Her eyes flared with panic. "I barely have magic."

I didn't need her abilities to know she was lying, both to me and to herself.

"Yet the carpet happened. And last night, the palace magic was desperate to keep you safe."

"It was?" She gaped at me, then chewed on her lip. "I can't explain it either. I'm as plain as the Sahara."

"You're not plain, Zair," I said softly, "as the Sahara is anything but plain."

Her eyes became seeking. "How do you make me feel as if..." She halted. Drew a breath. "I need to go."

Stay. Another question that had bothered me all day surged.

"The coughing, the blood, they are because of Ibhar's hit, aren't they?"

Her eyes grew guarded again, and I hated it.

"You could visit an infirmary outside the palace. A small one if you prefer, where no one would pry, but you need a healer."

"I'll be fine," she insisted. "There's no time for infirmaries right now."

Like the sheols there wasn't. I pulled her closer until we were almost body to body and began to argue.

She cut in, "You holding Ibhar down helped me win in the arena. And bringing me up to my rooms after I was... pushed off the building saved me from a lot of trouble, and I thank you." She swallowed like the memory still haunted her. "I would repay you if I can. But it doesn't suddenly give you a right to poke into my affairs, Gergesenes."

"Seriously?" I demanded in low tones, holding her stubborn gaze captive. Until I saw what I searched for in her unusual eyes.

After she'd sent me away from greeting her family, I had suspected there was more to this behavior. The sharpness. The almost desperate need to scare someone off. Now I knew that it was a wall she put up when people came too close. Close enough to hurt her.

"We are rivals, but I am not your enemy, Zair," I said. "I'm not the man who pushed you off a building to die, but the one who carried you to safety."

A gasp of alarm broke our stare. "What in the skies are you two talking about?"

35

ZAIR

Mishan squeezed the two goblets of palm wine in his hands, his grey eyes fixed on me. "You were pushed off a *building*?"

My heart tripped even faster. *Oh saints.* How much had he heard? Would he expose this to the guards relentlessly scouting for Remmon's spy? What was I thinking, talking about any of that *here*? I'd slipped, lost control *again* in that way Dathan constantly made me do. Why did I keep letting him get under my skin?

Panic bitter in my throat, I said firmly, "You heard wrong."

Mishan glowered. "Don't insult me."

Dathan released my hand and it felt like I'd lost a valuable bracelet. I shook my hand angrily to throw off the feeling.

Dathan's silver betrothal tunic stretched over his arm muscles as he clasped Mishan's shoulders. "You cannot tell *anyone* what you just heard."

"*What* did I hear?" Mishan gestured his hands and wine sloshed over the goblets. "That the celebrants' private conversation isn't over, I don't know, your budding love, but about *assaults*?"

I glanced frantically around. People were starting to stare at us.

Dathan's jaw ticked. "We have it under control. Don't get involved."

Mishan shrugged Dathan's hands off. "Why hasn't anyone been

notified that Zair was pushed off a building? Was *that* why you were in her rooms this morning?"

Mishan was worried... about me. Angry on my behalf.

An unfamiliar but gentle sensation unfurled in my chest.

If he kept expressing his indignation publicly, though, it would only work against me. Should I step in and calm him? No, Dathan was the one with the abundant charm and honeyed tongue. Besides, it *was* his fault we'd been talking about this here.

And he didn't know it, but Mishan had provided me with the opportunity to escape Dathan.

Exploiting their distraction, I drifted into the celebrating crowd, a gentle motion amongst raucous ones. From my side vision, I glimpsed emerald eyes trailing me. Queen Yval.

My chest leaped. She wouldn't appreciate me escaping her party early. Could wonder why I was creeping out. But then I turned and *looked*, and the queen was in serious conversation with her sister. Had I—

A body bumped into me.

Lysias. "'Heading out' again tonight, *aiyena*?"

Tell a lie. But there was only concern in her exasperated expression. I whispered instead, "Were you there last night, with me and Dathan?"

Her presence would explain how I was able to move at all after the fall. Her *injector* would explain the hole in my wrist.

"Yes. I took your offer to experiment with my medicine on you. It seems to be working. You no longer look broken."

"Again, I owe you for your kindness, Lysias." My voice caught.

She smiled gently. "I'll take the truth."

"Yes, I'm 'heading out'," I admitted after a moment. Saints, please, let trusting her with this not be a mistake.

Her eyes dimmed with worry, but she only asked, "Does the incised area on your wrist hurt too much?"

"Only a bit," I lied.

"The needle is still too large. I need to design one smaller so that... Sorry. I get carried away." She shook her head at herself and said to me, "Be careful. You're not made of steel, alright?"

I gave a thankful nod and made it out of the hall without drawing more attention. My betrothal attire would serve as the perfect disguise. If I was caught someplace I wasn't supposed to be, I could play the drunk and blithe *aiyena* looking for Dathan.

Dathan.

You look wonderful.

How could he say things like that to me? Look at me with heat in his eyes. As if... as if he found *me* desirable. As if he would've kissed me.

Maybe I was a fool, or maybe it was because he had saved me twice now, but for a breath, I'd wanted to stay there. To listen to him whisper more sweet nothings.

Be present, Zair.

White hand-carved stone mullions swept past with each quick step through the long passage. But the pace worsened the soreness in my chest. Dathan might be correct that I should see a healer, and in any other situation, I would have. But tomorrow was the Crowning. The Gifting would follow, and end the coronation in two days.

If my diagnosis was as bad as it felt, the healing could take longer than I could spare. Remmon already knew someone was on his tail. He was likely working faster to meet his goal before his two-week deadline was up, or before he was caught. Every spare second needed to be invested in my mission. For Sarai, Nergal's missing students, and because the queen was attacked today, almost murdered by the audacious bandits.

By comparison, I was insignificant.

The desert evening would be a black ink without the lampposts reflecting golden light along the yard's pools. I 'innocently' traversed the ground floor lounges, looking for Colonel Remmon.

Could Dathan have seen him after I'd fallen unconscious last night? He hadn't mentioned it, but did he now know the Colonel was my target? Would Dathan start trailing him too, just in case my lead was the right one?

My stomach cramped. Urgency intensified in me, quickening my steps.

The Commandant of Nergal made it clear when she'd ordered an assassination that a traitor could only succeed with scheming in the palace, and right under the Ironteenth's nose, if they were as slippery as ice.

Such a person could only be caught once.

If you made the mistake of keeping them alive too long, they *would* escape and make sure you never caught them again.

Dathan could not get to Colonel Remmon first.

On nearing a grand exit, I sighted a gaunt man standing before a group on the palace's grounds. Their clothes were black and silver. The quality was notably fine, which meant the gauntness of their faces wasn't from poverty.

A stark figure in red tasseled silk, the Magistrate, stood opposite them. She held her palms out. "I vow we're doing everything in our power for Thalesai's students."

Families. My chest twanged. These were parents of the Nergal students abducted months ago. They must've traveled to the capital after failed efforts to find their children, to seek the king's intervention.

My heart ached from the grief contorting their faces.

"What *are* you doing?" the group's head asked. "What measures are being taken? My daughter is only twelve. I don't even know if she's still alive."

My throat tightened with tears.

"Now isn't the time for this discussion," the Magistrate said, empathy in her otherwise firm voice. "Please return to your homes. You will be summoned soon."

She didn't want the foreign ambassadors spotting them here. But some wraith and shifter lords were strolling along the second floor's balusters, murmuring in their languages as they watched the grounds.

I shook my head. The secrecy with which this matter was being handled was wrong. Parents' sandals paced. Hands were dragged through hair.

They wouldn't be patient much longer. And when impatience graduated to rage, when Baihan parents started forming groups and pointing fingers at the king for not caring about Baihan children, I hoped King Khasar and his advisors could curb the tribal battle that might ensue.

Tribal battles that the lower-class, my family included, would take the brunt of.

AFTER FAILING to find Colonel Remmon in his usual areas, there was only one place left to look. The night winds burned my sore lungs as I tore down the hill into Ciasille Square. The streets beamed and brimmed with entertainment, taming only in the compound of the tavern Colonel Remmon had visited the last time.

Swiping my veil across my face, I began for the last meeting spot. But Colonel Remmon stepped into the main tavern. My heart flipped. The meeting was finished.

His body brushed mine in passing. Memories of his grip on my shoulders as he'd shoved me down from the window froze me with fear.

Skies, he would feel *me, the snoop who knew his secret. He would grab me and finish what he'd started.*

The odd sulfuric smell clinging to him faded with his movements away until air filled my stomach.

Pull yourself together.

He carried a bag. One even smaller than the bag of *siyvas* he'd had with him the last time. I couldn't risk following him; there was no palace night magic to save me out here, so I navigated back outside and pressed into the shadows of the outhouse.

Moments later, a familiar figure in dark attire stepped out of the tavern's doors. His headscarf was low over his face, concealing those eyes.

With each step closer, his ears perked up with alertness. "Who's there?"

I lunged and tackled the Esan smuggler into the shadows, pressing my knife to the pulse in his neck.

"One errant move, and I'll have you gagging on your own blood," I said into his ear.

It was a miracle my voice didn't wobble. I'd never taken a hostage outside of training before. But there were parents at the palace drowning in grief over their missing children.

The smuggler released a harsh curse. "You're the snoop from the balcony."

"Tell me what your business is with the First Colonel."

He stiffened. "I have no business with any Colonel."

Bitterness curled through me. I couldn't bite my tongue. "*A ka megie l'a mase egbe oli emenakafi omoegbe ukomi enealafandes.*"

It's people like you who give the Esans a terrible reputation. When you could honor your people and use your skills earnestly, you help monsters grow fangs that will rip our kingdom apart.

A shocked breath escaped him as my Esh swirled around us, to have been captured by one of the few like him.

"You're a fool to be loyal to Thalesai, sister," he finally hissed.

"I'm not your sister. Only the fool with your life in her hands."

"You know nothing then," he snarled, indignant.

"Enlighten me."

"How many decent establishments in Thalesai are willing to hire the Esans? Or pay us wages fair enough that we can survive on? Tell me, sister. How many from the other tribes are willing to patronize our businesses rather than tip up their noses and walk away from our shops the moment they see our eyes? They hate our unique abilities and see them as poison. They'd sooner watch us starve than spend *siyvas* that will feed us. How are we supposed to survive like that?"

I didn't answer.

"I'll survive in this prison of a kingdom anyway I can," he spat.

Even if it meant weakening our defenses for nations who still enslaved Esans, and watching innocents lose their lives.

I slanted my knife closer to that pulse, felt its thrum on the hilt. "What are you smuggling into Ari'el for the First Colonel?"

"I know not what you speak of," he repeated, fidgeting.

I drew blood. His heart raced harder against my chest.

"Don't lie to me," I whispered.

The leverage of life was in its fragility. We liked to believe we were strong-willed enough to take our secrets to the grave, until that fragile moment when we found our lives in someone's palms. That was the true test of strong-will.

He cursed bitterly. "The Colonel wants whitebomb flint."

My muscles went weak.

Sensing my distraction, he shoved his elbows into my ribs to break free. I recovered, stiffening my blade against his throat.

Whitebomb flint was one of the deadliest types of magical weaponry from shifterlands. My grandmother had given us horrific recounts of how it had razed entire human villages to ashes in minutes during the Invasions.

And the accounts we read of the War described the manifestation of those bombs as '*Erratic lightning crashing and erupting with smoke and blood.*'

That was what the mercenaries attacked Nergal Healing Academy with!

It was the reason my arrow had *touched* the lightning. I'd been guided by the glimmers of my magic; therefore it had been aziza magic against shapeshifter magic.

Not mere arrow against lightning.

"Whitebomb flint is made only for the shifters' army," I said roughly. "How could you have acquired it?"

"Just as there are black markets across Thalesai, there are shady folk that run black markets in the shifterlands too."

My mind spun, because Colonel Remmon... he was smuggling in the same weapon the mercenaries used to attack the academies and villages. The use of whitebomb flint also explained how the mercenaries could've crashed through Jalin Base's defenses and killed scores of our best soldiers.

Weaknesses, Dathan had said. The First Colonel knew that Jalin Base had no defense against whitebomb flint. Our soldiers didn't have magic, and he'd betrayed the intel to mercenaries.

"What does the Colonel need the flint for this time?" I demanded.

"I don't know," the smuggler bit out.

I could feel my control slip as my knife pushed deeper into the smuggler's skin. My blood roared to kill the abettor.

Sensing my intent, self-preservation kicked in. From his shoulders down, he struggled against my hold, but above was still as wild movements would impale him on my knife.

"Tell me the truth," I snarled.

"I *swear*. It's not my job to question my patrons. I find them what they want, collect my *siyvas*, and go!"

Disgust soured my tongue. "How many times have you smuggled Remmon whitebomb flint?"

His heart pounded out of rhythm. "It's my first time working for him."

I cut deeper. Warm blood slid down the blade to soak my sleeve.

"I swear it! This is my first time conducting business with the Colonel and the first time I've ever sought whitebomb flint. With how he closely described it, it's... it's not his first time. He must've had some other smuggler working for him before me."

My senses detected no lies, still my spirit cried to rid the world of perpetrators of such evil.

He must've sensed my distraction as I battled within myself. His elbow rammed into my sore chest; it felt like death. Stunned with pain, I sliced my blade across his flesh before he could complete his turn on me. His form slackened with shock and pain.

"I can still kill you," I wheezed, "if you don't swear a blood oath to leave Ari'el tonight, forget Remmon, and *never* return."

Breaking a blood oath meant dying a mysterious, gruesome death. He fumed over having to abandon the rich grounds of the capital. Still, he must've decided his life was more important. He touched my measured slash over his throat and made the oath on his blood, shaking with fear and fury.

"Go." I shoved him off. Without a glance back, he ran and vanished into the night.

Wheezing, I swiped my sleeve across my bloody mouth and stumbled away. The world had just tilted very wrongly.

36

DATHAN

My bedroom walls hummed with the palace's activity as I traded finery for blacks. I used wet ashes and crushed leaf juice—elements I'd created during disguise classes, to my tutor's fascination—to change my eyes, nose, and jaw outline with a play on light and darkness.

Hello, stranger.

Ibhar hadn't been at the betrothal party tonight, which was for the best. Since Zair started coughing blood, my fist tingled to smash his nose in. Yet it didn't seem he was up in our wing either—so where was he tonight?

I had to make time to follow him and find out.

For now, I picked up the Royal Accountant's keys. It wouldn't be long until he knew they were gone. There were three in total, made of bronze and carved complexly like a stag's horns. Hopefully, one served my purpose. Otherwise tonight's mission, the risky theft of these keys, would be a failure.

One might call my scheme sheer madness. But if I wanted to find out what the Dynast of Bornoir desperately sought, I had to help him break into the Royal Accountant's office.

THE GUARDS MANNING the Royal Accountant's office had been doubled. Still the fact that there was no talk of the murdered guards meant the guards' disappearance was being kept secret.

Sarhedrin would've known of this tightening of security, though, as a prime member of the court. And he would come prepared for it.

Had King Khasar sensed by now that traitors hid within his Chambers?

The guards patrolled the Chamber of Wings office while I folded myself out the window of the hidden stairwell. The drop was deep, the sandstone walls seeming to stretch to infinity.

Armed guards patrolled the lamp-lit poolside with barghests below, but the shadows above them were my ally, melding me to the walls. With balanced motions, I scaled the narrow ledge of the Royal Accountant's windows.

I ran my hand over the cold surface of the closest window. Metal mullions. Attractively carved, but more reinforced than the bars of a dungeon. There was no breaking through them.

Winds hounded at me as I pulled out the keys.

Please, please work. I shoved the first key in. It didn't open. I tried the second. Nothing.

Barely breathing, I tried the last. I turned it. The lock clicked open.

I didn't make a sound as I pushed in the hefty window. Well oiled. No creaks.

I swung into the office, landing as silently as a ghost. Over the window, none of the guards looked up. *Well done, soldier.*

I pushed the window closed, throwing the office into darkness. The tentative trek through the mammoth space to find the main door might have well been a journey across the Geidam Dunes.

Finally, my fingers met what felt like a knob. I felt about for a keyhole and found six. Great.

Silently, I dipped the key in and one by one, unlocked them.

Once the sixth lock came undone, I waited with bated breath for a reaction from the guards outside. The madness of my plan crashed against me like a battering ram. My head pounded with the consequences if this plan failed. Jaziah's life. My school. My family...

All will still be destroyed if I fail.

I steadied myself and refined the thoughts into a flash of determination. I needed a hidden area that also provided good visibility.

I climbed the ceiling's beams and willed Sarhedrin to try and break in again tonight.

Could Zair have been in a similar spot when Remmon attacked her? If so, what had she sought to confirm from the Colonel? What was Colonel Remmon's dirty secret? I intended to shift focus to him too, but the Colonel hadn't murdered his own soldiers and hidden their bodies.

And there was still the puzzle piece that was the king's brother. Although, I hadn't sighted Sarhedrin with him since that first night. There was also the unknown *He*, who gave Sarhedrin permission to perpetuate his schemes. Was there a thread here? Connecting Sarhedrin even to Colonel Remmon?

There had to be. If not, then Zair and I were chasing the wind.

Faint sounds came from outside. I stiffened against the wooden beams, waiting. *Sarhedrin could be killing the new guards.* My blood ran hot with urgency but I made my feet stay still.

The keyhole clanked for a few seconds and the door opened. Easily.

So easily in fact that if the Dynast of Bornoir was smart, he should be suspicious. Wonder why he'd been able to pick the locks quickly tonight. But ambition often clouded wisdom.

I pressed against the beams as candlelight illuminated the office below. The Dynast of Bornoir wasted no second in ransacking the massive space, pulling out drawers and barely keeping from tearing through their contents.

He moved on to a shelf. His fingers *whished* against spines and then halted on a tome.

"Yes," he murmured.

From the tension in his arms as he pulled out the tome, it had to weigh a ton. He moved to sit at the desk, swiping the quill from the inkpot.

Gingerly, I leaned closer as he ripped out a page from what seemed like a tome of records. With more care than I'd thought the demon capable of, he glued on another page in replacement.

What in ten sheols?

He spent no more than a minute scribbling something onto the doctored page, and then he was up. He folded the ripped-off page into his breast pocket, returned the tome, and left the office. Gone as quickly as he'd come.

I waited a few moments, waited until there were no sounds outside, before climbing down the beam. This time there was no choice. In the darkness, I found the window and pulled it far enough inside to let moonlight in. Hopefully the poolside guards kept their attention down.

The tome was heavy. I flipped once and easily to the page Sarhedrin just glued on. The glued area was still damp but by morning, signs of the swap would be faded.

The details on the page showed accounts of Bornoir's town revenue and expenditure.

Why was Sarhedrin doctoring his own town's accounts? There was no doubt that the details on this glued page were different from what was originally recorded by the Royal Accountant. So Sarhedrin wanted some digit, some financial *expectation*, changed.

Funds were strictly monitored in the amalgamated Thalesai as the kings strove to ensure no tribe felt cheated or exploited. It meant that rulers at every level had to present explicit documentation on their profits, expenditure, and revenue. It left no room for embezzlement and looting.

That the Dynast of Bornoir had struck at the very head of accountancy had to mean that he'd tailored the result to create an opening in his own records. One with which he could steal Bornoir funds without notice from above.

But how much gap in funds had he created? Was it enough money to sponsor the mercenaries?

If it was a small amount then the theft could be for some other purpose, nefarious but not necessarily connected to the mercenaries. If that was the case, why go to these extraordinary lengths to cover it up?

I needed to compare the figures to ascertain the size of the gap.

I studied the first three columns of the page, committing the numbers and words to memory as taught at Gergesenes. Armed, I climbed back out the window and locked it. I'd need to sneak into the Royal Accountant's private suite to return the keys, but first I needed to get that ripped page from Sarhedrin.

The grotesque stairwell was empty; he wasn't following it. So I jogged down for the next main hallway. I threw my black tunic inside out so that it was lined with white and rearranged my hair over my painted face before popping out of the stairwell.

Mosaic tiles in brown-and-white shone under my boots. No sign of Sarhedrin from the railings. I jogged down the stairs, catching up to him on the busy second floor.

My heart raced against my ribs as I moved between people, straight for Sarhedrin.

He will see through your disguise.

The thought hit me like a brick. Before I could change my mind, I bumped bodily into the Dynast of Bornoir. *Too late.*

Hands grasped my arm, keeping me in place as the face of the man I loathed most leaned into mine. Orcus Sarhedrin stared as if to glare to death the peasant who'd dared touch him.

"Are you blind, boy?" he demanded.

His brows suddenly furrowed, as if some part of him recognized me. Whose son I was. Whose *grandson*.

Rather than flinch from it, hatred poured through me like venom.

Let him remember me. Remember the torments he'd wrought upon me and my family. The lie he'd made our lives become. Let him recognize the face of the man who would be his destruction.

"Who are you?" he demanded, intense in his determination to recognize.

I clenched my teeth to growl out who I was. My *real* name.

But like a soft wind in the flames of my mind, a vision of Asahel's face fluttered, the life in her eyes as she'd kissed my cheeks in the arena; my father's worried face. Their recovery after all we'd suffered forced me to look away. To hide *again* like I'd done for most of my life. Ashes coated my mouth.

"I apologize for my clumsiness, Khosa Sarhedrin," I gritted.

"See that it never happens again, boy."

I yanked my arm from his grip and strode off, the ripped page clenched in my fist.

The lamps in my bedroom illuminated my desk as I arranged the original document Sarhedrin had ripped from the Royal Accountant's records. The good side? He had torn the paper, tried to destroy it, in haste so it wasn't completely shredded. The not so good? Piecing it correctly together consumed the better part of an hour.

But once I had it pieced—it confirmed my suspicion.

The margin between the revenue the Dynast of Bornoir was expected to produce biannually, and what he'd doctored in the accounts, was so massive that I sank down in a cushion.

Sarhedrin was planning to steal hundreds of thousands of *siyvas*.

This was one of the wealthiest men in Thalesai. His generation down to the *third* would be richer than saints. What could he possibly need to steal this sum for...

...if not to fund a group?

A group—*like the mercenaries*—that was pushing a monumental cause, if they would need that amount of money.

This was the concrete evidence I needed. At last. At last, I could confront my tormentor. Perhaps this should've been the way all along.

My next order of business was to abduct the Dynast of Bornoir.

37

ZAIR

The dawn sky was a mirror to the gold and orange desert landscape with swaths of blue over the distant dunes. My balcony's tiles were damp against my outstretched legs as I soaked in what would be my last moment of serenity if my mission today failed. I pushed the soggy napkin against my nose as more blood soaked it. My body, mind, and soul all felt brutalized.

Soon, it would be King Khasar's Crowning, the next-to-last ceremony of the coronation. The palace would be bustling. The perfect scene to take down First Colonel Remmon.

What about Dathan's own prey? Could his target be *the* traitor? But the smuggler had said it wasn't the Colonel's first time smuggling in the flint. And whitebomb flint was, without a doubt, the mercenary's secret weapon. Only someone with a position as lofty as the Colonel could pull the strings needed for the mercenaries to acquire it.

The proof was the flint now lying in his possession. He was the traitor. The reason my instincts had screamed at the first sight of him.

I rolled the phial of poison between my fingers. The rare Ussi poison was so little, one wouldn't assume it was potent enough to kill a man. I'd wondered if I could do it. Kill someone who didn't have a chance to fight back. It wasn't the way of a soldier.

But after speaking with the smuggler, affirming that Colonel

Remmon was behind the attack that could've killed my little sister, that had ripped hundreds of students from their families? I understood my Commandant's resolve.

She didn't even want the traitor alive for an interrogation: she wanted him dead. Kill the shepherd and the sheep scattered. Cut off the snakehead and its body died soon after. Once their head was gone, the sponsor of their funds and intel, the mercenaries would grow sloppy. Our soldiers would without doubt catch them and free the students.

My gaze shifted two rooms down to an empty dawn-golden balcony.

I'm not your enemy, Zair.

After the assassination, I was to return to Nergal. My Commandant and her mysterious sponsor would make excuses to explain my absence. Remaining here for the rest of the coronation after Remmon died would be too risky for everyone involved in my scheme.

I *was* eager to leave this treachery-filled palace and longed for the simplicity of Nergal.

Why then did my chest feel completely hollow at the thought of never seeing Dathan again?

I knew. I would miss having him, a peer who didn't detest me, to challenge. I'd miss how he could look into my eyes and not recoil, but instead banter and tease me. When he'd asked about my magic, he had looked curious, not alarmed, and I had almost admitted to using it. Memories fluttered in, of dancing with him, of the kiss at the banquet, and deep loss flooded me.

Yet this was for the best.

During our vowing, courtiers had sniped to my face that Gergesenes' best student deserved better than me. I'd heard the Ussi noblewomen angrily speculate that I had forced his hand with a pregnancy. My skin flushed.

Dathan's mere presence made my pulse race. His every touch made my *entire* body come alive in a way I never imagined possible. Yet I couldn't bear a marriage where I would always be called unworthy of my husband and blamed for ruining his future. Where my children would be hated and left with almost zero opportunities to have good lives. I couldn't bear starting a family only to have them constantly look over their shoulders because there were people who killed Esans out of misguided fear.

My eyes burned and I blinked the tears back. Skies, I missed my mother. Missed placing my head on her lap when the world became too hostile and my worries fading as she stroked my hair.

It ate at me that my family didn't have the freedom of every Thalesain citizen to watch their king be crowned, but it was better they weren't here on the day I planned to assassinate the First Colonel.

I swallowed hard against the cold chokehold of fear.

Pushing gingerly up to my feet, I bit my lip against the sharp pains in my chest, and hobbled to the mirror. Today, I wouldn't be applying kohl over my brows as the symbol of the betrothal. Rather, I dropped *whal* into my eyes.

Tears pooled because, *blast*, the herb had a vicious sting.

Where the Commandant had acquired the herb was beyond me since it was rare and found only in Ussi lands. Seconds later, it served its purpose. Colored my eyes a deep blue, erasing the gold rings in them.

No part of me could be conspicuous today.

38

DATHAN

Dew glazed the palace's interior garden, its serene beauty a contrast to the chaos of my thoughts. It shimmered in the very center of the palace, flowing up the six floors to an open sky that made the vines of hydrangeas, wisterias, and morning glories glow. I tapped my fingers anxiously against the third floor's railings.

Above, the aziza lords circled the skies, sunning their glorious wings with the smug knowledge that they fascinated us humans. The soldier who gave Zair new arrows swerved around the clouds too with translucent black wings. While his eyes were too far off to see, I could swear he scrutinized me from the sky.

I had greater concerns. During the Crowning, I would risk everything to abduct the Dynast of Bornoir.

The mere thought hardened my gut. Had given me sleepless nights since my first step inside the palace. But he was scheming to loot Thalesai's funds. He had betrayed the Royal Accountant. And he'd murdered Thalesain soldiers.

I would go to any length to drag Sarhedrin out of here.

Unable to remain still, I paced around the garden as if strolling. My plan was straightforward and I'd started putting the steps in place since dawn. But if my disguise didn't work everything would fail.

Scarlet and gold gleamed on the second floor, drawing my

attention below. King Khasar and Queen Yval moved regally, their courtiers trailing after them, their energies excitable.

Today, Thalesai would have a king and queen in truth.

Would those who didn't want them crowned choose today to strike again?

The Ironteenth unit seemed to share that concern. Even in the palace, their hands remained around their hilts, their ceremonial armors a base for blades.

A palace guard suddenly bounded into the scene. Only the Ironteenth were allowed near the royals and that the guard almost broke that rule stopped me short.

Massive black wings drummed as they drew nearer. Zair's aziza soldier flew lower with his pondering stare on the king's party.

"Back away, butterfly," I warned heatedly, the inner soldier rearing to defend. The aziza had smelled the conflict and like a wolf to blood, had prowled closer to feast on it.

His lips tightened. For a long moment, I thought he would challenge me. But he ascended, watching me until he was in the sky.

The head of the Ironteenth Fighters, Captain Emeso, intercepted the palace guard with his huge form. The guard spoke tensely. Captain Emeso's face slackened with shock, then hardened. With a grim nod, he led the guard to the king and the Majesties came to a stop.

The guard spoke and King Khasar's exclamation echoed up the garden. Blood drained from Queen Yval's face.

What is going on?

King Khasar barked out something, swerving toward the northern wing. The palace guard jogged to lead him, and tension strained the air as the royal party hurried after the guard.

I followed on the floor above them, watching as they took turns and steps downstairs. As they emerged in a sunny courtyard, I emerged on the terrace just above it.

Courtiers stood there, lamenting as a small crowd placed a long object cocooned in white onto a blanket. Scarlet slowly stained the blanket.

Cold rolled through my veins. It wasn't an object that was being handled. It was a body.

Without thought, I moved closer to the railings.

"Move," King Khasar ordered, his tone sharp with anguish.

The crowd quickly parted, their faces anxious. King Khasar's hand hesitated, shaking in a way that made my stomach churn. He reached down and yanked the cloth from the body.

My stomach dropped to my feet. Ambassador Caiphas.

The king's brother was dead.

THE KING'S cry of anguish was raw. Agony and unchecked grief.

Wails of sorrow flooded the courtyard like a black river. I pressed my wrist to my mouth. Ambassador Caiphas's friends knelt around his body, heads in their hands. Questions were flung about but answers were sparse.

King Khasar seemed like he wanted to speak but each time he opened his mouth, looked at his brother, cries were the only sounds that came out. Queen Yval reached for him, her face a mask of sorrow, but First Advisor Maachah reached him first. He placed be-ringed hands on the king's shoulders, appearing to try to calm him.

"Who did this?" King Khasar cried. "*Who dared do this?*"

The rage and pain in his voice sent chills through the air. Who *had* dared?

Could it be Sarhedrin? Saints! I'd thought Sarhedrin and Ambassador Caiphas had been unlikely allies. Could something else have been going on that I'd missed?

Before guilt could choke me, Colonel Remmon shook his head vigorously. Torment lined his face as he stepped forward from the crowd.

Heads swiveled to him, especially when he rasped out, "I can no longer keep silent."

The king pulled away from the Advisors, pinning Remmon with a wild look. "What are you talking about, Colonel?"

"Your Majesty…"

"Spit it out!" the king yelled.

I'd never seen him like this. He always strived for composure, even at times when it was obviously difficult. But here, standing before his brother's dead body, he looked shattered.

Colonel Remmon drew a breath. "I wouldn't want to make premature accusations, Your Majesty. But what I can say... is that the Admiral's office should be searched. For answers."

Shock reverberated through the yard and flared in King Khasar's eyes.

My fingertips numbed. No way. Remmon could *not* be implying that the Admiral had murdered the king's brother.

"What are you saying, Colonel?" King Khasar whispered.

Queen Yval's hands covered her mouth, and her sister's arms came around her.

"Please, Your Majesty," Colonel Remmon said gravely. "Don't make me cause the downfall of my superior. Please, just... have his office searched."

"Indeed," Second Advisor Drake muttered in disbelief, "the Admiral has been meeting with Thalesai's ambassadors this week. Ambassador Caiphas and the Admiral were scheduled to meet today, before the Crowning."

The look that washed over the king's face said his brother must've mentioned a similar meeting to him.

"Your Majesty?" First Advisor Maachah prompted when the king had been silent for too long.

Without glancing away from the covered body, King Khasar deployed three of his Ironteenth to carry out the office search. "Search *every* corner. Bring me a detailed report in no more than an hour. Colonel, I won't have you out of my sight until I give you leave."

Grim, Remmon gave a bow. "Yes, Your Majesty."

"Get my brother's body," King Khasar choked on the word, "off the ground. Maachah, manage this. My father cannot know until I... until I tell him."

As the king scrambled for control, distributing hoarse orders that were instantly followed, white-blue eyes raised from the yard up to where I stood. The Spaeman's grave gaze met mine, like he knew I'd been there all along. The sorrow in his eyes was absolute and *old*.

What message was he trying to convey this time? If it was that important, he'd have to tell me himself. The time for mystery was past.

Saints. I ran a hand through my hair. Ambassador Caiphas was dead. Colonel Remmon believed that the Admiral, the man whose bidding I followed, was guilty of treason.

Could the Admiral indeed be the traitor in the palace? Could he have sent the Commandant and me on a wild goose chase? Not once had I considered he could be the snake in the palace. His position provided him the perfect opportunity to enable the mercenaries.

But he had served two kings loyally in the last decade.

I tugged at my hair, struggling to keep my wits. One thing at a time.

Right now, I needed to implement my plan. To pluck Sarhedrin from the Al'Qtraz.

I swerved and my nose flared. The aziza soldier stood there in the corridor, his face grim. He'd heard everything.

"The human Ambassador to the wraithlands was a good man," he said.

I charged for him with a growl. "I warned you to back off! I should run you through with iron for being here!"

The air steamed into mist as he hissed, "If you humans think whispering behind doors while constantly keeping us foreigners engaged does anything but stoke our agitation to glean your secrets, then you are fools."

"If you tell *anyone* what you overheard today, I will kill you," I vowed.

His jaw clenched, but the mist his anger conjured slowly dissipated. "I am a warrior, not a politician. I have no intention of revealing anything overheard that does not threaten my people."

My first instinct was to call him a liar, but azizas didn't lie.

"I am truly sorry for the Ambassador's death, Scholar Issachar. Just as I am sorry for the troubles still coming to Thalesai."

39

ZAIR

Although I had never attended a king's official Crowning before, the somber air on the dais confirmed the whispers I'd overheard about Ambassador Caiphas's death.

The Crowning was a success. The cheers were deafening. People from far and wide crowded the vast hall in their best garments. Friends stood in small groups: rich families, farmers and miners from distant villages, students from various academies. Children sat on their parents' shoulders to see the dais. Artists sketched swiftly on paper, capturing the historic moment so that they could create paintings later for purchase.

There was no discrimination today between classes or the four tribes. *Only against the Esans.* My teeth clenched as I envisioned my family setting up carts in the southern quarter's market. Eager to sell fabrics and teabags to the people gushing into Ari'el for the coronation. As if they weren't Thelasians also worthy of being here.

Through the crush of shimmering gowns and elaborate tunics, I made my way for Colonel Remmon. My plain blue eyes didn't draw hateful attention; rather, anyone who looked at me smiled in celebratory greeting.

It was a new sensation not to be loathed on sight, still, forcing a smile back was difficult. It took all my focus to pull my thoughts from Ambassador Caiphas's death. He hadn't fallen off his horse or perished from an illness. He'd been murdered this morning, right here in the palace. Right in the king's home.

Most people, clapping by my ears, were unaware of the terrible thing that had happened on this auspicious day. I wouldn't have known either, but while breezing through the palace earlier, ensuring no abrupt arrangements ruined my plans, I'd overheard the whispers between guards. Between councilmen.

There were also the quieter, shocking whispers: that the Admiral was involved in the king's brother's murder. It had to be the reason he was absent at such a prime event. They'd said he was arrested this morning. Likely to be interrogated after the ceremony.

Citizens must be wondering at his absence and would surely speculate later.

On the dais, King Khasar and Queen Yval's facades were shuttered despite the intense jubilation for them.

Dathan and Ibhar were absent. At this point, I was certain Ibhar was also a spy.

Medals glinted. *First Colonel Remmon*. The man with whom he discussed had the rank of Fifth Colonel etched on the brooch holding his cape. For someone who'd just accused his superior of murdering an Ambassador of Thalesai, Colonel Remmon seemed sickeningly chipper.

The bond of comrades ought to be such that bringing dishonor to a comrade should be a burden. Like the weight pushing down my chest as I closed in on him in the crowd. But eliminating Colonel Remmon would begin the mercenaries' downfall, Sarai would be free of those who'd marked her, and the stolen Nergal students would be found.

It was time.

Within my long sleeves, I pulled out the tiny needle from the phial and held it out. Harnessing my aziza speed, I swept closer.

Almost there.

Colonel Remmon's body heat warmed me as I sank my poisoned needle into his hand. So slight, he wouldn't think it more than the sting of an insect. He grunted, but I'd already dipped back into the crowd.

A lofty pillar cooled my skin as I circled around and leaned against it. It held me up as exhaustion from using the magical ability dimmed my vision.

A server moved past. I snagged a goblet of wine, if only to seem occupied with drinking as I regained my breath. I swirled the wine, my heightened attention on the soldier I now recognized as the Fifth Colonel Dishe, still speaking with Remmon.

"...I suppose congratulations are in order for you too," the Fifth Colonel said lowly, "Admiral-to-be."

I stiffened, wine sloshing down my fingers.

Remmon grinned. "If one wants something done right—like a swifter promotion—one must handle it themselves."

Handle it *themselves*? *Admiral-to-be*?

"The other tribes overlook the Mizsabs," Remmon said. "That will be their downfall."

Colonel Remmon's hateful look at the Admiral during the welcome feast; him hiding the Admiral's schedule; him sneaking into the Admiral's office and forging documents... The guards had whispered about the 'implicating evidence' found in the Admiral's office and how it was grievous enough to have him arrested for Ambassador Caiphas's death.

Colonel Remmon had planted it!

Remmon wanted the Admiral's position. But why? Was it solely because he would rather Mizsabs occupied that office than Baihan? Or could it be because the Admiral had had his foot on the mercenaries' necks? Because Remmon wanted the Admiral out of the way so that as the new Admiral, Remmon could send soldiers on a wild goose chase while the mercenaries succeeded in destroying more of Thalesai with whitebomb flint?

Blood roared in my ears. The Admiral was innocent! He would be executed while Ambassador Caiphas's murderer took up the mantle of Admiral of Thalesai.

A choked gasp yanked my gaze from my trembling goblet, past a group of Cur Philosophy Academy students, up to Colonel Remmon. His eyes widened with confusion as the veins in his neck bulged.

You lying murderer. You monster!

"Sir?" the Fifth Colonel asked with consternation. "What is it?"

Remmon placed a red-tattooed hand on his neck, struggling to speak. His skin paled.

"Colonel Remmon," the Fifth Colonel called louder now, but the cheers drowned out his voice.

On the dais, the Spaeman placed the Crown of Kings, hewn of hefty gold and engraved with five gemstones for the five tribes, on King Khasar's head. The crown that was crafted by the first King of Thalesai after decades of slavery, worn by every free king after him.

"All hail His Royal Majesty, Khasar Osomake Nogbaisi," the Spaeman declared, "the King of Thalesai."

King Khasar stepped forward, magnificent before his people.

At last, the true King of Thalesai. On the day of his brother's death.

"Hail to the king! Hail to the king!"

The Fifth Colonel clutched Remmon's shoulders, his eyes wild with panic.

Someone moved beside me and spoke words that stopped my world. "Why assassinate a man with poison that takes so long to kill him?"

I jerked at the familiar accented voice, as smooth and icy as snow on a mountain's peak. I didn't turn. Wouldn't show guilt to the aziza warrior, Arno Irmah, towering beside me.

He'd seen me. As discreet as I'd been, *he* would've seen it all if he'd been watching. My joints trembled.

The only... only positive in this complication was that the azizas had no love for us humans. He didn't care about the Colonel. Saints, don't let him blackmail me again. There would be no escaping that noose without bringing everything I cared about crumbling down.

"I don't know what you're talking about," I managed, staring so hard at the floor that my eyes watered.

"Do the human lands not have herbs that kill on contact? That would seem more effective for an assassination."

My heart tumbled to the ground.

Don't give him power. Don't give him a leash to control you.

I straightened my back. "Why do you care?"

He tilted his head studiously, his silver-and-turquoise uniform gleaming. "I don't. Not about him, that is."

My chest rigidified with hope. Azizas avoided lying like one would avoid a dagger to the heart. "Then about what?"

Let him leave me alone. Let him want nothing from me.

He spoke softly. "I'll be leaving Thalesai immediately after the Crowning."

My brows fused. "The Crowning isn't the end of the coronation. It's disrespectful for your party to leave now."

"Storm clouds are coming. Trouble taints the winds of the Western Continent. My king wants his noblemen far from this gathering and in Dahomey before the storm breaks."

There *was* trouble indeed, but my nape prickled for he could be speaking of one direr.

"I came to say goodbye."

"Why?" I set my jaw. "We're not friends."

He studied me for a moment. "No, but my senses tell me that you and I would be something even more than friends someday soon."

My head snapped toward his dark golden eyes.

His mouth quirked. "I know you are betrothed to the Scholar claiming the name Issachar, but I feel in my spirit that we would meet again. I can only hope it will be on fair terms. Until then, accept the magic you are *blessed* with, Zair Nebah of Ari'el."

With a brief bow, he strode off with ethereal elegance.

He disappeared from view and my breath rushed out. If the saints were kind, I'd never meet the one person who'd witnessed my greatest transgression again.

On the dais, King Khasar, Queen Yval, and their closest councilmen proceeded out of the hall. Guests soon followed. And Colonel Remmon crumbled, a spill of medals and cape. A server screamed as blood poured from Remmon's nose over the white marble.

I stared at him and... there was no sting in my chest. Instead, a great burden fell off my back. I'd succeeded. I'd done it.

Now get out of the palace. Escape before your luck turns.

I turned to the doors, but an underlying doubt halted me.

Screaming people swarmed the unmoving Colonel.

"Seal the doors!" the head guard barked. "No one leaves!"

Run, Zair!

I couldn't. Not *yet*. The doors shut, sealing me and the remaining crowd in as suspects for murder.

I swallowed hard, but I needed to speak with the Fifth Colonel. To pry from the Mizsab man every bit of Colonel Remmon's scheme to aid the mercenaries.

40

DATHAN

Orcus Sarhedrin emerged from his secluded rooms to attend the Crowning. He gasped at the sight of his two guards sprawled on the ground. Knocking them out had been difficult but urgency drove me.

Now Sarhedrin was mine.

I jumped off the ledge above his threshold, landing silently behind him.

"Who's there?" Fingers stretched tautly, he glanced across the space for his men's attacker. He took a step back and bumped into me.

I itched for him to spin around and *see* me, but I couldn't risk it. Grabbing his forehead, I pushed a cloth seeped in *kaiga* over his nose.

He struggled fiercely, his heels scraping on the floor.

"Don't bother fighting," I took no small pleasure in whispering.

The taunting order triggered memories, the present melding its oily fingers with the past.

Don't bother fighting or running, Sosthene. You have betrayed your own! Now we would turn the world over if need be, but you and your family will face cirai justice!

I saw Sarhedrin's vicious face calling the vow from our front gate the first night he'd brought his men down on us. Felt the terror in our home as my parents gathered my sister and me, leading us out through the window into the back alley.

Hurry, mihe. Don't look back.

Sweat dripped down my temples. My lungs quickly closed up.

Separate the past from the present.

You lose him, you damn Jaziah. I struggled to grasp the ropes of the present, to untangle them from the binds of the past, and find myself again. I wasn't in Kadnazi but in the palace. I wasn't the victim anymore but in control. I wasn't powerless—I was the predator.

Air eased through my tight throat.

The mission. Getting this traitor to the Commandant.

I pressed the cloth harder to his nose, ensured *kaiga* was the only thing he inhaled.

I'd 'borrowed' the anesthetic from Zair's rooms this morning, taking just enough that she wouldn't notice. It was the only way to guarantee I knocked him out without maiming him first. Had I used an adasword hilt to his head, I might've lost control and bashed in his skull.

His chest heaved twice and then his body deadened. I waited a few more seconds to be certain, then let him drop and moved to his guards.

Their capes swished against tiles as I dragged them into the suite and shut the door. Neither saw me during their assault, but once they woke up from a faint with their master gone, they'd know something was very wrong.

Sarhedrin needed to be far from the palace long before they started pursuing answers.

Throwing Sarhedrin over my shoulder pulled a grunt from me. I managed the weight, jogging down the empty passage for the hidden stairwell.

In its darkness, I lowered him and lit a small lantern. I opened the bag I'd stashed there earlier and changed into the stableman uniform I'd swiped. I plaited my hair back and painted enough wrinkles on my face that even my family would pass me on the street. I pressed on a mustache for good measure. Next from my supplies was a sack with the hays I'd sewn onto the hem. I pushed Sarhedrin in.

"The Dynast of Bornoir thrown into a sack like an animal. How the mighty falls."

I'd been accurate with the sack's length. It concealed him until the hays at the tips were the only things peeking out.

Tying it, I dragged him over my shoulder and jogged down for the outer yard. By the time I emerged in the afternoon heat, my shoulders burned from his weight. I followed the servants' path leading to the royal stables.

No one looked twice at me—a stable hand carrying a sack of hay for the horses—as I dipped into the first stall. *Almost there.*

My horse's ears perked up at the sight of me.

I patted his neck. "Time to go home, boy."

THE GATES of Gergesenes Military Academy swung open only after I peeled off the disguise and showed the sentries that I was their student. They had been uneasy about my reason for disguising and the strange, moving sack I'd brought. Yet they let me through with little questions asked. The Commandant must've had a word with them about me.

I galloped into my school. The paths were sparse since students and staff were all invited to the Crowning.

I swung off my horse and dragged the Dynast of Bornoir onto my shoulder. The sack wriggled; he'd regained consciousness. Good thing I'd gagged him. Rather than head for the Commandant's office, I took a path between tall buildings down to the rear watchtower.

The sentry would inform the Commandant that I was at the academy. Once they did, he'd know where I was.

The rear watchtower loomed like a giant sword. The archers manning it glanced down curiously as they ate their afternoon meal, but didn't stop me.

I pushed open the heavy door and jogged underground for the dungeons. I yanked open the bars of the first cell before lighting the torches. A pungent smell hit my nose. *Sheols*. The dungeons were stuffy and smelly enough that students avoided misconducts just to avoid spending days here.

Dropping the sack on a chair, I grabbed a rope and strapped Sarhedrin to it. He struggled in earnest now, garbled sounds coming from the sack.

The Commandant's booted steps echoed. I stepped out and dragged the bars shut, just as the Commandant made the turn that placed him before me.

I stood at attention. "Sir."

He nudged his head toward a small office and we went in. He rubbed the back of his neck.

I spoke before he could. "The Admiral has been accused of murdering Ambassador Caiphas."

His head perked up with disbelief, but he wasn't *stunned*. "How did you hear of it?"

"I was there when the king saw the body." I strove for composure. "And when Colonel Remmon pointed fingers at the Admiral as the suspected murderer."

The Commandant sighed, appearing a decade older. "I understand what you're worried about, Issachar. That you and I are perpetrating the desires of a criminal."

I didn't argue. He was correct.

"The charges against the Admiral are false," he stated, no iota of doubt in his voice. "I've been working closely with him to find the mercenaries' hideouts since the mercs' in his custody are choosing death over confession."

My brows knitted. "With all due respect, sir... why you? He has numerous active officers under him."

The Commandant surveyed me. I held his gaze fiercely. I was a student, yes, but I'd risked my life and that of my family to spy for him. I'd earned this information.

"The Admiral suspects the military itself has been compromised."

The statement was like ice water dumped over me. But why was I shocked? Zair's target was Colonel Remmon—a man who had tried to kill her.

The Commandant went on, "And while I can't say too much, I can assure you that the Admiral's loyalty to the crown runs deeper than any gorge. He would never betray His Majesty, least of all in this way. Ambassador Caiphas was an asset to the human kingdom."

Gathering my wits, I asked, "How did you hear about the accusations against the Admiral?"

The king had ordered the First Advisor to ensure the news didn't get out.

"I was at the palace with the Admiral this morning, about to leave when the Ironteenth barged into his office to begin a search," the Commandant said gravely. "He'd been cautious that something like this might happen, that the traitor in the palace would try to get him out of their way, and he bade me to leave immediately."

...So that if something happened to him, Gergesenes' Commandant could continue investigating from where he'd had to stop. This was why the Commandant hadn't attended the Crowning. He needed to keep the hunt for the mercenaries going even in the Admiral's absence.

"Do you know what 'evidence' they found on the Admiral?" I asked.

"I've sent a message to Captain Emeso to keep me informed. Although I can't guarantee it's a request that will be granted."

Captain Emeso graduated from Gergesenes six years ago and as the Captain of the Ironteenth Fighters, was Gergesenes' biggest success of the decade. He had a loyalty to the Commandant, but foremost was his loyalty to the Majesties.

The Commandant stared at me, waiting for what information I had.

And for me to decide where I stood now. If I believed that the Admiral was still worth trusting, or that he was guilty and I would rather step back. He wouldn't push me in one way or another. The Commandant taught us that we had to stand for something, because only when the roots are deep would there be no reason to fear the wind.

Unclenching my fist, I made a choice and told him. About Sarhedrin's success in breaking into the Royal Accountant's office, after I let him in. The Commandant couldn't decide if to be astounded, uneasy or impressed by the daring feat. I told him of the forged accounts and the massive sum he intended to steal.

Bafflement twisted the Commandant's face. He ran a hand over it. "There aren't many reasons a wealthy man like Orcus Sarhedrin would risk his *rank* to loot that amount of money."

The only solid reason was to fund the menaces' weaponry and camps.

His face hardened in a way I'd never seen as he tramped from the office. I followed. The Commandant's muscles bulged as he drew open the bars and strode for the shaking sack. The sight of Sarhedrin's earnest struggle for freedom made the atmosphere feel tight and hotter. My head pounded with the horrors that always lingered in my subconscious.

The Commandant shoved the chair so Sarhedrin faced the wall, placing us behind him. Pulling out a knife, a *ripping* resounded in the dungeons as he sliced the sack around the neck. Below the rip, the sack sagged to reveal Sarhedrin's torso. The top concealed his head.

"Let me do it." The words scraped out of my throat like gravel.

The Commandant halted, and then looked over his shoulder.

"Let me pull the information from him," I said.

I didn't know what was on my face, the intensity of the darkness he saw there. He rammed a hard fist into the Dynast's temple. Sarhedrin's head slumped to the side as he went unconscious.

"Do you have a history with this man, Issachar?"

While the Commandant didn't know the details of my past, he knew enough to discern that if the Dynast of Bornoir was involved, it was in a hideous way.

Did I have a history with him?

Such a simple question, one that had no simple answer. The man sitting there had obliterated my family's identity, made us living lies. Haunted our dreams in the night and destroyed our ability to ever feel safe in the day.

"No," the Commandant said.

My head snapped to him. "Sir, I'm trained to handle the situation," I gritted. "Let me do this."

I *needed* to do it. I needed to cause him this pain *searing* my chest.

The Commandant scowled. "What I need from the Dynast is

information to end the mercenary reign of terror, and to keep our students safe. I don't want him dead."

"I won't kill him," I argued stiffly.

"That's not a promise you can make."

He was right and I hated it. I tore my gaze from Sarhedrin, looking to the bars instead in a search for control. "When you get the information, what would be done with it now that the Admiral is under arrest?"

How would we get to rescue Jaziah?

He exhaled. "What matters right now is *knowing*. Who are the mercenaries? What they want and where their captives are kept. Who their sponsors are and how deeply the root of treachery runs in the Al'Qtraz."

At his pause, I frowned at him.

"And then," he said, "if it means taking the information to the king and Chambers at the cost of losing my head, it's a sacrifice I have to make. But the time has come for Thalesai's rulers to stop hiding its problems while these mercenaries burn our land to the ground."

41

ZAIR

"Step forward if you are armed and show your weapons!" the soldiers barked in the hall of the Crowning.

Ten of them had blocked the doors like pillars, gesturing the armed visitors to step forward. Twelve moved to the walls and six more jogged up the dais. They bristled as they perused the crowd for movements that betrayed Colonel Remmon's killer, like an attempt to hide, or drop a dagger or sword.

Four soldiers pulled Fifth Colonel Dishe away from Remmon's body and knelt around him. One of them, a military healer, meticulously examined Remmon's corpse. He had to be investigating the cause of his death. They would expect a bloody stab wound first. One they could match to the murder weapon and use to trim down the suspects until they pinned the assassin.

A soldier suddenly pushed a rangy boy to the wall. The boy sobbed as the soldier's scoured his body. "I haven't hurt anyone, sir."

He must have done something to spark the soldier's suspicion.

My heart slammed. People moved in a state of fear and shock. Those armed were summoned to step forward first, while others moved behind. Many armed men and women hesitated and the guards' cinched their focus on them, to see how they would react to the order.

I hadn't realized the man a few feet away had dropped his sheathed dagger on the floor, he'd been so stealthy about it, until a guard barreled into him from behind. The man fell on his face, breaking his nose. Blood slipped from his nostrils and someone screamed. The guard yanked the man's hands behind him and dragged him to the dais. Another guard picked up the weapon.

"How dare you manhandle me like this? Let me go!"

The man's beaded cap and furious demands proved he was a man of prestige from a Baihan village.

But the First Colonel had been murdered. Prestige meant nothing to the guards right now.

Hands shaking, I made sure to surround myself with people and passed a woman sobbing with fear.

"The First Colonel is dead, and the killer could be in the hall with us. Saints preserve us."

Keeping my head low, I moved marginally closer to hear what the soldiers around Remmon's thought. Whatever they deduced killed him, I had to present myself in a different light to escape the hall and get to Dishe. My heart beat in my mouth as I stopped ten feet from them, beside a clay flower vase. I kept my gaze on the door, but sharpened my ears on Dishe.

"Sir, there's no blood. The First Colonel wasn't stabbed," a soldier ground out.

"What are you *saying*?" Fifth Colonel Dishe asked in a shaky, disbelieving voice.

"Here. Look, sir." The military healer held up Remmon's limp hand, where a tiny piercing sat. He smelled the piercing and the skin around his eyes tightened. "Poison."

My heart kicked against my ribs. The phial seared against my wrist. The impulse to flee zipped within me. I held still against it. Any sudden, jerky move, and the guards monitoring the hall like eagles would not miss it. Besides, there was no *fleeing*. Only a calculated escape, if I stayed calm.

An angry, frustrated silence passed among the four soldiers, because...

"He wasn't attacked with a blade but a poisoned needle," the military healer said to the Fifth Colonel. "It'll be much harder to find the assassin than if the murder weapon was a blade."

"If its poison, the assassin most likely pierced and ran," another guard bit out. "The chance that they would stay behind after poisoning him is slim."

"I don't care," Colonel Dishe breathed, held in the grip of shock. "No one leaves this hall without being searched up to their *hair*. If the assassin *is* in here, they must be found and executed for this!"

"Yes, sir, but we also need to alert our comrades and expand this investigation."

"Those doors will not open unless we are certain the assassin is not here!"

I needed to discard the phial from my sleeve. Now. However, a guard on the dais swept her focus around this area. Her sharp gaze moved over our hands especially. Skies.

Create a way out or face execution.

Subtly, I skimmed the nearby area and cinched my attention on two distraught men striding toward me. Their robes fluttered closer. I straightened. Their backs blocked me from the guards on the dais. Swift and calm, I swept my phial into the vase as I turned around. The men walked ahead of me. I moved steadily away from the poison.

Three steps away. Five. Seven. No one called me back.

The roar didn't cease in my ears. I stopped three pillars away but didn't move closer to the doors. Dishe was the reason I'd remained here. I couldn't leave here—or the palace—without him.

The military healer left Remmon's body and jogged around the tense hall, telling the guards that the murder weapon was not what they assumed. Grim shock flared from the guards. They quickly formulated a new plan of search while others covered Remmon's body.

"The doors will be opened," the ceremony's head guard announced coolly. "However, no one passes through without a thorough search. If you don't comply, you'll be taken into custody as a suspect of murder. If you try to run... Do not try to run."

A chill rushed through the hall.

The doors opened and a thorough search began.

A high-ranked guard placed a hand on Dishe's arm, and exchanged words with the shaken Fifth Colonel. Dishe nodded almost absently, and I marked his distracted state. Finally, Dishe headed for the entryway.

I took out my dagger for the search and moved a few paces behind him.

I kept my gaze down, for if any of them stared long at the Nergal student, my ring-less eyes would become a problem. Earlier, I'd had an explanation tucked away if noticed: I was tired of sneers and wanted to enjoy the Crowning in peace. Now, however, the guards were after an assassin. They wouldn't accept that explanation at face value.

I stepped forward for a guard to search me. Gaze lowered, I could exude innocence with my true weapon at least twenty feet away in a vase.

"Place the weapon on the ground."

I complied. Face stony, the guard's hands ran up my legs, my hips and bust in the most uncomfortable search I'd undergone. He searched my ears. Removed and shook out my veil.

"Unbraid your hair," he ordered.

I did, shaking it out.

His gaze raked over me and my heart picked up pace under that eagle-like survey. Dishe had turned into a corner, gone from my view. I needed to trail him!

"You can go," the guard finally said and turned to the young woman behind me.

A sudden lightness blew through me as I retrieved my dagger. I completed my mission—and escaped capture.

But somehow, my mission didn't feel complete yet.

I held up my skirts and moved as quickly as I could without drawing suspicion after the Fifth Colonel. The floor was busy. I needed to isolate him so that I could stand a chance at subduing him.

With each step closer to him, thoughts of protocol swirled in my mind, and I estimated a certain distance. A plan clicked into place. *Saints please, let it work.*

I waited until he climbed the busy main stairwell of the east wing, then ran up after him in the throng.

"Fifth Colonel Dishe," I said with my head down, pausing hastily beside him like I had somewhere urgent to be. "The Fourth

Colonel wants to see you about a report, I believe. He's at the third level's atrium. He says he doesn't have much time to wait."

With the First Colonel dead, it was expected that the senior soldiers would desire to speak with the soldier who had seen it happen. Perhaps if Dishe had been in his right mind, less stricken by the murder of his superior and accomplice mere moments ago, he might have wondered why the Fourth Colonel had not sent a guard to summon him instead. It wasn't abnormal for a soldier to send a friend or family member to summon a lower-ranked soldier, but it wasn't the regular way.

"I'll be there, thank you," he answered like someone in a daze.

I held my skirts and hurried up ahead of him. The third level's atrium sat in the last corridor from the students' lounge. People were in the lower floors for today's events and, as I'd anticipated, the area echoed with vacancy.

I dipped into the servants' passageway between the atrium and the students' lounge. Heart taking a steady beat, I pulled out my dagger and waited.

The thud of boots echoed in the silence. Closer. Closer. I stopped breathing.

Dishe's shadow brushed past the threshold. I listened for another step, then swung silently out of the servants' passage. Too distressed to be alert, he never sensed the threat there until my dagger's hilt crashed hard into his temple.

His huge body began to slump like Colonel Remmon had moments ago. I threw myself under his chest before he landed on the ground.

A small groan rose in my throat. His dead weight threatened to crush me. Had I not estimated and staged this attack near the students' lounge, I might have *been* crushed. Using all my strength to hasten up, I dragged us into the vacant lounge and into my bedroom.

Still gripping his arm with one hand, I plodded over to a chair. My chest burned from his weight. I pulled the chair—and my feet—into my large wardrobe. Positioning us both in front of the chair, I pushed him off my back and he slumped into the chair.

Clutching my chest, I let myself draw in deep breaths. *My mission is still far from over.*

My heart raced as I grabbed ropes off the drapes, binding him tightly to the chair. My Commandant hadn't sent me to do this. In fact, chances were that she would expel me when she found out I'd taken a Colonel captive. This might be the straw that brought my entire scheme crashing down.

But, I had to know what Dishe knew.

Colonel Remmon hadn't died with his evil intentions. He'd passed them on to another who was also part of the palace and military. The poison had spread, tainting the water and if I wanted Sarai safe and free, I needed to drain all of it.

I locked the Fifth Colonel in the wardrobe. I closed the last window to darken the room and shut my door, praying the ropes held as I left the Al'Qtraz with the exiting guests.

THE COMMANDANT STOOD before her desk, her academy a den of activity as excitable students returned from the Crowning. A Baihan disciplinarian, her scar-splattered face retained the sort of composure that kept one wondering what went through her mind.

She fired questions at me, and I answered them. By the time a ponderous silence descended, I'd told her everything about Colonel Remmon. The Admiral's schedule hidden in his desk. Remmon framing the Admiral for the murder of Ambassador Caiphas; his colluding with smugglers and the whitebomb flint he'd been bringing into Thalesai. My belief that he hadn't just been arming the mercenaries with flint but had schemed to pull the Admiral out of power so that he could assume his seat for the purpose of giving the mercenaries even more leeway to succeed.

Different emotions edged her face, small glimpses into what she was feeling: shock, betrayal, disbelief, anger, grief at the mention of the ambassador's death, and then resolve. She would ruminate over it all after. Nergal's Commandant wasn't a woman who made her students privy to her thought process, but the events were such that demanded long rumination.

"You've done very well, Scholar Zair," she began, striding over to a window to stare down at her students. "I'm impressed by your diligence..."

While I wanted nothing more than to earn her approval, it was too early for praises.

"Something is wrong, ma'am," I interrupted her.

She turned to me, the slightest crease between her brows. "What do you mean?"

"It's something you need to see for yourself," I said.

For a moment I thought she would insist I spill all I knew, but she studied my face and gave a small nod. "Show me."

WITH THE AL'QTRAZ in an uproar over the king's coronation, two chambermen found dead in one day, and the Admiral's arrest, the Commandant of Nergal's presence in the palace with her student was not unusual. In the tightly-guarded hallways, the guards saluted the small yet respected woman and stepped aside, certain she had come here to ascertain my safety. Betraying nothing of her true intention here, she jogged up beside me for my rooms.

Barghests snarled along corridors, but her hard stare sent even the beasts prowling back.

The lounge was blessedly empty—but where were the other students tonight? I lit my room's lamps while the Commandant locked the door behind us.

I opened the wardrobe and used considerable effort to drag the chair out. Then we stood before the unconscious, tied, and gagged Colonel Dishe.

The Commandant's mouth parted and my hoarse chest pounded. Had I gone too far?

"Just how did you manage *this*, Scholar?" she demanded.

Not 'how dare I abduct a chamberman'?

Her boots were silent against the rug as she moved to survey the knots. "Not even the most skilled soldier could break out of these."

Was that baffled admiration in her voice? The Commandant

turned to me and for the first time in five years, it felt like she *saw* me. Zair Nebah. Not just the Esan student in Nergal's uniform.

But now wasn't the time for a happy dance.

"Explain yourself," she ordered.

I cleared my throat, my lungs burning. I stifled a wince and spoke Binhese in low tones. "I overheard Colonel Remmon speaking with Fifth Colonel Dishe at the Crowning. They are in league together. Fifth Colonel Dishe knows what transpired with framing the Admiral. I could be wrong but... I suspect Colonel Remmon was involved in Ambassador Caiphas's murder. And what Colonel Dishe knows might be the evidence that clears the Admiral's name."

The Commandant tilted her head. "You want the Fifth Colonel interrogated so we can learn the depth of Colonel Remmon's treachery and his goal."

"Yes, ma'am." I'd understood the necessity of assassinating the main traitor to ensure he was gone once and for all. But Colonel Dishe proved that there was more to be learned on this matter. While the Commandant might want him dead too, I believed that this time, it was better to ferret information from the traitor first.

"Bring me a jar of water," she finally said.

I hurried to the bath chamber and filled an urn. I handed it to her and standing behind him, she emptied it on Dishe's head. Water splashed, seeping under my boots as Colonel Dishe gasped awake. He made to stand, only to be jerked back by the binds.

"Who are you?" he muffled around his gag.

The Commandant yanked off his gag, and her face turned cold. She gripped his shoulder firmly and spoke in a whispery soft voice that could never be likened to her bold one. "I have questions for you, and you'll answer with haste if you wish to live."

"Release me this moment," the Fifth Colonel spat. "Do you know who *I* am?"

An accomplice. Her fist rammed against his ear. A ruthless blow that flung him sideway, almost throwing him and the chair to the floor.

Here wasn't the unreadable, disciplined woman who conducted students' affairs. No. Here was a brutal interrogator resolved to draw every piece of vital information from an enemy of her land.

"You'll... pay for that," the Fifth Colonel panted once he gathered his wits. "You won't get away with this!"

"Why did Colonel Remmon murder Ambassador Caiphas?" she asked him, not the '*had* the Colonel murdered Ambassador Caiphas?' I would've asked.

The Fifth Colonel was hard to crack. He took her blows, gritting his teeth to hold in groans—until she drew out a knife from her person and stabbed it into his hand. Blood spurted.

I barely stifled a gasp.

She clapped a hand over his mouth, muffling his cries as blood rolled over the armrest. She placed her mouth to his ear, using a whispery soft voice that could never be linked to her bold one. "Why did Colonel Remmon murder Ambassador Caiphas?"

"He wanted the position!" Dishe finally panted against her hand, restless with agony.

The Commandant released his mouth. "Say that again."

"Colonel Remmon wanted to be Admiral. He loathed taking orders from a Baihan. He wanted to be the first Mizsab Admiral in Thalesai's history."

Tribalism our old friend, here you were again.

"So he murdered Ambassador Caiphas here in the palace?" she asked.

A vigorous nod. "He knew it was a risk, but killing Ambassador Caiphas in the palace allowed him to point fingers at the Admiral while the Admiral was also here."

The schedule! It wasn't just for Remmon to know when the Admiral was absent from the city so that Remmon could infiltrate his office and forge documents. But also to know when the Admiral would be *in* Ari'el and vulnerable to be framed.

It came back to me now that the schedule also mentioned a meeting between Ambassador Caiphas and the Admiral *today*.

Skies. Remmon had planned his treachery with ruthless precision.

"What evidence did Colonel Remmon plant in the Admiral's office?" I asked.

The Commandant gave me a rebuking look. *Wrong voice!*

Dishe hesitated to answer, so she stabbed the knife deeper into his hand.

He howled. "It was a document requesting whitebomb flint."

The confession jarred through the room.

"The Colonel framed the Admiral as a smuggler of whitebomb flint?" the Commandant whispered.

A bumpy nod. "And he hid some of the flint in the Admiral's office and the rest in the Admiral's rooms. The Admiral's possession of mercenary weaponry, combined with the accusations of murder, would strip away his credibility. Make it harder for him to claim innocence. Then Colonel Remmon who'd brought these sins to light would be the hero of the day and be promoted to Admiral."

Nausea gripped me. The Commandant's face had gone ashen.

"So Colonel Remmon *was* affiliated with the mercenaries," she said more than asked.

Shock exuded from Dishe. "*What?* Colonel Remmon? He would never..."

She shoved the knife harder. This time it burst out from his palm. Her hand over his mouth muffled his roar of pain. "What kind of woman are you?"

"The mean kind."

When she pulled her hand back, he gasped, "He didn't tell me about an affiliation with the mercenaries! I only knew his plans for promotion and his promise to put me in his seat as First Colonel if I aided him. The whitebomb flint was for framing the Admiral! That's all I know."

I focused hard, but my senses smelled no lies on him. It meant Colonel Remmon had kept his other clandestine scheme from Dishe. It was clear Dishe didn't know that this wasn't the only time Remmon had sought out the flint.

Perhaps Dishe wouldn't have stood by Colonel Remmon had he known the full extent of Remmon's corruption. Or maybe that was only wishful thinking.

The same thoughts radiated from the Commandant's eyes. She believed he'd shared all he knew.

"What next?" I asked her quietly.

She straightened, turned to the squirming Fifth Colonel and landed a hefty blow to his head. As he passed out, she motioned for me to unbind him.

"We're letting him go?" I asked as I untied Dishe from the chair.

She blindfolded him. "There are too many dead today, both deaths connected to the three of us in this room. If we eliminate him, we'll be inviting trouble to Nergal."

I showed her the servants' stairs and together, we dragged the unconscious Fifth Colonel up floors and dumped him just on the threshold to the king's heavily-guarded private area. On Dishe's roped form, the Commandant tucked in a note with forged handwriting:

> *The Admiral of Thalesai is innocent of every accusation.*
>
> *Apply the right amount of pressure and Fifth Colonel Dishe will spill all he knows about Colonel Remmon's treachery—and the murder of Ambassador Caiphas.*

Once Dishe's body thudded on the marble, the Commandant called out for guards. At the clapping of their boots, we plunged back into the servants' stairway. We reached my room, the Al'Qtraz seeming to grow rowdier from every direction.

We scrubbed clean all signs of the Fifth Colonel's presence.

"Gather your things," the Commandant said. "Your work here is done."

I nodded and went to my wardrobe to pack only what I'd brought.

Although one ceremony was left—the Majesties' Gifting—I'd known I would leave the Al'Qtraz today if my mission was successful. Yet as we strode out of the one place I'd come to see my magic as a boon rather than an abnormality, the lounge where I'd played with my peers and danced with a young man, I couldn't help but look over my shoulder at their rooms. I wished I'd seen Dathan one more time. Or had the chance to tell Lysias and Mishan goodbye.

PART III

THE CROSSED SWORDS

42

ZAIR

"*Welcome back, Nebah.*"
"*You killed it at the Best of Ten.*"
"*We should celebrate during the holidays!*"

With each greeting, my eyebrows neared my hairline as the Commandant and I marched up the steps between the tiered buildings. I nodded tentatively in response to the greetings. I'd thought that by now, they would've forgotten all about the girl behind the Best of Ten's medal.

Most still saluted the Commandant and moved with noses in the air at a glimpse of me. This time, I didn't give them the pleasure of caring.

We reached the Commandant's office on the topmost floor of the highest building, where she could see everything from her windows.

I went alert. Three cloaked men stood by the door. These weren't Nergal guards, and they hadn't been here earlier.

But the Commandant simply opened her door and went in. I followed warily.

Under the light of a single carved lamp, the plasterwork forming rings of Nergal's fanged foxes were shadowed. By the visitor's seats, I saw the swirl of ornamented black satin first before Queen Yval lowered her veil from her face and rose to her feet.

I stumbled to a halt. What was she doing here?

Saints. Did she... did she know I was behind Colonel Remmon's assassination? *She was here to sentence me to death.* My heart slammed against my ribs.

Calm and unreadable, Queen Yval looked to the Commandant and said, "My First Colonel was assassinated today. Could it mean what I think it does?"

The Commandant nodded. To my disbelief, she recounted everything I'd told her concerning my mission up to our encounter with Colonel Dishe.

Queen Yval remained expressionless as she listened to my list of crimes. Treachery. Theft. Murder. Abduction.

She asked detailed questions. The Commandant answered each one.

What was going on?

"Please excuse us, Commandant," the queen said.

My throat closed up as I awaited my punishment.

But once the Commandant closed the door behind her, Queen Yval spoke with a gentle smile. "You've done very well, Scholar Nebah."

My head spun.

"I... I don't understand, Your Majesty."

"I know. You see, I had your Commandant send you into the palace to dig out the traitor."

I gaped at the softly-spoken young Queen of Thalesai and struggled to reconcile her with the sponsor who'd sent me to assassinate a chamberman.

Queen Yval walked toward a window overlooking the starry sky that stretched like a wall above cresting sand. "My husband has a vision of sealing the gaps between the tribes of Thalesai. And his approach includes seeing only the best in their leaders without bias."

I just gaped at her.

"While his tolerance has its merits, it also means that he refuses to see Thalesai's leaders as potential threats to be monitored. This has made many in the Chambers overly bold. They're taking his leniency for granted, and that is something that *I*, Yval Nogbaisi, cannot overlook."

There it was. The infamous Ussi pride. But her pride wasn't just for her own tribe. It was from her rank as queen of the people of Thalesai.

"The king has enough enemies." She stopped by the window, then drew a breath and twirled to me. "I don't want him to feel like he has to contend with his wife too, so I don't argue with him over his views on how to handle his Chambers. I stayed silent and supportive during our first year as royals, learning the ropes to inherit our crowns. But then the mercenaries emerged, and I saw signs in the Al'Qtraz that there were traitors in my home aiding them."

Traitors. Not *one* traitor?

"I need help uprooting them all," she said humbly.

I still struggled to digest the fact that Queen Yval was my sponsor. And now she needed more of *my* help?

But, "I'm Esan," I blurted, and my face burned. Yet it was the truth. As an Ussi noblewoman, she shouldn't want to breathe the same air as me.

"I can see that," she said with some amusement. "It's why I requested you."

She had requested me? *Specifically?* I'd wondered why the Commandant chose me for this mission after years of hardly noticing my existence. The queen had asked for $\underline{me}$. My heart wobbled.

"The Esans possess skills I believed would make you the perfect spy. Like a cheetah," Queen Yval said as if in thought. "And after Colonel Remmon's elimination, I believe I was right."

The queen considered my skills from my aziza blood an advantage, not an abnormality? A rumbling started in the very depth of my core, like giant puzzle pieces locking into their right places.

My abilities are an advantage. I'm not a dog as Ibhar claimed; I'm a cheetah.

I'm a cheetah.

Emotions swamped me.

It was the queen who had provided the rare Ussi poison I'd used on Colonel Remmon, the assassination weapon, and the other mixtures. And... and the reason she'd ignored me *utterly* during our first meeting in the palace was to avoid any connection that could stir suspicion of our liaison. Not because she thought that I was Esan scum.

She'd been protecting both of us from the king's wrath in the little ways too. The old wound in my heart from that day began to scab over.

"But," I wondered, "why did you invite me to your *vyji*, Your Majesty?"

"On the dawn of my *vyji*, I received news from my Ironteenth Captain that the First Colonel had guards searching for a spy who'd broken into an office. A female spy. I'd known there was a chance it was you. I couldn't risk warning you, so I decided to pull you out of the palace while his search was strongest. Inviting you to my *vyji* was the easiest way to do that."

My eyes widened, a flutter in my stomach. "I hadn't... guessed."

"Besides." A small smile. "It was pleasant having at least one person close to my age present at the most intimidating moment of my life."

Somehow, even after the revelations, all I could say was, "You didn't look intimidated at all."

A wry smile. "When living in a den of lions, you learn to hide your fears and roar back. But I don't think you're a stranger to that lesson, are you?"

An understanding, one that transcended ranks and tribes, passed between us.

"I also heard about the Best of Ten, how you'd won while others were distracted from the true prize. I think you and I favor the same tactics."

A smile danced on my lips, but then a thought came. Both she and Nergal's Commandant were absent during the Best of Ten. "Did you and my Commandant meet during the event?"

"Yes. I'd needed a report and hadn't had an opportunity to meet with her until that day. We were both sorry to miss your performance. You claimed the top spot in the Best of Ten without using your magical abilities. Perhaps if you were to accept and hone them, you would be unstoppable."

A knock came and the Commandant strode in, stepping aside for the cloaked man I recognized as the Ironteenth Archer's head. A man lethal with his bow.

Queen Yval's forehead fused delicately. "Captain Folarin, what is the matter?"

He glanced at me and the Commandant.

"Speak freely," she ordered.

"News just arrived at the palace," Captain Folarin said grimly. "The mercenary group broke into the Kurje prison this afternoon."

"What?" the Commandant and I exclaimed.

Queen Yval's hand rose to her mouth, her face blanching. "No."

"The group successfully freed their captured leaders from the prison." He paused. "During the break-in, other prisoners escaped into the forests. There were some casualties on our side, and although sixty prisoners were rounded up, over twenty escaped."

I struggled to imitate the Commandant's composure, but horror was a living thing in me. The Kurje prison was one of the most guarded prisons in Thalesai because it held depraved criminals. Now the mercenaries hadn't just destroyed another of our strongest institutions and rescued mercenary *leaders*, but murderers, defilers, and bandits were on the loose.

Queen Yval lowered herself into a chair. "First Colonel Remmon isn't the traitor."

The ground undulated underneath me.

My panic edged the Commandant's face as she said, "Your Majesty... are you certain?"

The queen nodded as if partly in a daze. "Colonel Remmon could not have known the prisoners were in the Kurje prison, so he couldn't have given the information to the mercenaries. After the Admiral caught the mercenaries, the king held a small meeting where he decided the prisoners were to be locked in Kurje. He insisted the information wasn't made public to avoid a situation like this, a prison break-in. He'd planned to travel to the Kurje prison himself after the coronation to see the mercenary leaders and was determined to have nothing ruin that.

"Colonel Remmon wasn't invited to that meeting."

Tension ripped through the office. I'd assassinated the wrong man. Bile burned my throat.

What do I do now?

Remmon's words came back to me. *Someone* had given him a

two-week deadline to achieve his goal of framing the Admiral and stealing his position. A *He*.

Without thought, I stepped forward. "Your Majesty, who was present at the meeting?"

Captain Folarin frowned at my forwardness while the Commandant gave me a look to be cautious.

Queen Yval lifted her gaze and surveyed me, before saying in a steadier voice, "Myself, the king, the First and Second Advisors, and Captain Emeso of the Ironteenth. Captain Emeso had carried the orders and reports between the king and the Admiral, rather than the emissary."

"Skies," I whispered.

The Commandant did the same. This narrowed down the list ruthlessly. And meant the traitor of Thalesai... was a member of the king's closest trusted circle.

Queen Yval rose and paced, her mind churning behind her beautiful face.

The queen suddenly turned to me. "You must return to the Al'Qtraz, Scholar Nebah."

The Commandant took a step forward. "The palace is no longer safe for her. Not only has she assassinated the First Colonel, but she also took the Fifth Colonel hostage."

Captain Folarin's head jerked back.

"That Zair managed to achieve those feats makes her the only one I can trust to find the true traitor amongst these lofty suspects," the queen insisted.

"I'll do it," I dared to cut in.

"Scholar Nebah!" the Commandant rebuked, and then turned back to the queen. "Your Majesty, with all due respect, Scholar Nebah is a student entrusted to my care. Her safety is my responsibility, and sending her back into the palace at this hostile time would be gambling with her life."

"You don't understand," Queen Yval said. "Those who were present at that meeting are men the king trusts. Now that this has happened, he'll know he's been betrayed by someone in his inner circle." She swallowed and lifted her chin. "And because I am Ussi, there is a chance that he might suspect that person to be me."

43

DATHAN

The desert was a grey canvas as I galloped back to Ari'el. The sun gradually peeked out from the horizon, the tallest dunes sparkling as the light reached their peaks. Camels and horses filed vibrantly in the distance as citizens made early starts back to their hometowns.

I should be avoiding the palace like a plague after abducting the Dynast of Bornoir. My mission was complete. But I needed to see Zair.

News had spread of the First Colonel's death. The moment I heard of it, I knew. She'd done it. And last night, after the Commandant told me *who* Sarhedrin was scheming with to steal funds for the mercenaries... the depth of treachery in the palace ripped my chest open.

I had to see for myself that her mission hadn't cost her freedom or put her in worse danger. If it had—that deep, unexplainable inferno of protectiveness blazed—then I had more fighting to do. I flicked my horse's reins, spurring him faster. It no longer mattered that our attachment was false. Zair had wiggled her way deep into this beating organ in my chest. That was the truth. The reason I'd felt like I couldn't breathe the night Remmon pushed her down a window. The reason I relived our kiss in the banquet hall over and over again. The reason I now spurred my horse against the winds like the world might cave in if I didn't find her safe soon.

I had intended to keep my guard up against her, but I hadn't stood a chance against a woman who beamed brightly with passion, resilience, and that flicker of vulnerability. I was done denying and fighting that I felt deeply for her, even if I had no idea where these feelings could lead. *If* it could lead anywhere, with the barriers of tribes and missions between us. My ribs seemed to clench around my heart.

But I had too many battles to face already to keep lying to myself.

Like the battle to stay away from the Gergesenes' dungeons as the Commandant ordered. Leaving the academy was also the only way to keep from doing something stupid, like stealing into the dungeons to end the man who'd had my father beaten almost to his death, whose men had defiled my sister, and stabbed my mother.

Whose mercenaries now tormented Jaziah.

The morning whitened as I gave the guards my arranged excuse for leaving the palace and rode into the palace's grand grounds. I looked up at the Al'Qtraz and my nape prickled. Uproars echoed through the ornamental windows, revealing heated debates within.

I jogged up the steps and through the ground floor. The division was deepening. Tribesmen converged, joining bobbing heads, some pointing fingers in arguments. There was no way the foreign ambassadors didn't suspect Thalesai was on fire.

Where is Zair?

Mishan conversed with an elegant woman by an archway. His mother. He spotted me, said something to the worried-looking woman, and strode over.

"Where have you been?"

"What's happening?" I asked him at the same time. Then answered his question truthfully, "I had to go to Gergesenes."

His eyes dimmed behind his eyeglasses. "Did you hear about the Kurje prison break?"

"I did," I said grimly. Not long after the Commandant's revelation about Sarhedrin. For a moment, it had felt like the world crumbled around me and I was running too late to save it.

"All the academies in the Kurje town are shutting down. The moment news of the prison break circulated, parents insisted their children were sent back home."

I ran a hand down my tired face. "I can't blame them."

Mishan rubbed his temple. "Yet humans' greatest weapon is knowledge. If the mercenaries keep attacking academies and obstructing schooling, we cannot study to become as advanced as the other kingdoms are. We'd be ignorant, as vulnerable as we'd been centuries ago."

My jaw ticked with the effort it took not to voice an agreement. "Don't grow defeated on me, Mish. We will never be that vulnerable again. Not when we have a prime scholar building us flying inventions."

"If only charm won battles, Gergesenes," Mishan said with a chuckle.

"Any signs of Zair today?" I asked with forced casualness.

Mishan peered at me with intelligent eyes. "I heard she took permission and left the palace to Nergal."

She wasn't here. I didn't know whether to be relieved or more bothered. What state had she left in?

Swallowing, I scanned the busy hallway. "Where's Lysias?"

Protecting the elite students was not part of my mission, but after that day in the butchers' cell, after losing Jaziah, and after all I'd seen here, their safety mattered to me.

"She left for Quartus this morning. The Headmistress insisted she leave the palace's tensions. It's why my mother is here. She wants me to leave too."

His mother spoke with a palace guard, seeming to query him while he tried to reassure her.

"Did something happen in the Al'Qtraz that carried to the civilians?" How else would city folk know the palace was creasing with tension?

"There are rumors in the city that families of the abducted children are planning a violent protest at the palace. Anything to make the Chambers start paying attention to them."

Sheols. I should've stayed away from here. If it was already this strained, any link between me and the missing Dynast of Bornoir would be pursued aggressively. "I have to leave, Mishan."

His gaze rested on my daggers and he gave a nod. "I understand."

He didn't quite, but I appreciated him not prying for an explanation. I patted his shoulder and made for the exit. "Stay safe, Mish."

Underneath a gothic vault, Zair's lithe form collided with me. "Dathan."

I held her elbows to steady her. "You're alright."

Relief shook my chest like a barrage of air. I barely stifled the urge to pull her into my arms. Our hungry eyes drank each other in, a hundred questions blazing between us.

"We need to talk," she whispered, took my hand without any prompting, and pulled me back into the palace.

It was a statement I never thought I'd hear from Zair Nebah. I let her lead me up the crowded stairs and corridors of the western wing. On a vacant landing, a wail heralded a little boy—a Kwali noble's son—with a scraped knee.

Walk it off, little one, there are worse things to cry over.

But Zair knelt beside him. She soothed him quickly and when his snot-covered face was smiling, she sent him to find his mother.

"You always do this," I mused as she took my hand and resumed her onward march. "Look after weaker ones."

"I like to show people who feel unseen or unloved that someone cares. Sometimes, that's all a person needs to keep going."

Emotions tinged her voice. She connected to these people, the unseen and unloved, so she did for them what people didn't do for her.

My chest seemed to expand with pain as we emerged on a flat rooftop with marble trellises and balustrades. There was no one to overhear us up here.

In the open morning light, I closely studied her and my stomach tightened until it ached. Her golden skin had a sick pallor and her face was drawn. Eyebags and slumped shoulders proved she hadn't slept last night either.

The stubborn girl wasn't well, hadn't seen a healer after her fall. I ground my teeth to keep from pushing the matter, then noticed the bare skin above her upper right brow.

She didn't wear kohl, or any sign of what we were to each other. Did she think *we* were finished because she'd completed her mission in the palace?

"You're my *aiyena*," I told her firmly. "We were vowed before a priestess with witnesses. Our union is set in the temple's stones. Until there is an annulment, we're bound to each other, Zair Nebah."

Her brows crinkled. I almost chuckled at the familiarity of her frown.

"Why are you bringing that up now?"

I crossed my arms over my chest. Over my heart. "Just a reminder."

A sad look crossed her face, but she shook it away and said, "Whoever you captured isn't the traitor in the palace."

I tautened, lowered my arms. Firstly, she knew nothing of who I'd targeted and Sarhedrin had revealed his guilt. Secondly, why would she suddenly share information with me? She'd always kept her cards close. Was she trying to mislead me?

She must've sensed the direction of my thoughts. She glanced away, seeming at war with herself. To let her rival in or continue to keep me locked out. Finally, she drew a breath and looked at me. "My target was First Colonel Remmon."

"I know," I said carefully.

She looked disconcerted by that fact but went on urgently. "I thought he was the one aiding the mercenaries, but he wasn't. Not the main schemer anyway. He smuggled whitebomb flint into the kingdom multiple times, yes. But now the only motive I'm sure of is that he used the flint to set up the Admiral, rather than to arm the mercenaries as I'd believed."

She was showing me her cards. Showing me that I could trust her.

"Wait a moment," I said as her words fully registered. "Colonel Remmon was smuggling in whitebomb flint?"

She gave a nod, watching me.

"Whitebomb..." My throat closed. "Saints above."

"First Colonel Remmon coveted the Admiral's rank," Zair confirmed my silent question, because I left my face open for her to read. "He framed the Admiral for the king's brother's murder and solidified evidence against the Admiral by planting the flint in his office. But I'd wrongly connected Remmon's smuggling of the flint to sponsoring the mercenaries instead."

The Admiral was framed a criminal by *Remmon*?

Only earnestness cloaked Zair's face. Despite the Commandant's confidence that the Admiral was innocent, relief rushed through me to have actual proof. The kingdom would've been finished if the *Admiral* sponsored the mercenaries.

But then, "None of this means my target is wrong," I challenged. "You don't even know who it is."

Hesitation skirted her face, but then she lifted her chin fiercely. "Vow you won't tell *anyone* what I'm about to share. Or else I'll hunt you down and kill you."

Furrowing my forehead, I said, "Can't let you finally have real motive." I touched a thumb to my tongue. "I promise."

Stepping closer, Zair told me about the king's private meeting concerning the captured mercenaries. Only five people had been present at the meeting where the king chose their prison.

"Colonel Remmon wasn't at the meeting, and neither was the Royal Accountant. Unless you were tailing the First Advisor, the Second Advisor, the Ironteenth Captain, or the Majesties, then you haven't found the traitor either."

I stared down at her, astonished. Sarhedrin wasn't the traitor in the palace... but someone higher up than him.

What was Sarhedrin's plan if the funds he'd stolen weren't to equip the mercenaries? Why had he been angry that some mercenaries were caught? And why had he murdered Thalesai's noblemen and guards if he wasn't an enemy of the land?

I looked to Zair, unsteady like the ground had shattered beneath my feet. How had *she* known about that meeting?

She didn't look smug, but regretful.

"Why would you reveal this to me?"

"I want to beat you, Dathan," she admitted, swallowing. "I want to find the traitor myself and be considered worthy of the Ironteenth. But more than my ambition... I don't want Thalesai to fall. I don't want our peers to die in captivity. And I can't bear the thought of my sis... my family, endangered. Our competition isn't worth it." She glanced away. "I believe that you and I need to work together, to save our peers and kingdom."

The vulnerable admission—that despite trying, she couldn't bear the weight of this mission alone, that she needed help—humbled me.

I took her hand. "Come to Gergesenes with me. I need to tell my Commandant about this and hear what other information he has wrung out from the Dynast of Bornoir."

Zair's head jerked up. "The Dynast of Bornoir. He was your target."

I watched her wonder how he'd never fallen under her radar. Wonder what he'd perpetrated that made him guilty to me.

She was right. Our competition to find the real traitor first was not worth Thalesai's damnation. She'd trusted me; I'd do the same.

I gave her the important details concerning the Dynast of Bornoir, the findings that made me attack him. She agreed he was affiliated with the mercenaries somehow, even if he wasn't the main traitor.

"And there is Ambassador Caiphas," I carefully added.

"Ambassador Caiphas?" she exclaimed.

Grimness settled over me. "During his interrogations, my Commandant found out that Sarhedrin planned to steal money from the Royal Accountant... for Ambassador Caiphas."

Zair gasped, stumbled backward and caught my hand for balance.

"I know," I said.

"*Why?*" she stuttered. "What would Ambassador Caiphas want that amount of money for? *Why* would he collude with an Ussi bigot?"

"We don't have those answers since Sarhedrin himself doesn't know Ambassador Caiphas's motive. Only that..." I hesitated. Sheols, I hadn't realized how much I liked Ambassador Caiphas or wanted to see good in him. This realization was a hard draught to swallow.

Zair held my arm, an almost hidden line of hurt on her face. She thought I was unwilling to completely trust her. "Please. Tell me."

With my thumb, I brushed that line of hurt from her lips. "Sarhedrin wanted Ambassador Caiphas to vote for him as ruler of the new town the king plans to build. Apparently, the king put together a committee to cast votes on who'd be granted the land gifted to us by the wraithlands. It was a small committee of nobles with no interest in ruling the land, and Ambassador Caiphas was part of it. Caiphas agreed to vote for Sarhedrin if Sarhedrin paid for Caiphas's vote. So Sarhedrin tried to steal hundreds of thousands of *siyvas* from the Royal Accountant to buy Caiphas's vote."

Zair's hand dropped, disappointment weighing her features.

"Ironic, isn't it?" she said. "That Sarhedrin did all that, risked everything he has, to sway Ambassador Caiphas. Now the Ambassador is dead and risking his rank for all that money has been for nothing."

At the last statement, we both stilled. Realization flooded in like a burst dam.

Zair lifted her wide gaze to mine. "You'd said the Dynast of Bornoir was planning to steal hundreds of thousands of *siyvas*."

"Ambassador Caiphas wouldn't demand that amount for a vote. Even if he had, Sarhedrin would've been right to call him mad and walk away from the deal."

"No, the amount he'd planned to steal wasn't *just* for the Ambassador. He gave your Commandant half-truths, Dathan." The gold in her eyes flashed. "The money was intended for *something* else too."

"Or some other group." I turned for the exit, paused. "We need to meet my Commandant, Zair."

She hesitated, then said, "Alright."

There was no time to be surprised by her agreement. We quickly asked for passes to leave the palace and rode hard for Gergesenes.

44

DATHAN

"Two weeks," Zair murmured, her veil fluttering in the hot breeze.

Our horses trotted between giant red rocks, back to Ari'el, after I'd informed my enraged Commandant of Sarhedrin's false answers. Zair hadn't followed me into the Academy to secure her identity.

At her words, my head jolted up from praying Jaziah could withstand the torments just a bit longer. We were so close to finding the real traitor. The Commandant was wringing the entire truth out of Sarhedrin now.

The man my family feared the most was now helpless in a dungeon.

I put him there.

Spared my family from him because I had risen up and *gone* after him, rather than keep my head down. If a bold stance had rid us of Sarhedrin and could help me rescue Jaziah, how could it be selfish?

Pulling myself to the present, I asked, "What about 'two weeks'?"

"I'd overheard Colonel Remmon say that. He was given two weeks by his 'timekeeper' to reach his goal."

I stiffened but eased my muscles when my horse shook its head in reaction. "Sarhedrin said similar words."

She raised her brows, sickness still limning her face.

"He'd also been given two weeks by a man. He worried about not meeting his goal by the deadline."

Zair stared ahead in thought as we exited the rock walls onto flat land scattered with cacti. "Do you think Colonel Remmon and Dynast Sarhedrin spoke of the same person?"

"I do. Also that this person was in the secret meeting with the king."

She nodded. "Whoever he is, we have to find him before the coronation is over. The Gifting is tomorrow and everyone will leave the palace in only four days."

I couldn't help but smirk at her. "*We?*"

Her cheeks pinkened, but she kept her gaze seriously ahead and nodded. "Together."

It sounded like a foreign phenomenon the way she said it. And I would've been amused if I didn't suspect that having a partner felt that way for her. I could imagine her last five years at Nergal, lonely with her schoolmates refusing to partner with her for trainings and assignments.

It was interesting how the wind blew. Since our meeting, we'd worked around and against each other. Now we had to work together to actually succeed. Our Commandants would be enraged to learn of this decision to partner, but at this juncture, knowing how deeply entrenched in the Chambers the traitor was, there was no luxury for rivalry.

"We can cross out the Majesties from the list," she continued as Ari'el's gates gleamed into view. "Which leaves First Advisor Maachah, Second Advisor Drake, and Captain Emeso."

"Captain Emeso can be crossed from the list too."

She narrowed those spectacular gold-encircled eyes at me. "Why? Because he's a Gergesenes graduate?"

Partly. Gergesenes didn't raise traitors. But also, "As Captain of the Ironteenth Fighters, he can't go anywhere the king isn't or doesn't send him. There would be time, even after the coronation, to investigate if he's the traitor. We have no such assurance with the Advisors. Their duties allow more flexibility."

"True." Zair bit on her lip in that sweet way she did.

I thirsted to lean in and soothe it with my mouth. She looked up at me. When I didn't temper my thoughts, her cheeks filled with color.

It was her shyness that made me force my gaze away. I'd kiss her if she would let me. The yearning I felt for her wasn't like anything I'd ever felt before. The fire wasn't a flicker but a growing blaze, but while Zair could assassinate a man at the heart of the palace, intimacy was still foreign to her. It scared her.

I reached for her veil instead. She caught it before I could steal it, playfully wrinkling her perfect nose at me as she adjusted the article back over her eyes.

"Veil-stealer."

Heart stealer.

We rode into the busy main road in the Tiz Valley, speaking lowly as we joined travelers with groaning wagons. The thick traffic locked us in for hours until my Commandant's hefty carriage arrived. His guards cleared up the route, and the carriage passed.

Why is the Commandant going into Ari'el?

Perhaps it wasn't him in the carriage, but his second-in-command.

"I think our time would run out if we pursued the advisors together, only one at a time," Zair decided, pulling my attention.

"Agreed. We need to split, share targets to effectively cover ground."

My chest still clenched that one of the king's closest advisors might be Thalesai's traitor.

"Second Advisor Drake is mine," I said. He was Ussi, which was enough reason for suspicion in my book. But I'd also seen enough in the palace to know he supported Ussi supremacy. He could be sponsoring the mercs to discredit the king. If Zair knew that Drake was most likely the traitor, the competitive side of her would rear and she'd argue. I wasn't trailing Drake for glory so much as I was because Zair was ill. I didn't want anyone else pushing her off buildings.

She agreed. "I'll trail the First Advisor."

The Al'Qtraz glowed in the sweltering late afternoon as we rode our horses into the outer yards. I swung off mine first. Zair's foot tangled in her stirrup and a small laugh escaped her as she freed herself. The light, almost secret, sound whispered through me, and I couldn't help it.

I wanted to taste that reserved joy, wanted her to share it with me.

I stepped closer to her, watching her face as I rested a hand on her waist and leaned in. She didn't pull away but stared eagerly at my mouth. I brushed my lips over hers and almost groaned from the sweet softness of her.

"Kiss me, Zair," I whispered against her lips.

With an expression as drugged as I felt, she wrapped her arms around my neck, rose up on her toes, and kissed me. I groaned and gripped her waist. Fire blazed in my blood as I tasted her lips and then her warm mouth.

More. But there was only so much kissing we could do on the palace grounds. Even betrothed, gasps and chidings would soon follow if we stayed here longer. Zair would clam up under the scrutiny.

After having her soft and open in my arms, I couldn't bear her pulling away again.

I broke the kiss and took her hand, leading her past scented hedges.

"Dathan?"

"Too many eyes, Nergal. Students' lounge."

Laughter danced in her eyes, but she let me lead her on. If I was dreaming, I never wanted to wake up.

We entered the ground floor and with each step, each worried noble we greeted, I couldn't pretend the world wasn't on fire around us anymore.

Zair went from relaxed to rock-stiff as nobles glared at her walking beside me. I wanted to growl at them all. Her face became an unreadable mask. She would pull away from me in every way if I didn't hold tight, and it was too early in the day to trail the Advisors. *Think fast.*

Chambermen streaked through an exit leading to the Chambers building and I whispered to her, "No more lounging for us. The chambermen are having a meeting."

She tautened as my breath brushed her cheek. I tamped down my frustration. *Ten steps forward and nine steps back within a space of minutes*. Yet if I wanted to make any headway with Zair—and without a doubt, I did—I couldn't rush her. I had to be patient and show her that she could trust me. I'd always been a patient man.

"It's bound to be important," I added temptingly. I still hadn't figured out a way into the Chambers, but perhaps she had.

Her eyes moved with interest. "You want to... attend?"

"It's a crucial time. Whatever they discuss will be vital, yet would most likely never leave those halls."

Understanding the unspoken implication, she gave a nod. "I know a way in."

45

ZAIR

The servants' stairs twisted up the Chambers—a historic building we'd been taught about at the academies. It fizzled with tension. Servants clustered on landings, speculating over what today's meeting could be about. Apparently, they served victuals during Chamber meetings, but today the doors were shut to everyone who wasn't a chamberman. Palace guards included.

Preoccupied, and assured only fellow servants took this route, the servants paid no attention to Dathan and I heading quietly up. With each step on the smooth oak, Dathan's full attention burned into my back.

His attentiveness to me made the spite from the courtiers who believed I didn't deserve him sting worse.

My chest shriveled within that Dathan, the first man who had kissed me, witnessed people treat me like scum. I kept my chin up, hid the sadness, and pretended I wasn't shaken. But it felt like Dathan had an ability to see right through my walls, like they were really made of glass.

I didn't want that. I didn't want an *airran* to constantly witness the humiliations I tried to forget. But I would never be the *aiyena* who people celebrated and honored, to the joy of her *airran*. I was the *aiyena* that brought shame to my betrothed. Once the main traitor was exposed, this was just one more reason I had to go to a temple for an annulment of our vows before my heart grew any more entangled in this false betrothal.

The servants grew sparser and on the third floor, the stairs were vacant.

"The Chambers has four floors and halls," Dathan recited thoughtfully, a part of our *Amalgamated Thalesai* lessons. "The ground hall for legislative purposes, the second hall for executive purposes, while the third..." He halted before a servants' door of white and brown spirals. "For judiciary purposes."

The door vibrated with the activity behind it.

"Judiciary hall means today's meeting is to pass judgment on something." I stood beside him. "Or someone."

Certain the servants' door would be positioned at the hall's rear or someplace unimposing, Dathan pushed it slightly open. It moved quietly, revealing eight tiers of sinuous sachnisi seats arranged like a giant sickle. Chambermen in uniforms and boubous sat rigidly in half of them.

Our door rose behind a drape, setting us out of their line of sight. I couldn't use my magic to conceal us both, so I moved silently behind the drapes to the stairs curving up to a balcony of seats. I sidled into one of the back seats, and let out a long breath.

The ceiling spread wide and was of carved wood with intarsia blue crystals glinting between beams like stars. The mauve-and-peach geometric wall tiles shone under the sunlight from the curved windows.

Dathan slipped into a vine-green upholstered seat beside me, shadows on his scabbing knuckles that had beaten Ibhar off me at the Best of Ten. Our focus moved to the high table. King Khasar and the Chamber of Wings occupied it, their faces stern as they watched the Admiral who stood before the hall.

"It's his Hearing," I whispered. "They'll decide his fate today."

Although he looked wrung out, the Admiral's voice resounded, collected yet angrily, through the hall. "...is false. I've never had contact with whitebomb flint. I've been out of the capital for the better part of two weeks. It creates the perfect window for my framing."

"He knows someone is out to get him. He won't give in just yet," Dathan said with conviction.

The hall didn't seem convinced by the Admiral.

"And what do you have to say to the accusation that you murdered Ambassador Caiphas?" the Magistrate asked, her voice bold but without judgment. "And then had a henchman assassinate Colonel Remmon after he exposed you?"

My stomach lurched. The Admiral was facing accusation for my assassination?

Dathan's head snapped to me, but I couldn't look away from the Admiral.

"Also false," the Admiral said severely. "I maintain my stance that I am being framed by someone with an ulterior motive."

King Khasar clearly detested the implication that more traitors hid in his Chambers.

Where was Fifth Colonel Dishe? Hadn't they interrogated him? Hadn't he told them what he'd told us about Colonel Remmon and his framing of the Admiral? Or had the guards seen Dishe, a senior soldier assaulted, and hurried to help him rather than question him?

My stomach roiled; my vision blurred. I clutched the headrest before me. "Oh saints."

"Zair," Dathan called, his deep voice solid in the turbulence of my mind.

"This is my fault. He's taking the fall for me..."

"*Zair*." His hand settled over mine. I realized mine were shaking like leaves in a storm. "Breathe. We *will* fix this."

I obeyed and sucked a breath, managed a nod. *We*. I wasn't alone anymore.

"You were to meet with my brother on the morning of his death," King Khasar spoke, his face cold and composed. "Are you saying you didn't see him at all that day, Admiral?"

"I did see him, Your Majesty," the Admiral admitted, rigidly, as though he knew he'd just added a nail to his coffin.

Disapproving murmurs loudened the hall. My stomach flipped, and Dathan's steady grip tightened on my hand.

"We had our meeting," the Admiral said, "and then parted ways."

"Did anyone see this meeting, Admiral? Did they see you leave him?" Second Advisor Drake sneered.

"It was a private meeting, so no." Something shifted in the Admiral's tone. Something he *wasn't* saying. "It was only us in his office, and with preparations for the Crowning I doubt anyone was watching when I'd left."

"His office," the First Advisor, my new target to investigate, repeated thoughtfully.

The Admiral nodded. "Yes."

"Ambassador Caiphas's body was found outside, on the blood-soaked courtyard," the First Advisor said to the hall. "He was indubitably murdered there."

"I hadn't stepped outside the palace walls by the time of his death."

There was silence as the hall ruminated on this. Bits of hope fluttered in me.

The Magistrate asked, "Do you have anything else to say for yourself?"

The Admiral rotated slowly to King Khasar with his shoulders squared. The king's face was like stone.

"I'm sorry for the death of Caiphas Nogbaisi, Your Majesty," the Admiral said. "He might not have been perfect, but his intentions were always fair, for the good of Thalesai. I respected him and hope that whatever fate befalls me, he receives the justice he deserves."

Grief flickered in the king's eyes, but he said nothing.

I looked at Dathan's focused frown. Had he read between the lines of the Admiral's statement? I wasn't certain what the Admiral was trying to say, but there was definitely more to it.

'*...might not have been perfect, but his intentions had always been fair.*'

Was there a chance the Admiral knew all along that Ambassador Caiphas had intended to sell his vote to Sarhedrin? Even more, could he have known *why*?

Dathan's frown intensified on the person being led into the hall next.

Fifth Colonel Dishe.

My skin stretched taut. Would he say the truth, or would he heap more lies on the Admiral? The Admiral had too many odds stacked against him. A false testimony from Dishe would seal his grave.

"I would have to step forward if Dishe lies," I realized.

Dathan's body went tauter than the pillars. "I'll use *kaiga* to make you unconscious and carry you away from here before I see you do that."

"If I frame the Admiral for Colonel Remmon's death, then I'm just like Remmon."

Captain Emeso began leading the Admiral out of the hall. King Khasar lifted his hand in silent order and Captain Emeso stopped. "Have a seat, Admiral. There would be no secrecy with this hearing. All involved would be privy to everything."

Murmurings brushed over the tiered seats.

The Admiral's face wasn't visible as he settled on an ottoman in front. Was he curious to hear the lies his own comrades were heaping upon him? Or did he wish he was spared them?

"You shared some... interesting information with the Ironteenth last night, Colonel Dishe," the Magistrate said.

I couldn't draw breath. Dathan's arms tautened. What information?

"Now, we ask that you share it with the Chambers."

Fifth Colonel Dishe's hand was bandaged where my Commandant had impaled him, and his face looked scraggly.

My throat closed up as he opened his mouth.

And then he told the hall what Nergal's Commandant had wrung out of him last night. He started from when Remmon made him a deal to help uproot the Admiral from his rank in exchange for Dishe's rapid promotion. Dishe told them in detail how he'd found the Esan smuggler for Remmon, and how Remmon had thrust a dagger through Ambassador Caiphas's heart while Dishe kept watch.

Shocked noises resounded through the hall. Wrathful yells followed.

How could you?

You're a disgrace!

My stomach churned.

Dathan rubbed a hand over his forehead. "Somehow, it's even worse hearing it from him."

King Khasar looked murderous, clutching his armrest as if to keep from lunging for Dishe's neck. Captain Emeso mustn't have shared with the king what he'd uncovered from the Fifth Colonel prior to the hearing.

"Is he leaving anything out, Captain?" the Magistrate asked Captain Emeso, shock in her otherwise composed voice.

"No, Magistrate," Captain Emeso said.

"Why didn't you tell me?" King Khasar demanded.

"It was only in the past hour that we were able to pry the information out of him, Your Majesty," the head of the Ironteenth explained, and understanding skirted the king's face.

It wasn't until Captain Emeso resorted to torture that Dishe cracked.

The Chamber of Fangs—the military's heads—looked pained that soldiers of Thalesai had committed such grievous treachery.

"And who killed Colonel Remmon?" First Advisor Maachah asked.

"I don't know," Dishe said.

"Not the Admiral, then?" Maachah pushed, as if determined to exonerate the Admiral—his Baihan tribesman.

My heart raced hard enough to crack free from my chest.

"It couldn't be," Dishe rasped. "The Admiral is an upright leader. I believe most from the Chamber of Fangs can vouch that he isn't one to use assassins. If he'd had qualms with Colonel Remmon, he would confront him openly."

The Admiral's back remained stiff as he stared at his Colonel. The senior officers agreed loudly, most fueled with the relief that they *could* freely stand for their Admiral now that there was solid proof against treachery.

My throat eased until I could breathe. He might not be persecuted for Colonel Remmon's death.

"Who else was an accomplice in these schemes?" King Khasar asked Dishe.

Chambermen shifted on chairs, glancing at each other. The very thing King Khasar had not wanted, for his court to be contaminated.

"No one else that I know of, Your Majesty." Dishe's head was bowed as if he couldn't bear the condemnation. "First Colonel Remmon kept his cards close."

The hall buzzed as King Khasar conferred with his advisors. Chambermen joined heads to lament.

I looked to Dathan, almost lightheaded with relief. "I'm not dreaming, right?"

He smiled, wincing slightly. Blast, I was fairly crushing his hand.

I released him. "Sorry."

Holding my gaze, he spoke softly, "You're brave and loyal. Don't ever compare yourself to men like Remmon who don't hold a candle to you."

Emotions made my throat lump. "You're growing soft, Gergesenes."

"Only for you, Nergal." He winked, but something deeper unfurled in his green-brown eyes.

Wild birds took flight in my stomach.

We watched as Dishe was sentenced to life imprisonment, to be moved immediately to the hideous Serra dungeons.

"Your Majesty, please!" Dishe cried, falling to his knees.

Captain Emeso hissed a warning to him before dragging him away.

"Your work is done." Dathan took my hand and shook it. Because my prey and his accomplice had faced justice. "We appreciate your service to the kingdom, Nergal."

"You're welcome, Gergesenes," I said benevolently.

He lifted my hand, placed a kiss on it, and my breath hitched. He held my gaze for a moment, causing flutters deep in my chest. Seeming satisfied with what he saw, he released my hand.

I swallowed, grappling for composure on the havoc he wrecked against my senses.

A union with him is impossible.

Next, King Khasar exonerated the Admiral of the charges against him. The Magistrate apologized on behalf of the Chambers for the misjudgment he had faced.

"We better leave before we're sighted," Dathan whispered.

Indeed two Ironteenth now patrolled the hall, the afternoon sun gleaming on their ruthless armor. As if they were preparing for whatever was coming next.

I pushed on my armrests when the Magistrate's bold voice called, "Bring in the next offender, Captain."

Dathan and I exchanged confused looks. And then the Dynast of Bornoir scowled ferociously as Captain Emeso shoved him into the hall.

46

ZAIR

ow? Had Gergesenes' Commandant brought him in? He must have. But how did he explain taking a *Dynast* hostage to the Ironteenth? How did he explain setting a spy loose in the palace to accomplish that?

Every intention to leave fizzled, replaced with a hunger for answers.

Dathan fell back into his seat, a shaky hand clutching his chest. The intensity of the pain and rage twisting his face splintered my heart. "Dathan?"

He stared wildly at Sarhedrin.

The Dynast of Bornoir, while hard-faced, didn't look so high and mighty now in rumpled clothes. His face was so discolored that it was clear the Gergesenes Commandant had been ruthless in his pursuit for answers. Ussi chambermen bristled in silent affront to see one of theirs manhandled, despite knowing he was a suspect.

I didn't know how to pry into other people's feelings with how deeply I hid mine. But Dathan's pain was so... *old*. So raw. I had to take it away somehow.

"Dathan." I put my face in front of his so he had to look at me. "What is it?"

His eyes met mine but he wasn't seeing beyond his mind. "Nothing. It's nothing."

Stubbornness sparked. Before I could insist, the Magistrate's voice rang out.

"...Dynast Orcus Sarhedrin of Bornoir, facing charges of embezzlement, infiltration, and murder."

Dathan shook his head, veins bulging in his hands. "I can't be here. This is not the crime I want the monster punished for."

He rose and stormed off. I started to go after him, to make him tell me who Orcus Sarhedrin was to him. But I had to be here for the hearing. Dathan had said the Gergesenes Commandant hadn't uncovered why Ambassador Caiphas requested the Dynast's bribe. That truth might come out now. And maybe the Dynast would reveal who was aiding him and what the rest of the money he'd intended to steal was for.

King Khasar's mask was shattered. First Advisor Maachah said something to him, and the king drew in a deep breath as if he'd been urged to breathe.

"Would you confess to these crimes, Dynast Sarhedrin?" the Magistrate asked.

Even battered, the Dynast kept his mouth pridefully shut.

It was then I glimpsed Gergesenes' Commandant sitting on the fifth tier. He must have brought Sarhedrin to Captain Emeso directly. And now Captain Emeso was posing as the main interrogator to save his former Commandant's neck, and Dathan's by extension.

When the Dynast remained doggedly silent despite all the prompting, the irritated Magistrate asked Captain Emeso to share with the hall what he knew. Captain Emeso cast an intimidating image of obsidian before the hall, his adasword glinting at his side.

He told the hall of the Dynast's crimes, beginning with his collusion with Ambassador Caiphas. Gasps resounded as Captain Emeso grimly told about the vote and bribery. King Khasar looked stricken.

Captain Emeso's face grew even harder as he talked about the courtiers and palace guards the Dynast of Bornoir had murdered in a bid to break into the Royal Accountant's office. The Chamber of Fangs exclaimed with anger. Captain Emeso talked about how Sarhedrin had doctored the records in the Royal Accountant's office. Betrayal marred the Royal Accountant's scarred features.

Emotions were running high in the Chambers. The Magistrate asked the Dynast, "What do you say about these accusations?"

Chambermen spat angry words.

The Dynast of Bornoir said, "Captain Emeso was not my interrogator, nor had he abducted me from the palace. Find out first *who* in the palace is sniffing about, spying, when the Al'Qtraz was declared a neutral ground by the King."

Oh saints.

King Khasar would want to know now. He'd order Captain Emeso to tell him where he'd gotten the information, and Captain Emeso would have to expose the Gergesenes' Commandant. I clasped my hands tightly.

But King Khasar wasn't having the Dynast of Bornoir's insolence. "Answer the question," he barked. "Are the charges true?"

The Dynast raised his chin and stared down his nose at the Baihan king.

Heat flushed through me. Baihan chambermen, and even the Kwalis and Mizsabs, raged at the Ussi man's daring.

"He should be whipped for his insolence!"

"Open your mouth and answer your king, you bloody snake!"

Sarhedrin stood, beaten and prideful.

I wanted to fling a chair at his bald head.

"What did Ambassador Caiphas want the money for?" King Khasar asked, an ache in his firm voice.

The Dynast's words dripped with bitterness. "I didn't care about the reason for your brother's greed then, and neither do I now. Your brother was willing to sell your trust for *siyvas,* and I was happy to find him the funds as long as he served my interest."

He might as well have slapped King Khasar for how the king recoiled.

How *dare* he?

Voices rang out at once, condemning the disrespect to the King. The Ironteenth moved to stand by the Dynast, lest chambermen shot from their seats and attacked him.

The Admiral suddenly rose and the king lifted his hand. The hall quieted.

He asked the Admiral, "Are you ready to tell us what your meeting with my brother yesterday was about, Admiral?"

The king had sensed the undertone in the Admiral's earlier words too. Perhaps the people of Thalesai didn't show King Khasar enough faith.

The Admiral nodded firmly, as if bracing himself. "Six months ago, I'd been on a security inspection at the human settlement by wraithland's borders. While there... I found out that Ambassador Caiphas was expanding his settlement."

Judging from the furrow of King Khasar and the Chamber of Wings' foreheads, the information wasn't common knowledge. But an expansion wasn't a crime either.

"What aren't you saying, Admiral?" King Khasar queried impatiently.

"The new settlement, Your Majesty, was for the Esan tribespeople."

A chill of hate and condemnation swept through the room, icing its corners until I shivered in my clothes.

"The Esans have been facing persecution now more than ever, having their homes burned and massacred by villagers who don't want them as neighbors. They're captured and sold to aziza skintraders as slaves."

Skintraders? It had been years since I'd heard about the plight of Esans living in rural areas, but this was the first I was hearing of Esan skintrading. My mother's tribe was so hated that the deaths of Esan families weren't deemed important news or something to be taken action against! Even now, most in the hall were unconcerned. I wanted to *scream* at them.

"Ambassador Caiphas didn't think they deserved that. He tried inviting Esan refugees who could travel. To live under his protection in his settlement, but... the other settlers there didn't want them. So he decided to build them a settlement far enough not to disgruntle his settlers, but close enough that his protection covered them. He told me his plans. He wanted the Esans to have safe homes, food stores, academies, and infirmaries."

My throat thickened with longing and sadness.

"The ambassador never shared this plan with us." First Advisor Maachah rubbed his candle-white beard, his eyes doubtful.

"He knew most in the Chambers would have no interest in investing in an Esan settlement. And his concern was that if he proposed this plan and it was shut down, he'd have no choice but to send the refugees away."

A boulder lodged in my chest. The hall sobered as the truth of Ambassador Caiphas's goals sank in.

"I'd wondered how he planned to raise the funds, knew he would try to stretch the allocated funds for his settlement to include the Esans. And that it wouldn't be sufficient. I'd warned him not to do anything foolhardy. Then he came here for the coronation, and I found out he was making plans to purchase lumber and steel in large quantities from Irua.

"It reminded me of his plans for a settlement. It had to mean that he'd received the funds to build one. But I also knew he hadn't proposed the plan to the Chambers. I'd been concerned about the route he was taking. Ambassador Caiphas was a savvy and compassionate young man. An asset to Thalesai. I didn't want a mistake to cost us him." The Admiral drew in a breath.

Chambermen made mournful murmurs of agreement.

"When we spoke yesterday, he wouldn't reveal where the funds were expected from, but he admitted he *had* found a way to get them." He scanned the hall. "He must've believed selling his vote wasn't so wrong if it was for the good of a neglected group. And I suspect he'd presumed the Dynast of Bornoir would readily have the funds he'd requested, and not that it would've been stolen from the royal coffers."

The revelation stunned me, stunned the hall.

Ambassador Caiphas had planned to sell his vote, but not out of greed or because he didn't love his brother. It was to help my mother's people. Give them a safe haven. And even though the men in this hall didn't care one whit for the Esans, no one could deny that Ambassador Caiphas's motive was fair.

He was ten times the ruler most here would *ever* be. Now, he'd been murdered.

King Khasar cleared his throat but his voice remained hoarse. "Thank you for bringing that to light, Admiral."

The Admiral gave a bow and returned to his seat.

"Is there anything else you would like to share with us, Captain?" the Magistrate asked, scribbling on a document.

Captain Emeso said, "Yes, Magistrate. After the interrogation we discovered the amount of *siyvas* Dynast Sarhedrin had intended to loot. My men and I have reason to suspect the Dynast isn't being completely honest about his intentions for the money."

The Dynast went still. Whispers skirted the hall while the Chamber of Wings leaned forward in their seats. Even I leaned forward as much as I dared.

"Speak plainly, Captain," King Khasar said quietly, seeming to ready himself for the worst.

"The Dynast doctored the records to allow him to loot two hundred thousand *siyvas* without notice. Ambassador Caiphas couldn't have asked for more than fifty thousand *siyvas*, and that's if he was being greedy. I'd like the Dynast to tell us what his plan for the remaining money was," Captain Emeso said frigidly.

He didn't need to spell it out, and the strain in the hall said that everyone knew where the suspicion steered. That the Dynast could be a traitor and the money could be going to the mercs.

"Dynast?" the Magistrate asked coldly.

The Dynast kept his chin up. "I don't know what the Captain is implying, considering he wasn't there when the deal was made between the king's brother and I."

It was a tactic, his constant referral to Ambassador Caiphas as the king's brother. To imply that disloyalty tainted the entire royal family.

"So you're saying Ambassador Caiphas asked you to pay two hundred thousand *siyvas* for his vote," the Magistrate asked.

"Yes," the Dynast said.

"And you didn't think it was an outrageous sum he was demanding."

"I didn't think he cared what I thought when he decided on the amount. Perhaps, *he* had other plans for the funds than to build a settlement for filth. Perhaps," he met the Admiral's gaze, "he *isn't* the martyr he's being painted as."

He'd take his secret to his grave then. Protect the mercenaries at all cost. Bastard.

King Khasar's jaw hardened at the implication that his brother was aiding the terrorists. He shot up from his seat. "For your crimes against the kingdom, Orcus Sarhedrin, I strip you and your family of every title and privilege that comes with Dynast.

And I sentence you to death by hanging in the Golgotha Valley by Yule."

The Dynast jerked with shock but then struggled for a hard mask. He accepted his sentence to be hung in the Valley of Traitors without pleading.

Ussi chambermen jumped to their feet to protest his family's sentence. The other tribes rose and snapped at their defense of a criminal.

Time to go. An Esan girl caught eavesdropping on a top secret meeting would only intensify their wrath, and I couldn't risk arrest. I had to investigate First Advisor Maachah and stop him if he was the true traitor. I sidled down the stairs, heart in throat, until I made it out of the servants' door.

And there Dathan was, sitting with his head in his hands. His focus shot up at the door's click.

"You're still here," I said, surprised.

"I couldn't leave you," he said gravelly as he rose to his towering height.

I gave him a grateful smile but Dathan wasn't... present. No, he was in his head. Lost in whatever darkness raged there.

We hurried from the Chambers building without incident. My chest felt sorer as we reached our wing. He tried to shut his door, but I pushed it wider, entered, and closed it behind me.

He didn't even seem to notice as he paced, like a leopard caged in his own skin. His own mind.

I'd never seen him like this, and my walls rose. I'd learned to avoid agitated people years ago. Once someone was agitated, they hurt the first offensive thing in their path. As an Esan-eyed girl, that offensive thing had often been me.

Dathan ran his fingers through his hair, seeming like a lost boy. Something cracked in my chest. I forced the spiraling thoughts away, the chant to leave before he did something to hurt me.

Dathan Issachar had had numerous opportunities to be hurtful, but he'd never used them. Hadn't even acknowledged the opportunities were there. Instead, he looked after me and returned to the perilous palace after his mission was complete, *stayed*, because of me.

Drawing in a stinging breath, I placed a hand on his chiseled jaw.

His gaze snapped to mine, dark brown and so tortured that it awoke a powerful need to *help* him. But how? How could I take this pain away?

Share it with him.

So pushing up on my toes, I placed my other hand on his face and kissed him. Softly yet insistently.

He tasted of fire and spice and pain. *Saints.*

I caressed the thick hair at his temple and soon, his wide shoulders loosened.

I pulled back, joined my forehead to his, and whispered words I'd never said to anyone before. "Let me in, Dathan."

A dangerous request, but I felt almost helpless against the sensations swelling inside my chest. My heart raced as I waited, expecting a rejection.

His hazel eyes searched mine, the darkness deeper than the Niger. "I will, but only if you let me in too, Zair."

I suddenly itched to pull back and hide like a wounded bear in a cave. To thicken my fences until I was gone from his sight. His hold tightened on me, because he sensed my need to pull away.

But he was hurting, and I wanted—*needed*—to help him.

I swallowed. "I will."

47

ZAIR

Dathan led me to the saffron cushions forming a sitting area by his open balcony. Ari'el's roads still thronged with visitors. Were most still in the capital to explore its splendor... or because they were afraid to go back home where mercenaries could be lurking?

Dathan sank into the cushion beside me, his leg almost brushing mine. Awareness of him made the hair on my skin stand.

"The king sentenced Dynast Sarhedrin to a hanging in Golgotha," I said, making the opening for his confidence.

Dathan stared out his balcony, and when he spoke, his voice was so quiet I almost didn't hear him. "What I'm about to tell you... Right now, I feel like I'm going to lose my *mind* over Sarhedrin's sentence if I hold it all in any longer."

My chest tightened. "You can talk to me," I said softly, sensing the weight pressing down on him.

He hesitated, then murmured, "Somehow, I feel I can trust you with my secrets."

Something inside me clenched, sharp and unexpected. No one outside my family had ever looked at me like that—like I was safe. Like I was someone worth trusting. The realization snagged deep in my heart, drawing me even closer to him.

"I would never betray anything you tell me," I vowed, my voice steady.

And I felt the shift, the invisible threads winding between us, tightening, pulling us toward something inevitable.

He sighed and raked his hand through his hair. "My family... We aren't Baihan."

I stiffened with shock.

"We're Ussis, from the town of Kadnazi."

My stomach clamped. "*What?*"

His chiseled face stayed fixed on the balcony. "Both my parents are Ussis, heirs of renowned families in the north. My father is the sole son of an Ussi elder, a prime person in the Council of Fifty."

The Ussi Council of Fifty. When Thalesai was amalgamated, some Ussi leaders lost their ranks because the new Thalesai had restructured the human kingdom into cities, towns, and villages, rather than the numerous clans the independent Ussi Caliphate was grouped in. So, rather than reduce the removed rulers and their families to mere commoners, the Council of Fifty was formed. To retain their prestige and ability to make decisions for the welfare of the Ussis, and Ussis alone.

But the Council of Fifty was also known as the *Council of Bigots* by other tribes.

"I was still a child when my father and grandfather started arguing bitterly, seemingly out of nowhere. I hadn't understood then that my father could no longer stomach the schemes the Council perpetrated to hoard Thalesai's powers among the Ussis. My grandfather, a staunch Ussi fanatic, believed my father was betraying his roots by advocating for the other tribes. Eventually, my father quit the Council of Fifty. It had never been done and was a slap in the face of the members. The elders were enraged but willing to forgive, and told my grandfather to talk sense into him."

He paused, his eyes moving like he was trying to figure out how to articulate what came next.

"My father was the most skilled healer in Kadnazi town. And when the Council's bandits returned injured from their missions to burn down Baihan settlements or Mizsab farms, he healed them. Many of these bandits were sons, nephews, and nieces of the elders. But after my father pulled out of the Council, he felt treating the terrorizers just so they could return to wreaking chaos on innocents was still being a part of their evil. So he banned them from his infirmary."

His jaw clenched, his face going bleak, and my heart cracked worse.

"I was ten when Sarhedrin, an elder, marched down on our home with his bandits. To execute us under *cirai* justice for being traitors to the Ussi cause."

Saints. *Cirai* justice was Ussi list of laws, one they still practiced in the far north despite the reformed Thalesai law.

"Execute your family because your father wanted a clear conscience?" I demanded. It wasn't like he'd tried to kill an elder or declared hate of his tribe.

Dathan smiled humorlessly. "Turned out he didn't have that right. My parents gathered what they could that night, and we snuck out of our house into the streets, mere moments before our house was blown up with explosives."

I gasped.

"Our parents took us to their friends and asked for help. A place to hide or even just to sleep for the night and plan. No one would help us."

Skies.

"Some 'sympathized' with our plight but didn't want to be involved," he said bitterly. "My parents realized we had to flee our hometown for any chance of survival. But Sarhedrin made that impossible. When he learned we weren't killed in the explosion, he had his men paste my parents' images across town as wanted criminals. Soon after, he placed bounties on our heads, and almost everyone in the town hunted for us. He made them believe we were traitors who wanted the other tribes to thrive over the Ussis, and in the north, there's no greater misdeed."

My stomach cramped with images of a young Dathan and his family, terrified, fleeing their own people.

"My father did everything to ensure our survival. We hid in the stables and cellars of homes whose owners were absent, went days where we didn't utter a single word for fear of being heard."

"Saints, Dathan."

"Sometimes, we had to stay in caves, went too many days without food or water. I remember how *terrified* my parents were that my sister and I would perish from starvation. My father tried everything, but we just couldn't escape the borders of Kadnazi. Sarhedrin had his bandits patrolling for us. He wasn't the Dynast of the town but he'd taken our persecution upon himself like a sacred task. His men caught us a few times. One of those times my father was beaten almost to death. My mother..." His throat bobbed. "She was stabbed and left to die. And my sister..."

He ran a hand over his tormented face, his breath ragged, and I knew what had been done to her. A breath of horror shuddered out of me.

"I was too weak," he said roughly. "Even when I fought, it was never enough to help them."

Sorrow wrenched through my chest. "Oh, Dathan."

"It took weeks of watching us be hunted like animals before my grandfather intervened. Even then, it was in secret. He told my father we were dead to him. He demanded that we forfeited the family name because we didn't deserve it, before helping us escape Kadnazi in wine casks."

"What about your mother's family?"

"Her mother sent a message telling her to leave her 'traitorous husband,' annul their marriage, and return to her family with us. It was the only way they'd help her, but she refused to desert her husband. She'd wanted to send my sister and me to them, but Asahel and I refused to go live with people who condemned our father.

"After we escaped the town, my father decided Ari'el was the only place we could find refuge. It was a gathering of tribes and *cirai* law didn't hold here. It was our first glimpse of hope in too long. But then the days traveling here were rife with fear. We constantly looked over our shoulders. Afraid someone would recognize the only son of Asahar Sosthene. That was when it dawned that despite escaping Kadnazi, we'd have to spend the rest of our lives hiding."

The blue in the sky had slowly faded, leaving the vermillion of the desert sunset to dominate. Now the sky was a dark purple, as if mimicking the aura of Dathan's room.

"On reaching the capital, we couldn't risk claiming our heritage. We lived without identity for months. Not certain where we'd fit in, yet avoiding everything Ussi. Then one day, during a skirmish between gangs at a bazaar, a boy was stabbed in the throat. People believed he was done for, but my father was there and saved him. It later turned out that the boy was a Baihan councilor's only child." Dathan shook his head in marvel as if up till now, he couldn't believe that stroke of luck in his family's desolate history.

"The councilor felt indebted to my father, so he helped him find his footing as a healer in the city. Because of the man's kindness, one we hadn't known for too long, my father decided we would take on the identity as Baihans. We changed our last name, perfected Binhese and the way of life, and moved into the eastern Baihan quarters to be chameleons. Safe, as long as no one ever saw our true form."

Pretending to be from a tribe... There was nothing more grievous in a land where tribal identity was almost sacred. Dathan and his family lived in constant peril, not knowing if and when their truth would be unveiled. Even here in the Capital, Baihans would rage if they learned Ussis had fooled them and infiltrated their midst, and the Ussis would *kill* them if they knew their own had taken on a Baihan name.

My very bones trembled.

This is not the crime I want the monster punished for, he'd said. But for what the Dynast did to his family.

And here I'd been, thinking Dathan Issachar was solely the pride of Gergesenes. A Baihan prodigy with a glaringly bright future and no care in the world. Once I'd looked at him—and been oblivious to the reason behind his frequent hair change, or avoidance of the Ussis. I had thought he couldn't understand the pains I faced. But it seemed some people were just better at hiding pain than others.

"Your family's hiding in the cellars, was that why you'd been... unsettled in the storage cell that day?"

He rubbed his temple, shame edging his face. "I suppose you know my weakness now."

"I would never use it against you. And hating cages is hardly a weakness if it makes you fight harder for freedom."

He shook his head. "It's not only that. I'm brimming with too many memories that could make me useless at crucial moments. I can't even guarantee I'm reliable enough to catch the real traitor."

"You're Gergesenes' best student," I insisted. "You wouldn't be if you were weak."

He shook his head again. "You know, the world shines brighter in the eyes of dreamers. It doesn't mean you're delusional. Far from it. Rather that you find beauty even in dark things and don't let sorrows kill your spirit. I've never been a dreamer."

He thought *I* was a dreamer? Maybe I was, since my heart still loved a nation that despised me. And my soul still prayed for acceptance amid centuries-old rejection.

"The Dynast deserves a worse fate than a hanging in Golgotha Valley. He deserves to be mobbed by everyone he's ever hurt!" I snapped.

To my puzzlement, in the bleakness of Dathan's eyes, a light like the glimpse of dawn sparked. His mouth curved ever so slightly. "Thanks for the solidarity, Nergal."

I nodded firmly.

His smile grew, but then he released a long breath and his face became serious. "After so many years of secrecy, I needed to let this out to someone..." He rubbed his chest. "The things I've just told you, Zair..."

"No one will ever hear of it," I promised. "Not from me. And if they did, you could say I'm lying and they'd never believe me."

Dathan didn't laugh. I shifted self-consciously.

"They are all fools," he finally said. "We still have hours left before we go after our targets. Your turn. It's high time I learned something about my *aiyena*."

My stomach fluttered to hear the title. I ran my hands over my skirts. "I thought my family had a harder life than anyone. Now, I'm not so sure I have much to tell."

Dathan folded his long legs and straightened his powerful back as he faced me. "There's much I want to know about you."

"Like what? No one has been curious about me before."

"You shut everyone out before they have a chance to come close. When someone teases or acts in a non-hostile way, you regard them with suspicion. Like there has to be an ulterior motive for them treating you like a person. Why? I know there are cruel bastards in the world, but I like to believe there are also good people. Who made you defensive against the entire world?"

I couldn't hold his gaze, so I shifted mine but kept my shoulders squared because I wasn't a coward. Dathan Issachar, with his gorgeous face and keen mind, overwhelmed me sometimes.

"You know I'm Baihan," I began.

"Not because you bother telling anyone. I found out at the temple, and I was shocked."

I shrugged weakly, suddenly exhausted. "I have both my parents' blood."

"Yet in Thalesai, we're identified by our father's tribe. Ibhar wouldn't be so audacious if he knew."

I bit on my lip for a second. "Constantly correcting people and insisting I'm Baihan when they think I'm Esan feels like saying I'm ashamed of my mother. Ashamed of resembling her. If I'd had an Ussi mother and someone mistook me to be Ussi, I wouldn't rush to correct them. Doing so because my mother is Esan... it just doesn't feel fair to her."

Sad understanding filled his eyes. And while he was still tense, the torment on his face had eased. So I went on, opened up in a way I never had, if only to distract him from his suffering.

"My mother lost her parents during the Esan tribes' final attempt to build their own settlement. Members of the other tribes burned down the settlements because they couldn't have Esans ganging up against them with 'demonic wiles'." The memory always crushed my mother's heart. "Now, the Esans have to live isolated from each other. It makes them completely vulnerable. My family is the only Esan family in the capital, and the reason we have not been murdered in our sleep is because my father is Baihan.

"My mother had hoped Sarai would take after my father, so he would have one child at least who wouldn't bring him grief. But by the saints' unexplainable will, Sarai took after my mother too. And my father's family told him he had destroyed our futures by choosing an Esan woman. His Baihan heritage is what keeps us alive, but it doesn't stop the hate."

"And so you built up walls," Dathan said quietly.

"The higher and thicker my walls are, the lesser the scorn

hurts." The moment the admission left me, I felt raw. Like my defenses were shattered for the first time in my life, and I was without armor in the thick of battle.

It terrified me.

While Dathan might be living with a false identity, he was still a wealthy Baihan loved by most, and I was still the loathed Esan girl that was spat at on the street. I imagined his father wouldn't want his family to have anything to do with mine. Hated people that drew attention and could bring the ruin he'd escaped, back upon his family.

One way or the other, Dathan and I would have our betrothal annulled. I didn't want him to see so far behind my armor.

As if sensing my withdrawal, Dathan reached for my hand.

I quickly stood. "We're spent. We should sleep if we hope to be focused enough to catch the traitor."

There was just one event left, one final shot, to free Sarai of the mercenaries. I couldn't lose it.

Dathan stood too, his jaw ticking, and mischief glittered in his eyes. He went to his door, locked it, and shoved the key in his pocket.

"What are you doing?" I queried.

He sauntered over to stretch out on his bed and patted the blanket beside him. "You said we should sleep."

"*Gergesenes*," I gritted threateningly.

He sat up and brown locks fell over his serious face. "I'm not going to take two steps forward with you, only to fall back three steps, Zair."

My neck flushed. He threw off his tunic and kicked off his shoes.

"Why are you undressing?" I exclaimed, unable to keep my eyes from running over his flat abdomen. My mouth dried.

That mischievous glint. "I can't sleep well in a shirt."

"Dathan, open the door," I ordered.

Heat filled his eyes as they ran over me. How did he make me feel... desirable? How could he look into my eyes and still want me?

"You've let me in some," he said seriously. "I can't bear you shutting me back out. Not tonight."

Maybe it was the look on his face, the silent urge to trust him, the plea not to leave him to face the night alone, but I drifted over to him.

He eagerly lifted the blanket and I crawled into the soft bed. "How can you find calm in me?" I whispered.

He stared into my eyes, my soul. "Broken souls know how to soothe each other."

He closed his eyes. I continued watching him, partly waiting for him to fall asleep so I could steal the keys and escape, partly because he was the most beautiful man I'd seen.

"Sleep, *aiyena*," he murmured against our shared pillow.

Only a fool hostage would sleep in her prison.

Yet soon, surrounded by his warmth, my body hummed a new rhythm. Dathan rubbed my back, pulling me even closer and then sleep was dragging me into its gentle depth.

48

ZAIR

I jerked upright as the clock ticked past eight, rushing off Dathan's bed. How did I sleep so late?

Alright, considering how much the past few days had drained me, it wasn't shocking. And there was sleeping in Dathan's arms.

We'd ripped open the scars of our festering torments, bled out our pains before each other last night. And then lying together in his bed, I had felt complete. A wholesome feeling I'd never had with anyone. And now, scanning the room and not finding him, my stomach hollowed.

Why had he left?

I shook off the question, striding to the door. Last night was a pleasant reprieve from the chaos, but the queen had entrusted her fate to me and my sister was more unsafe than ever with the traitor losing his accomplices in the palace.

I needed to catch the real one.

I dressed fast, chest burning with pain as I stepped out of the lounge. The halls were tenser today, quieter too. I roamed silently, trying to listen for news as chambermen broke their fasts, but they were tightlipped. Speaking only about return plans to their towns after the Gifting.

I was losing hope of finding the First Advisor in the accessible areas, when finally I sighted his snowy beard. On a balcony on the second floor. Just by the stairwell.

I reduced my pace as I went up, tilting my head subtly to spot who he spoke with.

Ibhar?

Why was a Baihan chamberman entertaining the Ussi star pupil? A boy that would soon occupy a position in the palace, leaving one less for the Baihans?

Maybe it meant nothing.

They gesticulated easily, not at all like they were avoiding notice. The balcony doors were wide open and maids streaked past.

Yet my mind niggled. Since I arrived at the palace, when people from different tribes privately entertained each other, trouble lurked.

Besides, First Advisor Maachah *was* my target now. To cross him out as innocent of treachery, I had to investigate to the last detail.

My heart pounded as I neared them. Should the First Advisor be the traitor, he would do worse than Remmon had if he caught me stalking him.

He patted Ibhar's shoulder, and I swiftly spun toward a painting as he strode out of the balcony, down the hallway. Thank goodness, he didn't glance my way. Ibhar headed for my stairs next. Once his big form disappeared down the landing, I swerved after the First Advisor.

His bronze jewels flashed before he rounded a passage, out of my view. I held my skirts and hurried after him. My chest resumed aching. The bells in my head *gonged*, urging my feet faster.

The passage he'd turned into was oddly dark. The windows were shut.

I took a tentative step in, and gales churned. My veil flew off my face. My hair fell loose, pouring over my eyes as a dark aura spread like ink.

Light flashed. Out of thin air, a huge form jumped before me. Catching me completely off guard, he grinned like a demon.

I gasped. "Ibhar..."

He lunged for me. I spun on my heels, dodging his grasp and sweeping behind him. I didn't know what was happening or how

Ibhar had *appeared* here, but every instinct pealed and screamed at me to fight. I kicked the back of his knees. He dropped on the floor, but instead of landing on his face, he did a forward flip and returned to his feet. He swung a fist at me. I ducked under his arm and shoved my elbow into his back. He grunted. I made to kick the back of his knees again, needing the hulking boy flat on the ground to restrain him. But Ibhar moved fast. Reaching between his knees, he grabbed my foot and yanked. I lost balance and landed face-down on the ground.

Pain snapped up my chest. I flipped to my back, but not quickly enough. Ibhar threw himself on me like a web and pinned me down, just like at the Combat Arena. But this time, his thighs cinched my hips so tightly, I couldn't shift them to forcefully create room.

"Get off me!" I screamed, desperate to alert anyone nearby.

His fist slammed into my temple, and darkness yanked consciousness from me.

49

DATHAN

The balcony's balustrade cooled my waist as I monitored the washroom door the Second Advisor had disappeared behind. I'd been trailing him since two in the morning when he left his rooms.

So far, there was nothing remotely suspicious about him.

He'd left his rooms like a man restless, grumpy as he'd made his rounds checking on the night guards. Then he'd gone downstairs to the library, picked a book and read under a lamp. Utterly unaware I watched him from the shadows.

His restlessness, which alerted me at first, could've been from the tension everywhere. As advisor, it *was* his place to worry.

Besides, with the guests leaving in four days, he should've been using every second to move his schemes along. Now, as morning slowly colored the palace grey, I doubted the Ussi advisor was the traitor. That left First Advisor Maachah.

My heart picked up tempo. I clenched my teeth, struggling to form an answer from the new puzzle pieces. No, it didn't seem plausible. The First Advisor was Baihan like the king. And like the Ussis, the Baihans were loyal to each other to a fault.

Maybe Zair and I had it wrong. Maybe Captain Emeso shouldn't have been crossed out from that quaint list of suspects. I still didn't want to believe he could be the traitor, but at this point it was precarious to be sentimental.

Yet if the First Advisor was destroying Thalesai from within its palace, a Baihan man betraying not just his kingdom but his own tribesman, then he was a savage Zair shouldn't be tailing alone. My blood ran cold.

Pushing off the railings, I headed back to our wing. I'd dressed in normal clothes to blend in, and as I passed the busy palace staffs preparing for the big day, they smiled at me without suspicion.

I entered my room and... Zair wasn't there.

I rapped my knuckles against my desk. It was past eight and Zair was nothing if not efficient. Still, the part of me that wasn't rustled with agitation was disappointed to have missed another sight of her curled delicately in my bed.

I washed quickly, dressed in finery, and went to knock on her door. Thrice. No answer. I drew out my lockpicks, to affirm her absence, but a maid sashayed into the lounge.

"It is time for the final ceremony of the coronation," she announced. "The Gifting."

Zair

A RAIN of icy water yanked me awake like teeth biting my skin. I gasped and made to jerk to my feet, but ropes dug into my body.

I was tied to a chair.

Panic flared like wildfire. I struggled to tamp it down. I'd been spying about the Al'Qtraz for weeks. I was lucky trouble took this long to find me.

I can still get out. Sarai isn't safe.

I scanned my musty surroundings to assess the situation. Fabrics sprawled down walls. The only bit of light came from a lantern dangling overhead. My teeth clattered as the cold sank in.

I shook in the chair, seeking allowance in the ropes; too tight. I tried to move my fingers and failed.

A soft chuckle sifted over the dimness. Boots thumped, and then Ibhar stood before me.

My chest staggered like rocks crashing down a slope.

"I'd fantasized of this," he said. "Esan scum at my mercy."

"What are you doing? Release me!" I hissed through clattering teeth.

"Do *not* presume you can give me orders."

"Let me go this instant."

He yanked my hair, ramming my head to the headrest. I swallowed back a cry.

"I'll be asking the questions and you'll be answering them, understand?" He flung my head aside and straightened.

Fear was acrid in my throat as I raised my head. Ibhar grabbed a fabric and wrapped it around his hand, looking scarier than he ever had.

Why was he here? I thought frantically. He'd been speaking with the First Advisor who I'd been tailing, and then he'd appeared like a ghost.

"You're in league with the First Advisor," I determined.

His blow sent my head darting to the side. For a moment, the world was of pain and fright.

He yanked my head back to him. "You are a spy, *aren't* you?"

I gulped the blood in my mouth. His eyes searched mine, waiting, and when it became clear I had no intention of speaking, to betray those I served, an ugly sneer twisted his face.

"Someone planted you in the palace to ferret out information," he gritted, "yes or no?"

I looked away defiantly, even as despair rushed in. "You're delusional, Ibhar."

"You intend to be gallant. *Noble*." He laughed. "You know what I think of you Esan abominations: the world should be rid of your presence. So if you plan on holding out thinking I'll go easy on you, think again. Because were it left to me, I'd cut you up into bits."

"Who is it left to then? The First Advisor?" I spat. How had I been so fixated on Remmon that I'd missed Ibhar right under my nose? If I'd caught on to him, I would've found who he worked for. I would've saved Sarai by now. But I'd missed *everything*.

"I ask the questions!" Ibhar barked. "Who gave you the

audacity to slither through the palace, amongst your betters thinking you've any right to Thalesai's affairs?"

The words struck deep. "I *am* Thalesain, as much a citizen of this kingdom as you are."

"You want to play first?" He turned, and just as quickly whirled and rammed his boot against my chest.

A raw cry escaped me. I writhed, gasping for air, seeing only blackness. It already hurt to breathe. Now, it felt like dying.

This was why my senses chimed constantly against Ibhar. Unlike Dathan who I'd misjudged, Ibhar could really kill me.

His cheek pressed against mine as he snarled into my ear, "Who do you work for? Who *sent* you?"

I managed to choke in air but *it stung. It stung. It stung*. Warm liquid slid from my nose as my head lolled, but I managed to rasp, "Go to the sheols, Ibhar."

50

DATHAN

Where was Zair?

In the tessellated hall filled with leaders of different sects in the kingdom, the elite students presented gifts to the Majesties on behalf of our academies. The Majesties and nobles frowned as only four of us bowed and returned to our position at the dais's left.

No, Zair knew we had to remain inconspicuous until our goal was met.

Something was wrong. A roaring filled my ears. I needed to get out of this hall and find her.

"This is the most hostile Gifting ceremony in history," Lysias murmured.

Indeed the atmosphere was tauter than a bowstring, the cheerful music barely hiding the citizens' anger from the foreigners.

"Save the Baihans, the other tribes are displeased with the king. The last thing they want to do is shower him with gifts."

Lysias and Mishan had emerged from their bedrooms after the maid announced it was time for the Gifting. We'd been surprised to see the other back in the palace.

"*It doesn't feel right for us to revel in the perks of being special guests, only to tuck tail and run when things get dire,*" Mishan had said when

I'd asked about his return. Lysias agreed, and my admiration for them grew.

"I don't know why he's determined to continue his silent approach when it's agitating the people," Mishan replied to Lysias now. "At this point, they're certain he doesn't care about the missing students."

"He does care," I insisted.

As the last sect danced their gifts to the thrones, I surveyed the Ahimoth student standing in Ibhar's place. Why was *Ibhar* absent too, replaced by this other boy?

The hall slowly cleared out.

Mishan asked, "Where's Zair? She's going to be in trouble for missing this."

Lysias saw my temple tick.

"Are you worried about her?"

I opened my mouth to say that I was *losing my mind* with worry, that I needed help searching for her. Then I remembered who I was speaking with. If I even implied that something was wrong with Zair, I couldn't put it past Mishan to raise an alarm to the guards. His intention would be good, but it'd only put her in worse trouble.

Frustration burned through me to forfeit their help, but I said, "I'm sure she's somewhere. I'll find her."

"We'll help you," Mishan insisted.

"It's fine, Mish. You and Lysias look after each other."

I didn't wait to register Mishan's disappointment as I plunged into the crowd, weaving for the exit. The First Advisor was here and if I hadn't known it was him Zair should be tailing, I would've taken his angry reaction to her absence to mean he had nothing to do with it. But the traitor was him, Captain Emeso, or the Majesties. And whichever of them it was hadn't stayed secret this long by being lousy pretenders.

Finally bursting out of the crowded threshold, I almost growled when Khosana Meah blocked my path.

"Scholar Dathan, your queen would like a word."

"Khosana, I cannot…"

"Now, Scholar." She turned, leaving me little choice but to follow.

Body taut, I did, scanning for signs of Zair. None.

We reached a parlor overlooking the distant river. Khosana Meah had barely shut the door behind us when Queen Yval rose from an ottoman.

I gave a bow. "Your Majesty."

"Where is Scholar Zair?" she questioned before I finished speaking.

My shoulders stiffened protectively. "I don't know."

She tilted her chin up, yet fiddled with the sleeve of her silken overdress. "Where and when was the last time you saw her? Please be precise—and honest."

"In my rooms early this morning," I said before thinking better of the answer. Sheols. I did *not* have the time to be chided for spending the night with my *aiyena*. I rallied for a cover up.

Queen Yval raised a hand and spoke gently, "You're vowed. I hold no judgments. If anything I'm glad to see that you care for her."

She was?

"You didn't see her at all after that?" Khosana Meah probed.

"I didn't."

Why did they want to know? To rebuke her for her absence at the Gifting? My muscles twitched to shield Zair.

The queen's face held deep worry as she paced. And it finally dawned on me who Zair's sponsor was.

Queen Yval.

But no time for shock. If the queen didn't know where her spy was and was bothered, then Zair was in trouble. A furnace deep in me howled, churning to devour everything if Zair was harmed, and I barely held it inside.

Queen or not, the king would rage if he knew his own wife broke his rules and had set a spy loose in his palace. Learning of Sarhedrin and Colonel Remmon's treacheries had made him more hating of secrecy under his roof. And while the Majesties seemed to have a decent relationship, the queen was still Ussi. She would lose his trust if he learned she'd gone behind his back like his enemies had.

Queen Yval stopped her pacing. "Find her. I know you care for your kingdom and king. I can't tell you how much both might be at stake if she's not found soon."

The soldier in me kindled. With a low bow, I followed Khosana Meah out. Once we reached the door, Khosana Meah whispered, "Finding Scholar Zair might save her life—and the queen's. Please, do not take this task lightly."

Her fear for her sister affirmed my conclusion. If Zair was in trouble, Queen Yval was too. Their fates were now bound.

"I don't intend to," I vowed.

THE PROTESTERS angry about the missing children marched down on the palace at sundown.

Although the guards who were far better skilled and armed easily subdued them, the sheer number of protesters left the Al'Q-traz shaken. There were hundreds sloping down the hill with torches, yelling their demands for their children in the guards' faces.

All they had to do was throw one torch, and the sheols would break loose.

I'd been moving through rooms, listening in on conversations, for anything that involved Zair. In the daytime it was difficult and slowed how much ground I covered. With each passing minute revealing no trace of her, that fire burned hotter inside. If she'd been captured she wouldn't have been left alone.

Whoever her captor was would resort to torture to wring information from her. And just like Jaziah, Zair wouldn't yield. Was she facing the same torments Jaziah did? My body shuddered. Were hers worse?

Calm down. You can't help her if you lose your head.

I drew in a rough breath to calm the destructive rage and continued to track First Advisor Maachah. He headed upstairs while I climbed up balusters and pilasters on the palace's exterior like a leopard in pace with him. He entered into a room, and I sidled down the windy ledge to press my back against the wall by the window.

"Your Majesty," he greeted.

A quick glance into the room confirmed it was just him and the king in the parlor.

King Khasar paced. "I can't just send them back home without an address. These parents have been beyond patient. I should at least speak with them."

"Your Majesty, it still isn't the time to bring the issue of the kidnapping to light."

"Today was the Gifting. The coronation is officially over."

"The foreign ambassadors are still our guests for the next three days."

"To the *sheols* with the ambassadors!" King Khasar shouted, and I'd never agreed more with him. "So occupied I was playing host to them that my brother was murdered under my nose while men I trusted betrayed me."

"I understand that biding time has been difficult, Your Majesty," Maachah insisted, "but being king comes with sacrifices. If a crown was easy to bear then anyone would be king. The saints chose *you* to bear this burden. Now you must do whatever it takes to keep the kingdom safe."

A sound like the brush of hands through hair. A clatter followed, like the king's coronet dropped.

"If we give the ambassadors fore seats to the problems in Thalesai, let them see there are mercenaries tormenting us from within, there's no guarantee whatsoever that they won't run back to their palaces to begin scheming to exploit the problem. You know how tentative the Treaty is. While Thalesai has advanced since the War of Beasts, our neighbors still possess weapons and abilities that could grind us to ash if they come down on us again. Who knows when or *if* we would recover this time..."

"Watch yourself, Maachah. Do not underestimate me or my people," the king warned, but defeat lined his voice. The advisor's words had gotten to him.

"Forgive me for getting carried away, Your Majesty. The one who roars and the desert answers," First Advisor Maachah hailed.

The apology seemed humble, but outside with no view of them, I could also hear the sharp edge.

He made a strong argument, but his advice was more poison than cure. The people doubted the king, but King Khasar *wanted* to take action. Unfortunately, he was also trying to be a fair ruler, one who listened to the counsel of his advisors. Too bad that the counsel he followed was the one shattering the land.

Maachah seemed falser by the second.

As cold wind hounded into me and I shuffled off the ledge, it didn't escape my notice that the king was conferring in private with the Baihan Advisor only.

This was where his trust ultimately lay.

While King Khasar strived to show otherwise, the tribal bias was also in him. A bias that could rip him from his wife too, and cause him to lose faith in her, if I didn't find my *aiyena* in time.

I climbed in through a window and dropped into the shadows of the stairwell. Moments later, the king exited the parlor, and then the First Advisor stepped out.

His movement was extremely keen. Like if I breathed loudly he'd hear me. *Advisors should not have a thief's guardedness.*

Rather than proceed for some passage, he surveyed the area. As if daring any being to exist there at that moment. He drew something from his jacket and splashed it into the air.

A pale powder. It scattered and then expanded like drops of oil smearing over the air's surface. The spreading powder merged into a larger pool and then hollowed to create a hole. A rippling pitch-black door within a white frame.

Wind busied the halls, flinging my hair over my astonished face.

This wasn't human ability. It was magic.

The First Advisor stepped into the black hole. I recoiled as it shrank like a mouth swallowing itself.

He could have Zair.

Doubts vanished. I lunged forward. So close. But the hole disappeared into nothingness; Maachah gone with it.

Zair

"I should've known better than to let filth into the palace."

The disgusted mutter pulled me into consciousness. I wished instantly for the darkness. Everywhere hurt. Each breath. Fever burned through me.

First Advisor Maachah's visage came into blurry focus as the darkness gathered me again. I didn't fight it.

He leaned in. "Who sent you here to look for me?"

To look for me? It was him.

"Why?" I demanded weakly. One word that conveyed a dozen meanings. *Why* would you betray your kingdom? *Why* would you betray your king and queen? *Why* were you aiding the abduction of Baihan children? *Why* did you allow Colonel Remmon to murder Ambassador Caiphas, let Dynast Sarhedrin kill those guards?

Why?

He surveyed me as if to see into my mind. Know who else was on to his treachery, if the person was like me. Someone he could easily claim was a liar. Or if it was someone whose words held weight. Someone who could bring his schemes to an end.

And the depth of his treachery hit me again. This man armed the mercenaries with weapons, information, and funds. Saw children brutalized and defiled. Used great men like Sarhedrin and Remmon as mere puppets. Was the reason Sarai was marked for capture. And I was at his mercy.

What could he possibly stand to gain from this? The king trusted him!

If I couldn't tell the queen and Commandant what I'd found, if I died here, he *would* succeed in destroying everything.

"Torment either kills or changes a person, girl. In my time, it changed me for the worst."

"You were behind our abduction in Secruvi," I said weakly more than asked.

His face remained cold. "To undermine the Majesties' strength and cause further strife to weaken the Chambers. But indeed, I underestimated you students."

Saints. "A man who will harm innocent children for ambition is a man without a soul. And a man with no soul is but a dried riverbed, full of ashes and dust."

"I'll enjoy killing you," he said, then snarled at Ibhar, "When I return next time, you *better* have answers, Ghed."

Ibhar bristled. "Are the Yomadin plans still in place? It's still happening before the nobles leave the palace, right?"

My very soul stilled. *Yom-adin* translated to *sheols day* in Uhese. It had to be a codename for another attack.

Maachah said, "It is. Now, focus on your assignment with the girl to make sure there are no disruptions."

If it was anything like the attacks on Jalin Base or Kurje prison, it could shatter Thalesai this time.

"I'll be back in a day," the First Advisor warned.

"No," I said, a hoarse plea. "No."

As he moved out of view, I fought the urge to beg him to come back. To not leave me with Ibhar and his wicked fist. Part of my hazy mind knew that facing First Advisor Maachah might be worse than Ibhar, but I couldn't take any more beating.

Tears scorched in my eyes. I shut them. No magical ability I possessed, not speed or camouflage, could break me out of this situation.

Would anyone come? Did they know I'd been captured?

A fist suddenly connected with my jaw, knocking thoughts from my mind.

Tears slipped, stinging the wounds on my cheeks.

"Who sent you here?"

I said nothing.

"Why were you following Maachah? What were you trying to find? *Start talking*."

I forced my lids open and more tears rolled down my face. Ibhar's eyes gleamed. His thumb brushed over my tears. He brought it to his mouth and flicked his tongue over it.

I shuddered. "Why are you helping him destroy Thalesai, your kingdom you're sworn to defend?"

"'*Thalesai*' is a pipe dream. There should never have been an amalgamation. A Baihan man will never be the ruler of the Ussis."

"The First Advisor is Baihan."

"Maybe." He grabbed another cloth and wrapped it around his fist. "But whatever he is, he serves a cause that benefits my tribe."

51

DATHAN

I watched from the shadows as Maachah returned through the strange door. Thank the saints I'd waited. He strode off as the raging hole rapidly shrank.

Instinct warned me to flee. Far from whatever darkness this was. But some old, rooted sense within blazed like a smoky black message that Zair was in danger. If *this* man using darkness had taken her...

I flung myself from the shadows into the hole moments before it disappeared.

The world flashed black and white. The cries of dark winds pierced my ears.

My body abruptly collided with a stone floor. My fast breaths resounded as I unfolded blindly to my feet, waiting for my vision to clear.

The dim room was empty but cavernous and rich in adornment. Arcades of marble supported granite ceilings. Rising walls gleamed with white-and-purple tilework. In corners, quartz urns glittered. A repeated rushing sounded close, like waves rolling over the shore.

While decadent, a thick, musty sense clung to the place. Like a building shoved underground.

My entire body stiffened. Not underground.

Sweat beaded on my brows. Memories rushed at me like eager ghosts.

Too small, too enclosed.

Once we go into that cellar you mustn't say a word, mihe. Else they will hear us and hurt us again. Do you understand?

Tartness filled my throat from the terror of our hunters, of endangering my family by not being silent enough. Of being the reason they were tormented again.

"Who sent you?" the vaguely familiar voice echoed.

It yanked me from the dark mind pit. I couldn't let the nightmares cost Zair. It was time—to start confronting them.

I'm not powerless. I'm the predator.

Gripping my dagger hilt, I moved with a scorpion's silence. More elaborate architecture twinkled in the dimness. Carved stucco. Ivory statues and plaques. It was like a maze, one passage constantly leading to three, like errant tree roots.

At the end of a passage, a sudden dark shimmer caught my eye. The head of an abstract statue. The closer I got, the more unbalanced the head looked. Like it didn't *fit* up there.

A strange yet powerful force pulled me to it. I reached out and easily tugged it off.

Bleeding skies. *Big orbs, blacker than night, and covered in spikes.* Exactly as the books described them.

The... lost dragon egg.

Shock jarred through me as I turned the weighty egg in my hands. *I...* found it.

Now go find Zair.

Reeling back the waves of shock, I strapped the egg onto my back and kept moving, following the trail of the voices. Now wasn't the time to dwell on the enigma. The voices were faint, but wherever this underground place was, it echoed enough that the voices remained a guide.

A nauseating suspicion of where this could be arose. Within the base of the Plateaus of Rahbat, by the greenery stretching down to the river, lay the Saifa Tombs. Where past Kings and Queens of Thalesai were buried.

Sweat dripped down my brows, but I clung determinedly to the present.

At the end of a passage where the voices centered, I halted and peered into the next passage.

Two guards stood by a doorway there. Two *scythed* guards dressed like the bandits who'd murdered the palace guards for Sarhedrin.

Past them, in a room covered in fabrics, a single lamp illuminated two silhouettes. A male's frame blocked whoever he barked at on the sole chair in the room. The slightly unobstructed view of the other person's face was so bloody it was hard to recognize.

Saints, do not let that be Zair. Yet my instincts roared like a hundred raving lions, sorrow rising in me.

"You heard the First Advisor's impatience. We're this close to killing you if you don't start talking," the male snapped.

My body tensed.

Ibhar?

The slimy bastard!

He was the First Advisor's pawn?

Those odd moments of absence, when I'd thought he'd been out spying for his Commandant like me, for Thalesai's sake, he'd been working for the traitor.

A ragged cough. "Doesn't your... head ache from all this yelling? Mine does."

My heart felt close to eruption. It was her.

Ibhar strode around the chair, giving me a clear view of his captive.

Zair. Her face was swollen with gashes leaking blood, her form unmoving as she slumped like a broken doll held up only by the ropes.

Ibhar Ghed was dead.

I yanked out my dagger and charged, an animal broken from a leash.

Hands clamped tightly over my shoulders from behind.

On impulse, I rammed my elbow into my attacker's gut. The person jerked with a silent sound but didn't release me. Instead, their head leaned to my ear and hissed, "Go in there and you will *both* be dead!"

52

DATHAN

I twirled on my restrainer, and bitterness masked my face. The Spaeman.

Placing two fingers to his lips, he moved three steps back, silently pushed open a door and pulled me in.

The moment he closed the door, I shoved his arm off me.

"What do you want?" I demanded as I faced him in the vacant crypt. The stone door was sealed. Noise would neither go out nor in.

The Spaeman must have *seen* that all this would happen. That we'd been going after the wrong men. That Zair would be captured and tortured. He hadn't warned us. And now he thought he could keep me from going after her?

"I don't intend to keep you from rescuing Scholar Zair."

"Stop reading my mind! Why are you here? *How* are you here?"

He only answered the first question. "To keep you from making a foolhardy decision. One of you made a grave mistake stepping into the viper's pit. Now she's paying for it. I'd be remiss in my directive if I allowed you to make the same mistake."

Fury and fear for Zair writhed inside my chest.

"Convenient how you pick and choose when to follow this directive." He hadn't even stepped in to save Ambassador Caiphas. "You could've stopped this. Did you see her in there? Ibhar is killing her."

Sadness edged his face. "I don't see every man's fate. And it's not my place either to alter every future that I'm shown."

I growled at that.

"I'm not here to make you understand the Spaeman ways. While you are Gergesenes' prime student, you cannot singlehandedly bring down beings of magic."

The air knocked out of me. "*Magic*. Those scythed guards…"

"Are not human." Anger sparked in the depth of his eyes. He closed them and when he reopened his white-blue eyes, there was only control.

"What are they?" I breathed. These beings prowling our palace's secret passages, killing guards, were from other nations.

They'd infiltrated our land while we'd stayed utterly oblivious.

"There's no time to dissect that trouble."

"Spaeman…"

"You are a clever young man. *Think*. You need help. The traitors have revealed themselves to Scholar Zair. They will fight bloody to keep her from making it out of these Tombs alive."

"There is no time."

"Chaos travels on the clouds. A strike so terrible that it could create the channel our enemies need to invade Thalesai again. The kingdom needs both you and Scholar Zair alive to stop it. You cannot rescue her alone, Issachar, and I cannot let you both be consumed."

"I'm *not* leaving her here."

His face lined with admiration and sympathy. "I ache for her too."

And then the world went blinding white around us, winds ripping at my hair.

No! "Don't!" I lunged for him.

He moved out of my reach, and curtains of white fluttered over him. "Favored are the seeds broken and rejected. They shall form the roots of the white tree."

"Khosa Spaeman!"

"That dragon in your possession, guard it. Give it not even to the king. He is yours and you are his."

He disappeared into the curtains. I grasped after him, found nothing. Rage snarled through my chest. I didn't care about dragon eggs or parables right now. I needed to find Zair! The sensation of falling gripped me before my knees slammed into the ground.

I glanced wildly for the Spaeman, but I was back in my bedchamber.

I JOGGED down the Al'Qtraz's stairs to the second level and marched through the doors, into the Chamber of Fangs. It was time the palace guards knew what I had seen of First Advisor Maachah. They needed to ride to the Tombs with me to free Zair and destroy those magical bandits. First Advisor Maachah's *men*.

The military offices echoed with my steps, sparse, until I reached the wide foyer where general briefings held. Twelve of the palace's head guards stood in a semicircle—and addressing them with his hands in fists and eyes flashing was the First Advisor.

Heat sped over my skin, nostrils flaring as I stepped backward and took in the serpent standing out in the open. Moments ago, he had been using what had to be magic in the palace. Now, he dared to stand in righteous anger before our soldiers. Flames rumbled in my head.

"The palace's security has never been weaker than in the past few weeks—when it should be strongest," the Baihan man snapped, his face reddened around his white beard. "His Majesty is greatly displeased with you, head guards. *I* am greatly displeased with you."

Steam simmered in my chest. No, he was enraged that they hadn't stopped Zair before she and whoever sent her caught up to his schemes. And now... this meeting was to manipulate the situation to his favor. The guards would strive to obey *him* now, believing whatever he told them. Until his ultimate goal was achieved, he could deflect any accusations of treachery against him. After all, he had just ordered the palace guards to improve the palace's security out of his 'loyalty to the king'.

I clenched my fists to keep from launching my daggers at him in the Chamber of Fangs. The soldiers would instantly turn on me.

"This is your last chance, head guards," he said. "Keep the Al'Q-traz and our nobles safe, or be dishonorably stripped of your ranks."

The words dropped like a boom of thunder, and the soldiers dipped their chins in contrition.

A head guard cleared his throat. "We understand, Khosa. We have vowed to give our lives to protect the Majesties and Thalesai's dignitaries, and we'll keep that oath."

The First Advisor sniffed, then said, "You can begin with the servants' complaints that there has been a person lurking around their passageway."

Zair. He was priming them up against Zair. They—no one—would ever believe anything Zair had to say after this. All he had to do was point her out as a spy in the palace and have Ibhar and the servants corroborate it. Her words would mean nothing. The guards straightened, anger coiling from them.

I'd heard all I needed to. I turned and strode back to the students' lounge. Until I had irrefutable evidence and testimony against the First Advisor, he was a mastermind that would untangle himself from any weak binds. And the palace guards would stand behind him. I needed a new plan to free Zair now before the First Advisor returned to the Tombs.

"I NEED YOUR HELP," I said as I pushed open the door of my bedchamber, four daggers tucked into my boots and at my waist, my adaswords sheathed at my back.

Mishan and Lysias halted their intense discussion in the lounge and turned to look at me. Realization sunk quickly into those brilliant minds.

Lysias's hands lifted to her mouth. "Zair is in trouble, isn't she?"

Mishan stood too, bristling with impatience, ready to snap at me to tell them what was happening with our fifth peer. I didn't need any convincing this time.

"She has been taken by bandits. Not just any bandits but…

beings of magic. She's in very bad shape." My voice cracked. I cleared my throat, allowing only the predator to rise in my chest.

Their faces twisted with shock as each word sank in.

"Bandits with magic?" Lysias breathed. "How? How did they find Zair?"

"What... what sort of magic?" Mishan stuttered, his face pale.

I shook my head. "I haven't found out yet, but I need your help to get her back. *Yours*, no one else's."

They might not have been sent to the Al'Qtraz on missions to find the traitor, but Mishan and Lysias grieved over the abduction of Thalesai's youths too. I wanted to believe they wouldn't let the same fate befall one of our five under their noses if they could help it. And they might not be fighters, but they were intelligent, and their skills had been pivotal in the War of Beasts.

Fear and concern warred on their faces as they struggled to keep up with my words. I watched them with my heart beating faster. Would they agree to help Zair? Or would they decide the danger was too much for them?

I said quietly, "I would have gone to the guards if I could, but right now, there is no one else to help me save Zair but you."

Slowly straightening his shoulders, Mishan stepped around the settee toward me. "Alright. What do you need? Where is she?"

Lysias swallowed, but she stepped forward too. "How can we help?"

I let out a quiet breath, the clock on Zair's life seeming to tick in my head.

"I have a plan to take down the bandits," I said, my daggers burning against my skin. "But I need you, Mish, to make me a defensive tool. A mirror shield that can also block throwing knives."

The weapons the bandits had killed the First Accountant's guards with.

Mishan halted as the weight of the danger barreled into him again. We had escaped the Secruvi knife-throwers by a hairsbreadth. There was no guarantee we would escape a similar situation again, this time against magical beings, alive.

I spoke on to Lysias. "She's wounded. I need a healer with me."

Mishan ran a hand over his face. "Dathan..."

"No, the palace guards *cannot* help with this," I cut him off, reading his tone and expression. "I already went looking for them. I'll explain everything later, but right now, I need an impenetrable shield. Can you help me make one?"

His eyes moved over me, his mind reeling behind his glasses. Finally, he nodded and strode to his bedchamber. "I think I can craft something for you."

Lysias didn't need further convincing and was already hurrying to her door. Then she paused and looked at me with a frightened yet pensive expression. I could almost hear the pounding of her heart across the lounge and wished I didn't have to pull her into this.

"I have a draught. I formulated the mix to protect myself if I ever encountered street muggers. I brought a little of it to the palace, just in case our foreign guests decided to break protocol."

Brows lowered, I turned fully to her. "What kind of protection is this draught?"

"One that dispatches men faster than a knife can. One of the herbs is deadly to all living things and incredibly difficult to source, but I think I have enough to help Zair."

With that, she turned into her bedchamber.

I would never put Lysias or Mishan in the line of danger, but I didn't dispute her need to protect herself. I paced the lounge like a great cat, thinking of the times the four of us had been in the lounge while Ibhar was off somewhere. Betraying his kingdom.

I wanted to *gut* him. And I would, but first I would wring out everything he knew from him.

Mishan reappeared wearing a dark cloak and handed me a thick object. "This should do the work."

I surveyed what had been an oval wall mirror, mystified. "You could not have just built this for me, Mish."

He shifted on his feet. "Perhaps not."

We all had similar metal cabinets in our rooms, and Mishan had cut out his drawer box bottoms—apparently, all four of them—and whittled them to fit the shape of the mirror's other side. Then he'd sealed all together in one of the cleanest metalwork I'd seen, leaving a leather grip dangling from the center. The result was a makeshift oval mirror shield that would protect my neck from throwing knives, but also more.

"You made this for yourself, didn't you?" I asked.

"Yes." He lifted his chin stubbornly, neck reddening. Because just like Lysias, he had built himself a defensive tool in case our magical guests decided to break the truce. This shield wasn't just to stop the kind of knife-throwing bandits we faced at Secruvi but to weaken wraiths. I wondered what other tools he had stashed in his bedchamber.

"I'm the last person who would criticize you for protecting yourself, Mish. And *this* is exactly what I need if I'm going to be facing wraiths," I said, testing the shield's grip.

"Good." He pulled out two makeshift daggers with leather grips from his cloak. "Iron blades in case they are azizas. You take this one, and I'll keep the other."

The bandits didn't have wings hence couldn't be our southern neighbors, but I didn't dispute strapping on one more blade. The remaining object was the napellus should the beings be shifters, but the herb was too rare to find in such short time. And if all went according to my plan, the bandits shouldn't see me coming.

Lysias ran back out, wearing a dark purple cloak and holding a rattan basket. "I'm ready."

I paused even as my body strained to be on the move. "We can distribute herbs and bandages in our pockets. Excess load will draw attention to us that we can't afford."

She took the oval mirror, gasping at its weight as she placed it in the basket.

Deep thought seemed to run through her mind as she pointed to the swords at my back. "When we reach the gates, we'll tell the guards that Mishan—who won at the Best of Ten—has some tools he urgently needs for his project. You and I are escorting him to get it. It *can* wait, but the next few days in the palace will be idle as guests leave, and Mishan will rather keep busy. With this excuse, there's a decent chance they will let us through with little qualms."

"She's right," Mishan said. "You look like a man going to tear down an army by himself. The guards will grill us with questions if they see you."

I'd been so restless to get back to the Tombs, I hadn't even thought of the palace's gates. All I knew was that Ibhar was tormenting Zair and nothing would keep me from getting her out of there.

"Put your tools in the basket," Lysias coaxed. "I'll cover it and the guards will assume the basket is for the tools we buy."

"You're right." I placed my adaswords in the basket and took it from her. "Let's go."

We hurried down to the stables and mounted our horses. At the great gates, Lysias employed her sweet mien and explained our brief excursion to the head guard. Mishan had just won a sponsorship from the king himself for this project. It was now important to all. Besides right now, the city beyond was less capricious than the palace. The head guard gave me a trusting look, *'Look after them, scholar.'* I had every intention to. Ibhar wasn't taking anyone from me tonight.

Instead, I would take everything from him.

The guard ordered his men to step aside for us. As we cantered down the hill, I summarized the hideous situation Thalesai was in and the First Advisor's orchestration of it all. Blood drained from Lysias and Mishan's faces as they struggled to absorb the revelations. Once we reached the hill's base, I nudged my horse into a gallop for the Saifa Tombs.

The northern end of Ari'el flew past—busy avenues and thronging restaurants—and finally, the stone walls of the Combat Arena filled the landscape. Dodging carriages, we rode around the arena, through the labyrinthine streets of the residential area just beyond it, until the Plateaus of Rahbat surrounded us in rocks and earthy smells.

I tugged on my horse's reins a good distance from the Tomb's entrance. Mishan and Lysias followed suit.

"Wait for me here," I whispered meaningfully.

In the dimness, they read the reason on my face and nodded.

Armed with my daggers, I moved silently along the rock walls. Stepping on neither twigs nor rocks that would hint at my presence. The gold and white marble entryway of the Saifa Tombs stretched tall and wide before it merged into the natural rock walls of the Plateaus.

Close enough for decent visuals yet far enough to stay unnoticed, I stopped by a boulder and scanned the perimeter. Took my time with it. I didn't expect Maachah's clandestine thugs to set themselves as open guards of the Tombs. No, they would keep silent watch in the dark and eliminate unwanted guests before the guests knew what hit them.

There. Brief movements deep in the shadows fifteen feet away from the entryway, where the moonlight's reflection on the marble didn't illuminate them.

I palmed a dagger hilt. If I engaged head-on, it would be two against one and take up the time I could be using to face the bandits in the Tombs. This vantage also wouldn't allow the aim I needed. I scanned the jagged rocks beside me and marked the stone ledges I needed a few meters ahead.

The movements halted in the shadows, but I knew that they were there. I made out the hints of limbs and fabrics in the dark.

I climbed up the rock as Jaziah and I had done multiple times. Fast, fast, fast. An owl hooted somewhere. The body shapes were to my lower left now.

I released the holds and leapt to the ledge with the best vantage point above them. They had the ears of eagles, catching even the slight thud of my feet. But before their heads finished tipping upward in my direction, I hurled the two daggers.

Steel split skin and bone as it lodged in their necks. Bodies dropped.

The mission had barely started. I swung off the rocks and ran for the bodies in the dark, triggering no disturbance in the gorge. I retrieved my daggers, wiped the blood off on a bandit's jacket, and went to get Lysias and Mishan.

Hang on, Zair. I'm coming.

I led my horse by the reins and the three of us reached the front of the Tombs. From Lysias's fluttering lashes, I knew she caught the whiff of blood in the air and prayed she held her wits amid the danger. I held her gaze with a question as I reached up and assisted her off her horse. She gave me a firm nod. We tied the horses behind a huge rock that had been carved into a fluid shape some paces from the entrance.

"These bandits are alert," I said as the ripples of the River

Niger filled the night. I gestured regretfully to their heeled shoes. "Once we're in there, we need to be silent."

Lysias immediately nodded. Despite their wealthy upbringing, neither hesitated to slip off their shoes, stash them on their horses, and stand barefoot on the sand.

I took my weapons from the basket and strapped them on. "Breathe slowly and shallowly. Only speak when we're sure the bandits are subdued. Stay behind me at all times."

Lysias pursed her lips tightly as I handed Mishan a sheathed dagger to add to his makeshift knife. He strapped it to his thigh like someone who knew how to use one. Good.

"Once we draw close enough to the cell, I'll show you an open crypt to lie in wait. I'll summon you when it's over. Come out and help me with Zair and Ibhar. Not a moment before, alright?"

"Wait, Dathan," Lysias blurted as if she couldn't keep her thoughts to herself anymore. "I have an alternative plan."

I frowned. "What plan?"

Lysias pulled out thick, wool cloths from the basket and handed them to us. She tied the third around her nose.

"I feel the storm of your anger and have seen you with a sword. I almost fear for those men standing between you and Zair. But my draught can make this faster. Safer, for all of us. Once it permeates the air, it makes anyone who inhales it unconscious and weakens them even after they wake up. None of us—including you—has to risk being hurt tonight."

"That isn't my plan," I said, shaking my head firmly. I'd thought the draught had been protection for herself. Not to throw out my entire plan.

"But it's a *foolproof* one if you'll try it," she said.

"You've tested it before and it works?" Mishan prompted.

"*Biksod*, vinegar, *kaiga*, and soeflower. What effect do you think such effervescent mixture would create?" Lysias quizzed him, holding my gaze, seeing the itch for a fight.

Mishan's eyes moved as he mentally catalogued the ingredients, then flared as if understanding clicked. "Where in the skies did you find soeflower?" To me, he said, "It has an odor that kills every living thing when inhaled in large amounts and weakens in smaller quantities. No being is immune to its odor."

Lysias said, "I traded an arm and eye with the tutor who taught my class to use the herb. This draught has the last of my soeflower. I wouldn't offer it if I weren't certain it would work, Dathan."

"Will it release fog or smoke? Anything that will give us away?" Mishan queried.

"It smokes lightly at first. In the darkness, it's impossible to notice, as I intended. If we carefully trigger it, the bandits would have inhaled enough to paralyze them before it starts to smoke."

Mishan nodded, convinced. "I can vouch for this formula, Dathan. You asked for our help. Let us help you."

Two against one.

I'd planned to keep exploiting the element of surprise and Jaziah's weapons of choice, throwing knives, to whittle down the bandits before facing Ibhar. I wanted only Ibhar to leave this place breathing, but battered and in binds. Yet these were two smart students vouching for this plan, and Zair's life was more important than my retaliation.

Jaw clenching, I looked at the marble entryway.

I quickly drew the image of the wraiths' formation by the cell. The two of them had kept close proximity to Ibhar—and if any more had joined them, the passage was narrow and would force them into close range. If the draught worked as Lysias and Mishan believed, the close proximity would ensure they all inhaled it.

But if somehow the draught didn't work, my blades and shield were ready.

"Alright. We'll try your way," I said. "If it doesn't work, I'm returning to my original plan."

Lysias squeezed my arm in appreciation, pulled back, and handed me another cloth. "Both of you please make sure you don't inhale it. The last cloth is for Zair."

If we find her alive.

I ignored the words hanging like a fog over us and wrapped the wool around the lower half of my face. Mishan did the same.

"If I don't cut them down, I still need them restrained, Mishan."

Mishan swallowed and nodded. "My cloak, shredded, can make a mean bind."

"Thank you," I said earnestly to the both of them.

"It's what friends do," Lysias said.

Steadying myself to face the cave-like tombs again, I turned to the entryway. Sounds of rushing water echoed as I led them into the dim maze. Deeper through the route imprinted in my head. The walls seemed to move, closing in on me, but I knew now that I would walk a hundred caves to find Zair.

The soft echoes of footsteps came first, followed by deep voices in a different language. Startled by how close and real the threat was, Lysias's breath hitched. I halted my steps. It was the slightest sound, but these bandits were sharp.

The rapid conversation continued without pause.

I turned to Lysias, lifting a calming hand in the dimness. She pressed her hands to her mouth, apology written all over her. Her pulse raced in her neck. Mishan mimicked a breathing gesture. She drew in deep breaths, then nodded. *I'm ready.*

No, this was too much for them. I scanned the passage, returning to my first plan. I would leave them in one of the crypts until the fighting was over and...

Mishan grabbed my arm and shook his head firmly. *We're not leaving you and Zair.*

Fine. I pressed my finger to my lips again, and continued the silent trek. We reached the end of the last passage and pressed our backs to it. I placed the shield on the ground and held out my hand for Lysias's draught. It didn't look at all like I had imagined—a sizable bottle filled with dark, syrupy liquid. This little bottle was wrapped in a sponge and had translucent liquid that resembled water.

Lysias gave a silent demonstration on how to handle it.

Primed to lodge my daggers into more necks, I shook the sponge, then squeezed it. In my palm, I felt the silent snap of the bottle, cushioned by the sponge. I dropped to my haunches and rolled the little sponge down the passage. Nothing seemed to happen.

Face mostly hidden by a wall and its shadows, I surveyed the bandits. There were three of them now. Two leaned against the wall with scythes, discussing tensely in Turanci. I released my shield and reached for my daggers. The largest one stood by the room's threshold, listening to the other two while scanning the perimeter. Swift aims of my daggers at the first two's necks would take them down before the third reacted. My shield would block his own throwing knives, forcing him to face me man to man. I'd cut him down, then get Ibhar last.

I finally let myself look inside the cell. Ibhar leaned in and placed his grimy fingers on Zair's throat, as if searching for a pulse.

My heart stumbled. Why wasn't she moving?

I channeled that wild fear and rage into razor-sharp precision, gripping my daggers and rising. Time to move in.

Mishan grabbed my hand and widened his eyes. *Don't.*

I shook his hand off. The sponge made a *fizzing* noise. Mishan and Lysias leaned closer and from above me, peeked over the wall's edge. The smoke erupted into the passage and Lysias let out a breath, touching my shoulder.

It works.

53

ZAIR

"Stay with the living," a familiar voice soothed in the depths of my mind.

Spaeman?

"Your light will shine. As brightly as the stars that pour over the dunes."

The pain had become my sign of wakefulness. Heated conversations from my captors stirred me awake.

What is that thing on the ground? they were barking at each other, alarmed.

Why is it smoking?

"Who cares? Throw it back out!" Ibhar's growl.

My heart stumbled.

A faint, odd smell grazed my nose, worsening the spinning in my head. Three hefty thuds followed, like falling bodies.

"They're all down!" another familiar voice hissed. *Mishan?* "Your draught worked, Lysias."

"Good. Tie them up, quickly."

Dathan? No, I couldn't dare hope. Opening my eyes to find I was still alone with Ibhar would crush me.

Hands touched my face and fabric covered my nose. I tried to recoil, but my sickened body was beyond my control. I needed water.

"Zair, can you hear me?" The frantic voice made my heart lurch. "Zair."

I forced my eyes open as far as they'd go; it was only a sliver, my lashes still touching. Curly umber hair. Wild hazel eyes. His masked features were grim as his blade sliced through my binds.

Dathan. I wanted to speak, to sob with relief, but I couldn't manage anything beyond staring through barely opened eyes.

"She doesn't look good," Dathan said hoarsely as he swept ropes off my battered body.

He gathered me into his arms and the pain worsened. The world blackened around the edges, but if I was hallucinating my rescue, then I didn't want to wake. I forced my eyes open another sliver and this time, sighted Lysias. A scarf veiled her nose, but I couldn't miss those caring blue eyes. Mishan was here too, his face also half concealed as he handled ropes as if tying up something. No someone.

How? Dathan had told them about our missions? He trusted them.

Lysias's hands tormented my chest area.

"Oh saints, they broke her rib," Lysias whispered. "She needs a healer. Now!"

Dathan moved. From this angle, I caught a glimpse of dark red hair on the huge body sprawled in front of Mishan. Ibhar.

Fear skittered through my veins. I dragged my focus to Dathan's face. He looked like the angel of death as we moved past Ibhar. "Drag him to the Tomb's mouth, Mishan. I'll handle his movement from there."

Wait... First Advisor Maachah. Ibhar wasn't the sole villain. We needed to warn the Majesties of First Advisor Maachah. I tried to speak but again it was futile. I was a slave to the sickness.

THE DEEP-BROWN WALLS of my home were such that my mind, however lucid, would always recognize. *I was home.*

Was Sarai here? In my aching chest, joy and alarm battled.

Dathan tenderly adjusted me against his strong chest and knocked once he reached the lit porch.

The door opened and Niah cried, "*Zair? Mama!*"

From that moment, the world moved in flashes. Fabrics and hairs and colorful walls swept about my vision. Cries of alarm and horror made my head pound.

"What has happened to my daughter?" my father shouted—Dathan must've removed his face covering.

"Is she breathing? Is she *alive*?" Niah's voice pitched high with terror.

"Bring her in here!" my mother cried. "Niah, bring my healing bag."

Sarai was here. Safe for now. She sobbed with panic, as swept up in the chaos as I was. I wanted to reassure them, to rage at Dathan for bringing me here and putting them through this. Yet all I could do was cling to consciousness.

Dathan carefully lowered me to my bed. The worn but clean canopy in my shared bedroom with my sisters wobbled above me. When he pulled away from me, cold emptiness surrounded me. My mother and Niah crowded my bed and my mother pulled out herbs and bandages from her healing bag.

My father thundered at Dathan from the door, "How did she end up in this state?"

"Benhal, don't be brash with him." My mother's voice was hoarse with tears.

Don't cry, mama.

"No, Zillai. He cannot bring my daughter home gasping for breath," he shouted and his voice cracked, "without explanation!"

"I understand your anger, sir," Dathan spoke in Binhese, his voice rough but composed enough to get a wrathful father's attention. "I should've looked after her better. The palace has become unsafe, and Zair fell victim to the hostilities unfolding there. I didn't reach her in time. I'm sorry."

He hadn't lied. He respected my parents too much to lie to them, I realized with a tremble in my heart.

My father cursed. I could imagine what he was thinking. That the academy he'd entrusted his daughter to, the royals he'd entrusted me to, had neglected to protect me because I had Esan eyes.

"She's barely breathing," Niah whispered.

"We need to take her to an infirmary," my mother said. "I'm no healer and my baby does not look okay."

Fear coated my tongue, of being found by the First Advisor. Of being taken back to that dark room.

Tell them they can't, Dathan.

"Take her to a small infirmary that people from the palace cannot easily find," Dathan stressed, agreeing with my mother. "If anyone asks for her, tell them she hasn't come home."

No one questioned that directive. At this point, my family wanted to protect me from the entire world.

"Ask the healer to examine her breathing," he added insistently. "Since the arena, she's suffered effects from the contest."

"What do you mean?" my father asked.

Don't tell them, Dathan.

Dathan hesitated, like somehow he could hear my thoughts, but then spoke grimly as if shaking them off. "She's been coughing blood."

My mother wailed.

My father hurried over to her. "Clean her up, Zillai. We'll take her to a healer immediately. Zair will survive this."

Niah pulled away, and then Dathan's unique scent teased my nose. His lips grazed my forehead, a balm in my fevered state.

His breath brushed my ear, his deep voice a remedy. "Forgive me, but I could trust no one to care for you better than they. *S'neh gi dhala.*"

The room had fallen completely silent with shock as they watched his intimate care for me.

"It's not finished, Dathan..." I rasped. "Another attack is coming before the nobles leave the palace. Maachah... A bigger one."

Dathan stilled. He must've said my name, but while I tried to fight it, unconsciousness won.

54

DATHAN

"This way, quick. Zair warned that something bigger is at play," I said urgently to the Commandants of Gergesenes and Nergal.

We jogged down the steps into the Gergesenes Military Academy's dungeons. Ibhar's demands to know where he was greeted us.

The Commandants still bristled that Zair and I disobeyed their explicit orders and allied. But Nergal's Commandant was also stricken that Zair's mission had led her to be brutalized in captivity.

"All those years under my tutelage," she said hoarsely, her voice almost lost in the *thuds* of our boots, "and I never let myself pay attention to Scholar Nebah. Yet all along... she truly had been my best student."

I pushed down my own emotions to destroy everything for Zair's suffering. At least Zair hadn't simply been Esan cannon fodder to Nergal's Commandant; the woman cared about her.

My Commandant shot frowns at me that I ignored. I'd brought our competition into the loop. But Zair had taken dangerous risks for *our* mission. Her Commandant deserved to know what Zair had discovered as much as my Commandant did, and at the same time that he did.

More than their anger, doubts radiated from them. They questioned our verdict. Struggled to believe that First Advisor

Maachah, the king's closest advisor, was the traitor of Thalesai. But the Commandants were two of the few people who could bring Maachah down. I'd needed to bring out my strongest witness to convince them. Ibhar.

I said, "He's in this cell."

This time my Commandant didn't try talking me out of handling Ibhar. He could see it on my face that Ibhar was mine.

My Commandant nodded gravely, permitting me to carry on.

I grabbed a cup, filled it with water from the pump and went into Ibhar's cell. The Commandants stood outside the bars.

"Gergesenes," Ibhar breathed with surprise as I stepped into his view. "You..." His face reddened. "Untie me right now, you bastard."

I kept the rage and disgust from my face, and spoke coldly. "Tell me everything you know about First Advisor Maachah, and I will consider it."

He paused. "You and the azishit. You were *both* spies."

I tamped down the urge to growl at him for torturing her, yet still having the *guts* to condescend to her. Instead, I brought the cup of water into his view.

"What's that?" he demanded.

"This?" I furrowed my brows on the cup.

Outside, the Commandants peered with puzzlement and impatience.

"Ah. It's *atashe*," I said. "A special Esan potion."

Ibhar went as stiff as the stone walls. "Get that thing away from me."

I planted my boot beside his knee, looming over him. "No, you piece of rubbish. My intention is to get it inside of you if you don't start talking. You see, *atashe* was created by the Esans to exact revenge on those who mistreat them, without it tracing back to them. You hurt them and all they have to do is drop this into your wine. It eats you up from inside, slowly, until it melts your stomach open."

Although his jaw remained stubbornly taut, his eyes brightened with horror.

"And don't think you'll be dead by then," I went on. "No, the agony keeps you wide awake so you watch your insides pour out of your body to drop at your feet."

He struggled against his binds. "Curse you, Issachar!"

Gripping his jaw, I yanked his face up, pressing the cup closer to his mouth. He struggled harder, making strangled sounds of panic.

"You don't have to suffer through that, you blackguard. Just tell me what you know of the First Advisor."

He pressed his lips together, his eyes wild. I lowered the cup to his mouth.

"Alright! Alright, I'll tell you!" he cried and his eyes flared with bitterness. "What do you want to know?"

Good. "Is First Advisor Maachah in league with the mercenaries?"

"Yes."

I glanced over his head to the cell's bars. The Commandants stood with hands clasped behind their backs, their faces hard.

I asked, "And why is the First Advisor of Thalesai in league with mercenaries? Did he send them?"

Ibhar laughed bitterly. "*Him* send *them?* You all are so clueless it's almost painful to watch."

My fist slammed into his stomach, the force ripping a shout from him. I hit him again for Zair, and again for our mates whom he betrayed. He howled.

I grabbed his jaw again. "*What* is his business with the mercenaries?"

"The mercenaries are wraiths, not humans!"

I swiftly concealed my shock. Didn't give Ibhar the pleasure of knowing he and his master truly had us utterly blindsided.

Wraiths. Bleeding *wraiths*. That's why the Spaeman didn't want me to dare attack them by myself in the Tombs. Without exploiting the element of surprise and Lysias's mixture knocking most of them out, their shadow magic might've overcome us.

The Commandants' shock was palpable.

"You know this, how?" I probed.

"Because I'm the First Advisor's messenger. Because I traveled using geas to the mercenary camps to deliver the funds and information the First Advisor had for them."

Geas. Bleeding sheols, it was what Maachah had used to transport himself to the Tombs. Geas were wraith magic made solid for transporting.

"The mercenary cell that the Admiral and his soldiers stormed didn't have wraiths," the Commandant of Gergesenes suddenly said, doubt rising from him.

"And if they were wraiths, they would've transported themselves out of the dungeons," I snarled at Ibhar. Didn't want to believe this revelation about wraiths infiltrating Thalesai.

"They have some humans within their group, Ussis like me, that are fighting for our independence. But the wraiths rule the group! It's *their* geas we use."

It explained why Sarhedrin's scythed guards constantly had darkness around them. They were *shadows*.

"What's being done with the abducted students?" I growled. "Why hasn't anyone demanded ransoms?"

"Because they weren't taken to be exchanged for money! The mercenaries take the students to shatter Thalesai's peace, and as camp slaves while they focus on their main goals."

A harsh taste clogged my throat. "Camp slaves?"

"The boys are reshaped into mercenary warriors. The girls are used as... caretakers."

So the brutality the students suffered was the mercenaries' tactic to break their minds and spirits. To force them to submit to the mercenaries as their masters and then turn against Thalesai. My heart twisted. Could they have succeeded? Was Jaziah now their puppet, willingly training to become *their* fighter?

No, Jaziah would rather die.

Yet that wasn't all. Ibhar's glower said he held plenty back.

"What else?" I ground out, bringing the cup back into his view. If I hit him again, I could kill him.

His ears twitched with alarm. "And wives. The older girls have been married to the mercenaries!"

My throat clogged with bile. Nergal's Commandant released a choked sound. The cell's gate slammed against the wall as my Commandant barged in, thundering, "Where are the children? Where are these mercenary camps?"

Despite his wrath, he retained enough control to remain behind Ibhar and out of view.

Ibhar's frantic eyes remained on the cup. "I don't know."

"You said you traveled to meet with them," I snapped.

"I traveled from the Tombs right into their camps in caves. It was how they made the geas work, like a direct door. And the mercenaries constantly travel to avoid capture. I was never led outside the camp or around it to tell precisely where in Thalesai they were."

"Crafty bastards," the Commandant spat, pacing now, his dark face pale.

"What is Maachah's motive?" I asked Ibhar.

"To dissolve Thalesai. Make the tribes split and return to being independent entities again, rather than be one kingdom subject to rulers of other tribes."

Curse it.

"*How?*" I pushed. How did he and the wraith mercenaries intend to break the kingdom apart? Did the wraiths merely want the humans to separate, or did they want to destroy us entirely? And were these wraiths working under the Wraith King's orders, or were they radicals taking matters into their own hands?

"I don't know," Ibhar shouted. "That was all he told me. It was all *I* needed to know to help him."

"So... it was you who took the mercenaries' intel on Jalin Base's weaknesses?" Gergesenes' Commandant realized roughly. "And Kurje prison's too?"

Something flashed in Ibhar's face, like uncertainty. Indignation quickly replaced it. "I did what I needed to for my tribe. The Ussis should never be ruled by the Baihan."

"Your father might be Ussi, boy," Nergal's Commandant said tightly, "but I can assure you that he, more than anyone else, would be ashamed to know that his own blood betrayed his kingdom to the wraiths."

More uncertainty dimmed Ibhar's skin until he resembled a boy with his world crumbling.

Hate poured through me, but I had one more question. "What major attack is Maachah planning in a few days?"

"Yomadin."

My eyes flared. "Sheols day."

"When is 'a few days'?" my Commandant demanded, face blanched.

"I don't know the specifics," Ibhar said, "but he is bringing destruction to Ari'el soon."

Bringing destruction. Soon. What did that mean? But Ibhar had served his use.

Leaning closer to his ear, I said, "That 'Esan girl' that you love to insult? She has more honor in the tip of her toe than you will ever have in your entire body."

Yanking his jaw open, I emptied the cup into his throat. He cried out, liquid splashing over his nose and mouth. He continued screaming in horror as I dropped the cup at his feet and strode out.

Eventually, he would figure out *atashe* was a hoax. Until then, he could languish in mental torment.

"WE MUST TAKE the boy to the queen," Nergal's Commandant said when we returned to my Commandant's office, clasping on her cloak to leave.

"The Admiral is the more practical option," my Commandant countered, pulling paper and a quill from his inkpot to write a message in code.

I took a step forward, my forehead creased. "The king should be the first to know. 'Yomadin,' whatever that will be, is close."

It was a bold stance, yet the familiar guilt was faint, the whisper that I was a bad son. Catching Orcus Sarhedrin was proof that hiding and suppressing myself, my potentials, was not the way to live. I would never have found Zair or the lost dragon egg if I hadn't braved the Tombs.

He is yours and you are his.

If I made myself lesser instead of stronger, who stood to gain but those who'd caused my family pain to begin with?

I wouldn't live my life hiding or with my head bent any longer.

And while the voices of guilt still whispered, I would learn to silence them. A rightness settled in my core with the decision.

"The king is mourning the death of his brother and the reveal of two traitors in his nest. He's not likely to handle this matter with the rationality needed. I won't chance it," Nergal's Commandant said staunchly and left the office.

"The First Advisor is also the closest person to him right now. If it comes down to it, him against us before the king, the king is likely to choose the person whose betrayal would cause him less grief," my Commandant added.

"You're giving the king too little credit," I insisted.

My Commandant looked up from his paper, surveying me. "With information of this enormity, we can't risk chancing that he won't favor First Advisor Maachah. If he refuses to believe us, those students may never be found and 'Yomadin' may consume us all.

"You've done your job, and done it tremendously. Now let us handle the rest."

Coming to attention, I saluted. "Yes sir."

"And stay *away* from the palace henceforth. It's no longer safe for you."

Another affirmation, and then I left his office. But it was another order I'd have to break. I'd overheard Maachah's conversation with the king. He abused the king's trust, feeding him lies to buy his accomplices time to destroy Thalesai. King Khasar *wanted* to do the right thing. Maybe he just needed a chance to.

Was it a huge risk I intended to take? Yes, but the alternative didn't settle with my conscience.

My body ached with exhaustion, and I felt close to dropping. Tomorrow, I need to consult with Zair—my ally. Saints, I just needed to see her and know she would be all right. Afterward, I would go to the palace.

55

ZAIR

It had been two whole days since my parents rushed me to the infirmary. And still, there were no announcements of the students' release.

No news of the mercenaries' destruction.

Had my warning been too silent for Dathan to hear me? I needed to get to Nergal's Commandant and the queen.

The streets in the southern quarters were nearly too narrow for the public horse-drawn carriages, but my father had insisted one brought us back home since his wagon had a broken wheel. He said I wasn't recovered enough to walk the distance, and... he wasn't wrong.

As he and the driver discussed the fee, he kept Sarai close. My mother and Niah stayed near me to see if I would need help as I set my crutch on the pothole-riddled footpath. My mother talked about going to clean at the small temple along our street tomorrow, an offering of her time to pray for my recovery. But if Yomadin wasn't stopped would there be tomorrow?

Calm down; focus on climbing off the vehicle without falling on your face.

My first time using a crutch, I was set to toss aside the object that now permanently engaged my bow hand. But my leg hadn't yet healed from Ibhar's assaults, and the healer insisted I used it for a week.

Relief eased bits of my trepidation at the sight of our home, still standing.

My family had stayed with me at the hospital. When I'd regained consciousness, I'd worried that the First Advisor's men might have burned down our house to punish me, leaving us homeless.

We trooped to the door—and the lock was broken.

My stomach twisted. Niah and my mother gasped.

They'd come. They'd come here searching for me.

"Stay out here," my father ordered us and went in.

I squeezed my mother and Sarai's hands as we waited.

Moments later, he came out with relief on his face. "Someone came searching, but nothing is lost."

My mother and sisters rushed in to see. I hobbled in with my crutch and a sudden *BOOM* shook the foundation of our house.

My father frowned. "What was that?"

My mother, Niah, and I shared agitated looks. Our Esan instincts howled like watchdogs forewarning *danger*.

My mother clutched her ear. "It's the sound of trouble."

Sarai started to sob, horrified. "They've come for me."

My father's pupils flared. He pulled her to him.

Another *boom* rattled the furniture, and we stumbled from the impact. My father bounded for the front door as noises poured in from the streets. I hobbled after him. My mother and sisters shoved open the windows to look, and my joints quaked.

The entire sky rolling over Ari'el morphed like a sea churning with blood. It slowly tainted from blue to peach to deep scarlet, coating the city in the hue of destruction. Sulfur drifted on the air to my nose and churned my stomach. Whitebomb flint.

"The mercenaries," Sarai cried.

Outside, parents hurried children into crooked houses; young girls cried in fear as they abandoned their buckets by the well and ran; people mounted horses to go find loved ones. Red lightning sparked and crackled like veins from black clouds. The winds yowled, ripping awnings from poles and cracking windows.

It was like the underworld had been unleashed in Ari'el.

"This is what *Yomadin* means," I breathed.

"Everyone into the cellar!" my father shouted.

"Zair!" someone shouted from the streets.

Clutching my crutch, I whipped toward the voice.

Dathan ran against the wind and dodged a rain of glass as the winds shattered the window above him.

"Dathan!"

"Hurry in, son!" My father barely kept the door from shutting under the wind's hounding.

Dathan dived into the house. My father released the door and the wind slammed it with such force that Sarai jumped.

"You're standing," Dathan said to me with emotion.

He was fine. I'd twisted myself in knots when I'd regained consciousness and realized my parents knew nothing of how he was.

We eagerly drank each other in, lips smiling with relief, eyes fraught with terror. Still, we couldn't utter a word about our missions in my family's presence.

My father noticed. He started to dispense orders. "Zillai and Niah, shut the bedroom windows and shield them. Zair and Scholar Dathan see to the kitchen and parlor. Sarai, let's go find a solution for the wagon."

Everyone sprang into action. My family cleared the parlor, and Dathan and I moved to shut the windows.

"It's First Advisor Maachah!" I yelled over the slapping wind.

"You told me. About him. About Yomadin," Dathan gritted out as we shoved the final window shut.

He'd heard me. He always did.

Gales squalled against the house, flinging people about the streets with ghostly fists.

"Gergesenes' Commandant told me there's an estimate of five-hundred wraith mercenaries on Thalesai soil," he said grimly.

"What? How?" I cried.

"That part was Maachah and Colonel Remmon's handiwork. They'd blindsided the soldiers along the Gais Mountains with bogus orders, diverting their attention while the mercenaries gradually infiltrated the borders."

"And Sarhedrin stole the funds that catered to five hundred of them." My head pounded. "Have defenses been set up for Yomadin?"

"Ibhar couldn't give the exact day or *what* was coming before the Admiral threw him in the prisons. I don't think defenses have been set for *this* manner of attack."

"I think Maachah wants to destroy the city," I said.

Dathan stared at the crackling lights streaking like gnarled branches across the bloody sky. These were the thin sparks that flickered when stone and steel were struck, before a larger spark emerged and created fire.

"Not the city," Dathan noted, mind working. "His entire family is here and demon that he is, he won't want them hurt. His target is…"

We looked at each other, spoke at once. "The palace."

"If he kills all Thalesai's leaders, the kingdom will split," Dathan discerned.

"That's the reason this flint is of such intensity, Dathan. It's evening and aziza magic guards the palace from all forms of magic. Even that of whitebomb flint."

"And Maachah aims to wrought a destruction so volatile that even the aziza magic can't save the palace from obliteration," Dathan realized.

"We need to go to the palace."

He jerked, his focus settling on my crutch. "You're staying here. I'll go warn of the First Advisor at the palace."

He turned, but I caught his arm.

"I think I can fight this thing," I said urgently. "I've fought it before."

My magic was good. My abilities were good, the thoughts ran through my head. *How could it be freakish if it saved us? Why had I let myself be ashamed of it?*

"How does one fight lightning?" Dathan asked. "All we can do is attack its aftermath."

I held his gaze critically. "I fought it in the Nergal Healing Academy with my arrow."

His eyes widened. And then shook his head firmly. "You've suffered through enough at Maachah's hand. I won't take you to be killed by him."

I squeezed his arm. "I *won't* be. I have Gergesenes' best with me."

He began to argue fiercely but clocked an even fiercer determination on my face.

"There's no way to battle magic except with magic. I have magic in me not even the Ironteenth do. If the palace falls, the city falls. *Thalesai* falls, Dathan. I cannot allow that to happen without trying to stop it."

He swore and ran his fingers through his hair. "This is what the Spaeman had spoken of in the Tombs. Fine. But only if your parents agree."

I started to argue, but there was no shaking him on this.

My father ordered everyone into the cellar. I told him where I was headed instead. It took three resounding *Nos*, before we convinced my parents to allow me to go to the palace. They'd seen what I'd done in the Nergal Healing Academy. If that skill would save Ari'el today, they couldn't in good conscience stop me from trying.

Even then, my father insisted on following us. My mother kissed my face and begged me to be careful while Niah brought me my weapons. My father only left after my mother gathered my sisters to the cellar.

Our neighbor gawked at us like we'd gone mad as we climbed into his wagon borrowed by my father. He steered the horse down the emptying streets for the red-washed palace.

Scarlet painted the city. Hundreds of soldiers maintained strategic positions beneath arches and in turrets, primed for an invasion. With each *boom* from the sky, our wagon jerked and my body throbbed while my nerves strung tighter.

"The streaks of lightning are snappier!" my father called. "We might not reach the Al'Qtraz before the main bolt strikes."

Then the palace would fall.

Needing a distraction, I whispered to Dathan, "Were Mishan and Lysias really there that night in the Tomb, or did I imagine it?"

He managed a tense smile. "They were there. When this ends, I'll tell you all about the fiercest healer and engineer I've met."

When.

A stall's canopy snapped under the force of the gales and flew straight for us. My father steered the horse, barely dodging a collision.

"My sisters said that Nergal's Commandant visited me in the infirmary," I rushed out to Dathan. If we didn't make it back tonight, I needed to know this.

They said the Commandant had offered for my fees to be handled by the academy. My father stubbornly declined, saying Nergal hadn't taken care of me when he'd entrusted them to. There was no need for them to pretend to care now. Still the Commandant had set up guards to watch after me in case the First Advisor's men found us.

"Did you speak with her?" I gripped my wooden seat as a *bang* cracked the street, flinging debris over my face.

"Yes." Dathan looked at me. "It's only fair that she received the information you'd suffered so much to find, isn't it?"

We'd set aside our rivalry and become allied partners. Still, it surprised me that he hadn't hoarded the information to be done with as he and his Commandant willed.

The emotions must've shown in my eyes because his softened.

"We're here," my father called.

And my stomach twisted as another problem rose like a mountain before us.

"We won't get through," Dathan said.

Sweeping up the Al'Qtraz's hill were daunting lines of defense, row upon row of soldiers in armor. Spearmen on foot. Swordsmen on horses and camels. Archers on the ramparts and balconies. Weapons glinted. Barghests growled ferociously, standing before giant, hideous beasts of wings and claws I never imagined existed in the palace's cages.

They stood, terrifyingly magnificent.

"That host would slash us down before they allow anyone anywhere near the Majesties," my father called.

Thunder cracked like a slave master's whip. A thin thread of lightning broke free from the sky and slashed against the plateaus. It exploded. I gripped my seat as the wagon rocked.

A wheel jagged off and clattered away. My father jumped off his seat to grab it.

"Papa, be careful!"

Another whip of lightning slashed closer to Ciasille and verandahs crumbled. Cries heralded people rushing out from their homes into the breaking streets. Bodies dangled from broken walls, young and old, and blood poured down walls like rain.

Oh saints, the deaths had begun.

Determined, Dathan pointed to a turret. "Can you only fight the magic from the palace? What if we used a turret with a good vantage?"

"I'm not certain *what* magic I have in me or how I managed to destroy the lightning the first time I did. But if I'm around the palace, if its night magic fuels mine, there's a better chance I could succeed again."

He grabbed my weapons and hopped off his seat. "I saw some carpets in this wagon."

I navigated down the unsteady steps, confused. "Our neighbor is a carpet weaver."

Dathan kept his head low as we hurried around the wagon.

"This could be our way into the Al'Qtraz." He stared meaningfully, hopefully, at me.

His thoughts registered. Myth said the entire Al'Qtraz hill was doused in the night magic. While the low vantage point here set me at a disadvantage as an archer, if the myth was true, the hill's base could fuel the magic I needed to soar to the palace's top.

Dathan dragged out a wide round carpet. He ran as close to the hill as we could without drawing the legion's attention from the sky. Following him with my crutch, I gulped hard. He trusted me. I could fail him. Fail the city if the palace's magic shunned me.

Dathan dropped my arrows and his blades on the carpet.

Osime. Please, let this work.

My knees had barely settled on the carpet when the magic in the hill hummed. As if it had been waiting for me, the sole being in the city it could fuse with to fight the palace's enemies. My skin tingled like sunlight dazzling over mist. Dathan gaped at the white glow flowing over my arms.

"We need to reach the roofs!"

Magic threaded through the carpet, and the fabric stretched out like a tautening palm as it levitated with us.

We exchanged determined nods. The carpet swerved like an indigo bird and we were off, flying swiftly as if catapulted around the hill and away from the soldiers' aim.

The carpet—the palace magic—struggled against the wicked current, almost flinging us off to our death. Dathan held tightly to my hand with one of his and the carpet's edge with the other.

The carpet finally brought us to a tiny cupola, and we climbed it. Around us, archers lined every top-level balcony. Beyond was the city I loved so much, tainted red and frailer than glass.

A city Maachah and his henchmen were ready to destroy today.

The sky was a swollen bruise sinking lower to the earth to bleed out grief. I froze under the enormity of the magic I was about to battle.

"I'm not sure I can do this!"

"Zair!" Dathan shook my shoulders.

I looked to him, hair whipping around our apprehensive faces.

"*Miracles can happen*, remember?" he called, even over the clash of lightning and fire. Even over the vicious roar of damnation.

I nodded jerkily.

"I'm here with you. You're *not* facing this alone." With each passionate word, he looked deep into my eyes, into my spirit, poured his fears and worries and determination and faith into my very soul until I was not alone. Until he was there in the very bedrock of my existence.

And this bond between us... it was solid. I was not alone.

"Together, Zair?"

I nodded, courage rushing through my chest. "Together."

He quickly set me up with my weapons.

More errant threads of lightning snapped free, destroying structures and the people in them. But the main streak, a reddish silver trident, was only just unfurling from the terrible sky.

Dathan breathed, "Maachah, you bastard."

If even the finger of that light grazed the Al'Qtraz, the palace would be obliterated.

Desperation and anger welded in me, to smell the fear in Ari'el. To see human vulnerability. With blades and explosives that were ready to fight to defend the people and land they loved, yet were disadvantaged against this magical weapon. Just as we had been disadvantaged during the decades of oppression.

Raging emotions kindled the magic in my bones. My magic hummed, but it wasn't the Al'Qtraz that roared back in answer. It was a greater force than anything else that existed. A force greater than greed and hatred and wickedness. It burst forth from the bond *blazing* between Dathan and me. A shining pure light that glowed over my fingers and weapons.

It was unity.

Unity that went beyond lifetimes.

The trident pierced through the sky, descending directly above the palace.

"For peace," Dathan said softly.

"For Thalesai," I said, and let the arrow fly.

My magic-laced arrow flew higher and higher, and I held my breath. The arrow ripped into the solid light with a loud, splitting sound.

"Bull's eyes," Dathan breathed in awe.

I started to laugh in disbelief, but fell quiet as the giant bolt split into two, then four, then six. The whole world seemed to stop as the sky released a deep rumble and shook, lowering down to the earth.

"The sky is falling down!" a woman screamed.

My chest quaked as I took in the dipping clouds. "What is happening?"

Face pale, Dathan took my hand and drew me close to him where we stood at the highest point of the city. The fire started from the center of the sky and a shout escaped me. Dathan curved himself over me and the entire city shook as the lightning bolts burst into wildfire that swallowed up the sky.

56

ZAIR

Sitting on the pure gold of the palace's cupola, at the highest point of the city, Dathan informed me of Ibhar's revelations on the scheme to dissolve Thalesai. I ground my teeth.

The queen and Admiral knew the truth now, I reminded myself as ashes coated my hair.

The scarlet sky was gradually morphing into a plain night. The city was a field of agitation, teetering between shock and relief as ashes drifted in the breeze. People wept and my soul mourned as the dead and wounded were carried to infirmaries. Separated families reunited in the scattered streets.

My magical arrow had struck true... and Maachah's lightning had burst into flames and ash across the sky.

I would never let anyone shame me over my magic again. Every part of me was useful... and precious. That was the only truth to believe.

"The issue now is that the Admiral and the queen won't take this information to the king," Dathan said with the giant mountains behind him, deeply bothered by this.

"The king *cannot* find out they were working behind his back," I argued.

We'd sighted Maachah charging back into the palace after the whitebomb flint died away. None of the guards had stopped him. They were still unaware of the monster he was. And after almost destroying the city, he'd wormed his way back into the royal court. My blood boiled.

"Yes, but I *want* to tell King Khasar about Maachah," Dathan said seriously.

My spine locked. "Why? We're speaking of King Khasar's most trusted advisor. You and I, on the other hand, are mere students," I added because I could see now that Dathan revered the king, a loyalty I understood as I felt the same to the queen.

Would we always lock horns over which royal we supported?

"We won't know how much the king can handle unless he's given a chance. He is the king. The ultimate decision-maker of Thalesai. He can't grow into that role if everyone tries to shelter him."

"He chose to keep quiet about the abduction of children and ignore their hurting parents' plea for his intervention," I countered.

"That was all Maachah's influence. I overheard them talking. The king was anguished to do nothing for his people while prioritizing the foreigners. But Maachah used the king's trust to manipulate him."

I rubbed my aching temple. "I don't know."

Dathan turned to me, his muscled form blocking part of the sky. "If Maachah suddenly disappears without the king knowing what he's done, if he's told some lie that Maachah fell off a horse to his death, think of how easily it would be for someone else to deceive him again. This is a man that just tried to blow the Al'Qtraz to smattering using whitebomb flint. The king should know this.

"'*Suffer to learn*' is one of the rules we're taught at the academies. Maybe that doesn't apply only to war commanders. Maybe it applies to kings too."

I searched for an argument to that. Found none.

Curse it, he was right.

Keeping the king in the dark was the safer way to get rid of First Advisor Maachah, but perhaps telling him the truth would be the wiser way. For the king and the kingdom.

"Why ask me?" I wanted to know. "Why not tell the king regardless of what I think?"

"Because you are my partner."

Not rivals anymore, but partners.

"Alright," I relented with a firm nod. "I trust you."

An intense look filled his face. Dathan knew I was a walking fortress. I hadn't even known when the words left me, but we had been through enough together that I didn't feel a panic to take the words back.

I trusted him.

A small smile curved his mouth. "Well, that only took baring open my soul and a few near-death experiences."

I chuckled and his gaze fell to my lips, darkening into a near black. On the cupola, my body inched closer with longing. He placed a broad hand on my waist, his breath brushed my skin. I shivered in anticipation.

But then he leaned slightly away so our gazes met. There was a question deep in his beautifully haunted eyes.

"What is this, Zair?" he whispered amid the rain of ashes.

A weighty question. And I didn't know the answer. I was afraid to. A deep yearning had grown from within to remain in his life, even with the coronation over. The only boy I trusted. The one who made me feel like something wonderful with the exhilarating emotions he drew out of me. Whose pain I ached to take away.

But how could our betrothal continue? We lived different lives. He had too much to lose being with me. I couldn't live the rest of my life hating myself because I ruined my husband's future.

So swallowing, I made myself pull away, clearing my throat as I asked, "When do you want to go to the king?"

Dathan retrieved his hand, concealing his disappointment. "Tonight."

"Tonight?" I exclaimed.

"The Admiral won't wait any longer to destroy Maachah after this attack. My hopes of sparing everyone King Khasar's wrath when I tell him the truth can only work if he knows before they uproot Maachah."

So we barely had any time at all.

57

DATHAN

After telling a guard who I was and that I had urgent intel for the king, an Ironteenth Fighter came to lead us to the king. His pace was brutal.

Zair tried to hide her discomfort, but she struggled with her crutch. I would've carried her, but she'd likely punch me if I dared. Bringing the dragon egg along might've been a great gift to mollify the king, but the Spaeman's directive remained in my head. Finally, the Ironteenth Fighter halted before carved double doors manned by Ironteenth Spearmen, and two guards who served the Chamber of Wings.

Before I could process that fact, the doors heaved open.

The office was brown-themed. Shelves of scrolls lined the walls, and the king scribbled over piles of documents on a desk. Captain Emeso paced by the window behind him.

And First Advisor Maachah rose to his feet.

Fire surged in my chest, but—he was leaving. I fought for that soldier control. Zair tensed beside me, bowing as if in greeting while hiding from his view. Saints, what was she feeling? Seeing the man who ordered her torture?

I grappled for control as the greatest traitor of Thalesai—who had Jaziah in shackles—neared us. He glanced at Zair with a frown. I stepped in front of her, shielding her entirely from his view like a dune.

Looking distracted, Maachah continued on out. Captain Emeso strode over to close the doors.

And it was just the four of us. That the First Advisor still had private meetings with the king meant we still had some time.

We greeted King Khasar, and he halted Zair's attempt to bow. While his face remained tense, almost harried, as he set aside his quill, his eyes grew warm.

"Scholar Dathan. I'm relieved to find you safe after tonight's... After tonight."

"I'm relieved Your Majesty is safe as well."

"Her Majesty," Zair blurted. "Is she also well?"

"She is." His gaze shifted to Zair and grew thoughtful as he took in her crutch. "I suppose your injury explains your absence at the Gifting. I hope you're being well cared for. If not, I will call for my healers."

Zair quickly hid her surprise at his concern. She glanced at me before squaring her shoulders and saying, "Actually, Your Majesty... my absence at the Gifting wasn't by any choice of mine. Even if I'd been wounded then, as the representative of the Nergal Academies I would've found a way to be present. I wasn't able to attend—because I was taken from the palace."

Straight to the point.

The calmer mood snapped like a cane.

Confusion and displeasure filled the king and Captain Emeso's faces.

"Your Majesty," I said candidly, placing my fate in his hands. "Regardless of what is happening in Thalesai, I believe you're a good man. A king who wants only what is best for his people."

Something sad filled the king's eyes.

"That's the reason we've come to you with this," I went on. "I urge that you consider this matter as a grey point, because I don't think that in a land like Thalesai much can be black or white."

King Khasar's face closed, partly impatient. "Will you lecture me further, or will you tell me the reason you've requested an audience at such a dire time?"

It was an order. Zair and I exchanged grim looks. Once we revealed our secrets, this meeting would either bring justice to the First Advisor, or see us imprisoned.

Saints, let me have made the right call.

Before either of us could speak, there was a sharp knock on the door.

I stiffened, waited for the Admiral to barge in, to tell the king that Zair and I were bleeding liars.

But the Spaeman stepped in, immaculate in white, his overlong limbs brisk in their movements.

He held my wary gaze, and gave me a deep nod.

A single gesture; a wealth of approval. He supported my choice to come to the king.

Taking a position behind Zair and I, he clasped his hands behind him and bowed to the king.

"Why are you here, Cesen?" the king asked with confusion.

"To confirm the truths that they tell you, Your Majesty. And to alert you of lies, should there be any. If you suspect they speak untruths, you know that I'm bound to ever be true to you."

Joining his fingertips, the king's mood fell sterner.

The Spaeman's presence and his intention to vouch for us was a bolster. Maybe I wouldn't get Zair thrown into prison after all.

"No one else is welcome here and there would be no interruptions," King Khasar finally said. "Captain, inform the Ironteenth outside." He gestured to Zair and I. "Speak."

The tensest night of our lives began; and we waded into its shadows together.

ZAIR BEGAN by explaining the reason she'd been absent at the Gifting. Where she was magically transported. Why. She'd noted suspicious behavior, followed the suspect, and was taken to the Tombs where she'd been tied up by wraith bandits.

Minutes, and then hours, flew past with all we unloaded.

There were obvious moments where the king wanted to believe we were spinning tales. Each time the Spaeman stepped in to confirm our recounts. From the smuggling of whitebomb flint for the mercenaries, to generating funds for them by tampering with financial records, to the geas used to transfer messages and resources from the Al'Qtraz to the cave camps. To tonight's attack primed for the palace and why it had *suddenly* ceased.

As Zair and I efficiently wove our recounts and discoveries into a concise thread, we were careful not to mention the queen, the Admiral, or the Commandants. I'd warned Zair that if we made it before the king, we could only implicate ourselves. No one else.

So without lying and putting the Spaeman in a tight corner, we gave the impression that we'd taken it upon ourselves to help find our missing mates. And when we were chosen as representatives for our academies, we decided to find information from the palace.

Three hours later, the sky was dark but not as dark as King Khasar's face. His face was devoid of the shock and pain that contorted it an hour ago. Now it was as hard as steel and just as cold.

"You were spies in my palace," he demanded.

I braced myself. "Yes, Your Majesty."

"You disobeyed your king. How dare you?" he roared.

We had no answer, so we waited with barely concealed dread.

He looked over his shoulder to a shaken Captain Emeso. "Captain, by the next half hour, I want the queen, the First Advisor, and every chamberman in the palace gathered at the Chambers." He called out to the Ironteenth outside. Two of them entered. "Take Scholars Dathan and Zair to the western holding cell. Lock them up," he ordered. "If you dare lose them, I will have your head."

Sheols.

I glanced at the Spaeman as the Fighters' massive hands clamped like shackles on us, but it was clear that even he knew not what the king was doing, what his plan was, or what decisions he would make.

58

ZAIR

My stomach hardened as the Ironteenth Fighters thoroughly searched us. They relieved us of our weapons, handling us like criminals.

Barghests circled, red eyes ferocious.

Now that the Fighters knew we'd been spying in the Al'Qtraz for weeks without notice, we were major threats.

They seized my crutch to avoid me using it as a weapon—a fact that incensed Dathan until I begged him to let it be. The first Fighter's black armor glittered as he dragged open a door of metal lattice.

"Get in."

I limped ahead, biting my tongue as pain shot up my leg with every step. Ibhar had targeted it in the Tombs when he'd realized using my chest as a punching bag would kill me sooner than he wanted.

The cell reeked of uncertainty and fear. Was small and bare save for the long bench under a tiny window that was built high on the wall.

Prisoners. We were prisoners. We might never go back.

My stomach flipped.

The king was holding a meeting. He *wanted* to hear the First Advisor's side.

But the First Advisor would be backed by the Baihans and all in league with him. At the end of that meeting, the king could choose to believe him. His kingdom wouldn't feel on the brink of collapse if he sided with Maachah rather than us.

He would likely order us thrown into the prisons, or executed immediately for breaking his rules and falsely accusing a member of the Chamber of Wings.

My stomach spun, and I feared I would retch.

Desperate for a distraction, I turned to Dathan.

He moved resignedly to the bench.

"Tell me about the Nergal students." My voice shook. "What did the mercenaries want with them? Why didn't they ask for ransom?"

"Come sit," he urged.

Submersed in panic, I'd forgotten about my aching leg. I limped over. A shaky breath left me when I sat.

He sat beside me and told me what had been done to the female students. Horror rippled through me.

"The older boys are... fed on to keep the wraith mercenaries stronger. And for the younger boys, the mercenaries have been working to indoctrinate them. Teaching them that humans are inferior and that the wraiths are here to repair the world order. Their goal was to release them back into society once they had their minds warped, to use them as their little henchmen to perpetrate strife."

Blood drained from my face. All this time, this was how the students were living? What they had been *suffering*? And the First Advisor had tried to make us *forget* them in captivity!

"My friend is among them," Dathan added quietly, rubbing his forehead. "I'm trying to hold on to hope that in spite of everything, he's one of the survivors."

His friend was the main reason Dathan was here, just as Sarai was mine. I told him this, about her marking at the healing academy.

Needing even the slightest glimpse of light in this black hole, I said, "A-and the Admiral has plans in motion to bring them back?"

As if he understood why I needed to know, he said, "Yes, and very soon."

"But if the king chooses to believe the First Advisor," I swallowed, "what happens to them?"

"Regardless of who the king chooses to believe tonight, Maachah or us, the Admiral's plan to rescue the students will hold. Our soldiers have infiltrated their camps using Ibhar's geas. They have marked trails to get the students to safety if matters become volatile."

My knees shook with the depth of my relief. My sister would be safe. Finally.

"Okay. Thank the saints." And then, "What did the Admiral find out about the weapons taken from Jalin Base and the abducted officers?"

Dathan shook his head, running his hand over an anxious face. "The officers were made to teach the mercenaries how to operate the weapons and then killed. The weapons were smuggled into wraithlands, but we don't know if these mercenaries are acting under orders of the wraith king."

So the wraiths now had some of our strongest weapons, as well as their own magic. A problem for tomorrow. Right now...

"We saved them," I whispered, the biggest positive in this dark situation, and looked at Dathan. "Whatever happens to us today, we saved the students."

His sad eyes held understanding. If we were executed or imprisoned tonight, it would be a worthy sacrifice.

Dathan took my hands and kissed them. A hot shiver went through my spine. He said softly, "If tonight is our death day, I'm honored to have been your partner in this life, Zair Nebah."

Tears filled my eyes. "We face what comes next... together."

This time when his gaze fell to my lips, he didn't ask questions of a future that might not be.

His soft, gentle kiss sparked a blinding light inside my heart, solidifying this new bond that pulled us together. He drew me carefully onto his lap. In his arms, the pain, the fear, the grief, gave way to fragile hope.

I slipped my arms around him, felt an almost transcendent completion as our bodies joined.

He broke the kiss to brush his lips over my cheek, my temple, and neck. I wrapped my arms even tighter around him.

"Zair. Zair. Zair," he murmured over my skin like my name was beautiful nectar. "My adversary, my *aiyena*, my ally."

I soaked in his deep voice, and then a deep sadness unfurled in me. There would be no exploration of these feelings if the king declared us criminals. And if we were allowed to leave, our betrothal had to end.

This moment was all we had.

Sensing the shift in me, he pulled back, his eyelids heavy with passion. "What is it?"

The door heaved open. Dathan's arms tightened protectively around me.

The Ironteenth didn't blink at our position as he said, "You've been summoned."

"By who?" I asked. *Where?*

The Fighter didn't answer.

My heart picked up speed.

"Her crutch?" Dathan asked, clearly set to raise sheols if I was denied it.

The Ironteenth brought it in. I took the crutch and carefully stood. We were flanked by blades and restless beasts. My heart charged and howled in my chest.

I'd expected we would be led back to the office or to some private room to receive the king's verdict. We weren't.

We were led into the lamplit evening. I slowed from the struggle to keep the brutal pace the Ironteenth set.

Dathan moved closer and placed a hand on my back.

"They're taking us to the Chambers," he said grimly when the building filled our vision.

Skies, this was *worse*. I couldn't pretend to be brave anymore. My leg ached even more. Sweat beaded on my brows, and my heart raced like it would rip out of my chest.

With each step up, Dathan's apprehension and sorrow surfaced.

"I could carry you," he said hoarsely in my ear, his body half behind mine, basically keeping me up.

"That would make quite the entrance," I panted. A slight smile eased the hardness of his face. Tears stung my eyes.

"Save that humor for me when this is over, Nergal," he said gravelly.

"You think we'll make it out?" I said as we reached a great door of metal and oak. Even the Fighter shoved it open with considerable effort.

The chambermen would take one look at me and decide I was guilty. There was no chance of me leaving this hall free. I only hoped that if there was even a chance that Dathan would be granted a pardon, my presence beside him wouldn't make him lose it.

"I want to believe that there's justice in the world," Dathan said quietly. "And I want to believe in our king."

FIFTEEN.

Those were how many pairs of eyes pierced into my back. Judged me. I felt small and exposed in a way I hadn't since I was an untrained little girl.

Outwardly though, I drew from Dathan's brave mien as we faced the king, awaiting our sentence.

Queen Yval sat on the high table, along with the Admiral, the Second Advisor, and the Royal Accountant. Her eyes were harder than I'd ever seen them when they focused on me.

They didn't radiate hate. Only deep disappointment and reprimand. I'd gone behind her back. Now she could do nothing to help me.

The Admiral regarded Dathan with that same underlying anger.

Maybe they had been right. Perhaps rather than save the day, we'd given the greatest threat of Thalesai a hole to slither out of their carefully laid trap.

Regret was a harsh taste in my throat.

King Khasar raised a hand and the speculating, angry murmurs of the hall died.

This was it.

"Scholars Issachar and Nebah," King Khasar said, "are the two who uncovered the First... Uncovered Maachah's ploys. They are the reason the greatest foil of Thalesai's progress is now in the dungeons, rather than at my table dining and spinning his webs of lies."

Dathan and my heads jerked up, our shock impossible to hide.

The king looked grim, as if hiding the hurt of the worst betrayal yet. Still I thought that was also gratitude in his eyes as he looked at us. My head spun with confusion.

He spoke directly to us. "What you both did was daring, some might even call it foolish. But I believe that you'd felt you had no choice in your desire to help your fellow students. I believe you had honorable intentions for your disobedience—and it saved us."

I was so shaken that dust could have knocked me over.

But perhaps after his brother's death, the circumstances of it, King Khasar was choosing to see grey. To understand that sometimes even good motives led people through desperate routes.

Skies, was this truly happening? He believed *us* over Maachah. And now he commended us before the rulers of the kingdom.

Commended *me*.

Before I could digest it all, another burning question heaved in my mind. What decision had been made concerning the former First Advisor, then? Did he reveal his motive? Would he be punished in secret? His misdeeds hidden from the people?

"For the bravery and loyalty you've both shown to your peers and to Thalesai," King Khasar continued, "I'm granting you positions in the Ironteenth Fighters when you graduate from the elite drill camps. I've learned from my Spaeman that Scholar Dathan has aspirations for the swordsmen, while Scholar Zair has aspirations to join the queen's archers."

My world paused.

My ears had to be deceiving me.

Dathan looked stunned, his eyes widening beautifully with joy and disbelief. He looked at me and whispered, "Miracles are happening."

Behind us, a chamberman jumped to his feet. The loud buzz of disapproval permeated my shocked haze.

"An Esan girl cannot be trusted to protect our queen!" the man protested. "Their kinds have proven *repeatedly* to be untrustworthy."

My stomach cramped. This was it. The reality. The shake from the dream.

"Untrustworthy?" Queen Yval pondered. "Haven't we just agreed that if it wasn't for Scholar Nebah's discoveries and sacrifices, that more of Thalesai's young would be abducted from their schools? That mercenaries would still be ravaging our land without us knowing their enabler—a Baihan elder—was right under our nose?"

The chamberman's mouth flapped like a fish's. He fell back into his seat, flushing. While disapproval radiated from the chambermen, no one else vocalized their protests.

Queen Yval looked at me. She gave a small smile, albeit strained with a weight that hung over the entire Chamber of Wings.

It was then my instincts picked up on a daunting current. It dimmed my elation. Something was wrong. Maachah must've confessed something else to them before we were summoned.

59

DATHAN

Zair and I were separated the moment the hearing ended. The queen sent for Zair, while the Admiral ordered with a head tilt that I follow him.

There was no choice but to follow, but impatience pricked at me to get back to Zair. She was in pain, barely keeping on her feet. I wanted to take her home and away from the glares of chambermen who loathed the thought of an 'Esan' occupying any position in the Al'Qtraz.

The moment I closed the Admiral's door behind me, he leaned against his desk and said, "You disobeyed my orders and went to the king."

I stood at attention. "It was the right thing to do, sir."

"You could've risked your friend's rescue."

"He would want me to trust my instincts, sir."

He surveyed me for so long that my stomach hardened. He might think me dogged, hence unfitting for the king's elite guard. He could withdraw his support of me and talk King Khasar out of his reward.

Everything I'd worked for over the past five years could go down the drain.

I parted my lips to speak, to explain further my reasons for making the choices I had.

"I'd been wrong to underestimate the king as I had," the

Admiral said, shame brushing his features. "And it was very insightful of you to see that beyond his age or experience, we have a good man for a king. You would make a fine addition to the Ironteenth Fighters, Scholar Issachar."

Relief and another potent emotion settled in my throat. "Thank you, sir."

The Admiral didn't move or dismiss me. He knew there was more I needed to know.

"My friend, Jaziah..."

"The abducted students will be brought to Ari'el in two days. If he's alive, I promise he will be returned to you."

I tamped down the urge to insist on joining the rescue. I had to trust that Jaziah had survived.

"Did the former First Advisor explain the reason for his treachery?" I asked. "Why there are wraith mercenaries in Thalesai?"

The Admiral's face darkened, seeming to age a decade in a second.

The atmosphere grew thick enough to suffocate as he said, "The wraith king has declared war on Thalesai."

The words dropped in the office like an explosion.

"First Advisor Maachah was his servant, positioned to begin the destruction of Thalesai from within; collapsing structures like the academies, food sources, military bases, and prisons. While also breeding mercenaries that could rip it open from within when he's ready to bring his armies down on us from our borders."

By all the saints.

"Why?" I breathed. The ground felt unsteady. "Hadn't the wraith king... Why would he gift the king land if he seeks to destroy us?"

"The wraiths have always seen humans as beneath them. No better than slaves. Our blood makes their magic stronger, so they are adamant we should be nothing but blood sacks for their sustenance and workers for their fields. The new wraith king has chosen to disregard the Treaty his predecessors honored with the staunch belief that there should never have been one signed to begin with.

"As for the land, Maachah confessed to have told the wraith king that a succulent piece of land gifted to the kingdom would cause dissent amongst its rulers and tribes, keeping the king and

Chambers occupied with internal conflict while the mercenaries carried out their schemes." He shook his head. "Maachah knew too much about the kingdom, its weaknesses, and he told everything to the wraith king."

"*Why?*"

"Fifteen years ago, Maachah and his family were abducted on a journey outside Thalesai. His first wife and children were tortured and killed one by one in his presence, and then he was tortured almost to death for two years. When he returned, he told of all this but the recount was never complete. I realize now that he never told who his abductors were or how he escaped. Now, we've learned it was wraith bandits who abducted them. They knew he was the son of an elder. They broke him with mental and physical torture, warped his mind, and charged him to contest for prime positions in the kingdom. To become their informant.

"All this was decades in the making. Slow poison. Now, the wraith king would use the knowledge Maachah has leaked to bring Thalesai to its knees."

I'd thought bringing Maachah down would be the beginning of security and stability in the kingdom, but it wasn't. We'd only cut a finger off Thalesai's enemy's hand. Now the entire fist was ready to crush us.

My next question was one I hesitated to ask, but I needed to know. "Has only wraithlands declared war, or is it like the Invasions? Are all our neighbors preparing to invade us?"

The Admiral heaved a sigh. "We don't have that answer yet. Maachah spoke only of the wraith king."

My mind streaked to my family, to my sister. After what we'd faced and escaped, to be thrown into a war.

"Will this be publicized to the people?" I asked the Admiral. I didn't want to hide this from my family.

"The king has decided to address the people soon. On the mercenary rampage, the children's rescue, the treacheries in the palace. He'll make it known by using Maachah as an example, what happens to traitors of Thalesai. He intends to tell his people that war is coming. He's following his instincts now, taking steps *he* believes are right."

The world felt as fragile as a lizard's egg when I half-staggered out of the Admiral's office. Every second was a countdown, like soon the beauty of the Al'Qtraz would be nothing but rubble. The laughter of clueless courtiers would be wails and the wood of beams would be for coffins.

I hadn't even realized my legs carried me down the hallway until I found Zair.

She stood on an upper landing, the railing in a death grip, about to make her way down. From the haunted look in her eyes, the queen had told her of the coming war. She was thinking of her family just as I was thinking of mine.

I wrapped an arm around her back and bore her weight as we climbed the steps.

"The queen told me Maachah confessed to pulling Sarhedrin and Remmon's strings," she whispered, sweat beading on her temples. "He discovered they craved more power in the Chambers and used their greed to recruit them. His goal, to divide the tribes, made them eager to work for him."

"I'll be the first at their executions," I muttered.

We were passing a seating area when we sighted Zair's father there, monitored by guards. While Zair obviously hoped he'd gone home when we didn't return, I knew he wouldn't have left her.

He paced the tiles. When he sighted us, anger and betrayal darkened his face.

"Zair Nebah, I step away for one minute and you vanish for hours. Explain yourself this moment," he erupted.

"I'm sorry, papa," Zair said. It wasn't her intention, but as she limped toward him, the anger on his face melted into worry. "I promise I'll explain everything once we reach home."

"You had better."

He deserved an explanation, but how much would she share?

Satisfied she was in good hands, I apologized too for keeping him in the dark and excused myself to begin my journey back to Gergesenes. Where my Commandant could tan my back and throw me in the dungeon for weeks for my blatant disobedience. But Jaziah would be rescued soon and Maachah had been exposed. It would be worth it.

"It's not safe to travel for the Dades Valley this late." Zair's father frowned. "Those dunes are rife with the organ-harvesters."

Even after I'd lied to him and put his daughter in danger, he was concerned about me?

"I'd rather not spend the night in the palace, sir." The Ironteenth Fighters were discomfited that we'd slinked around them for days. They now watched us like hawks. "And I'm not with enough *siyvas* to stay in an inn..."

"You'll come with us," he decided. "You'll bed down in the parlor and eat at our table. It's the least I can do to thank you for bringing Zair home."

Again, his fatherly warmth and approval touched the part of me that was parched for it. If my own father knew what I'd done, how I'd helped save my mates and exposed Thalesai's traitor, would he be impressed? Be the father I'd once revered again? I hoped so. Maybe I'd risk finding out tomorrow, before returning to the academy to get my back tanned.

I looked to Zair, half expecting a protest. All I saw was exhaustion as she struggled to stay upright, her grip shaking on her crutch.

"Alright, sir," I quickly said.

Apparently, the queen had a carriage awaiting us and the lavish vehicle drove us to Zair's house.

Throughout the drive Zair stared at me with a soft expression and I gazed back at her, neither of us needing words to express the hopes and fears and the deep yearning.

Twenty minutes later, we drove into the Nebah's street in the Southern quarters.

And the sight of Zair's mother and Niah running toward our carriage, tears gleaming on their cheeks, iced my blood. They were missing one more person.

"Stop. Stop the carriage," Zair's father told the coachman. The three of us were out of it and rushing to Zillai and Niah before the wheels completely halted.

"Mama, what's wrong?" Zair called, struggling forward with her crutches. I kept pace behind her, pushing down the urge to rush ahead.

"Where is Sarai?" her father demanded, glancing wildly toward their house.

"She's gone!" Zillai could barely utter the words through her tears, her hand pressing her chest like she could barely breathe. She fell to her knees as my heart rattled down my ribs. "The mercenaries took my girl. She's gone!"

"No." Zair's crutch dropped from her grip. I caught her from behind before she could stumble to the ground.

DEAR READERS,

From the bottom of our hearts, thank you for being part of our journey. We're Stacy and Du'Sean, the husband-and-wife duo behind our small but passionate publishing house. Our mission is to uplift diverse voices, especially those often overlooked in the romance genre, and bring their beautiful stories to life. We know how challenging it has been for authors of color to find a place in the industry, and we're committed to changing that, one book and one story at a time.

Your support means everything to us, and we'd love to stay connected! Join our **newsletter** for updates on our new releases, giveaways, and promotions. And be sure to follow us on **Instagram**, **Facebook**, and **TikTok** for all things romance.

We adore love stories and hope you'll fall in love with the books we're honored to publish.

Reviews are also gold to authors, and we would appreciate your honest feedback on Amazon, Goodreads, and even Bookbub.

Warmest regards,
Stacy and Du'Sean

A DESERT OF BLEEDING SAND

ACKNOWLEDGMENTS

A Desert of Bleeding Sand was snatched up at the 11th hour, a moment when it seemed I would soon run out of publishing doors to knock on. The unwavering support of the people below was the reason I was able to persevere and why you are now holding my book in your hands.

First, I want to give all the glory to the Lord God who answers prayers. In the hardest moments, You stayed close to me, telling me to hold fast because at Your set time, You will do it. All of this is You.

My family has been a huge blessing throughout this journey. My parents encourage and pray for me. My siblings, Naomi, Bella, Peter, and Benjamin are my confidants, empathizing and celebrating every milestone. Listening to my new ideas and weighing in with great insight! You guys learned publishing terminology because of me. I love you all and wouldn't be here without you.

I also want to thank Maddie R. for the unwavering support, love, and critiques. I am super blessed to know you! Thanks to Jasmine for the fantastic feedback that helped polish vital details to this book. Bella, I'm thanking you again here because you've been the most consistent beta reader and each time your notes are awesome!

Thanks also to Tomi Oyemakinde, Mariana Rios, Allegra, and Jordan for the reads and great feedbacks that ranged from the full manuscript reads to the first chapters. Laurel, you haven't read this book yet, but you read every other manuscript before your travel and discussed them with me in a way that made them feel real. You also continued to encourage me after; I'm grateful for you!

Ayobami, thank you for helping me review the contract! A random midnight phone call discussing contracts was something I never thought I'd do, but everything is fun with you, dear friend. I want to thank Mrs. Ada B, our pastor's wife for the prayers and listening ear. I want to thank Pastor Nathaniel Bassey, and the Hallelujah Challenge team! I am now a part of the 'water-to-wine testimony' gang.

The ladies in the blogosphere who have followed this journey and encouraged me, I have to shout out to you: The Lily Cafe (Kat), Jennifer M, Isabel, and Words and Coffee (Sarah)! I wish you all successes with your writing!

Thank you, Joy—my dear friend since high school who was my first reader and book supporter, reading my handwritten stories and making tweaks with your pen. Now they are forever entwined with my earliest stories. Thanks for still believing in me long after.

Laura S. used her editorial wisdom and kind feedback method to help me wrangle A DESERT OF BLEEDING SAND into good shape. She also told me, at the 10th hour time when I got really anxious, that she believes deeply in my story. This was one of the best things you said to me. So thank you so much, Laura!

Chinelo and Asheree, thank you beautiful ladies for all the support. Appreciation to the Path2pub team, both past and current for coming on board to share publishing/writing advice with the writing community: Amber, Mariana, Alex, Briana, Michelle, Kelly, Christine, and others! Thanks to my *wonderful* street team, the Desert Stargazers. For your enthusiastic support, the super fun cover reveal, and for making the countdown to release day especially fun. May the torches in your heart never burn out!

My entire publishing team was, of course, also a vital part of this 11th hour success because it was their yeses that finally pulled my story out of the submission trenches. Thank you!

Everyone who'd told me at one point or the other that they look forward to reading this book: it kept me going. And everyone who picks up this book: Thank you!

AUTHOR'S NOTE

I initially did not think I would write an author's note for A DESERT OF BLEEDING SAND, even as a Historical Fantasy book. As a reader, I often researched intriguing aspects of historical fiction and checked out the authors' interviews long before I got to the ending and author's note. With a similar mindset, I thought I wouldn't have to write a note.

It wasn't until I came back after a yearlong break from A DESERT OF BLEEDING SAND—which I'd spent submitting the book for publication—that I realized some of the book's events need an extra bit of light shed on them. Before I proceed, keep in mind that the note is filled with spoilers.

I first drafted book 1 in 2022. And as many of these events happened, I wrote them into the manuscript in real time. Two years later in 2024, other than the main happening of the students abducted from their classrooms, some of the minor events slipped from my mind. Revising the book reminded me of them, and I realized friends and relatives had also partly forgotten them, hence I knew I had to highlight them in an author's note.

You see, my birth country is filled with hardworking people that have always had to work hard because of poor governance. There is no real reward for striving. Instead, things just get harder. And this generation of youths—my generation—is starting to inherit this difficult and sad reality.

AUTHOR'S NOTE

Over ten years ago (April, 2014), the *Bring Back Our Girls* movement started after terrorists invaded the country and promptly started kidnapping hundreds of students from their schools. The country had faced some challenges in the past, but nothing like this terrorist invasion and strange attack on children. As is revealed at the end of the book, the little girls were taken into their forest hideouts to be married off to the terrorists and forced to become their wives/caretakers. The terrorists had been brought into the country to stay, you see, and this was part of their plan for settling in. Despite all the supposed efforts to free the girls, a good number of them never came back but have grown into wives and mothers for their tormentors. These are girls whose parents sent them to school to learn and have a chance at a bright future.

Forward to 2022, the elections were coming up. The bad people are at their most soulless during this period, willing to do anything to win. Mercenaries were hired and unleashed on unassuming citizens who were struggling to make ends meets, either for monetary gains or to discredit their opponents. The terrorists again went into classrooms, kidnapped hundreds of children, from toddlers to university students, and demanded outrageous ransoms. Millions of naira that the parents had to beg, borrow, and sell everything they owned to pay off. These ransoms would then be shared, some given to the bad politicians to fund their campaigns, the rest used to equip the mercenaries with hefty weaponry for their reign of terror. Sarhedrin, Remmon, and Maachah were fully inspired by such politicians.

I remember feeling sick, shocked, and so helpless as the news came in daily. My younger brother was in a private university, which is often located in remote areas. My family and I couldn't find any peace, worried that one day we'd get a call hearing that their school had been raided too.

I mention this to show that while my book has funny moments and fantastical elements—because many Nigerian youths are wonderfully witty and humorous too!—the message is serious and real and cannot be understated. The events were not made up for shock factor. Real children faced the atrocities written here and some that we cannot even imagine. Some of them died while some are still in captivity.

AUTHOR'S NOTE

The Jalin Base invasion in the book also happened at the time I was writing it. We got the news, in addition to other horrible news, and the only way I could cope was to write it in. One of our most important military bases was attacked, weapons were stolen and senior officers were abducted by the insurgents using intel. It was not created/added just to heighten stakes in the book.

The Kurje prison break happened literally a few miles from my former estate. Between my house and the airport, there's a district I hadn't even known had a huge prison until this happened. Proof that the guards there were doing their duties without qualms for decades. But because of the hunger to win the elections, the insurgents were given the intel and tools needed to break into the prison—armored tanks, advanced weapons, money, etc. They broke into the prison, killed innocent people, distributed large amounts of money to the prisoners, and drove off with their apprehended leaders. Till now, two years later, the escaped terrorists have not been caught. This happened; it is not a fictional event for stakes.

The tribal system is based on the tribal makeup of Nigeria, although we have many more beautiful tribes than five. This aspect is hopefully to show how tribalism in an amalgamated country is often our biggest enemy. During the elections, I was shocked at how much tribal bias came into play and the division it brought.

The external kingdoms are inspired by two nations that oppressed/exploited Nigeria before it became one nation, and another kingdom that often had clashes with my tribe before the Amalgamation. Dahomey has a fascinating history that I look forward to exploring more of in the coming books. I also chose Dahomey to represent a thriving African kingdom, rather than have all the powerful kingdoms in the story be from other continents. Learning the mystical *azizas* originated from Dahomey was one of those magical moments in writing where things click beautifully.

I made Thalesai's king and queen good leaders because it's something I deeply hope for, and I made them young because I believe it's way past the time for youths to begin to occupy offices. I came up with the plot of Zair and Dathan going to the palace to fight for their peers because during the abductions, I ached for a nation where we the youths had more power. Where we couldn't

AUTHOR'S NOTE

be silenced with a ban on social media or policemen sent to shoot us down during peaceful protests.

While many of the book's elements are inspired by true history and Nigerian/African culture, certain elements are also made up. I am a fantasy author, after all.

I refuse to give up on Nigeria or call it hopeless. It has too many diligent, good, and hardworking people to lose hope for us. I believe my country will be great someday and that the future will be bright for its youths.

If you want to learn more about these events, you can read up on the Bring Back Our Girls and EndSars movements, from the point of view of the people.

ABOUT LUCIA

Lucia Damisa is a fantasy and romance writer who discovered a passion for writing at age 13 and has amassed stacks of notebooks filled with handwritten stories. She has a BA in Mass Communication and has experience as a journalist and freelance writer for websites around the world. When she is not world-building and sobbing over her characters' plights, she is reading or taking photographs of nature.

- amazon.com/stores/author/B0DHXZXCYK
- instagram.com/luciadamisa
- tiktok.com/@booktok_authorlucia

www.ingramcontent.com/pod-product-compliance
Lightning Source LLC
LaVergne TN
LVHW091527060526
838200LV00036B/511